Dave —
My continued appreciation
for your years of support —

Tom Kidwell
2015

Other books by this author

"Above The Red"© 2013 ISBN 978-1-4817-6761-3
"Loweja"© 2013 ISBN 978-1-4817-6763-7
"A Certain Superstition"© 2013 ISBN 978-1-4817-6765-1
"A Parting Of The Clouds"© 2013 978-1-62994-687-0
"The Wolves Of Calamity"© 2013 ISBN in production
"Beyond Absolution"© 2014 ISBN 978-1-4897-0215-9
"Lang's Paradox"© 2014 ISBN in production
"Running The Distance"© 2014 ISBN in production
"Stepping Stones In The Dark"© 2014 ISBN in production

Non-Fiction:

"Just Another Old Bowhunter"© 2009 ISBN 978-0-692-00281-0
"Another Old Bowhunter"© 2010 ISBN 978-1-4575-0977-3
"The American Feral Hog"© 2012 ISBN 978-1-4575-1405-0
"First Footsteps West"© 2013 ISBN in production

Forever Will

...From the Ashes of War

Thomas Kidwell

Edited by Allyson Keats Brookshire Assoc., LLC

Although the characters, places, and events portrayed herein have been inspired by true events and actual places, the content conveyed to the reader is entirely fictional. Any resemblance to actual people or places is purely coincidental. Any slanderous or otherwise offensive dialog between the characters portrayed within this book regarding ethnic slanders, do not reflect the opinion of the author or the publisher, and are described herein only to illustrate the climate of bitterness existing between ethnicities during the era portrayed.

Scripture taken from the King James Version of the Bible.

LifeRich Publishing is a registered trademark of The Reader's Digest Association, Inc.

LifeRich Publishing books may be ordered through booksellers or by contacting:

LifeRich Publishing
1663 Liberty Drive
Bloomington, IN 47403
www.liferichpublishing.com
1 (888) 238-8637

Because of the dynamic nature of the Internet, any web addresses or links contained in this book may have changed since publication and may no longer be valid. The views expressed in this work are solely those of the author and do not necessarily reflect the views of the publisher, and the publisher hereby disclaims any responsibility for them.

Any people depicted in stock imagery provided by Thinkstock are models, and such images are being used for illustrative purposes only. Certain stock imagery © Thinkstock.

ISBN: 978-1-4897-0343-9 (sc)
ISBN: 978-1-4897-0344-6 (e)

Printed in the United States of America.

LifeRich Publishing rev. date: 11/18/2014

About this book...

By July of 1963, only a cursory number of doctors in the rural Virginia countryside still made house calls. Dr. James Russell Boldridge was one such doctor. His office was on the ground floor of his Culpeper County antebellum home, but Dr. Boldridge was best known for his willingness to come to his patient's home— night or day—rain or shine. He was seventy-six years old at the time, and still practicing medicine. (He practiced medicine beyond his eighty-ninth birthday) He was a slightly gruff old gentleman, tall, lanky, and his method of sterilizing a syringe was to hold it under a water faucet for a moment or two, then wipe it off with his handkerchief. His bedside manners varied greatly with his moods, he was armed with a well-used vocabulary of inappropriate words that on occasion, would have caused a Barbary Coast sailor to blush, and the white porcelain medicine cabinet in his office was filled with mysterious brown-glass bottles (some with no labels) containing God only knew what, and for God only knew how long. But Doc Boldridge was cheap when compared to his younger, office-entrenched colleagues, charging only eight dollars for a house call to tend an adult, and six dollars to administer to a child, which included a needle filled with whatever kind of medicine he happened to have deemed necessary at the time.

I was a newly-married, telephone company lineman on a particular hot July morning, struggling to raise my family on a very austere income. I was home in bed, running a fever, and I needed help. My beautiful bride, Glenda, pleaded with the blabbermouths that were hogging-up our eight-party telephone line to get off, which they compliantly did, and she called for good ol' Doc Boldridge to come to the rescue. He soon arrived in a cloud of dust with his dirty brown doctor's satchel full of... whatever—the same kind of satchel you would have expected to see any doctor carrying... in the early 1900's maybe. Anyhow, with the same old painfully dull needle that he jabbed everybody else with, he soon had me taken care of, and I paid him the eight-dollar fee. Almost four hours later, he bid my wife and I good day and left in his old sedan. What happened during his four-hour visit was something that I've remembered ever since.

Doc Boldridge was the son of a doctor, descending from a family of devout southerners, which included many old civil war veterans there in Culpeper County, and the good doctor enjoyed nothing more that talking about the civil war to anyone who would listen. In my sickened state, I was a captive audience. In that four hours, he shared many stories with me, and I have somehow managed to forget every one of them—save for one. With a goodly portion of condescending disdain in both his voice and his fiery eyes, he told me the story of two "*wretched, low-life, widow - bitches,*"[sic] living on a tobacco plantation in a county southwest of Culpeper, that had taken a badly wounded "*Yankee bastard*"[sic] into their home under the guise of him being a wounded Confederate soldier, and over a period of a year, nursed him back to health. The doctor went on to say that the wounded Yankee never went back north to "*his own kind,*"[sic] but actually married one of the ladies, and eventually fathered children with both women, and lived there on the farm the remainder of his life. The doctor did not speak fondly of the Union soldier or the ladies who harbored him and nursed him back to health, but I have always assumed that his ire was fueled by the residual hatred that was instilled in him through his Confederate ancestry.

Dr. Boldridge never outgrew his bitterness toward Yankees.

In his heart, as well as the hearts of many others, the civil war still raged on. His shortages of medical etiquettes notwithstanding, Dr. Boldridge rendered a valuable service to the community over the many years he practiced medicine in Culpeper, Rappahannock, and Fauquier Counties, and even with his occasional moments of social 'sourness,' people in the community my age or older remember him with fondness. My family and I moved to northern Virginia shortly thereafter, and I never saw the good doctor after that special day when he shared so many stories with me. He was recognized far and wide as being the region's supreme Civil War Historian, knowing the exact location of every battle, every skirmish, and every encampment. I wish I had taken notes and recorded actual names, dates, and precise locations, but I did not, and the story that I have so unpretentiously pieced together is but the product of the fragments that have remained imbedded in my mind for more than a half- century. I have no doubt that the story is true, excepting of course, the literary elaborations that novelists are guilty of.

Dr. James Russell Boldridge died in a nursing home in 1983 at the age of 97, and as shameful as I am, I must confess driving past the nursing home many times, without ever paying him the courtesy of a visit. I've often wondered how many other taunting stories he must have carried along with him to his grave. May he rest in peace, assured that at least one of his recollections, whether imperfectly embellished or not, will linger in print.

Author

A Brief Introduction

by Dr. David Landis, PhD

Thomas Kidwell's saga of *'Forever Will—From The Ashes of War,'* irresistibly beckons modern man to take a broad step back in time through a small portal in which to view the day-to-day drama and challenges that befell an entire citizenry living in the South during the Civil War and in the frightful years thereafter.

Tom's literary rendition doesn't rehash the horrors of that grizzly war that have already been so well documented in many fine historical works. Instead, this author takes us deep into the hearts and minds of one family, a unique family, a family who was truly of Southern gentility, but who regarded all men as the Bible commands, as *Brothers in Christ*. It becomes a microscopic journey into the thoughts and minds of a family that came together by non-conventional circumstances, yet they were circumstances which galvanized them into a sovereign family unit defined by their faith, their understanding, and their love.

This tale delves into the harsh realities of the great losses, incredible grief, and the hardships of losing fathers, husbands, brothers, and sons to the horrors of grapeshot cannon fire, devastating wounds from mini-balls, and gangrenous infections, butcher shop amputations... it takes us far beyond the stench of cordite and decaying flesh of countless horses, and into the hearts and souls of those who managed to endure.

We're led through the battleground of the mind and heart...

where Christian realities clash head on with human anguish, resentment, anger, and the full range of normal human emotions stirred by such losses. We are gently led thru the eyes and heart of one woman and one man. She is a woman of incredible character, insight, and Christian morals who steps beyond her and her family's personal losses to consider the destitutions of another creature in need, a fallen human, regardless of the color of his uniform or his unknown past. And he comes to her as a man with no name, no past, and a future that is at best, uncertain.

Forever Will inspires us to willingly or otherwise, examine our own hearts and ask ourselves the thought provoking question, *"What would I have done in such a circumstance?"* ...while challenging us to be better people—to cast aside our hypocrisy, examine our own hearts and become renewed, to the betterment of our country and ourselves. We would do ourselves a great justice if we simply lived our lives in accordance with the first chapter of James, verses one and two:

"Judge not, that you be not judged. For with the judgment you pronounce you will be judged, and with the measure you use it will be measured to you."

Contents

Prologue

God willing, there will never be a more dismal chapter in the history of The United States of America than that ugly period composed of the violent years of 1861 through 1865. It has been long thought that the tally of casualties stood at 450,000 during that era. However, research completed in 2012 has revealed that the American Civil War cost the lives of 750,000 Americans, which doesn't include those maimed and horribly disfigured during that period of conflict. Nor does this figure include the numerous victims who contracted diseases such as tuberculosis during the war and died later. Also absent in these figures is the unknown thousands of civilians who died as a result of hate crimes committed by the non-military, and otherwise '*good citizens*' of our great nation.

America suffered more casualties during the Civil War than the combined casualties of World War I, World War II, and the Korean War. Because the issues that ignited the war were so compelling in nature, so engrained in the very culture of the society of the respective regions of North versus South, hatred between the North and the South was the accepted norm during this period and lingered on through the Reconstruction Era and even into more modern times. An unambiguous line of demarcation was drawn in the sand, and everyone was expected to stand on one side or the other. As they still have the propensity to do today, political zealots fanned the fires that led an entire citizenry into the bowels of hell.

Southern residents who were committed to the same philosophies and deeply seated convictions that had inspired Northern allegiance, dared not make their beliefs known to their Southern neighbors. Men were dying by the hundreds each day, and families who had lost a loved one in the conflict of battle were understandably prone to seek retribution among folks of opposite beliefs, especially those within easy reach, such as a neighbor. Voicing such anti-patriotic sentiments in the wrong places or at the wrong time could result in having one's house burned, or their family's senior members hung from a tree by one of the myriad of vigilante groups that sulked in the shadows during the daylight hours and spit forth their poisonous venom in the dark of night. In October of 1862, in Gainesville, Texas alone, for example, forty suspected Unionists who opposed secession from the United States were brought in and hung. Two others were shot as they tried to escape. And the terrible irony of the crime, was that all but seven of the men were completely innocent of the charges.

Likewise, Southern sympathizers living in the North could expect harsh retaliation from their neighbors if they were to publicize their Southern fidelity. As the war progressed, and men from both sides started dying by the thousands, emotions and hatred grew even stronger. Nearly a quarter million widows and about as many orphans were left behind to carry on with their lives without a family bread winner or father. Some of these widows lost their husbands, as well as many or all of their sons. There was scarcely a family that had not been touched tragically by the war in one way or another.

This book is about one such family. Inspired by a true story, or at least the 're-telling' of a true story, the theme of this book was conveyed to the author without elaboration in 1963, by Dr. James Russell Boldridge. It pays tribute to the men and women who, in the aftermath of war, struggled daily and endeavored to rebuild their homes, restore their crop fields, and bring some form of Christian normalcy and peaceful productivity back into their lives.

The American Civil War was about much more than just the issue of slavery. It was about much more than just the issue of state's rights to govern themselves, or federally imposed taxation. The American Civil War was about a people learning to live with themselves, a struggle to determine what was morally right from what was wrong, so that we, as a united people, could provide the most sovereign future for our following generations. One needs to realize that not every conflict that took place during the American Civil War occurred on the battlefield of valor—some were fought within the heart and soul. When the final shots had been fired and the smoke cleared, the only certainty that prevailed was that the South would never be the same as it had been during the antebellum era, nor would the North.

Ironically, after the war, the Reconstructionists imbued the pious concept that *"to the victor belongs the spoils of war,"* and demonstrated the same reprehensible disregard for human rights toward the vanquished citizenry of the South that was the theoretical Northern justification for the war in the emancipation of the black slaves. The act of exploiting people for the purpose of personal gain is as old as mankind itself. Our sentiments of compassion, understanding, and love for one another are too often set aside when there is a profit to be made by our apathy and indifference. In the book of Genesis, we read about Joseph's brothers selling him into slavery for twenty pieces of silver. And in the book of Matthew, we read about Judas betraying Christ for thirty pieces of silver. It's amazing how mankind's conscience takes a holiday when there is money to be made, but such greed remains well-documented throughout the ages.

Change comes slowly in a climate where emotions run deeper than mutual respect. Atrocities and mockeries of justice were commonplace in the post-war South, on both sides of the issues. They were common among those vanquished, and they were common among those who came to the South to rule and prey. In the horrible midst of this epic conflict, a family begins a great journey—a journey of discovery—a journey of the heart and soul... and it's a journey in which hope emerges, from the ashes of war.

Uninvited Guests Arrive

"And ye shall hear of wars and rumours of wars: see that ye be not troubled: for all these things must come to pass, but the end is not yet." Matthew 24:6

Several battle-weary Union officers had ridden to the large three-story farmhouse on top of the hill to visit the upstairs bedchamber where a young corporal lay wounded and in a comatose state. Two Union surgeons had haphazardly attended to setting the young corporal's broken leg and bandaging a severe head wound, but they had done precious little in the way of rendering the attention that the young man's broken body really needed. The house in which the young soldier lay was the plantation home of devout southern sympathizers; two widows and their two daughters, and an old, feeble gentleman who had once been the owner and master of the farm. War is never very pretty, nor is it ever sterile or discriminating, and although the war had thus far spared the home of the Montgomery family, it had previously cost the lives of several of the menfolk there in this prominent southern Virginia household. Mrs. Abigail Montgomery had lost her husband and her only son at the battle of Manassas and the first battle of Bull Run two years previous. Her Sister, Agatha Martin had lost her husband in a skirmish just south of Centreville, Virginia the year before. Now, Abigail, Agatha, and Abigail's two daughters struggled daily along with

5

their elderly and feeble grandfather, Phillip Montgomery, Sr., to eke out a meager existence among the ruins of what had once been a thriving and profitable tobacco plantation. Phillip Montgomery, Sr. was old and frail. Today, we would refer to his condition as, *Alzheimer's*, but in the 1860's, it was known simply as '*the aging illness.*' Each year found his mind growing progressively weaker and his frail hands trembling more. From a leadership standpoint, Phillip Montgomery had almost nothing to offer his beloved granddaughters in the way of support or protection, thus bequeathing such governance responsibilities to his eldest granddaughter, Abigail. Phillip Montgomery was but an ineffective figurehead, symbolizing a bygone era.

In a smaller house, a hundred yards behind the main house, a middle-aged African man and his wife were all that remained of the enslaved workforce that had once produced the annual tobacco crop that had enabled the plantation to survive and actually prosper. The other slaves had all fled to the north at the beckoning and encouragement of the invading General Malcolm Kirkland. The two workers who remained had been residents of Montgomery Farm for more than twenty years, and had no desire to sever their relationship with the Montgomery family by fleeing with the multitude of emancipated slaves, even though their two sons had voluntarily left. Besides, in their opinion, they were already free, having gained their freedom nine years before the war had even started through a program initiated by Mr. Montgomery, by which an enslaved worker could earn their own freedom after as little as five years of crop sharing indenturement. Phillip Montgomery's neighbors had scorned him for eagerly providing such readily available liberties to slaves. Such liberal and generous Christian theology in the antebellum south was unpopular among the men of wealth and prominence, but Phillip Montgomery was steadfast in his belief that all men were created equal... a rather rare and unusual conviction for a man of deep-seeded southern gentility. His political allegiance was with the south, but his heart yearned for freedom for all men. Though his family was considered well-to-do by most people of the region, his anti-slavery beliefs had prevented him and his family from achieving the same high level of wealth as the aristocracy of some of the larger southern plantations that exploited slavery to an extreme. Despite Montgomery's refusal to increase his profits at the expense of slaves, their family holdings and their annual profits had allowed them and their workers to live life quite comfortably there at Montgomery Farm for more than a generation. Most of the commodities they required, and the necessities of life, were manufactured, produced, or grown right there on the farm. Nothing was allowed to fall to waste. Theirs was an industriously thrifty family.

The battle that had taken place the day before on Montgomery Farm property was a short, albeit a very violent and bloody battle, and it had concluded when the Confederate forces had retreated through the woods to the southwest. As was commonplace following battles such as this, the armies would bury their dead, lick their wounds, and fight again another day. There were eight dead among the Union casualties and twice that many among the Confederate forces. The carcasses of eight horses littered the fields. Two of the surviving Union horses were wounded so badly that they were led into the woods and shot. Most all of the surviving Union casualties were well enough to walk along with General Kirkland's company of infantry as they prepared to leave and go in pursuit of the retreating Confederate forces. All of the soldiers but the young corporal who was now lying in Abigail Montgomery's upstairs bedchamber had been able to march, or limp, along with their company, having received relatively minor injuries. The eight dead were buried quickly in shallow graves at the edge of the woods, and the wounded had received the immediate care they needed to continue on. The dank smell of gunpowder still hung in the air, and the stains of blood could still be seen among the grassy pastures of Montgomery Farm as the Union forces prepared to leave.

The young comatose corporal was the exception among his

comrades. He would not be leaving with the other troops, and his immobile circumstances posed a dilemma for General Kirkland. Had the young man been a soldier of the Confederacy, he would have most likely been shot and disposed of in the nearby woods, and Kirkland's troops could have hastily proceeded in pursuit of their Confederate prey. But this badly wounded young man was one of Kirkland's own. The young man had distinguished himself in battle time and time again, and having gained Kirkland's esteemed admiration, the general could not bring himself to disregard the soldier's magnificent contribution as if it had been nothing of consequence. The young man could not be carried along with the advancing Union forces, and leaving him behind in the care of biased Confederate sympathizers at Montgomery Farm, although seeming to be an option of ill conceivement, was the only option available. Leaving the young man behind in such a helpless condition seemed nothing short of a death sentence. General Kirkland studied deeply over the subject the evening before his company departed, and with little choice in the matter, he summoned the landowner, Mrs. Abigail Montgomery and her sister, Mrs. Agatha Martin to the front porch of their home for the purpose of engaging them in a conversation of stern warning. With the fire of Union hatred in their eyes, the two women stood on the porch with defiantly folded arms, and listened to what General Kirkland had to say. Without paying the ladies the courtesy of removing his hat or dismounting from his horse, General Kirkland spoke to them from his saddle.

"Mrs. Montgomery, my troops and I are ready to depart from your farm here."

"I would suppose that you've come here to pay me for our two cows that your men butchered last night." Abigail Montgomery had the most compelling urge to draw the revolver which was concealed beneath her apron and shoot the general, but she did not. Her daughters were in a clever hiding place in the house, and if she were to shoot the general, she knew full well that the soldiers would kill her and her sister and set the house ablaze, thus killing her innocent daughters as well.

"Butchering the cows was necessary to feed my men, Mrs. Montgomery. Consider yourself fortunate that we did not kill the other five cows. I've come here merely to inform you of our departure, as a courtesy to you."

"And it's with good riddance from where we stand. And if it's your pleasure to ask for our permission to leave, then you certainly have it."

"Mrs. Montgomery, I shan't waste either of our time by debating the cause of this war, nor my purpose in being here, I will simply appeal to your Christian charity for the life that I will be leaving in your hands..."

"And what life is that, pray tell?"

"I'm referring to the life of the wounded young corporal in your upstairs bedchamber."

"You're leaving him here? Aren't you going to take him with you?"

"Mrs. Montgomery, my surgeons tell me that he cannot be moved, that he will surely die before the sun sets this evening if we attempt to move him."

"So you're leaving him here, in my home? A Union soldier in a southern home? That's absurd!"

"I agree that it's a regretful decision indeed. However, I have no choice but to do just that, Mrs. Montgomery."

"And exactly what is it that you expect of our Christian charity, General? Do you expect for us to nurse the man back to health so that he can rejoin your soldiers and kill more of our sons and husbands?"

"I expect for you to treat him as a human being who is in need of compassionate attention, and not as that of an enemy soldier."

"General Kirkland, you ask too much of us. I have lost my husband and my only son to your wretched Union bullets. My sister here has lost her husband to Union bullets. And now, you ask us to render aide to a Union soldier, perhaps the very soldier who has killed one or more of our loved ones? No! We cannot and will not do it! I demand that you remove him from our home immediately!"

"And how many bullets were fired by your southern menfolk that took the lives of northern sons, brothers, and husbands, Mrs. Montgomery?"

"I simply cannot provide care for the man, General. Such assistance would be a betrayal to the memory of our dead patriots... our sons, and our husbands, and I shan't do it!"

"Oh, but you will indeed render the assistance the young soldier requires. Allow me to state my position in a slightly more definitive manner, Mrs. Montgomery... and you and your sister would do well to listen to what I am about to say. We will be returning this way in a few weeks. If I find that the corporal has been well attended, I will repay each of you for your efforts with money from my own purse. Perhaps my surgeons will advise me that he can be safely moved then, and we will take him with us at that time. As for now, I will not endanger his life so that I can afford you and your sister the convenience of his absence."

"And suppose the man should die before you return, General, what then?"

"When we return, if we find that the young man has died, Mrs. Montgomery, then I will assume the worse—that he died either from your negligence, or at your own murderous hands. I will see that you and your sister are both delivered into the hands of my men, and I will turn my back and keep a blind eye as I allow my men to have their way with you. My troops will burn your house and everything in it to the ground. Your barn will be burned and your horses and mules will be shot and thrown into your well. I will make damned sure that you are left with nothing but ashes and ruin here. Have I made myself clear, Mrs. Montgomery, or do you require a more vivid description?"

"You've made yourself quite clear, General."

"Knowing my full intentions as you do now, might I ask

what your current position on the matter is at this time, Mrs. Montgomery?"

"You've given me little choice in the matter. My sister and I shall do nothing which would encourage the man's death, I give you my solemn oath to that affect. We can attend to his broken leg quite easily, I suppose. But the injury to his head is well beyond our meager capabilities here. This is a farm here, not a hospital. I overheard your very surgeons discussing the gravity of his condition, and his condition is perilous, at best."

"I would imagine that you and your sister here suppose yourselves to be some sort of Christians, do you not, Mrs. Montgomery?"

"Of course we are Christians, what of it?"

"Then perhaps it would be a good idea for you to familiarize yourself with *Romans 12:17*, and *Ephesians 4:32*, and exercise your Christian faith by praying for my corporal's recovery. After you have read these scriptures, stand in front of your own looking glass, and see if the person looking back at you is in fact, a Christian. You've heard my position, and I will not discuss the issue any further with you."

"You threaten my sister and I with such evilment and from the same mouth you quote scripture from the Holy Book?"

"I make no imposed threats. I have only made a solemn promise, and have thus provided you and your sister with a most excellent incentive to be charitable... for once in your miserable lives. Good day, Mrs. Montgomery, I'll see you in three or four weeks. The fate of you and your sister, and the fate of your farm, is in your own hands. Do with it as you will. Good day to you."

As the Union troops vanished in formation, into the woods to the south, Mrs. Montgomery and her sister went back into the house and quickly opened their Family Bible to find the scriptures that General Kirkland had made reference to. Agatha read *Romans 12:17* aloud. *"Recompense to no man evil for evil. Provide things honest in the sight of all men."* And then, *Ephesians*

11

4:32, *"Be ye kind one to another, tenderhearted, forgiving one another, even as God for Christ's sake hath forgiven you."*

Abigail Montgomery took a deep breath and went back to the porch and carefully surveyed the fields and woods surrounding her home to satisfy herself that all of the Union forces had in fact vacated Montgomery Farm. The only trace of Union presence was the smoldering remains of their campfires and the scattering of provisional debris that they had left behind. Satisfied that the Union soldiers had completely gone from their property, Abigail Montgomery addressed her sister, Agatha. "Agatha, please go to the attic and fetch Elizabeth and Sarah from their hiding place. Tell them that it's safe for them to come down now. I'm sure they are probably scared to death up there, bless their hearts."

"Yes, Abigail."

Abigail Montgomery's two young daughters, Elizabeth and Sarah were summoned from a far corner of the attic where they had remained in a clever hiding place behind a loose wall panel the entire time that the property had been occupied by Union soldiers. The four women sat in the parlor of Montgomery House to discuss the disposition of their badly injured and comatose guest. Even though Abigail was only thirty-two years of age, she had always been the strongest and most dominating presence among the family of four womenfolk at Montgomery Farm since all of their younger menfolk had left to fight in the war. Being the mother of both Elizabeth and Sarah, and the older sister of Agatha Martin, she was now considered to be the matriarch and binding agent of what remained of her family, even at her young age. Although she was only thirty-two years of age, the duty of authority had fallen upon her shoulders and she was staunchly determined to provide the leadership that was necessary to hold the remnants of their family together and somehow continue the operation of their farm, without which they would have no income. After all, life on Montgomery Farm had been the only life that any of them had ever known, and the farm had provided them with the essentials to maintain life. As their family leader and spokesperson, Abigail Montgomery was provokingly feisty in nature when conditions warranted, yet gentle and compassionate when circumstances would permit her to embrace the more feminine aspects of her being. Her extraordinary beauty and small stature was misleading, extruding the image of a woman who was both vulnerable and defenseless. But such was not true of Abigail Montgomery. She was combative when necessary, and had always been endowed with steadfast determination and the grit of her ancestral forefathers. She now represented the sole remaining strength and leadership behind the Montgomery family name. Even someday in the future, when the war would finally be over, there would be no menfolk returning to fill or resume a leadership role. They had all been killed, save for Phillip Montgomery. If the family was to have any future whatsoever, it would be only by the grace of God, and Abigail Montgomery's incredible strength and fortitude.

Abigail's daughters, sixteen year-old Sarah and seventeen year-old Elizabeth, had perpetually demonstrated the strictest of obedience to their mother, regardless of the fact that in happier times they had often frolicked playfully with their mother as though they were all adolescent sisters. Theirs had always been a loving and happy relationship before the war, and the deaths of their father and brother had given them an even higher sense of loyalty toward what remained of their family. If and when the war ever ended, there would be no menfolk returning there to assume leadership of the family. Agatha Martin, Abigail's younger sister, was also of strong fortitude, though always compliant and obedient to Abigail's directives. And now, their family and their farm was all that remained for them. Their two Negro servants who had voluntarily remained behind to live on the family plantation had always been regarded more as an aunt and uncle than any type of subservient unequal. Ezra and Vivian had even assumed the last names of their former master, Phillip Montgomery, but spelled their name, *'Gomery.'* They had been granted their freedom sixteen years earlier by the benevolent Phillip Montgomery, and remained at Montgomery Farm as freed tenant farmers under the generous crop-sharing agreement of the Montgomery's. It was an arrangement that was mutually beneficial to all concerned. Ezra was indeed a giant of a man, standing nearly six and a half feet tall, and weighing more than two hundred fifty pounds. His powerful hands were quite capable of performing even the most strenuous of tasks on the farm, yet his nature was that of a gentle man, prone to compassion and unwavering family obedience.

A meager crop of tobacco, corn, wheat, and vegetables was still planted and harvested there each year despite the war, but in the absence of their antebellum workmen, it was now necessary for all family members to join in the farm work. Even the young sisters, Elizabeth and Sarah worked diligently in the fields from time to time in order for the family to have an income to carry them through this difficult phase of their life. Union blockades prevented them from having access to many items of food that they traditionally craved, such as coffee, spices, and processed grain meal, but their income from their tobacco crop enabled them to at least buy the essential amounts of food that they needed to sustain life. Most all of their crops were necessary for the sustainment of life there on the farm, but it was the tobacco crop that afforded them the income needed to purchase the more sumptuous items in their life. Among these objects of opulence, coffee had always been a most treasured family favorite, and in its absence, it was the most coveted of all the missing luxuries. Even in earlier days when the farm had operated at its peak, life had never been overly lavish at Montgomery Farm like it was on so many of the large southern plantations. The Montgomerys had always been prudent with their resources as well as their spending. Consequently, the hardships of war had not presented nearly as severe an impact in their lifestyle as it had for so many other plantations in the region.

Considering the fact that there was a wounded northern soldier in their house now, it became necessary for the family to conduct a consultation, for the purpose of discussing a proper strategy for dealing with this new and discomforting situation. As the young family matriarch, Abigail sent Sarah to fetch Ezra and Vivian to the house, as they were using mules to drag the last of the dead cavalry horses far away from the house. Once they had finished, the six of them sat in the parlor to discuss their current predicament. Exercising her authority of command as well as her inbred leadership skills, Abigail Montgomery addressed her family with a markedly feminine, yet authorative and unwavering voice.

"Having a wounded enemy soldier upstairs in our house now, I think it would be advisable for us to discuss our situation here and make a decision as to how we will best deal with the dilemma that we now have before us. The presence of a Union soldier in our home places us in an awkward position among our countrymen, especially if the young man's identity as a Yankee was to be discovered. I would like to hear suggestions from each of you before we determine our approach in dealing with the situation that has befallen us."

Ezra was the first to bring forth a possible solution to the problem, by asking, "Do you want me to go upstairs and kill the man, Miss Abigail? I'll go up there and do it if you tell me to."

"No, of course not, Ezra! I gave my solemn oath to General Kirkland that we would not harm the man. Enemy or not, we are not barbarians here. Besides, General Kirkland said that he will be passing through here in a few weeks when he returns to Fairfax. He has vowed to burn everything here to the ground if the soldier has been harmed in any way... not to mention the horrible things he will encourage his men to do to us. No, Ezra... our only chance is to try to keep the man alive. God willing, the man will live long enough for Kirkland to return, and he will carry the man away from here at that time."

"How bad is the man wounded, Miss Abigail?"

"I don't know, Vivian. I have not seen the man very close yet, nor have I even inspected his injuries. He was attended by two of

General Kirkland's surgeons an hour ago. I only watched from the hallway as they set his broken leg in place and wrapped it with tobacco staves and bandages. They discussed the possibilities of amputating the man's leg, but said that they were too pressed for time. If the leg doesn't heal correctly or it becomes infected, then I suppose the duty will fall to us to remove the leg."

Sarah, Abigail's youngest daughter, quickly spoke out and asked, "Mercy, Mother! How could we bring ourselves to cut off the leg of a living human being?"

"We will pray that something that drastic will not be necessary, Sarah, but we will do whatever we are forced to do, if such a thing is required in order to preserve the man's life."

"Does the man have full knowledge of how badly he's injured?"

"No, Sarah, he's aware of nothing at the present time. He sleeps soundly, and has been sleeping soundly since he was brought here yesterday afternoon. For all we know, he could be in the final moments of his death sleep. I only know that I overheard one of the surgeons telling General Kirkland that the man's condition was not good. I would like for everyone to accompany me upstairs so that we can go into the room and see the man's injuries for ourselves. Perhaps between the six of us, we can make our own assessment as to how we can best attend to his broken leg as well as the injury to his head."

"Yes, Mother."

Abigail arose from her chair and said, "Everyone please follow me."

The group ascended the creaky old stairway to the second floor where the family bedchambers were located. They entered the room and quietly assembled around the bed where the wounded soldier lay. He slept quietly, and by all outward signs he appeared to be more dead than alive. Elizabeth, perhaps thinking that the soldier was going to be a much older man, was stunned when she first saw the man's face.

"I had imagined him as being a much older man, Mother, he's really not much older than a boy. I've never seen a Yankee this close before, but he surely doesn't look like someone who would be capable of posing any sort of threat to us."

"He's at least twenty-five or twenty-six, Elizabeth. He's a good ten years older than your own age, and quite capable of aiming and pulling the trigger of a rifle. This man is an enemy soldier—of that, there can be no doubt. Look at his uniform, Elizabeth, not his face. Despite how innocent he might look while he's lying there asleep, he's a Yankee and a killer. They all are, and you would do well to remember that... we would all do well to remember that."

Raising the bandage on his head to look beneath, they saw a large lump with dried blood caked in his hair. Sarah looked closely and announced, "His scalp is torn quite deeply here above his ear. It needs to be stitched together so that it can heal properly without becoming septic."

Abigail leaned forward, took a closer look, and said, "It can't be stitched closed until the wound is properly cleaned."

Elizabeth touched the bottom of his right foot and commented, "His foot below the broken leg is somewhat cold to the touch, and might indicate that there is a poor flow of blood below the broken bone."

Sarah spoke up quickly with a recommendation of her own, "Perhaps we can massage his foot three or four times a day and apply warm compresses, Mother. That might aid in the circulation of blood."

"Very well, Sarah, we can do that, but I don't think the broken leg is an issue of such great urgency at present. I see no reason why the Yankee surgeons would have even considered amputating the man's leg. This poor devil doesn't even realize it, but he is very fortunate that the surgeons left him here with both of his legs still attached. The entire leg has a reasonably good color to it. In my estimation, it's the head injury that will take his life if he is to die. What do you think, Vivian?"

"I don't know, Miss Abigail. He don't look none too good to me. He even looks like he's almost dead already. All them dirty clothes next to them open wounds ain't doing him no good, neither. I think we got us a bunch of work to do if we're gonna save this man's life... that's what I think."

Abigail raised the bandages on his leg and immediately proclaimed, "My dear God! Look at this!"

"What is it Mother?"

"Under the splint... see here? His leg has not been set straight! I doubt the bones even match where they're broken. We'll have to re-set his leg, and try to clean that nasty wound better. We'll put a new splint on his leg—a proper splint! Those filthy Yankee scallywags have quite a nerve calling themselves surgeons!"

"Mercy!"

"His uniform is so ragged and torn that it's not worth saving, and I would rather dispose of it than to risk having a Yankee uniform discovered in our home. Our neighbors could easily assume us to be traitors if such a thing was to occur."

"What should we do about improving the man's condition, Mother?"

"We need to get started immediately if we are to save this man's life. I would like for everyone but Vivian and I to leave the room. Vivian, you and I will bring some hot water up here and remove the man's torn clothes and try to bathe him somewhat. Once we have removed all the blood and dirt, and re-set his leg properly, we can make a true assessment as to how badly he's injured. I want his bloody uniform burned. If the man is discovered in our house by anyone of southern conviction, we must tell them that he is a soldier of the Confederacy. Otherwise, he'll be killed, and we'll be left here alone to answer to General Kirkland when he returns. We've all heard the horrible stories of what the Yankees will do to women when their lustful anger is aroused, and we must do everything within our power to prevent losing Montgomery Farm to Kirkland's ravenous appetite for revenge."

"Yes, Ma'am."

"Elizabeth, you and Sarah go to the kitchen and heat up some water in the two largest kettles. I will also need a clean needle and some bleached thread. After Vivian and I have finished bathing him, and have covered his personal area with a bedsheet, we'll call you and Sarah into the room and we'll clean that wound on his head better, stitch it together with needle and thread, and put a clean dressing on it. Those despicable Yankee surgeons should be ashamed of themselves for doing such a poor job. I've seen better dressings than this on horses. Meanwhile, let's go back down to the parlor, and while the water is heating perhaps we can discuss this some more. Agatha, will you please fetch one of the older bedsheets, and cut it into strips for bandages?"

"I am opposed to rendering aid to this man, but I will do as you say, Abigail."

"Hurry on, there's not a moment to lose!"

Elizabeth and Sarah put two large kettles of water on the stove and while they waited for the water to heat, everyone gathered in the parlor again, as Agatha sat there cutting a bedsheet into strips for bandages. Abigail had been thinking, and had formulated a plan in her mind.

"Ezra, I would like for you to make sure the large tobacco wagon is in proper order for a long journey. If the man dies, we must quickly load our most cherished items onto the wagon and flee to Richmond. We can all ride in the carriage, and you and Vivian can follow along behind us in the wagon."

"Yes Ma'am, Miss Abigail."

"If General Kirkland comes back and finds the man dead, Elizabeth and Sarah cannot hide in the attic again for fear of being burned alive, and I would rather die than to see them fall into the filthy hands of the Yankees. If the soldier dies, we have no choice but to flee Montgomery Farm for our lives and pray for God to have mercy on us as we do."

"Yes, Ma'am, Miss Abigail."

"Elizabeth, I would like for you and Sarah to carry the large rocking chair upstairs and place it by his bed. Beginning tonight, I want one of us to be with him at all times. We'll take turns watching over him. We also need to keep the flies away from his open wounds. If he dies during the night, we will immediately make preparations to leave here for Richmond. We can try to make it to the home of Jack and Margaret Stallings. They will give us refuge in their home. Otherwise, we'll have the insidious wrath of General Kirkland to fall upon us. Does everyone understand?"

"Yes, Mother."

"Very well. Let us make haste and tend to our duties."

With a plan firmly established, the young man's wounds were attended, his body bathed, his broken leg was re-set, and everything was properly bandaged under reasonably sterile conditions. When the soldier had received the attention that his wounds required, everyone went about their work much as they had prior to the arrival of the Union invaders. The young man continued to sleep, uttering not a sound or disturbance of any sort, and still appearing to be more dead than alive. Even after the blood and dirt was washed from his body, he appeared to be a gaunt figure of a man... just waiting to take his final breath. By the end of the third day, the swelling had gone down somewhat in his head injury, yet there still appeared to be little hope for the young man's recovery. The women became concerned over the fact that the man had not been drinking water, so they attempted to raise his head slightly so that he could drink without choking. By squeezing small amounts of water from a small rag directly into his throat, he would take short, involuntary swallows that seemed not to be more than three or four ounces during the course of a day. A puzzling improvement developed on the third morning when it became apparent that the man had gained the ability to drink small amounts of water from a glass held to his mouth, yet he did not have the ability to hold the glass or even open his eyes. By the fifth day, there were still no noticeable signs of improvement in his condition other than the fact that the swelling had gone down considerably in both his leg and his head. Outwardly, his body appeared to be going about the process of healing itself, yet inwardly, he remained in an unresponsive and comatose state.

By the end of the fifth day, the women had resolved themselves to the fact that even though the young man was drinking more water now, he was not awake to eat, and would probably continue to emaciate and eventually starve to death. Abigail and her daughters had already begun packing some family heirlooms and keepsakes into trunks in preparation for the man's death and their inevitable journey to Richmond. They made painful and heartrending decisions as to what they would take with them and what they would have to leave behind for Union plunderers. There were many items of bulky furnishings that had once belonged to Abigail and Agatha's mother. Their mother had played the old piano since Abigail and Agatha had been children, and the old piano represented fond memories of their mother. But the old piano would have to be left behind if they were to flee to Richmond. It saddened them both to know that if they had to flee to Richmond, these treasured items would have to be left in place to suffer a fate of theft or destruction. Their situation was desperate, and nothing was more important than their lives.

Then a minor revelation occurred. On the sixth day, in the middle of the night, Sarah rushed into her mother's bedchamber to awaken her. She bore an encouraging announcement.

"Mother! Come quickly! It's unbelievable, but I think the man might be waking up!"

The ensuing ruckus had awakened everyone in the house, and the four women were soon dressed in their nightclothes and standing at the side of the young man's bed. Two oil lanterns supplied enough light for everyone to see that the man's condition still appeared to be unchanged. Puzzled as to why her daughter thought the man was awaking, Abigail asked, "I thought you said that he was awaking, Sarah?"

"I honestly thought that he was, Mother, he actually moaned out the name of Jesus! At least I think that's what I heard him say."

Abigail leaned closer to the man, and from only seven or eight inches away, she spoke loudly to him. "Sir? Can you hear me, Sir?"

There was no response to Abigail's question, so she spoke to him again, "Sir, if you can hear me, then say something, or move a finger... or open your eyes."

Again, there was no response. Agatha soon retired back to her bed while Abigail, Elizabeth, and Sarah continued to look down at the unresponsive and benign face of the young man. Taking her mother by the hand, Sarah asked, "He's going to die, isn't he, Mother?"

"Only God knows for sure, Sarah, but it would certainly appear that way. If he does die, at least we'll have the comfort in our hearts of knowing that we provided for him the best that we could. You and Elizabeth had best go on to your beds now and try to get some sleep. The sun will be rising in another two hours, and I'll watch over him until morning."

Abigail turned the oil lamp to its brightest setting and spent the next hour looking upon the face of the young soldier. She tried to remain objective as to the character of the person there before her, but for some reason the man's face seemed to project the essence of innocence and purity, rather than that of a bloodthirsty and dangerous enemy. An unsolicited warmth of sympathy swept over Abigail's heart as she looked down upon this helpless man. Gently, she picked up his hand, and looked at it closely, and quietly asked, "Sir, did you kill many of my countrymen with these hands of yours? Would you kill again if we should nurse you back to health? Would you repay our Christian benevolence by killing more of our sons and husbands? Perhaps you'll simply die, without providing us with answers to our questions. Still, for some reason I cannot help but wonder about you..."

Oddly enough, even though the man remained unresponsive, Abigail had the strangest sense that he could hear her words. In a moment of arbitrary and spontaneous kindheartedness, she reached forward and gently touched his face while speaking quietly and almost lovingly to him, "Your face is badly in need of a shave. I suppose that you have fought in many battles. God only knows the horrors that you must have witnessed." Continuing to study over the man, Abigail softly asked, "Who are you, Sir, and what kind of a man are you? I know not who you are, and I suppose that I shouldn't even care, but... for some reason I do. Are you really my enemy? Did you kill my son or my husband? Have you ever derived pleasure in raping a defenseless woman, or killing one of my countrymen, or burning a family out of house and home? If you should die, it would give me comfort if I thought that you knew that I do not hate you. It's true, I hate the war and I hate what the war has done to me and my family... but for some odd reason, I cannot find it in my heart to hate you, Sir. Perhaps if I knew you I could easily hate you, but alas, I know nothing about you, save for the color of your uniform... I will pray that you are indeed a gentle man, and I will ask God to bless and heal you. If it will bring comfort to you to know that someone on this earth cares whether or not you live or die... just know in your heart that I care, and I will be praying that you will live, and that you will recover from your injuries. Does it surprise you to hear me say that?"

Then, almost as if she had embarrassed herself by offering such a sympathetic oration to a comatose and dying enemy soldier, she placed his hand back at his side, leaned back in her chair, and resumed watching over him. If ever a man's face portrayed the essence of innocence, such innocence was somehow conveyed to Abigail on this one very touching occasion.

Early the next morning a full company of battle-wearied Confederate infantry and artillery came along the dusty roadway near the house as they quickly advanced northeastward. Abigail and her daughters carried water and biscuits to the troops as they passed by, while the elder grandfather Phillip Montgomery talked with two of the Confederate officers. The officers carried startling news that General Kirkland and his army had been overwhelmingly defeated just two days prior at Stuart's Draft. Rumors carried word that General Kirkland, along with two thirds of his men had been killed in the two-day battle. Three companies of Confederate troops were now advancing northward toward the town of Culpeper, and there was but one thing on the family's immediate horizon that was certain—General Malcolm Kirkland nor any of his army would ever pass this way again. The family had been spared the impending threat of plunder and rape, at least for the time being.

Abigail Montgomery's immediate thoughts were drawn to the wounded soldier lying in the upstairs bedchamber. She had come dangerously close to telling the Confederate troops that there was a wounded Union soldier in their home, but at the last minute, her conscience had taken command of her actions, and she had withheld such information. She suspected with some degree of certainty that if she had relayed such information to the confederate troops, the young man would have most likely been unceremoniously dragged outside and disposed of. Perhaps this mysterious soldier was deserving of such a fate, she did not know. Because of her uncertainty, she withheld any mention of his presence there. There was another, even more compelling reason why she withheld any information regarding the wounded soldier's presence. She felt an anomalous sensation that told her that God was watching her. Divine intervention was taking place, and she could not help but recall the scripture that General Kirkland had made reference to before he had departed, *"Recompense to no man evil for evil. Provide things honest in the sight of all men."*

Upon hearing about General Kirkland's demise from her feeble grandfather, Abigail Montgomery had personally confirmed the validity of such information with two Confederate officers, and after the brigade of Confederate troops had left Montgomery Farm, she called for another meeting in the parlor with the womenfolk and Ezra and Vivian. The elder Phillip Montgomery was also in attendance, yet his feeble state of mind prevented him from being fully aware of all that was said, or contributing to the discussion in a positive manner. Abigail quietly addressed the gathered assembly with a refreshing new confidence that the state of their wellbeing at Montgomery Farm had just improved considerably.

"Once again, all troops have vacated our property here, and we are alone again with a wounded man upstairs. General Kirkland and most of his army have been defeated just two days south of here at Stuart's Draft, and we only have God to thank for that. General Kirkland, himself, was killed in the battle. He shan't be passing this way again, and for the time being, we are freed of any threat of having our farm burned to the ground. Therefore, we have been granted the liberty to do with the Union soldier as we see fit. I have my own opinion of what we should do, but I wish to hear suggestions from each of you before making a final decision. Before discussing the matter, please join me in prayer, as we thank God for delivering us from evil."

Abigail led the assembly in a brief but sincere prayer, and after which she asked, "Agatha, do you have any suggestions as to what we should do with the young man now that General Kirkland has met his doom?"

Displaying a fiery temper, Agatha quickly responded, "Yes, I think we should do away with him, bury his body in the woods behind the tobacco barn, and go about our lives as though this nightmare had never happened. Giving aid and comfort to the enemy is deplorable conduct for a southern patriot. Such a thing might even be perceived as an act of treason, and we could be subject to the reprisal of our countrymen. We should be ashamed of ourselves."

Sarah sprang back at her aunt's suggestion with immediate opposition, clarifying her recommendation with a sobering definition of Agatha's despicable proposal, "So, Aunt Agatha, you're suggesting that we murder the poor man in his sleep and be done with him, is that it? My, my, but God must be terribly disappointed to hear you talk in such a sinful manner!"

"He's not a poor man, Sarah, he's a filthy Yankee, and it wouldn't be the same thing as murder! He's a soldier, an enemy soldier, for heaven's sake! If he recovers, he will be quite capable of killing and burning and raping... just like all the others of his kind!"

Maintaining jurisdiction over the conversation, Abigail looked directly at Agatha and asked, "Agatha, if you really think the man upstairs should be killed in his sleep, why don't you go ahead upstairs now, and do it yourself? He's unconscious and weak, and should offer you little if any resistance. You could simply hold a pillow over his face and smother him quite easily as he sleeps. The rest of us will wait here until the deed is done, and you can call us to come upstairs after you've killed him. Would that satisfy you? Is that really and truly what you want to do with the man?"

"No... I could never bring myself to do such a horrible thing, Abigail. I just..."

"Would it help your conscience to feel better about our killing him if we asked Ezra to go upstairs and tend to it for us?"

"No... I wasn't thinking when I spoke out just now. It was the devil speaking through my lips, and I'm sorry for suggesting such a thing... I was angry and frightened... Forgive me."

"In that case, Agatha, what do you think we should do?"

"I don't know... I would suppose that God would want us to continue caring for him... as we would want someone to care for us, if we were wounded, helpless, and dying."

Abigail looked around the circle and asked, "Elizabeth, what do you think we should do?"

"I'm sorry, but I side with Sarah on the issue, Mother. The Holy Scripture clearly tells us that it is wrong for us to kill another human being. I see nothing evil on this man's face when I look upon him... nothing! He needs our attendance desperately, and..."

Agatha immediately voiced back a response, "And what does the Holy Scripture say about your father, and your brother, and my husband? Was it not equally as wrong for the Union soldiers to kill them? Men die during war, Elizabeth, and we are at war! The Bible says, *an eye for an eye!*"

"Elizabeth immediately erupted, "With all due respect, you

have no idea what you're talking about, Aunt Agatha! You're quoting a passage in Exodus, which Jesus himself rebuked in the fifth chapter of Saint Matthew, saying that we should, '*love thy enemies!*' I would suggest that you study your Bible before attempting to use scripture to support your sinful motives!"

Abigail tried to ease the increasing tension between her daughters and their aunt. "Let us remain calm, and discuss the issue without resentment toward each other or the display of undue emotions. All we have left here at Montgomery Farm is each other, and we should never raise our voices in anger at each other like this. Ezra, what do you think about all of this?"

"It don't make no never mind to me, Miss Abigail. If you wants the man dead, just you say the word, and I'll go upstairs and carry the boy out to the woods so's that you womenfolk don't have to see what's done or clean up any kind of mess."

Sarah immediately lashed out again, "Oh, wouldn't that be just dandy?! Ezra can do our killing for us! How handy! That way, all we have to do is change the bed sheets upstairs and wash our hands of the entire matter! Isn't that convenient?!"

"Control yourself, Sarah. We can accomplish nothing by raising our voices and criticizing one another. Ezra was simply trying to help us in our situation here. He meant no malice."

Sarah replied, "I can't believe that I'm sitting here among the people whom I love, discussing whether or not we should go against God's Holy Word and kill someone! I'll not have any part of such evilness if you should decide to kill him!"

"You will comply with whatever the family decides, young lady!"

"That's where you're wrong, Mother! I'll damn well make my own decision when it comes to murdering someone!"

"Sarah! I'll not tolerate profanity or insulting behavior in this house! Control yourself, young lady!"

"I apologize for both my profanity and my insolence, but I will not apologize for my beliefs! You yourself taught me to be a better Christian than to take part in a murder, Mother! And what about you, Mother? We've not yet heard your opinion of what should be done with the man."

"I believe that killing the young man would be a sin against God, and we should continue to administer to him as best we can."

"Well, God bless you for your Christian generosity, Mother!"

"Sarah! I'll not tolerate your sarcasm either! You are a young lady now, an adult, and I expect you to start acting as such! If you can't control your tongue, then I'll ask you to leave the room!"

"I'm sorry, Mother, I just find this type of conversation very distressing. That poor man is lying helpless in the bed, entirely dependent on us, and we're calmly discussing the merits of killing him, as if we were talking about killing a chicken for dinner!"

"As long as I live and breathe and I am charged with leading our family, there will be no action taken against the young man that will harm him in any way! I will entertain all options that we might have, short of anything that might be in violation of God's law! Is that clear?"

Hearing Abigail's voice raised in anger, the elderly Phillip Montgomery suddenly rose to his feet, and shaking his fist in the air defiantly, he shouted, "I'll gladly wager any man alive that my horses are the finest and fastest horses in the county!"

Abigail once again regained control of the discussion. "I'm sure they are, Grandfather. Agatha, would you please take Grandfather to the side porch and fix a chair for him there? We shall finish our conversation when you return and our emotions have subsided a bit."

"Yes, Abigail."

Abigail was thankful for the brief interruption, and hopeful that tensions within the family would ease, and their conversation could continue under more peaceful conditions. Agatha soon returned after helping the old gentleman to a chair on the porch, and their discussion continued in a more pleasant forum. Abigail looked around the table at her daughters and her sister and quietly asked, "Has everyone had sufficient time to calm down, so that we can resume... peacefully?"

Everyone responded apologetically in the affirmative, and Abigail soon offered, "In truth, the man upstairs will most likely die of his own accord in another day or two, without any need for our violating God's Commandments. Tomorrow will be the sixth day that he has been here, and he's not eaten a bite the whole while, nor has he shown even the slightest sign of recovery, other than drinking small amounts of water. Ezra, in preparation for the probability of his death, I want you to carry the man downstairs, while he's still alive, to the small chambermaid room behind the kitchen. Sarah, prepare the room and the old bed for him there, please."

"Yes, Mother."

"Elizabeth, please change the bloody sheets on the upstairs bed and give them to Vivian to be boiled and washed thoroughly. We will confront each day, one day at a time, as we always have; as a family, and tomorrow, we will see what tomorrow brings."

"Yes, Mother."

"Has the man's uniform been properly disposed of yet?"

"No, Mother, I hid it behind the woodpile on the back porch the first day that we tended to him."

"I want it destroyed immediately... burn it... every trace of it, and scatter the brass buttons in the woods behind the chicken house."

"Yes, Mother."

"We will continue with our nightly bedside vigils until such time as he either awakens, or passes to the great beyond."

"Yes, Mother."

"Ezra, would you please prepare a grave in the woods behind the barn? There seems to be little hope remaining that the man will survive another day, if he even survives that long. When the young man expires, I would like for his body to be wrapped in one of our oldest blankets for burial. I would like for him to be taken from the house and buried as quickly as possible, so that we can put this unpleasantness behind us and go on with our lives. Do you understand, Ezra?"

"Yes Ma'am, Miss Abigail."

"Agatha, I would like for you to watch over the soldier from nine o'clock until midnight tonight, if you would please."

"Of course."

"Sarah, Would you please relieve your aunt from midnight until three o'clock in the morning? Elizabeth, if you would, please relieve your sister at three o'clock and stay with the man until six. I will look in on him from six o'clock and throughout the daylight hours as I attend to my kitchen duties."

"Yes, Mother. Do you feel confident now that it will not be necessary for us to amputate his leg?"

"That's one of the unfortunate aspects of this man's situation, Sarah. His leg appears to be mending perfectly so far. The ghastly injury to his head will be the injury that claims his life, of that, I am almost certain. As long as the young man remains alive, however, we will continue to tell any visitors that he is a wounded soldier of the Confederacy. In the unlikely event that our property is trespassed by those Northern scavengers again, we will tell them that the soldier was a corporal in Kirkland's army, and politely encourage them to take him away from here. In the meantime, as long as he is in our care, we will administer to him as God would expect any good Christian to do. We will pray for him to recover, and when he dies, we will pray for God to have mercy on his poor, wretched soul."

O   O   O

The following two days passed uneventfully. The young soldier had been under the women's care for eight days and nights. In the performance of their Samaritan obligations, the lady caregivers had become understandably endeared to the helpless young man. During the many hours that they had administered to him, his face had become a familiar sight to them, and his presence in their house posed no apparent threat to the occupants there. As senseless as such a thing may have seemed to an onlooker, each of the ladies had conversation with the man as they tended to his wounds and watched over him. He was but an anonymous and nameless individual who was completely dependent on the mercy of his hosts, yet the ladies there at Montgomery House spared no compassionate attention to the young man's needs. They gently talked to him as they tidied his bed, trimmed his fingernails and toenails, washed his face, and combed his hair. Even Agatha talked sweetly to the man and began to have high hopes that he would indeed recover from his injuries.

With the burden of leadership continuing to rest squarely upon her young shoulders, Abigail Montgomery and her family now lived in the same household with two men—one of which was feeble and troubled greatly by the discordance of senility, and the other one wounded, helpless, and entirely unresponsive. There was no one to provide the women with the comfort of protection or the reassurance of governance and leadership. That duty belonged solely to young Abigail Montgomery, and no one else. Outwardly, Abigail provided the family with the leadership and direction that they needed, but inwardly, the role of leadership was a burden which she despised, and it was an encumbrance that was taking a toll on her. It was a burden that denied her the ability to freely embrace the more feminine aspects of her life. She wanted to enjoy the womanly splendors of daintiness and moralistic primness, yet that was a luxury which circumstances had stolen from her. She had never wanted to accept what had been traditionally acknowledged as being a man's responsibility in the first place. Nevertheless, fate had thrust such an unwanted role upon her, and she had risen to accept the challenge. After all, she was of a stronger constitution than her sister, Agatha, and there was no one else among them to accept such a pronounced responsibility.

Everyone had done precisely as Abigail had instructed them. The downstairs chambermaid room was cleaned of the items which had been stored there, fresh bedsheets were put on the bed, and things were re-arranged somewhat within the small room to allow for a chair to be brought in and placed next to the bed. The chair was intended to serve in more of a *death watch* capacity than anything else. It was a place where a vigilant family member could observe the young soldier when he breathed his last breath, and thus carry word of his passing throughout the house to the other family members. The blood-stained bedsheets from the upstairs bedchamber were stripped from the bed and taken outside to be boiled and washed. Everyone busied themselves that afternoon in making the preparations to move the wounded soldier downstairs, and all preparations were successfully completed more than an hour before sunset. Ezra had been told by Abigail to carry the man as gently as possible when the time came to move him, so that the move would cause the young soldier no additional stress or unnecessary trauma.

Elizabeth and Sarah had obediently followed their mother's instructions and burned the soldier's badly torn uniform in the same fire that was used to heat the caldron of water to wash the bloodstained sheets. Then they threw the brass buttons from the uniform into the woods. Ezra cleaned the soldier's blood-spotted boots, oiled them, and stored them under the chambermaid bed. As soon as the room was in order, Ezra returned to the man's bedside upstairs. When all preparations had been completed, they were ready to move the young man's motionless body downstairs. Abigail had given some thought to rummaging through some trunks in the attic to retrieve some clothes for the young man, but with such little hope resting in the man's recovery, she thought that such a thing as finding clothes for him would be a futile effort. To Agatha, Abigail commented, "God sent him into this world naked, and I suppose that it's only befitting for us to return him to his Maker naked."

The Examination Chamber

"Beloved, I wish above all things that thou mayest prosper and be in health, even as thy soul prospereth."
3 John 1:2

xercising the greatest of compassionate care, Ezra did as he had been told, and wrapped the soldier's naked body in a bedsheet. With Abigail, Sarah, and Elizabeth assisting him, they carefully carried the young man downstairs to the small chambermaid room behind the kitchen, a place that was nearest to the back porch door. Ezra carried the bulk of the man's body in his arms and Sarah and Elizabeth each held the man by his ankles, while Abigail carefully cradled his head in her hands. The small room had been used as the sleeping quarters for a chambermaid twenty years earlier, at a time when there were servants in the house. In Abigail's way of reasoning, when the man took his final breath, it would be a relatively simple task for them to load his body onto a wagon there at the back door, and Ezra could take him to the woods for burial. Continuing to follow Abigail's directives, Ezra did as he had been told, and prepared an appropriate grave in the woods behind the barn to receive the young man's body when he expired. It was an exercise that bore grim testament to the fact that the man's remaining time on this earth was at best, grievously uncertain, and his recovery was thought to be well beyond any imaginable hope.

On the second morning after the soldier had been moved into the chambermaid room, Abigail and Agatha looked in on their guest and spoke with each other about his condition. Sarah and Elizabeth had gone to the barn to milk the cows and Abigail and Agatha were awaiting the milk so that they could separate the cream and churn butter. Their normal workday was just starting as they stood there over the sleeping young man and exchanged their sisterly thoughts.

Agatha looked down upon the young man with a pitiful expression on her face and sympathetically said, "You know, Abigail, it sorely shames me that I once suggested that we should do away with this helpless man. I'm ashamed of having suggested such a dastardly thing. Yankee or not, the longer I find myself watching over him at night, the more attached I seem to become to him for some reason. It comforts me to know that I haven't the slightest of doubt that we are doing everything we can possibly do to affect his recovery."

"I feel the same way, Agatha."

"I have the oddest sense of responsibility that I should do everything in my power to protect him... as a mother would protect their own helpless child. It's really quite strange that I should feel that way..."

"I understand perfectly how you must feel. One cannot help but feel obligated to render assistance to someone who is as helpless as this man is, Agatha. In the same odd sort of way as you, I'm finding myself becoming attached to him as well, and like you, I don't know why I should feel that way. I wish that I could be provided with some assurance that all our efforts were benefitting him. I sometimes feel as though our best efforts are only prolonging his eventual death."

"Perhaps God will surprise us all, and allow this man to recover soon, Abigail."

"While we cannot rule out the possibility of his recovery, try not to raise your hopes too high, Agatha. He's shown us very few encouraging signs of recovery so far. His wounds appear to be healing, and he's certainly drinking more water each day, but other than that..."

Agatha held the man's head in her hands and tilted it forward slightly while Abigail slowly gave the man some water, which he swallowed without difficulty. "Look at how well he drinks now, Agatha. I don't understand how he can swallow, and yet remain completely asleep at the same time." With sadness in her voice and eyes, Abigail continued to say, "It seems so strange to me that the man can show such encouraging signs of improvement outwardly, yet remain so unresponsive in all other respects. He has shown only the faintest sign of any fever, his complexion appears to have improved, and he even seems to be drinking more water nowadays, yet he passes no bodily fluids whatsoever. I don't understand how it's possible for him to drink water with such prolificy and never pass any fluids."

"You're mistaken, Abigail, he does indeed pass fluids."

"Why would you say something like that, Agatha?"

"I said it because it's true, that's why. I've witnessed him passing fluids with my own eyes. He passes fluid quite willingly. When I've sat with him the last three evenings he's urinated perfectly for me each time that I've asked him to."

"Each time you've asked him to? You're not making any sense to me, Sister, he can't hear you."

"Don't you tell me that he cannot hear, Sister, I know better! He hears me perfectly! And he urinates for me every time that I ask him to."

"If this is true, why does his bedsheet and mattress remain perfectly dry? I've noticed no wetness upon his bed. The cloth padding we have under his body remains perfectly dry as well. We seldom have to change his bedsheets, and when we do, it's always because his wounds have drained blood, not because he has passed any type of fluid. What on earth are you talking about, Agatha?"

"Once a day, for the last three days, he's urinated for me each time I have requested him to do so."

"And exactly how is this accomplished without so much as a trace of wetness left behind in his bed, pray tell? How might you explain that to me?"

"I'd be glad to explain that. Three times now, I have carefully eased him onto his good side so as not to cause any stress or undue pain to his injured leg. Then, I've simply propped a pillow under his injured leg, pulled his bedsheet down, and held a six-ounce jar in place for him. At that point, I've simply said, *'go ahead and pee,'* and he does it for me without hesitation... perfectly... every time. He's neither opened his eyes nor has he ever said a word to me, but he seems to know what he's supposed to do, and he simply does it, every time that I ask him to. He's really quite cooperative in that respect."

"Lord have mercy, Agatha! I don't believe a word of this! If it's true, then why haven't you told me about this before now?"

"I didn't think it was all that important, Abigail. He's never opened his eyes or spoken so much as a single word, but I swear to you that I'm being truthful!"

"Well it is important! It's very important! If you're being truthful with me, it's an encouraging sign that he may be making some progress in his healing. You should have told me about all of this three days ago when it first happened. I've been aggravatingly puzzled over his ability to drink water and pass no fluid. Perhaps there is more hope for his recovery than I thought possible."

"I hope and pray that's true, Abigail. Nothing would please me more than to see the man make a complete recovery... unless of course, he becomes fit enough to fight again. I shudder to think that we would somehow be instrumental in enabling him to kill our countrymen again."

"Only God will determine what becomes of him. Tell me something, Agatha, when you assist him in performing this function, is it necessary for you to actually touch his... his... male part... you know... his private thing...?"

"Well of course it's necessary to touch him down there,

Abigail. How else could a sleeping man be expected to point himself into the jar when he pees? It's essential that I point his member into the jar while he urinates. I simply hold the jar with one hand, take his member into my other hand, then point it into the jar. It's necessary so that the bed doesn't become wet and fouled. Otherwise, we would be changing bedsheets and washing and airing out mattresses and padding every day, and the room here would probably have the offensive odor of a privy."

"Couldn't you simply place a chamber pot beneath him somehow without having to touch anything personal?"

"I've already tried using a chamber pot, and it's too big to fit under him without bending his leg in a manner which would cause undue stress to his injury. The night I tried it, he moaned out loud with pain. The jar works perfectly, though, and it's not as though he is awake to witness me touching him down there."

"Mercy sakes... This is good news indeed! With his body functioning normally like that, this is the most encouraging thing that has happened since he has been here! We should continue to encourage him to drink as much water as possible, and I would appreciate it if you would continue to assist him in urinating, but we must not mention this to Sarah or Elizabeth. I surely wouldn't want them to think that something as vulgar as assisting a man to urinate would ever be required of them when they're watching over him. That's a chore which should only be performed by you or me, or perhaps Vivian. It's our duty to protect Sarah and Elizabeth's innocence of men until they are older. They have come of age now, but I do not want them to have knowledge of a man's nakedness until they are wed, if that is at all possible. It's important to me that they remain innocent... especially after what you and I had to endure in our youth."

"I agree, no one should have to go through what we went through. And as far as attending to the man's private needs are concerned, such a duty should only be relegated to women who have been married before, like you and me, and possibly Vivian. But Vivian is seldom available here at the house."

"Then the duty belongs to you and I. Perhaps you could instruct me as to the correct procedure, and you and I can attend to such matters ourselves, during the times when we are responsible for watching over him. You could attend to him in the mornings, and I could attend to him in the evenings. Does that sound like an agreeable plan to you?"

"Yes, of course it does."

"When could you teach me the proper procedure? I'm still having a difficult time believing that such a thing is even possible."

"I'll demonstrate the procedure right now if you like. I haven't attended the man since last evening, and I feel certain he is in need of urinating by now. It's really a very simple procedure, and as I said, the man is entirely cooperative. I keep the jar over here under the bed. If you'll close the door in case Elizabeth and Sarah come back from the barn, I'll get the jar and show you exactly what I do each time. There may be a better method to accomplish this, but the method I use has worked extremely well for me."

"What on earth gave you the idea to attempt this... the very first time you did it?"

"I was watching over the man three nights ago and simply realized that he had not been wetting the bed. I thought that to be very odd, and decided to see if he would cooperate by using the jar, and to my utter surprise, he did. If you will recall, Abigail, he began drinking greater amounts of water three days ago."

"This is amazing, to say the least, but I still find all of this very difficult to believe!"

Agatha and Abigail locked the bedchamber door, eased the sleeping man partially onto his good side, pulled down his bedsheet, and Agatha positioned the six-ounce jar into place as Abigail studiously looked over her shoulder. Agatha then whispered to Abigail, "It's important for you to have his member pointed down into the jar like this before you ask him to start. He starts peeing fairly soon after you ask him to. You need to be aware of that so you don't accidently cause him to make a mess on the bed."

"I'm afraid that I'll believe all of this only after I've seen it occur with my own eyes."

"Then prepare yourself for a surprise, Abigail, and watch this."

Agatha leaned very close to the man's ear, appearing to be almost close enough to touch the man's ear, and very softly and lovingly said, "Sir, it's me, Agatha. I'm here with my sister to attend you now. It's alright now, I have the jar in place for you. You can go ahead and pee now. Come on, it's alright... go ahead and pee now... Let's show Abigail what a big boy you are. That's it, oh my goodness, yes! You're doing just fine. Just keep peeing all you want to... Have you finished already? Good! Well now, that's the best you've ever done! I'm so proud of you!" Abigail watched in complete astonishment as Agatha demonstrated the process with a remarkable three or four ounces of success.

"That was incomprehensible, Agatha! I'm utterly amazed! The poor man slept soundly through the entire process, yet he responded to your commands with perfect obedience! This is unbelievable!"

"I told you so! Oh! I almost forgot... watch this..."

Then Agatha surprised Abigail even further, when she leaned forward over the man and kissed him on his forehead!

"Agatha! My Lord Sister, have you lost your mind or something? Was that really necessary?!"

"Yes, it was indeed... it's a very important part of the process. It's simply the way that I reward him for his cooperation. Such a reward seems appropriate for someone as compliant as he is. It only seems fair."

"Land sakes alive! I hardly know what to make of all this! I'm almost speechless! If it was your intention to stun me with all of this, you've certainly succeeded!"

Agatha carried the jar outside and promptly emptied it, rinsed it out, and sat it back under the man's bed to be used again the next time.

"That's all there is to it, Abigail. What do you think?"

"I'm impressed beyond words! I shan't begin to tell you how encouraged I am now. I really think the man is showing remarkable improvement."

"Do you think you can attend to the task yourself without difficulty?"

"I don't know why not. It seems simple enough... Yes, I'm confident that I can do it without a great deal of difficulty. The most difficult part seems to be rolling the man onto his side without causing distress to his injured leg."

Abigail and Agatha were both greatly encouraged by the man's progress, and for the first time, Abigail gained new optimism that the man's recovery might be forthcoming. As they had agreed, they never mentioned the procedure to Sarah or Elizabeth.

Late that evening, as everyone was in their bedchambers preparing for bed, Abigail entered the soldier's room a half hour before Sarah was due to arrive for her regular nightly three-hour vigil. Abigail locked the door, carefully eased the man partially onto his side, propped a pillow under his injured leg, and pulled the young man's bedsheet down as far as his knees. She retrieved the jar from under the bed and held it in place with one hand, just as she had seen Agatha do that very morning. But then she found herself becoming hesitant to touch and hold the man in the same brazenly uninhibited manner that Agatha had so willingly and unashamedly demonstrated to her. Her hand was hovering a mere inch from the man's groin, and poised to do its duty, but she was nervously reluctant. Twice she opened her fingers to take the man into her hand, yet each time she withdrew her hand without actually touching him. She told herself, "*It's utterly ridiculous for me to hesitate like this. This man needs my help. It is my responsibility to administer to his needs. This is something that has to be done, and if Agatha has the courage and fortitude to touch him in such a manner, then so do I!*" She closed her eyes momentarily, and said, "*Lord, as desirous as I am to see this man awaken from his injuries, please let him remain asleep while I'm attending to this unpleasant duty."* She took a deep breath and softly said, "Sir, don't be alarmed, but I am about to touch... you... uhhh... for the purpose of pointing you into the jar. We have no male attendants here at Montgomery House, so the duty has fallen to Agatha and I. Please bear with me, and please don't do anything quite yet..." Gingerly, she forced her hand to do its duty, and with an unfamiliar and indisposed grip on the man, she delicately pointed him into the jar, just as Agatha had done. Her embarrassment had risen to a level much higher than she had anticipated, but she had mustered the audacity to do what she had to do. *"Thank God,"* she said to herself, *"the hard part has been done..."* With the situation seeming to be well under control now, and with both of her hands apprehensively occupied, she took another deep breath and positioned her mouth close to the man's ear, using the same technique that Agatha had so professionally demonstrated to her that morning, and softly said, "Lord give me strength... Uhhh... Sir...? Uhhh... This is Abigail Montgomery... I'm Agatha's older sister. I'm here for the worthy purpose of assisting you in urinating, and although it discomforts me greatly to do this, I'm ready anytime you're ready... I think. You may begin relieving yourself at any time now, if you wish to do so. Please commence."

Nothing whatsoever happened. Through the clear glass of the small jar, she could distinctly see that the young man was not responding to her prompting in the same manner in which he had so readily responded to the prompting whispered to him by Agatha that morning. Abigail waited for a moment or two, until she was certain that the man was not going to respond to her initial request, then, she took another deep breath and tried to offer him further encouragement.

"Sir, have you no need to relieve yourself at the present time, or did you simply not hear me? You may begin now." Still, nothing happened, and Abigail began to feel as though her efforts were an embarrassing failure. In her estimation, the only positive aspect of her present circumstance was that no one was there to bear witness to her humiliation. Not wanting to admit defeat this early in the process, she tried once more.

"You may commence with relieving yourself, Sir. I swear to you that you are in the correct position to do so, and it is safe for you to proceed now. Please, Sir... this is not an easy thing for me to do when you refuse to cooperate like this. I've seen you drink a goodly amount of water since this morning, and I feel quite certain that you have fluid to expel, so please commence at any time."

Once more, nothing happened. With there seeming to be no available recourse, Abigail practically pleaded with the man. "Sir, I shan't begin to tell you how compromised and embarrassed I feel at present, holding your... thing like this... If the women at my church could see me now, I would be... banished for all eternity, I'm sure."

Again, nothing happened. Abigail thought back, trying to remember the exact words that Agatha had used with such resounding success. She vividly recalled how sweetly Agatha had talked to the man, almost as though she had been talking to an adorable baby, and decided to speak as lovingly to him as she possibly could using the same tone of sweet baby talk. As embarrassing as it was for the prestigious widow, Abigail Montgomery, to speak loving baby talk to a man while holding a jar in one hand and his...

"Sir, you can pee now. Honestly you can. Come on and pee for Abigail... You pee'd perfectly for Agatha this morning, won't you please pee for me? I'm begging you, Sir... Come on, show me what you can do... be a big boy now and go ahead and pee for me... please pee for me... Oh! Mercy! That's it! You're doing it! You're doing a marvelous job! I'm so proud of you!" Initially, Abigail was pleased with the man's compliance. But after a moment or two, the tone of Abigail's voice changed, and she became concerned. "Sir? Sir? Uhhh... Sir?"

Abigail's concern heightened, as she watched the level of urine in the small six-ounce jar rising closer to the top. "Are you just about finished, Sir? Sir, the jar is getting full... Please stop now... Sir, please stop! I beg of you! Oh my Lord! The jar is going to overflow if you don't stop, Sir, Please stop now! Oh... my goodness!"

Desperate to bring the situation under control, Abigail quickly announced, "I'm very sorry to do this to you, Sir, but you've given me no choice!" With that, Abigail tightened her grip on the man significantly, to such an extent as to cause the knuckles of her fingers to turn white, thus stopping the flow almost immediately. "I'm sorry if this is hurting you in any way, but you've given me no choice!" In a near panic, she looked around the small room, trying to conceive of her next move, but had no idea what to do. Now, she was faced with a disturbing predicament. One of her hands held a jar of urine that was very nearly filled to the brim, and the other hand held tightly onto the man's... well... As if to make matters even worse, as Abigail frantically tried to conceive of a plan which would allow her to release the constricting grip that she now had on the man, Sarah arrived at the bedchamber door, and found it to be locked from the inside. Having both hands fully occupied, Abigail couldn't go to the door or even leave the poor man's bedside. She was helpless, and could do nothing but maintain her awkward and embarrassing grip on both the man and the jar.

"Mother? Are you in there?"

"Oh my goodness! Uhhh yes, dear, I'm in here."

"The door is locked, Mother."

"Uhhh... yes, darling, I know it is..."

"What are you doing, Mother?"

"Me? What am I doing? Well... at the moment... Uhhh... I'm doing nothing really important, dear. I'm just in here taking care of the man... that's all..." In her desperate state of mind, she wondered, *"Dear Lord! What can I do?"*

"Will you please unlock the door for me so I can come inside, Mother? It's almost ten o'clock, and it's time for me to start watching over the man."

43

"Uhhh... The door? Uhhh... No, as a matter of fact, I can't unlock the door right now, dear."

"Why not? Is everything alright in there, Mother?"

"Uhhh... Yes, dear, everything is fine, it's just that... I'm uhhh... experiencing a minor difficulty at the present time, and both of my hands are occupied at the present, that's all. It's nothing to be concerned about, dear. Listen to me closely, Sarah, I need for you to go upstairs and tell Agatha that I need for her to come down here as quickly as possible. I want you to remain upstairs in your bedchamber until I send for you, alright, dear?"

"Why? Mother, what's wrong in there?"

"**Just do as I say, Sarah**! I'll explain things to you later, dear. Now there's not a moment to lose, go quickly! Please!"

"Yes, Mother."

A short while later, when Agatha arrived at the bedchamber door and found it to be locked, Abigail asked her to go outside to the bedchamber window, where Agatha removed the window screen and stood there on a wooden crate. When she looked inside and saw her sister balancing a full jar of urine in one hand and holding the man's ... in the other, she lapsed into an immediate fit of hysterical laughter. Her laughter caused Abigail more than just a little humiliation, not to mention her immediate anger!

"**This is not a laughing matter, Agatha**! Stop it! Stop it right now! Please reach in and let me hand you this jar to be emptied. Careful! It's filled to the brim!"

"Why do you have such a tight hold on the poor man's member, Abigail? It's turning blue!"

"I can't help it! The jar is full to the brim, and if I loosen my grip he'll pee on the bed, that's why! It's too late in the night to be changing bedsheets and mattresses! Just empty the jar please and hand it back to me, and stop your insane laughter at once! There's nothing humorous about this situation whatsoever!"

"Oh, but I must disagree with you, Sister! This may be the most humorous thing I've ever witnessed before! If Sarah and

Elizabeth could only see their prissy and sophisticated mother at this moment... holding a man by his... Ha! Ha! Ha!"

"So help me, Agatha, if you don't stop laughing this instant and help me, I'll throw this jar at you! I swear I will!"

Still laughing so hard she could barely contain herself, Agatha reached inside to carefully accept the full jar.

"Hurry and empty the jar, Agatha, the man is starting to groan."

"I'm not surprised that he is groaning, Abigail, you're squeezing his poor member so hard it's turned blue! He's probably in excruciating agony, poor soul!"

Agatha emptied the jar behind the house and hurriedly handed it back inside to Abigail, who replaced it under the man so that he could finish his natural endeavorment. Finally loosening her firm grip significantly, she again encouraged the man to resume his efforts. "I'm sorry that I had to do that, but it's your own fault for passing so much fluid at one time. The jar is back in place now, and you may resume peeing. I hope that I didn't hurt you too much..."

With the jar once again in place, there were only a very few residual drops produced by the man at that point, and Abigail assumed that her resolute grip had most likely gotten the man out of the mood to cooperate.

"Thank you, Sir! God bless you, and thank God that's over."

Abigail arose from the bed and unlocked the door for Agatha to come inside. She explained in detail everything that had happened to Agatha who immediately burst into such violent laughter again, that her face became red. Ignoring Agatha's insane laughter, Abigail quickly went into the kitchen, and when she returned, she placed a larger, twelve-ounce jar under the bed for future use. She eased the man over onto his back, recovered him with his bedsheet, and before she could stop herself, she gently kissed him on his forehead, and said, "You must have drank a lot of water today. That's good, and Agatha will see to your personal attendance from now on." With the impending arrival of Sarah, Abigail raised the man's bedsheet one last time, long enough to assure herself that his ------ had returned to a normal color. When Agatha's irritating laughter had subsided somewhat, Abigail pounced on her with immediate harsh words.

"I shall never do that again! From now on, I wish for you to assist the man in the evenings! I will attempt to administer to him in the mornings only, but only as long as he cooperates with me. He cooperates for you much better than he responds to me, and I shan't compromise myself in such a horrid circumstance ever again!"

Still laughing at her sister's embarrassment, Agatha paused in her laughter only long enough to respond, "I'm sorry that I laughed at you, Abigail. Please forgive me, Sister."

"Very well... you're forgiven..."

"Oh... might I ask you one question before I go upstairs to my bedchamber, Abigail?"

"Yes, what is it?"

"You do intend to wash your hands before you make our biscuits and bread in the morning, don't you? Ha! Ha! Ha! Ha!"

Agatha was still laughing hysterically when she turned to go upstairs to get Sarah, and Abigail was still seething in anger. Abigail was not given to the use of profanity, and thought surely that if she had made any additional comments to her beloved sister that night, her comments would most certainly have been riddled with words unbecoming a Christian lady. Instead, she only said, "If you ever mention this to Sarah or Elizabeth, I'll tie you to a tree with your own tongue and take an axe to you! I swear it!"

Agatha's incessant laughter could be heard throughout the house as she climbed the stairs to her bedchamber. Abigail could faintly hear Sarah asking Agatha, "What is so humorous?" Agatha simply answered, "Ask you mother." Sarah soon arrived for her nightly vigil and despite her repeated pleadings, Abigail refused to tell her why Agatha had been laughing so much, nor anything about the embarrassing events that had prevailed during the previous half hour. She went upstairs to her bedchamber for the night, leaving Sarah extremely curious, and completely unaware of the confusion that had transpired earlier.

○　○　○

Two evenings later, on the eleventh day of May, Sarah sat in watchful vigilance in the chair at the young man's bedside awaiting Elizabeth's arrival to relieve her. It was Sarah's eighth night of such observant vigilance since the man had been there. An oil lamp was nearby, casting a kerosene-fragranced dim light, and she gazed intently at the young man's face as she had done for so many hours and so many nights before. Like all of the other ladies at Montgomery House, she had become familiar with every feature of the man's face as she looked for encouraging signs of life; a twitch of the mouth, an opening of an eye, or the sound of his voice. In the distant hallway upstairs, Sarah could faintly hear her mother when she knocked on the door of Elizabeth's bedchamber and softly called, "Elizabeth, dear?"

"What is it, Mother?"

"I dislike having to wake you, darling, but it's almost three o'clock, and it's time for you to go downstairs and relieve Sarah."

"Yes, Mother. I'll be down as soon as I dress."

Sarah could barely hear the sounds of her sister stirring upstairs as Elizabeth scuffled around in her room to don her slippers and bed robe. Then, she heard the creaking of the boards in the stairway as her sister descended the steps. When Elizabeth came into the small bedchamber, Sarah remained seated in the chair instead of immediately arising to go to her room. Elizabeth moved the man's feet slightly to the side, and sat quietly at the foot of the bed as both sisters looked down upon the injured young man in the dim light of a solitary oil lamp. It was shortly before the stroke of three as the sisters quietly talked, so as not to be heard in the rest of the house. Sarah continued staring at the young man's face, and asked, "Do you think that he is a married man, Elizabeth?"

As Elizabeth replied to her sister's question, the old clock in the parlor struck the hour of three.

"We've no way of knowing one way or the other, Sarah. But if he is a married man, I can't help but feel that his wife is a very fortunate woman... whoever she is... that is, if he lives long enough to come back home to her after the war. Are you going upstairs to your room?"

"Oddly enough, I'm not very sleepy tonight. I would rather remain here with you and talk for a while longer, if you don't mind."

"Of course I don't mind. I appreciate your company."

"Do you think this room smells musty, Elizabeth?"

"Yes, very much so, it's the kerosene odor more than anything else, I think. I'll open the window a bit. A little fresh air would probably be good for all of us, and it may even help comfort the man in his sleep."

Elizabeth raised the window as Sarah asked, "How old do you think he is, Elizabeth?"

"If I had to guess, I would say that he's most likely between twenty-five and twenty-nine. I think that he's much closer to Mother's age than he is to ours. Owing to the amount of hair on his chest, I would think that he is at least twenty-seven or twenty-eight."

"Elizabeth, may I ask you for your frank and honest opinion of something?"

"Of course... what is it?"

"I've looked upon his face for several nights now, as I've sat here next to his bed, and I'm sure that you have too, and I would like to know if you think he is a handsome man."

"Keep your voice down, Sarah. I have the oddest sensation that he may be lying there listening to our every word. And for all we know, he is."

"That's utterly ridiculous! He's not conscious of anything, Elizabeth. He's not made more than soft moans since he was brought to our house. He can hear nothing in his present state. Now, answer my question, please."

"Very well… Yes, I admit that I think he's a handsome man, perhaps the most handsome man I've ever seen. I've often looked at him myself as I combed his hair, and imagined what he would look like if he were clean shaven. How about you, do you think he is a handsome man?"

"Oh yes, very much so, and I've also wondered what he would look like if he were clean shaven. I've often wondered if a person's hair continued to grow when they were asleep at night, and after having watched this man for so many days now, I can plainly see that it does continue to grow. The hair on his face has grown considerably just in the short time he has been here. Do you think we should attempt to shave his face?"

"I don't know. Perhaps if he recovers we could. Such an effort would be a waste of time if he dies. I'll ask Mother tomorrow and see what she has to say about it."

"He's not going to die, Elizabeth!"

"Oh? And just what is it that makes you so certain of that, Sarah?"

"I think that God sent him here for a reason, and I just have the oddest feeling that he's not going to die."

"Why on earth would God send us a Yankee? Why would God not send us a dashing and debonair southern gentleman—one closer to our age?"

"I don't know, but I do feel that God has sent him here, and I don't think he's going to die, either."

"Perhaps he won't… at least I hope and pray he doesn't. I could think of a thousand questions that I would like to ask him if he ever awakens and is able to talk to us."

"Elizabeth, if I asked you another question, would you be perfectly honest with me?"

"I've always been perfectly honest with you, Sarah. You can ask me anything you like."

"During the many hours that you have watched over him, when you've been alone in the room with him, all by yourself, like we are now, have you ever raised the bedsheet and looked underneath?"

49

"Sarah! I'm ashamed of you for asking such an outrageous question as that! You're making my face blush just to suggest such a thing. Looking at a man in such an invasive manner would be sinful!"

"There's nothing sinful about merely looking, Elizabeth! And you haven't answered my question yet. Have you ever peeked beneath the bedsheet at him? Yes, or no?"

"No! Of course I've never peeked beneath his bedsheet!"

"Not even once? Be honest with me..."

Elizabeth responded quite sternly at Sarah's implied accusation, "No!" But then, Elizabeth suddenly grew suspicious of Sarah's motives for asking the question in the first place. She looked at her sister rather skeptically, and dubiously asked, "Have you?"

"Me? Only once... earlier tonight, for a very brief moment... or two. I was curious as to whether or not he wore an undergarment under the bedsheet, and to my surprise, I found that he wears nothing whatsoever."

"Sarah! I'm terribly disappointed that you would admit to such a wicked and outrageous thing as that! Suppose that it was you lying there, helpless and defenseless... would you want this man to raise your bedsheet and gawk at your nakedness?"

"Looking never hurt anyone, Elizabeth!"

"Land sakes, Sarah! Sometimes it shames me to hear the filthy things that come out of your mouth! If Mother could hear you now, she would be washing your mouth out with soap!"

"I'm an adult now. Mother would scold me, yes, but she would never wash my mouth out with soap. I'm only being honest with you, Elizabeth."

"This poor man is entirely at our mercy, and to think that you would invade his privacy like that... my, my, my..."

"I was curious, that's all. I've always been sort of curious about what a man looks like, I can't help it. I'm sixteen years old, Elizabeth! Lots of women my age have already married and had a baby, and I've never even seen what a naked man looked like before tonight. I've only seen the nakedness of small boys before tonight, never that of a grown man."

"Land sakes, Sarah! And is the nakedness of a grown man so much different than that of a young boy?"

"Mercy, Elizabeth! The difference is astounding!"

"Really? Exactly what do you mean by that, pray tell?"

"I don't know, I can't explain it."

"Please tell me that you didn't touch this poor man in an inappropriate manner... did you?"

"No, of course not! I only looked! I promise you!"

"This kind of talk is sinful, Sarah! If Mother knew that you raised the man's bedsheet you would be severely punished, and probably disallowed from ever being left alone with him again! You should know that!"

"You won't tell her, will you, Elizabeth?"

"No... of course I won't. We've always shared little secrets between us. I would never betray you, but you need to restrain yourself from such evil impulses. Satan is putting thoughts like that in your head. And suppose this man is aware of the fact that you took such liberties? How would you ever explain yourself to the man if he were to wake up suddenly and find you studying over him in such an intrusive manner?"

"He's sleeping quite soundly, and has been for more than eight days now. He's not aware of anything. You're a year and a half older than I, have you ever looked upon a man's nakedness before, not a child, Elizabeth, but a real man?"

"No! Never! Someday I'll have a husband to look upon, and I'm perfectly content to wait until I am married."

"Don't try to tell me that you've never been just a little curious as to what a naked man looks like, Elizabeth."

"Of course I've been somewhat curious... sometimes, maybe. Tell me, what did he look like? Describe to me what you saw."

"Such a thing is impossible to describe. Would you like for me to raise the bedsheet and let you see for yourself?"

"Sarah! Don't you dare! I'll scream if you do!"

"Think about it before you say *no*, Elizabeth. I won't tell Mother. This may be the only opportunity in your whole life to ever see something like this! You could be struck by lightning tomorrow and be carried to your grave never knowing what a naked man looks like."

"I suppose that is possible..."

"No one will ever know except you and me, and I swear that I shall never tell another living soul. It's truly a sight you will never forget, and once you've looked, your curiosity is immediately satisfied."

"You make it sound so intriguing, and I will admit that you have succeeded in placing a terrible temptation in front of me, but... I don't know... Are you sure that you can't simply describe what you saw?"

"The complexity of a naked man defies description."

"He sleeps so quietly and peacefully, Sarah, look at him..."

"I'm quite certain that Mother and Vivian looked at him thoroughly when they undressed him and bathed him, and it didn't kill either one of them. Aunt Agatha has watched over him several nights now, and if anybody in the world would peek under the bedsheet, Aunt Agatha would peek to her heart's content, I'm sure. I looked at him myself tonight for a very brief moment or two, and it didn't kill me. Come on, Elizabeth... give in to your curiosity just this once."

"Well... err... perhaps we could only look long enough to ascertain whether or not he is injured down there in any way. Do you think that would be sufficient justification for our looking...?"

"Of course it would. Perhaps I may have overlooked something when I looked at him earlier. I didn't inspect him for any injuries. I would treasure hearing your opinion. I only looked for a very short period of time because I heard Aunt Agatha stirring in the kitchen earlier. How about it, Elizabeth, shall we take another look... together, just you and me?"

"I don't know, Sarah. This is terribly embarrassing, but the more we talk about it, the greater my own curiosity is aroused.

I think that your enthusiasm in the matter has succeeded in corrupting me. I shan't be able to rest now, until I see what he looks like for myself."

"I'm going to raise the bedsheet and look again, whether you look or not. Will you look if I do?"

"Very well... I suppose there is no harm in just looking. Move the lantern closer so we can see well and let us inspect him for injuries. That's all we're going to do is inspect him for injuries, is that understood?"

"Yes."

"You may raise the bedsheet when you are ready."

"Very well. Take a deep breath. There! What do you think about that? Can you see good enough?"

"Oh my goodness! Land sakes! I don't quite know what to say... I've seen quite enough. Lower the bedsheet."

"Already?"

"Lower it immediately, Sarah!"

"Alright, but keep your voice down. Wasn't that kind of fascinating... in an odd sort of way?"

"Mercy! I may never be able to look at a grown man again without blushing, thanks to you."

"Did you see any injuries, Elizabeth?"

"Injuries? Oh! No, I saw no obvious injuries. I would suppose that everything looked to be in order."

"See, Elizabeth? Looking at the man didn't kill either one of us, did it?"

"Looking has succeeded in making me feel guilty and dirty. I wish I had never looked."

"Well I don't feel guilty or dirty. I feel... better educated in the subject of men, that's all."

"Mercy, Sarah! Now I know how you must spend all of your time when you're here alone with this man! I spend most of my time reading from the Holy Bible when I'm alone with him here, and you spend most of your time invading the privacy of this poor soul! I'm ashamed of you, Sarah."

"I'm sorry if I have shocked you, Elizabeth, and I haven't been invading his privacy... very much."

"Let us swear an oath that we will never tell another living soul about what we've seen here tonight, and you need to hold a tighter rein on your devilish curiosity, Sarah."

"I can't help being just a little curious, Elizabeth. I think it's just in my nature."

"Look at him lying there, Sarah. He has a peaceful look on his face, doesn't he? If one didn't know he was ill, one would almost think that he was merely sleeping peacefully. He's a very pleasant man to look upon."

"I hope and pray that he doesn't die, Elizabeth. I've sat here often at night wondering what it would be like to speak with him, and I really hope that he wakes up someday soon and is able to talk to us."

"Me too, Sarah. I even held his hand one night and asked God to heal him."

"I wonder if he is an educated man?"

"We've no way of knowing unless he wakes up and is able to talk to us someday. He might even be a man of some esteemed importance, a dignitary, a teacher, a university scholar, or even an ordained pastor. Oh my Lord!"

"What's the matter, Elizabeth?"

"I hope and pray that this man is not a pastor!"

"Why, pray tell?"

"I couldn't bear the guilt of having stooped so low in my life as to have willingly looked under the bedsheet of a pastor!"

"Don't be ridiculous, Elizabeth! If he was a pastor, it is unlikely that he would have been participating in a battle, for heaven's sake. Even Yankee pastors would be unlikely to partake in battle."

"Still and all, it's entirely possible that he could be a young pastor. Then again, he might just as well be a mortician or even an emissary of Satan... a murderer, or a thief. We just don't know, do we?"

"He's not a bad man! I can tell by the gentle expression on his face. I'll wager that he's a kind and compassionate man."

"I hope he is, Sarah, and I hope he recovers soon, and I certainly hope that he's not a pastor."

"Look closely at his hands and fingers, Elizabeth. They're soft and smooth. He's evidently not performed very much hard labor in his time."

"I agree. Even his fingernails and toenails are perfectly manicured."

"Ha! That's because I clipped and filed them two nights ago. They were in desperate need of attention until I completed the task."

"You've had a grand time amusing yourself with this man, haven't you, Sarah? It's almost as though you've been in here playing with your very own doll while you've watched over him!"

"It needed to be done, and I asked Mother for her permission first, Elizabeth. Do you think it was a sin for us to look under his bedsheet like we did?"

"I don't know, I hope it wasn't. We only looked for a very brief time. I don't know about you, but I've already forgotten everything I saw."

"I wonder what his name is, Elizabeth?"

"I would wager that it's probably John or David, or even Samuel. Those are very common names among Yankees, I think. When I've sat with him at night, I've often wondered what the color of his eyes are. I would guess they are brown, or perhaps even hazel."

"You're woefully mistaken, Elizabeth. His eyes are a very dazzling and deep shade of blue. They shine like crystals on a chandelier."

"Oh? And just how would you know this, miss know-it-all?"

"Because I raised one of his eyelids several days ago and looked at them, that's how I know. I've done so several times since, to see if he would respond in any way."

"Sarah! Is there anything about this man that you haven't looked at or touched, or experimented upon?"

"I was overwhelmed by my curiosity one morning, and I just had to raise an eyelid to see his eyes. It's not as if it causes him any unnecessary discomfort. He just lays there and lets me do it, and it doesn't hurt him at all."

"If that be the case, then raise his eyelids and show me his eyes. I would very much like to see the color for myself."

"Alright. Look closely, and bring the lantern here again so that we may see better. See there? Look at them, Elizabeth. This is the first time I have raised both of his eyelids at the same time. Can you see good enough?"

"You were right, Sarah. His eyes are a very beautiful shade of blue indeed. He's a strikingly handsome man for a Yankee, isn't he?"

"Very much so. He takes my breath away sometimes. And his teeth are perfectly white and clean as well."

"His teeth? Lord have mercy! You've even looked into his mouth, as if you were preparing to purchase a horse?"

"When I would give him small amounts of water I couldn't help but look into his mouth."

"After everything else that you've told me tonight, I suppose that I shouldn't be a bit surprised that you've looked into his mouth... Honestly, Sarah! You can close his eyes now."

Sarah released the young man's eyelids, but upon doing so, his eyes remained partially opened. She pushed his eyelids closed again, and held them in place for a moment or two, but when she removed her fingers, the man's eyes opened again.

"What's the matter, Sarah?"

"I'm not sure... his eyes won't stay closed now for some odd reason. Each time I close his eyelids, they open again."

She gently pushed his eyelids closed a third time, but when she removed her fingers, the man's eyes opened again on their own accord. She tried the maneuver a fourth time, with the same unsuccessful results.

"My Lord! Do you think he died just now, Sarah?"

"I don't know... I don't think so, he's still breathing. I can feel his breath going in and out of his nose. Put your finger here and feel for yourself."

"You're correct, he *is* still alive. I can even feel his heart beating here within his chest."

In a single instant of astonishment to the sisters, the young man's eyes moved to look upward at them, and for the first time, he uttered comprehensible words... "Ohhh... I'm not dead... I swear I'm not..."

"Lord Jesus! He's awake! He just talked to us! Go get Mother, Sarah! Quickly!"

"No! Not yet! Let's see what he has to say first. Can you hear me, Mister? Do you need anything?"

"Water... please... water..."

Instantly, the sisters assisted the young man in raising his head and taking a few sips of water. He drank nearly a full glass of water without any noticeable difficulty, uttered a few words that were mostly incoherent, and closed his eyes again. Sarah and Elizabeth gently lowered his head back onto his pillow.

"What did he say, Sarah?"

"I'm not sure. I'm certain that I heard him say his leg *'hurts like hellfire'* and was terribly painful. Then, I thought I heard him say something queer..."

"What? What did he say?"

"It sounded to me like he said that he didn't need for me to hold the jar for him right now... whatever that means."

"He doesn't need you to hold the jar? That doesn't make any sense, Sarah. You must have misheard him."

"I don't know what jar he could have been talking about... Perhaps I did misunderstand what he said, Elizabeth."

It was the second encouraging sign that the young man was perhaps not as close to death as everyone had assumed, and Elizabeth and Sarah were the only family members who had ever heard the young man speak intentionally. They marveled adoringly at their patient with newfound optimism as they stood over him and gently rubbed his foot below the injury in an effort to eliminate some of the man's pain.

"Do you think this is helping to reduce the man's pain, Sarah?"

"We've no way of knowing for sure, Elizabeth, just keep rubbing. It seems to be giving him some comfort. Please say nothing to Mother about this, and don't you ever tell a living soul that we looked under the man's bedsheet."

"I agree. Everything that has happened here tonight will be kept between us in the strictest of confidence. When the sun rises in a couple of hours, we will kill a chicken and prepare a broth for him. If he's able to drink the broth like he just drank the water, perhaps a broth will help to give him more strength."

"I'm so excited that he's finally shown some signs of recovery that I can hardly stand it!"

"Me too, Sarah!"

"Did you hear his voice, Elizabeth? It sounded so marvelously manly, yet so soft and gentle."

"I know... I thought his voice sounded heavenly, and if I live to be a hundred, I'll never forget his eyes!"

○ ○ ○

Abigail and Agatha came downstairs later that morning to find Sarah and Elizabeth preparing a fire in the stove. Elizabeth had already gone to the chicken house, killed and plucked a chicken, quartered it, and placed it in a pot to boil. Abigail seemed to sense that something was different on this particular morning and asked, "My daughters are up very early this morning. I've never known either of you to rise before me. Was there any change in the soldier's condition during the night?"

"Nothing very much at all, Mother. He moaned a couple of times during the night, and opened his eyes for a short time, that's about all."

"Opened his eyes? Really?"

"Yes... briefly."

"That's very encouraging! Why did you not wake me?"

"It was only for a very short time, Mother. He was asleep again in the time that it would have taken you to come downstairs, and Elizabeth and I didn't want to disturb your sleep."

"If he's opened his eyes, even for a moment, it's the most encouraging sign he's shown thus far! Why are you boiling a chicken at this early hour, Elizabeth?"

"Sarah and I talked about it last night, and thought that we might try to encourage the soldier to drink some chicken broth today, instead of just water. He drank a whole glass of water last night, and we thought perhaps the broth might give him some strength and aid in his recovery."

"That's an excellent idea. I should have thought about that myself. I'm going to go into his room and see how he's doing now. When I come back, we need to boil some water for tea and I'll make some biscuits and bread for us. Agatha will be downstairs soon, and we have many chores that we need to tend to today."

Sarah and Elizabeth mischievously looked at each other as Abigail walked into the tiny bedchamber to make her own assessment of the man's condition. It was her intention to lock the bedchamber door, retrieve the jar from under the man's bed, and assist him in urinating, as she had done the previous morning. This morning would prove to be distinguishably different than any of the previous days, however. She emerged from the man's room only a few seconds after going in, somewhat ashen-faced, looked at Elizabeth, and asked, "Elizabeth dear, would you go into my bedchamber upstairs and fetch my pistol from the table drawer, please?"

"Why, Mother? For God sakes, Mother, please don't shoot him! I beg of you! Please!"

"Mercy sakes, child, calm down! I have no intention of shooting him! But I have just found that our guest is awake now, and sitting upright on the bed, studying over his injured leg. He looked at me briefly, but I immediately left the room. I do not want any of us to go back into the same room with him without a pistol for us to defend ourselves if such a thing were to become necessary. Please hurry and fetch the pistol, and summon Agatha to come with us when we go back into the room. Elizabeth, button your bed jacket before you come back downstairs, please. With our guest being awake now, and apparently aware of his surroundings, we must always take every precaution to guard our modesty with all due humility whenever we are in his presence. Do you both understand?"

"Yes, Mother... Mother?"

"Yes, what is it?"

"Perhaps you should button your own bed jacket... I can see your bosom quite well."

"Oh! Yes, of course! Thank you for bringing that to my attention, Elizabeth."

As the pot of chicken began to boil on the stove, Agatha joined them downstairs, and the four women slowly and cautiously entered the small room, apprehensive as to what they might find inside. There was barely enough room for all of the ladies to fit inside. The soldier looked up at them. Nervous and uncertain eyes began to study over each other. The man's eyes moved back and forth among the ladies and finally focused exclusively on Abigail, as if he recognized immediately that she was the figurehead among the group. The pistol in her hand left no doubt in the soldier's mind as to who was in charge. Abigail looked at the young man and perceived his appearance as being that of a totally different man than the wounded soldier whom she and her family had become so accustomed to. With his eyes open now, he seemed to take on an entirely new personality—one that was much different than the personality of the comatose and immobile young soldier who had seemed to be more of a fixture in the house than a living and breathing entity. The family had become familiar with the sleeping soldier, and now they were faced with acquainting themselves with an entirely different man. Abigail took proper measures to let the young man see that she was armed. She was careful not to point the weapon directly at him, but she made certain that he saw it in her hand. The wounded man studied over the women with curious interest for a moment or two longer, looked at the pistol, and asked, "Are you ladies the angels of death? Has God sent you here... to kill me, and take me up to heaven?"

As the spokeswoman, Abigail stepped even closer and answered the soldier's query. "Mercy no! We've no intention of killing you, as long as you behave yourself properly and mind your manners. We're here to talk to you, that's all. We are the ones who have been attending to your injuries here, and trying to assist you as you mend."

"That's very kind of you. Thank you for not killing me. Might I ask you where I am? What place is this here, Ma'am?"

"You are in a servant's bedchamber in our home, at Montgomery Farm. You were wounded, and brought here to recover. As I said, we've been attending to your injuries here. What is your name, Sir?"

Abigail's question seemed to dumfound the young man, as if he had no idea what she was talking about. After pondering for a moment, he simply replied, "My name?"

"Yes, your name, what is it?"

He continued to look deeply puzzled by Abigail's simple and straightforward question, and once again he struggled somewhat and said, "My name is... my name is... I am..."

Abigail became frustrated at the man's apparent reluctance to answer such a simple, unassuming question. Initially, she didn't recognize the fact that he was making his sincerest effort to answer her. She asserted herself further, and asked, "Why do you take pause at such a simple question? We insist on knowing your name. What is it? Tell us."

Sarah spoke in the man's defense, saying, "Mother, please! Can't you see that he is confused? He's obviously having some difficulty trying to answer you."

The soldier looked pitifully into Abigail's eyes and said, "It's odd, but I can't seem to recall my name at the moment, Madame.

I should know my own name, I know, but... I don't. I'm truly very sorry."

The young man soon sank back into his bed and his eyes closed again. He gritted his teeth in pain, and moaned, "Jesus help me! My leg..."

Abigail continued to gently purge the young man for a response but achieved nothing for her efforts, as the man seemed to drift into unconsciousness again. Near midday, the young man awoke again, and Abigail went into the room to feed him some of the broth that Elizabeth and Sarah had prepared, along with some small, tender pieces of chicken. The appealing taste of the warm food caused the young soldier to become overly zealous in his eating, and he choked for a moment, cleared his throat, and resumed eating.

"Sir, you must eat more slowly, or you will only succeed in making yourself ill. Your body has been through a terrible ordeal, and I'm sure that you still have some very difficult days ahead of you. Are you in much pain at the present time?"

"Yes Ma'am. My leg hurts pretty bad, but it's fairly tolerable unless I attempt to move my right hip. My leg has been broken above my knee somehow, hasn't it?"

"Yes it has, but it appears to be in the early stages of healing now. I'm afraid that it's going to take some time for it to heal properly. I'm very sorry that I have nothing to give you that would help with the pain. Once you have managed to eat for two or three days, I will give you some bourbon spirits in an elixir. That will help with the pain, but if I attempted to give it to you now, it would only serve to make you violently ill."

"I understand, Ma'am, thank you."

"This chicken broth should help you to regain some of your strength."

"Thank you, Ma'am. This is the best tasting thing I have ever eaten, and I swear to the Almighty above, that you're the most beautiful woman I've ever rested my eyes upon. You look prettier to me than any angel that ever flew down from the heavens above, I swear you do."

"I'm happy that you are enjoying the broth, but I must insist that you to restrain yourself from making tactless and ill-mannered comments like that. I'll not tolerate such coarse annotations here in my home. Be forewarned Sir, we are all God-fearing women here, and this is a Christian home, so please remember to conduct yourself accordingly."

"I'm truly sorry if I offended you in any way, Ma'am. I meant to show you no disrespect, I was merely paying tribute to the truth. I'm still somewhat dizzy and confused, and it's difficult for me to focus my thoughts or maintain proper control over my words sometimes. For that, please forgive me."

"You've not eaten anything for almost two weeks. I'm not surprised that the broth tastes good to you, but you need to eat slowly or you will become ill and the broth will do you more harm than good. Try to make yourself pause a bit longer between bites, and chew the pieces of chicken more slowly."

"I will, Ma'am, and I sincerely thank you for your Christian charity and kindness."

"If you manage to keep the broth on your stomach we'll feed you some biscuits and milk a little later in the day. You've lost a lot of weight since you've been injured, and you need to eat as much as your body can tolerate after your stomach has had a chance to recover. Does that sound like an agreeable plan to you?"

"Yes Ma'am, it truly does."

"Do you feel up to the task of talking to us for a while?"

"Yes Ma'am, I think so... I'll do my best..."

"You have a very pleasant voice, but you speak so softly that it's difficult for us to hear you sometimes, you sound almost as if you are whispering."

"I'm sorry, Ma'am... this is my normal tone of voice, I think, but I'll try to remember to speak louder."

"Do not exert yourself to do so, we will stand close enough so that we can hear you."

Abigail motioned for the others to come in from the hallway, and Elizabeth, Sarah, and Agatha walked into the room from the kitchen and stood closely at the foot of the bed as the young man grimaced in pain and moved slightly in the bed to a more comfortable position. Such a small amount of movement seemed to drain most of his energy and bring beads of perspiration to his brow. Abigail was poised to answer the man's query as soon as he situated himself better in the bed. Wiping the perspiration from his forehead with a dampened cloth, Abigail said, "We have questions about you, and we're sure that you probably have plenty of questions about us as well."

"Yes, Ma'am, indeed I do."

They gave him a drink of water and he unavoidably choked, causing everyone but Abigail to back away from the bed as much as the small room would permit. When he had cleared his throat and taken a few more swallows with no ill effects, the small group of women again stood closely at his bedside. Elizabeth was the first to present a question to the man as Abigail wiped his mouth and face with a cloth.

"Is there anything that you would like? Is there anything that may help you to feel better, or assist you in being more comfortable?"

"Coffee... maybe, if that's not asking too much and if you happen to have such a thing here."

Abigail quickly responded to the young man's request, stating, "We have some tea that we could offer you, but we've not had coffee nor sugar here at Montgomery Farm since the Union blockade of the James River, more than a year ago."

"Blockade? I... uhhh..."

Abigail continued, "Earlier, we asked you your name and you were unable to answer us. Will you tell us your name now?"

"Yes... I must have a name... Give me a moment, please. [*a long pause ensued, as the man again struggled with the question*] It's strange, I'll admit, but I just can't seem to recall my own name for some odd reason. I am truly sorry."

"Perhaps it will come to you as we talk."

"May I ask a question, Ma'am? I'm terribly concerned about something, and hope that you can shed some light on the matter."

"Of course you may. What is your question?"

"Well... I'm just concerned about the situation here in your house, Ma'am... I don't wish to offend you by asking such a prying question, but I was wondering if you and your family here honestly have the means to feed me?"

"The means to feed you? I don't understand... Why would you ask such a question?"

"Well, it's just that I wouldn't want to eat another bite of your food here if I thought for a moment that you and your family were depriving yourselves in any way just to feed me."

"I see. Well... perish the thought, Sir. Our means here are meager, to be sure, but we certainly have been blessed with the means to feed you, and it is our duty as Christians to do so. We indeed have sufficient food for ourselves, as well as plenty to share with you."

"Please forgive me for asking such a meddling question."

"Nevertheless, we do understand your motives for asking the question, however, and we appreciate your concern. It's a definite credit to your character that you would ask such a question. Do you remember anything about how you were injured?"

"No, Ma'am, not really. I seem to remember being under a horse at one time or another, as if one had fallen on me or something, but that's about all that I can remember. I know that I've had my leg broken, and I've somehow been injured up here on the side of my head, but I don't remember anything about how any of it happened."

"Your head was injured by a heavy blow of some kind that caused a long deep cut above your ear. Your leg bone was shattered by a rifle ball, I think. You were injured during the battle that took place here twelve days ago. That's all that we know for certain."

"Rifle ball? Battle? You mean I was shot? What battle are you speaking of, Ma'am?"

"Surely you remember the fact that you're a soldier, don't you?"

"A soldier? No Ma'am... Begging your pardon, I think you must be mistaken... At least I don't think I'm a soldier. I think that I would certainly remember fighting with someone if I was a soldier, and I have no memory of any such thing."

Abigail began to recognize that the man was being entirely sincere and honest—that he really was at a loss for recalling much of his recent past, and that his mind had been damaged somehow when he had been injured. She asked, "Do you know what country we're in?"

"I assume this to be the United States of America, is that correct?"

"Yes. Do you have knowledge of the fact that our country is at war?"

"America is at war? My God, Ma'am! With whom are we at war?"

"Perhaps we should continue talking after you have had the opportunity to rest some more. Your eyes are beginning to look quite weary again, and we do not wish to over-burden what little energy you have. We will leave the room now, and allow you to rest quietly. We can talk some more this evening if you're up to it."

"How long have I been here, Ma'am?"

"Altogether, I believe this is the eleventh day."

Addressing himself to Abigail, the young man asked, "Before you leave the room, may I speak to you privately, Madame? It's about a matter of importance."

"Privately? Anything you have to say can be said in the presence of all of us. We have no secrets among us here in my house."

"I need to say something that's very personal in nature, Ma'am, and it may embarrass you in front of the other ladies."

"As I said, we have no secrets among us here. You may go ahead and say what you need to say and be done with it."

"Well, it's just that I am experiencing a rather urgent need to relieve myself before I lay back down again, Ma'am. If this is the eleventh day that I've been here, it's no wonder that I'm experiencing such an urgent need. Is there a man here in this house, someone who could somehow assist me in getting outside to a privy, or to a place where I can...?"

Abigail thought about the jar under the bed, but instead, she said, "Oh! I see. Well, in that case... Sarah, go quickly and fetch Ezra. Elizabeth, fetch a chamber pot for our guest from one of the empty upstairs bedchambers. Ezra will assist you when he gets here. Can you wait for a few minutes without difficulty?"

"Yes, Ma'am, I think so. Thank you... and I'd like to thank you again for the soup. It was delicious. I don't know much about my situation here, or the circumstances that have brought me here, but I clearly understand that you ladies have been very kind to me, and I thank you."

"You're perfectly welcome. You are most likely going to be bedridden for another four or five weeks, perhaps longer. You've already been here for more than eleven days, and you need to move around in the bed as much as your pain will permit in order to avoid bedsores. Try not to lie in one position longer than you have to, even if it pains you to change positions."

"Yes, Ma'am. I'll try to move around as much as my pain permits."

"Would you be more comfortable here in your bed if your face was clean shaven and washed?"

"Yes, Ma'am, indeed I would... but I'm sorry to say that I don't think that I am quite up to the task just yet. My arms are weak and my head seems to be spinning."

"I will return to your room this afternoon with some hot water and a razor, and attend to the task myself if it will aid in your comfort."

"Thank you, Ma'am. That would be very kind of you."

Ezra soon arrived, and the ladies adjourned to the parlor. With every effort made to avoid causing unnecessary pain to the young man, Ezra assisted him to his feet so that he could make use of the chamber pot. He also saw to the task of emptying the chamber pot and replacing it in the man's bedchamber. The young man was taken aback when he first saw Ezra's enormous size, but soon came to realize that by nature, Ezra was a strong, but gentle man. Meanwhile, the four women had gathered themselves in the parlor to discuss the dramatic and unforeseen improvement in the general health of their guest. As usual, Abigail guided the conversation.

"I am pleasantly surprised with the apparent improvement in our guest. It would appear to be quite likely now that our guest will eventually recover from his injuries, God willing, although his injuries may require a great deal of time to completely heal. I never had even the vaguest idea that he would have lived for more than another day or two at the most. It seems as though God has chosen to spare his life for some reason, and entrusted it with us here at Montgomery Farm. This means that it will be necessary for us to continue telling our visitors that the man is a wounded soldier of the confederacy. Otherwise, he may be taken outside and killed before he has a chance to fully recover from his wounds. I'm beginning to sense that there may be some evidence that this man might possess at least some redeeming qualities. He even expressed a concern over whether or not we had sufficient food here for ourselves."

Sarah poured each of them a cup of tea, and Abigail resumed her assessment of the current situation and the young man's condition.

"He remains perfectly weak, but seems to be conscious and well aware of what's going on around him—which is all the more reason for us to dress with modesty in mind whenever we are in his presence. He also seems to be quite harmless and meek, and extremely well-mannered, but I do not want any of us to take any unnecessary chances while we are in his presence. We still have many questions about our guest that remain unanswered, and until we have some answers to our questions, we will continue to take all necessary precautions."

Elizabeth asked, "What kind of precautions are you referring to, Mother?"

"I want the door to his room to remain locked at all times unless we are in the room there with him. We are no longer to go into his room when we are dressed in our bedclothes. As I eluded to a moment ago, he is now well aware of his surroundings, and I want him to know without a doubt that we are respectful in the way we present ourselves. We are not to go into his room unless there are at least two of us present, and one of us must be in possession of a pistol at all times whenever we are in his presence. And no one is to enter his room without my knowledge. Is that clear?"

Sarah responded to her mother's mandates, "He seems to be perfectly harmless to me, Mother. He was even concerned about our having enough food for ourselves. I can't imagine an evil person caring whether or not we had enough food to eat. He seems like the perfect gentleman to me, and I don't know why we would need to have a pistol in our possession while we are in the room with him."

"Until we know more about him, I do not wish to take any unnecessary chances. It is no longer essential, nor is it advisable, for us to perform a nightly vigil now that he is showing such remarkable signs of improvement. We will lock his door at night and unlock it when we carry him his morning meal. Is that understood?"

Elizabeth quickly responded by saying, "There's a window next to his bed in the room, Mother. If he wanted to escape during the night, all he has to do is climb out of the window."

"He's not able to leave here in his present condition, but if he wishes to escape, that would be just fine with me. I would gladly hold the door open for him and provide him with one of our horses. Let him do it and be gone from here. His departure would be a blessing for us all. He's not being held in captivity here, I'm merely taking precautions so that he cannot come into the sanctity of our house during the dark of night and bring harm to any of us. Yankees are well known to have an insatiable appetite for molesting women, and I'll not allow any of us to be put at risk. Until we know better, we will continue to regard this man as a threat and as the enemy soldier that he really is. Have I made myself clear on the issue? Does everyone understand what's required of them?"

"Yes, Mother."

Later that same afternoon, Abigail violated her own mandate, when she returned to the man's room unaccompanied, for the purpose of shaving his face. She had prepared a pan of hot water, and set it on the table at his bedside. Under the cautious scrutiny of the man's curious eyes, she positioned her pistol in such a manner that it was within her close reach. She prepared a warm soap lather in a small bowl, and applied it to the soldier's face. Abigail maintained a stringent, unemotional and stoic demeanor as she applied the lather, and would have never admitted to a living soul that she had actually become emotionally stimulated during the performance of the seemingly impersonal and perfunctory task. No one was aware of the increased beating of her heart, but her. This feeling of strange emotion was new to her. Had she known beforehand that the act of merely applying soap lather to the soldier's face would initiate such personal feelings, or imbue such fervent emotions, she would have delegated the task to Agatha, or perhaps Vivian. She had never comprehended that the simple act of shaving a man's face would stir such unfamiliar excitements within her being. Nevertheless, she was here with the man now, and had gone so far as to feel committed to the completion of the task, regardless of the mysterious sensations that it was creating. Using her father's razor, she applied it to the skin above the man's cheek and said, "If you'll remain perfectly still, I'll try my best to accomplish this without cutting you."

"I'll do my best to remain as still as possible, Ma'am."

"This is very new to me. I've never shaved a man before."

"This is very new to me, too, Ma'am. Although my memory is

faulty, I don't think I've ever been shaved by a beautiful woman before."

"Guard your attempts to produce flattering words, Sir, you're only succeeding in making me nervous, and I don't want to cut you."

"If you think that you might accidently cut me, Ma'am, I would much prefer for you practice up there on my cheek until you get the hang of things, rather than on my throat... that is, if you don't mind."

Before she could catch herself, Abigail unwittingly smiled, then quickly erased the smile from her face and said, "If that was an attempt to be humorous, I congratulate you, Sir. Humor is a good thing, and Montgomery House has experienced an absence of any sort of humor in recent years. However, it might be in your best interest if you were to cease talking until I have finished shaving you. Hold yourself perfectly still, and do not talk. I feel as though I'm starting to 'get the hang of this,' as you would say. Would you prefer to keep your mustache?"

"I'll leave that entirely up to you, Ma'am. The mustache can stay or go, whichever is the least trouble for you."

"Very well then, I'll leave your mustache intact. I'll merely trim it somewhat with the scissors afterwards, so that it doesn't interfere so much with your eating."

"Thank you, Ma'am, but if you leave my mustache long and bushy like it is, it might actually help me as I eat."

"How in the world could your mustache possibly help you as you're eating?"

"I was thinking that maybe I could use it to strain the flies out of my soup, Ma'am."

"That's very funny indeed. Now, if you will cease with the unnecessary smiling and joking, it will be of great assistance to me as I attempt to shave around your mouth."

Unwittingly, Abigail smiled again for a brief moment. She found the man's humorous anecdotes refreshing. It reminded her of an earlier time in which she had not been as reluctant to share a smile. It reminded her of a time in which she freely exercised her own sense of humor with her young daughters. The war had made it seem as though those days of carefree humor had been twenty years ago, when in fact, it had only been five years. Nervously, she proceeded with shaving the man. The man kept his eyes focused on Abigail's eyes and said, "I can't seem to remember much about myself, Ma'am, but I don't think I've ever been stupid enough to argue with a woman who was holding a razor at my throat, especially a woman as beautiful as you... but of course, I've never even seen a woman as beautiful as you before now."

"Then perhaps you'll obey me when I ask you to stop staring at me so intently, or making improper personal references to my appearance? In God's eyes, everyone looks the same. In God's eyes, everyone is beautiful, and no one is more beautiful than anyone else."

"I understand that, Ma'am, and I agree with you wholeheartedly, but you need to realize that I wasn't looking at you through God's eyes, Ma'am, I was looking at you through my own eyes, and as badly as I might be injured, I have no difficulty recognizing beauty when I see it."

"Your difficulty doesn't seem to be with your eyes, Sir, your greatest difficulty appears to be with your inability to control your tongue."

"You make a good point Ma'am. My tongue does seem to have the undisciplined nature of speaking my mind, I'm afraid. I suppose my tongue has a mind of its own."

"While I have the razor so handy, I can remedy that problem for you if you like. Would you like to stick your tongue out for me?"

"Mercy, Ma'am! You seem to have a special talent for controlling the behavior of unruly men. I'll put forth my greatest effort to exercise better behavior, I promise. But, nothing I do is going to change the fact that I think you're the most beautiful woman in the world."

"Be quiet! And stop staring at me!"

"You're so pleasant to look upon that it's very difficult for me to take my eyes off of you, but I'll try my best to do exactly as you say and remain as docile as a kitten."

"That's a very wise decision on your part. And I can assure you, Sir, emboldened comments such as that will purchase you nothing here at Montgomery House, to be sure."

"Yes, Ma'am. I'll remember that and keep my comments to myself. Oh, my Lord... Jesus, help me!"

"What? Did I cut you?"

"It's nothing, Ma'am."

"You just said *'oh my Lord, Jesus help me'* for some reason. What is it?"

"Well, I accidentally looked at your face again, and if I told you what I was thinking, you'd most likely cut my throat from ear to ear."

"Then be quiet, and say nothing! I'm almost finished!"

Abigail exerted every possible effort in order to keep from smiling at the man's innocent humor, yet failed miserably. Try as she did, a pronounced, uncontainable smile crossed her face as she contorted her lips in an effort to prevent the smile from becoming evident. She didn't want the young soldier to take notice of her smile, yet he did.

"Ma'am?"

"Yes?"

"Wouldn't you feel more comfortable if you just let yourself go ahead and smile, instead of puckering your mouth up like that? It must be terribly uncomfortable for you to do that. It makes you look like you smell something offensive."

"I shan't tolerate much more of your rudeness before I leave you here half-shaven and walk away. Now, be still!"

"In that case, would you please clarify one of your rules of conduct here at Montgomery House for me, Ma'am, so that I'll have a better understanding of exactly what's expected of me?"

"Yes, what is your question?"

"I was just wondering if you would consider it to be an

emboldened comment if I was to say that, even as beautiful as you are, I think you are even more beautiful when you smile?"

"Yes, I would indeed consider that to be another of your outlandish emboldened comments!"

"How about if I were to say that I think you have the most beautiful eyes in the world? Would that be out of order as well?"

"Yes, it would!"

"Very well then. In order to comply with your wishes, I shan't say either of those things to you, regardless of the fact that they are very true."

"Thank you for not saying it."

"Ma'am?"

"Land sakes alive! What is it now? At this rate, I'll never finish shaving you!"

"I was wondering if you would be so kind as to permit me to sit here and think about how very beautiful you are as long as I don't actually say anything out loud?"

"No! Please close your eyes and stop talking. I'm doing this purely for your benefit, and you are making things terribly difficult for me. Had I known ten minutes ago how difficult you would make this for me, I would never have undertaken this task."

"I'm sorry, Ma'am. And I'll also try very hard to stop thinking about how beautiful you are, despite the obvious difficulty I'll have in convincing myself to do so."

"That's another very wise decision you've made. I told my daughters and my sister earlier today that I thought you were well mannered. I may have been terribly mistaken in my initial assessment."

"If you'll be so kind as to forgive my previous transgressions, I will put forth my greatest effort not to offend you in the future. I promise."

"Very well, in that case, your transgressions are forgiven."

"Oh my Lord!"

"What?"

"Nothing, Ma'am... absolutely nothing. I think I had best close my eyes, before I get myself into more trouble."

Unintentionally, Abigail smiled again. The soldier said nothing, but merely smiled pleasantly back at her. The war, and the many tragedies that had befallen Abigail's household, had given her precious few reasons to display a smile in recent years. Yet this strange Yankee newcomer had forced her to produce a smile, even though it was only for a brief moment in time. Nevertheless, a tiny seed of speculation had been planted in Abigail's heart that her patient was a man of temperate and very pleasant disposition, with a unique flare for humor. Perhaps she would be more acceptant of his humor if she knew more about him. As it was, she knew practically nothing about him, except that he was a Yankee soldier, and he was in the midst of southern ladies, in a southern home.

Once she had completed the task of shaving the man, she used her scissors to trim his mustache, and then she cleaned his face with a warm, dampened towel. With a lethargic and unemotional expression on her face, Abigail looked at the man and said, "There, I've finished, thank God. Should I fetch a hand mirror for you to look at yourself?"

"No, thank you, Ma'am. I'm very weak, and the act of looking at myself in a mirror may be all it takes to send me to the great beyond. Tell me, Ma'am, would you consider it to be an emboldened comment if I was to thank you for what you just did?"

"No, of course I wouldn't. Politeness is quite acceptable— crassness is not."

"Then, thank you, Ma'am, and I mean that sincerely."

"You're quite welcome."

Having completed the task, Abigail picked up the pan of water and started to leave the room. Before she could walk through the door, however, the young man called for her. When she turned around to face him, she could see that he was holding the pistol that she had inadvertently left on the bed. He was holding it by the barrel, and reaching forward to hand it to her.

"Ma'am, you left this behind on the bed, and I certainly have no use for it, as long as you promise me that you won't come back here with the razor to cut my tongue out."

"Oh! Well... thank you... You have my promise to that effect."

Abigail gently took the pistol and hastily exited the room, careful not to look the young man in the eye again. She had taken notice of the fact that in his clean-shaven condition, his handsomeness was eerily attractive to her, and she cared not to entertain such foolish and idealistic thoughts. The notion that she would find any man's appearance to be appealing to her was utterly repugnant. For the first time in her life, Abigail was confused over her own subjective emotions. The idea that she was even slightly susceptible to the charms of this strange man was almost infuriating to her, and she was terribly embarrassed over the fact that her temporary enchantment over the man's sense of humor had caused her such capriciousness as to accidently leave her pistol within his reach. Nevertheless, the fact that the man had so eagerly given it back to her provided her with a measure of assurance that suggested the man meant no harm to her or her family.

When Abigail had left the soldier's room, she went directly to the parlor and stood in front of the mirror there. The young man had expressed his opinion that he thought Abigail was beautiful. She looked at herself in the mirror for a moment or two and thought, *"If he honestly and truly thinks that I am beautiful, then he must surely be burning up with fever! Still, it was nice of him to say such a thing. No one has ever thought me to be beautiful... at least no one has ever told me as much. This strange young man seems to possess rather... interesting mannerisms."*

In the ensuing days, Ezra furnished regular progress reports to Vivian relative to the young man's visits to the privy, and Vivian discretely assured Abigail that the man's body was now functioning healthily in that respect. Several days passed in which the young man slept much less and continued to eat very well. Abigail had found herself to be predisposed to the man's natural charm, and therefore avoided him whenever possible. Agatha and Sarah carried most of his meals to him so that Abigail could unnoticeably circumvent any need to look upon the man herself. Still, even when she was not in his presence, she found him to be in her thoughts often. Ezra continued to assist the soldier in the performance of his personal needs, and strength began to return to his body in small amounts each day.

○ ○ ○

As the four ladies sat in an upstairs bedchamber repairing a quilt one afternoon, Abigail's subconscious mind prompted her to present a question to the other ladies. She cleared her throat and coyly asked, "When you carry meals to our guest, or cater to his needs, does he ever say offensive things to any of you when you are in his room?"

The other ladies looked up from their sewing, and asked, "Offensive things? Such as what?" to which Abigail replied,

"The offensive things that men are prone to say when they are attempting to seduce a woman... such as telling you how beautiful you are, or how stunning your eyes are, or other emboldened things such as that."

The other ladies assured Abigail that the man had only expressed the perfect courtesies of politeness when they had been in his presence. Suspicious as to why her mother had asked such a question, Sarah asked, "Has he ever said anything brazen or improper to you, Mother?"

"No! Of course not! I would never tolerate such a thing in our house! No Christian lady would tolerate such a thing!" Her denial was untrue, yet her embarrassment over the man's endearing words would not allow her to make such an incongruous confession to her daughters or her sister. She kept such knowledge to herself, and hoped that the man would never again make such coarse remarks in her presence. Perhaps the poor man was not yet recovered to an extent that he was capable of guarding his every word, and with that possibility in mind, Abigail would give him the benefit of her doubt, and exercise patience on his behalf. Still, she wondered why the man seemed to '*single her out*' from the others, and direct such endearing words exclusively to her... No matter.

The ladies there at Montgomery House had always enjoyed cooking, even before the arrival of their injured guest. The man was so generous with his compliments that the ladies became even more enthusiastic in their preparation of their traditional culinary masterpieces. When it was all said and done however, everyone's favorite delight was hot biscuits, and there was not a woman within a hundred miles capable of making better biscuits than Abigail Montgomery.

Experiencing an urgent need to relieve himself one morning, the young man thoughtlessly tested his bad leg by attempting to use it to stand on his own two feet. His intention was to stand at his bedside and use his chamber pot without summoning Ezra for assistance. However, he quickly found that the pain was too intense for him to stand or walk. He involuntarily cried out in agony and fell helplessly to the floor, without the benefit of his bedsheet to cover his nakedness. Further adding to his woes, his head had struck the corner of the chair as he fell, causing a small cut above his right eyebrow which began to bleed freely. Hearing him fall, Abigail and Sarah quickly rushed from the kitchen into the small chambermaid room where they found the naked man on the floor. Abigail was shocked by the sight of a naked man lying there for Sarah's innocent eyes to see, and immediately reprimanded the poor soul as he writhed and contorted in excruciating pain, helpless on the floor.

"You imbecile! You'll accomplish nothing more from such foolish endeavors, than to delay your own healing!"

Grimacing in pain, from a fetal position on the floor, the pitiful man sorrowfully responded, "I'm truly very sorry Ma'am. I didn't realize how badly my leg was injured until I tried to put my weight on it."

"Why didn't you summon Ezra?!"

"Because it's humiliating for me to have to call on someone every time I need something! I thought I might be able to stand on my own accord without inconveniencing anyone or having to call upon Ezra for assistance."

"Maybe now you've learned how stupid that was!"

Abigail and Sarah each took him by an arm and assisted him back into his bed, where he quickly covered his nakedness as best he could with his hands. Abigail scolded him again for his imprudent attempt to walk and threw the bedsheet at him so that he could cover himself.

"Perhaps you'll think twice before doing anything that stupid again!"

"I was only trying to avoid inconveniencing anyone, I swear it!"

"You will only inconvenience us if you continue to exhibit such foolishness. You've even cut your forehead when you fell, and only succeeded in causing your leg to start bleeding again! The wound on your leg was healing perfectly—now look at it! Now, we'll have to change the dressing and just hope that you haven't disrupted the healing of the bone! And I don't appreciate the disgusting display of your nakedness in front of my daughter's young eyes!"

"I'm truly sorry, Ma'am. I promise that I will restrain myself from such foolish endeavors in the future, I swear to the Almighty I will, if you'll just have mercy on me and stop shouting at me."

The man's pitiful plea caused Abigail to consider how rash she had been in criticizing him so relentlessly. She calmed herself, and humbly said, "In that case, I apologize for admonishing you as I did. I suppose that you were only trying to help in your situation, and I didn't mean to sound so condemning in my words. My scolding was only intended to get your attention."

"Oh, you've got a lot more than just my attention, Ma'am, I swear you do. May I ask you a question before you leave the room, Ma'am, now that I've covered myself with this bedsheet and your scathing criticism seems to have subsided somewhat?"

"Yes, what is it?"

"I was wondering if you have any idea of how demeaning and humiliating it is to lie helpless and naked on the floor while someone you have come to greatly admire shouts coarse and offensive reprimands at you?"

"I..."

"Why is it that you seem to hate me so bitterly? It's breaking my heart! I swear it is! I may be helpless and stupid, but I still have feelings. Have I committed some great crime that I don't know about? Am I really such an evil and despicable scoundrel that I am deserving of your hatred?"

"Neither I, nor my family here, bear you any hatred whatsoever. And I apologize to you if I have given you that impression. We only want what's best for you. Your foolish attempt to walk on a broken leg caused me to lose control of my words. For that, I'm truly regretful. I will try to exhibit better control of my tongue in the future. Please accept my apology. I will return in a moment to change the dressing on your leg."

After leaving the man's room, Abigail spoke softly to Sarah in the kitchen.

"I have always hoped that you would remain innocent of men until such time as you were a little older. I'm sorry that you had to see the young man displaying himself in such a disgustingly naked circumstance as that, dear."

"That wasn't the first time that I've..."

"That wasn't the first time that you've... what?"

"Uhhh... that I've helped someone to their feet who had fallen, Mother."

"Oh..."

"Everything the man said was true, Mother, your words were very cruel and cutting. I felt so sorry for him. He didn't deserve such cruelty. He was only trying to attend to his own needs without being a bother to us."

"I've apologized to him for my outburst, and I am truly regretful for my harsh words."

"I've never seen such a hurtful expression on a man's face before, Mother. He was nearly in tears as he spoke, and lying helpless on the floor..."

"I said that I was sorry, Sarah, now dismiss it!"

"Yes, Mother."

Abigail was in fact very regretful for the way she had admonished the man. So regretful, that she walked to the side porch briefly, where she shed a tear in private and silently cursed herself for being so insensitive.

Shortly, Abigail returned to the man's room, cleaned the cut above his eye, and changed the dressing on his leg. The man was clearly heartbroken over the incident, and Abigail began to recognize that this man was perhaps the most considerate and kind man that she had ever come in contact with. She realized that harsh words were not needed when communicating with him. There were no words exchanged between them until she had gathered her supplies and turned to leave. The man merely said, "Thank you," and Abigail simply replied, "You're welcome."

That afternoon, Abigail returned to the chambermaid room bearing a piece of hot apple pie and a glass of chilled buttermilk from the springhouse. Her conscience had continued to torment her with guilt regarding the way she had scolded the man so severely. The image of the man grimacing in pain, naked on the floor as she scolded him was haunting her, and she found it necessary to make an attempt to ease her guilt. It was unlike

Abigail Montgomery to humble herself before any man, yet she knew that she could not live with herself until she had at least made an attempt to offer her sincerest regrets to the man. She entered his room with the pie and buttermilk, and apologetically asked, "Sir, may I come in?"

"Of course, please do."

"If you will be so kind as to permit me, I come to you bearing a peace offering."

"A peace offering? For what reason, pray tell? I don't understand."

"I know this will not make up for the way that I talked so cruelly to you this morning, but would you please accept this as my way of saying that I'm truly sorry?"

"This is awfully nice of you, but you didn't have to do this, Ma'am, I've already forgiven you for the way you shouted at me this morning. Besides, you had every reason to be angry with me this morning. Attempting to stand without Ezra's assistance was stupid of me. I should have known better than to attempt something like that this early in my healing."

"Still and all, I do apologize for my outburst, and I hope that you will enjoy the pie and buttermilk. Would it bother you if I sit here with you as you eat?"

"No, Ma'am, not at all... please do."

Abigail seated herself at the foot of the bed, and waited for the man to finish his pie and buttermilk. The young man ate as though the pie was the most enjoyable thing he had ever eaten. He also took advantage of the opportunity to do more than a fair share of occasional staring at Abigail. He did his best to conceal his adoring glances, but despite his attempts to be inconspicuous, Abigail was well aware of his fleeting glimpses of endearment. This caused her only a minor discomfort, and after the way she had scolded him that morning, she was more than happy to let him stare to his heart's content, without calling him to task as she normally would have.

"We've had no sugar here at Montgomery Farm for more than

a year. I had to sweeten the pie with maple syrup and molasses. I hope you like it. It's fresh out of the oven."

"It's delicious, Ma'am, truly delicious!"

For some strange reason that was unknown to her, Abigail felt extremely gratified as she watched the man eat so enthusiastically. Her thoughts dashed back quickly to a time a few days previous when the man was thought to have been in the final hours of his life, and she silently thanked God again for granting his recovery. Her deepest intuition told her that he was a good-hearted man, with admirable qualities, but she had no idea what was causing her to feel that way. When he had finished eating, Abigail took the plate and the glass and before turning to leave, she giggled lightheartedly and said, "I will return in a moment with a dampened cloth."

"For what reason, Ma'am? And what's so funny, if I might ask?"

Smiling pleasantly at the man, she chuckled, and said, "Your mustache has more than a fair share of buttermilk in it now. I'll be right back, and we'll tidy up your face a bit with a warm cloth."

"Thank you for the pie and the buttermilk, Ma'am, it was delicious... and thank you for taking the time out of your busy day to sit here with me as I ate."

"You're welcome. If you continue to eat like that, I'm encouraged that each day will find you growing even stronger. Your recovery thus far has been a miracle from God... I'll be right back with the cloth to clean your face."

"Ma'am?"

"Yes?"

"Something has been weighing heavy on my mind, and I was wondering if you would permit me to share it with you, in the way of an apology?"

"*You*... wish to apologize to... *me*... about something?"

"Yes, Ma'am, I surely do."

"Apologize for what, pray tell?"

"Well, it's just that, the other day when you shaved me... I said some things that were unbecoming a gentleman. A gentleman who cannot control his tongue is no gentleman at all. It's not my tongue that I have so much trouble with, Ma'am, it's my heart. But regardless, a gentleman should know better than to allow his heart to speak on his behalf, especially at the expense of embarrassing a very sweet and sincere Christian lady. I truly apologize."

"Your words are very touching, even with the buttermilk in your mustache. I accept your apology."

"And I apologize for making a mess of my mustache, too... I suppose we should have gone ahead and shaved the mustache off when we had the chance, don't you think?"

"I'll admit, when your mustache has so much buttermilk in it, you do have a rather comical appearance. But no, I'm very pleased that we didn't remove it. I like it just like it is... I suppose... I mean... I'll be back in just a moment."

Abigail emerged from her temporary entrancement, aware that her words had been bordering what she would have considered as being excessively complimentary. She wished to say nothing or do nothing that could be interpreted by the man as being imprudent or suggestive. Nevertheless, there was an attractive aura about the young man that she found strangely charismatic and refreshing, and she found it unsettling that she should feel that way about someone she knew almost nothing about.

It was on the eighteenth day of his recovery that Ezra assisted the man in dressing in a single-piece undergarment which had been provided by the family. The garment was very small for the size of the man. It had been owned by Abigail's fifteen year-old son, who had lost his life in the service of the South. However, the garment was so small that it was extremely uncomfortable for the soldier to wear. Nevertheless, he squeezed into the undersized garment as best he could and Ezra wrapped him in a blanket and carried him into the parlor where he could sit and attend a family discussion regarding the progress of his healing and his general circumstances there at Montgomery Farm. It was intended to be a session in which everyone could learn more about the soldier, and the soldier could likewise learn more about his hosts. As Ezra picked the young man up in his arms, the young man looked sincerely at him and said, "Ezra, I can't tell you how much I appreciate everything that you've done for me. I hope that I can find some way to return your kindness someday."

"Don't you worry none about me, you just worry about gettin' back on yer feet. You just call on Ezra any ol' time you need to, and I'll be glad to help you."

"Still, I know it's not easy for you to carry me around like this, and I really do appreciate it."

"Shucks mister, you don't hardly weigh nothing at all! You needs to eat you some of Miss Abigail's taters and cornbread!"

Who Is This Strange Man We
Have Here Before Us?

*"Be not forgetful to entertain strangers: for thereby
some have entertained angels unawares." Hebrews 13:2*

There remained a keen interest within the Montgomery household for everyone to know more about their new guest. With the current awareness that their guest was now conscious and had the long anticipated ability to communicate, there was a new sense of excited urgency that had aroused their interest to an even higher degree. Early speculation that their guest was in fact a gentle man who posed no immediate threat, had caused them a growing desire to learn more about him. There were many unanswered questions, and every day seemed to produce new questions—both on the part of the ladies as well as that of the wounded soldier. Abigail had requested his presence in the parlor in order that they might spend an hour or two discussing such questions and learn more about each other while the whole family was in attendance. Once Ezra had carried the young man into the parlor and helped him to be seated, Abigail mediated upon the discussion... a duty befitting her matriarchal responsibilities as head of the Montgomery household.

"Good morning, Sir," Abigail cheerfully said, as all eyes in the parlor were inquisitively affixed on the young soldier. He had obviously shaved himself for the occasion, and even though he was wrapped in a bedsheet, he appeared quite handsome to the ladies of Montgomery House. From the soldier's perspective, being wrapped in a bedsheet gave him the discomforting feeling that he was on display, almost as a freak at a carnival sideshow. Noticeably apprehensive, he answered, "Good morning, Madame. Good morning, Ladies."

"Do you feel up to the task of talking to us this morning?"

"Yes Ma'am, I surely do."

"While we're talking, if at any time you feel weary, please inform us, and we'll see that Ezra carries you back to your room where you can lie down. Would you care for a cup of tea?"

"No thank you, Ma'am. You have a beautiful home here. I appreciate being invited into your parlor this morning, and I'm especially thankful to leave the room for a change. The only time I get to leave the room is when Ezra carries me out to the privy to... I'm sorry..."

"There are no apologies necessary, Sir."

"I'm sincerely looking forward to speaking with all of you this morning."

"Good, so are we. If you're agreeable, let us begin with you telling us how you feel about the progression of your healing at the present time."

"Yes Ma'am. I feel as though I am making some good progress in my healing, thanks to your Christian hospitality and generosity. I grow stronger each day, and the pain, although quite intense at times, seems to be bothering me less each day, and most nights I can sleep through the night without being pestered with pain. Most of the pain that I have is in my leg now, as my head injury hurts very little at present. Thank you for caring enough to ask."

"We're very pleased with the progress that you're making. Ezra tells me that you did not call upon him for assistance even once yesterday. Is that true?"

"Yes Ma'am, it is true. I was able to attend myself quite well yesterday without his assistance, thank you. I can stand on my own, as long as I don't put any unnecessary weight on my right leg by attempting to walk."

"I hope you're wise enough not to do anything that will retard your healing in any way. It takes time for bones to heal properly."

"I'm doing fine in that respect, Ma'am. I know you must be anxious for me to remove myself from your home here, and I promise you that I'll concentrate all of my efforts on healing as quickly as possible."

"You've misunderstood our aspirations, Sir, if you think we are anxious for you to leave our home. Our anxiety lies only in our wishes to see you heal properly, and that your health is fully restored when you do leave, regardless of how long that takes. In other words, we only want what's best for you, and it doesn't matter to us how long that takes. Have I made myself clear on that issue?"

"Yes Ma'am, and I thank you for your concern as well as your generosity, I really do."

"Good. Let us move on to something else. Have you been able to recall your name as yet?"

"No, Ma'am, I'm sorry to say that I haven't. I have tried almost constantly ever since I have been here and you first asked me. I have searched my mind quite thoroughly, many times... yet... I cannot seem to recall my name. I cannot recall much of anything, save for a few faint recollections of my distant childhood, I'm sorry to say."

"It seems very strange to me that a man so well versed and so effective in his conversations could not remember his own name."

"I agree Ma'am, it seems very strange indeed, and I cannot explain it. I remember nothing about myself, save for a few small recollections of my childhood."

"Can you tell us what you can remember of your childhood?"

"Yes Ma'am, I can faintly remember the faces of people whom I think were my mother and father. I can remember sitting with them in a church, and I can remember singing hymns with them. That's not very much, I know, but it's about all that I can remember at present."

"If you can remember being in a church with your parents, can you recall with any certainty whether you are a Christian or not?"

"Oh, yes Ma'am, there's no question in my mind that I am a Christian. I can recall faint portions of my Baptism as a child, and I can also recall certain scriptures from the Holy Bible... such as, *Saint John 3:16*, and *Saint Matthew 6:9*, and a few such as that. I have asked God to restore my memory, and every night I ask God to bless you and your family here for all that you have done for me."

Abigail was immediately ashamed of the fact that she had erroneously prejudged the man in the beginning as being just another Yankee scoundrel, and she involuntarily uttered the words, "Lord... forgive me..."

"What? Ma'am, is anything wrong?"

"No... it's nothing. Tell us, do you have any preference for a name which we might use to address you, until such time as you can recall your proper name?"

"I don't know. I haven't considered the need for such a thing until this very moment, but I suppose it would be helpful if I had some kind of name. And I again apologize for not knowing my proper name."

"It is apparent that you will be with us here for an extended period of time as you heal, and we need to have some sort of a name that we can use to address you. Do you have any particular temporary name in mind that you would prefer?"

"No, Ma'am, I have no preference at all. You may call me by any name that you deem appropriate, and I'll gladly answer to it. If you'll be so kind as to select a name of your liking, I would appreciate it."

"Very well, until we know differently, we shall call you, *William*. Would that name be satisfactory with you?"

"Yes, Ma'am... quite satisfactory."

"As I said before, you seem to be extremely well versed in conversation, William. Your choice of words and the way you express yourself would seem to suggest that you are a well-educated man. Do you know whether that's true or not?"

"No Ma'am. I'm afraid that I can't answer that because I just don't know for sure one way or the other. I certainly have no specific recollection of being properly educated... but of course, I don't seem to have very many specific recollections of anything, unfortunately."

"Do you know whether or not you can read and write?"

"I would certainly think that I can, but again, I'm not sure, Ma'am... I'm afraid that I would not know for sure until I try. I know that sounds like a stupid thing for me to say, but I'm very befuddled with myself at the present time."

"Would you mind opening this Holy Bible for us, and see if you can read a random scripture or two?"

"No Ma'am, I wouldn't mind at all, I'll try. Let's see... how about this; *But when Jesus saw, he was much displeased, and said unto them, suffer the little children to come unto me, and forbid them not, for of such is the kingdom of God. And he laid his hands on them, and departed thence.* Should I read more, Ma'am?"

"Perhaps later. Surely you must be an educated man. You seem to read quite eloquently, William, and despite the softness of your voice, your reading is quite pleasant to listen to."

"Thank you, Ma'am, I appreciate that. Do I still sound like I am whispering?"

"No, we can hear you quite well at present."

"I'll try to remind myself to speak a little louder."

"William, I have instructed Ezra to make a crutch for you and bring it to your room. You need to be careful and take your time in attempting to use it, but when you are able to walk by yourself with the aid of a crutch, you may have the full freedom of the first floor of our house. You are not permitted to go upstairs to the second floor at any time, but other than that, you have full freedom to go anywhere you wish, any time you wish. You are invited to take your morning and evening meals with us at our family table in the kitchen if you choose to do so. The exercise of careful walking will probably contribute to your healing, and the conversation at mealtime may even assist you in the restoration of your memory."

"Thank you, Ma'am, it's most gracious of you to be willing to share your home with me. Would you mind if I asked you some questions... purely to satisfy my own ignorant curiosity?"

"Of course not. You may ask us any questions you like, and we'll try to answer to the best of our ability."

"I was wondering if I would be terribly out of place, or making another of my emboldened comments if I were to ask you your names?"

Abigail blushed with immediate shame for her rude oversight and said, "Oh, my Lord! I sincerely apologize for our rudeness, William! Of course you would not be out of place to ask such a thing. We should have properly introduced ourselves to you the first day you awoke from your injuries. In all the confusion, I suppose that it slipped my mind. I am Abigail Montgomery, this is my sister, Agatha Martin, and this is my oldest daughter, Elizabeth Montgomery, and this is my youngest daughter, Sarah Montgomery."

"I am very honored and privileged to meet you all. And the older gentleman whom I occasionally see walking by the door sometimes...?"

"He is my stepfather, Phillip Montgomery. He has been as a father to Agatha and I, but we've always called him 'Grandfather Montgomery.' He suffers from the old person's aging illness. He's eighty-three years old now, and is no longer in full possession of his mental faculties. I would ask that you exercise tolerance when listening to some of the confusing things he occasionally says. He is very feeble, and cannot help his condition."

"I understand perfectly, Ma'am."

William listened closely, and was making an earnest effort to absorb everything that Abigail was telling him. Understandably, with every new bit of information that he learned, he wanted to know more. He asked Abigail, "Might I inquire as to how I came to be here with you and your family, Ma'am?"

"You are a soldier, William, and you were wounded in a battle that took place here on our property and left here with us to recover from your wounds. You were in such a deplorable state of health at the time, that the army of which you were a part, could not safely transport you without fear of causing your immediate death."

"I was a soldier? Really? What state are we in here? Is this Kentucky or North Carolina?"

"No, it is neither. This is southwestern Virginia. At this moment, you are approximately a hundred and sixty miles southwest of Richmond, in the foothills of the Appalachian Mountains. Our family raises a crop of tobacco here on our farm each year, as we have done for the last thirty-five years."

"I see. Several days ago, you said that our country was at war. Can you tell me with whom we are at war? Are we at war with England again?"

"You're being entirely truthful with us, aren't you? You sincerely don't know anything about the war, do you?"

"In my confusion, I know very little about myself, Ma'am, but I do know without a doubt that I am not a liar. As kind as you have been to me, I would never intentionally deceive you in any way. Of that, I swear a solemn oath to you."

"I did not mean to offend you, William, and I was not insinuating that you were lying. The war which I spoke of is an internal war within the United States. Northern states are at war with the southern states. A state of war was declared more than three years ago. Men from both sides have died, and continue to die by the thousands."

"By the thousands? Do you mean to tell me that Americans are killing other Americans? On American soil? My dear God, how could this possibly be?!"

"That is a very compelling question... one that I often find myself wondering about, and I fear there is no simple explanation for the conflict, nor does there appear to be an end in sight at this time. There are important differences in beliefs between the south and the north. There are differences of opinion in how states should be governed and taxed, as well as the right of Washington to impose regulations and levy taxes on states. Northern states are demanding the abolishment of slavery, and while that's an issue with great merit, the south remains at odds with the other demands of the political tyrants of the North. There are other differences as well. We can discuss these differences at length when you have recovered more from your injuries, if you wish to do so. Do the names of General Malcolm Kirkland, President Jefferson Davis, or Abraham Lincoln mean anything to you?"

"No, Ma'am, they surely don't. Should they?"

"Perhaps that is a bit too much to get into right now. We'll save that for a time when you are more rested."

"Ezra told me that your family does not own slaves. Is that true?"

"Grandfather Montgomery freed the slaves on our farm more than twenty-two years ago. His Christian convictions demanded as much. Our laborers are paid, not owned, and our family has provided them with legal documents to support that."

"Thank you for telling me this."

"Do you have any concerns or personal needs that you would like to bring to our attention... anything at all?"

"Yes Ma'am, I do, but you have treated me so graciously and kind here already that I hesitate to be a continual inconvenience to you by asking for additional concessions..."

"Do not hesitate to ask for anything that you might need while you are here with us, William. If you are in need of something that we can provide, we will be happy to do so. If you need something that we cannot provide, we will tell you so. Is that agreeable with you?"

"Yes, Ma'am, thank you."

"What is the concern that you spoke of? Please tell us."

"Well, Ma'am, it's just that the undergarment which I was given to wear under this blanket appears to be the only item of clothing in my room, and it is very much too small for me. In fact, it's so small, that it's really quite painful for me to wear. Do I have any proper clothes here that might belong to me? Anything at all?"

"You were wearing a military uniform when you were first brought here, but it was so badly torn and blood-soaked that we burned it. I'm sorry."

"Would it be possible for me to obtain some kind of proper shirt and trousers somehow? I don't mean to sound so particular or demanding, but I would feel much more at ease in accepting your kind invitation to join your family for meals if I had something to wear besides a bedsheet or a blanket. I feel like some kind of Indian on display, and I can't help but feel embarrassed and inferior when I'm wrapped up in a blanket like this, especially when I'm in the presence of ladies who are always so properly attired."

"We understand. I will see that clothes are brought to your room. I think you are approximately the same size that my late husband was, and I still have most of his clothes stored away in trunks in our attic if the moths haven't eaten them. I will see if I can find a shirt and trousers for you. If they need to be altered, we can attend to that as well. Your boots are tucked away under your bed. I asked Ezra to clean the blood from them and store them there. They are quite worn, but will probably suffice for as long as you are here with us."

"To my knowledge, I have no means with which to repay you for your kindness, Ma'am, but I swear by all that's Holy that I will dedicate myself to finding a way to repay you someday."

"Your healthy recovery is all the repayment that we ask, William. Now, if you will excuse us, Ezra will assist you back to your room and I will see that clothes are brought for you to dress yourself. The crutch will be brought to your room as soon as it's finished, and you will then have our permission to go and come as you please, bearing in mind of course, that you are not permitted to go upstairs under any circumstances."

"I understand, and I'm truly indebted to you for all that you and your family have done for me."

"One word of caution before you leave, William... Our neighbors have become increasingly curious about the presence of the strange young man in our house. Evidently you were seen by someone passing by one day as Ezra helped you outside to the privy. We have contrived a story for curious inquirers, that you are a wounded veteran who has been rendered mentally incompetent by a head-wound. We've done this for your own welfare. Please do not be offended by this ruse. It would be to your advantage to portray yourself as such when we have visitors, and talk to no one. It's for your own good. Do you understand?"

William bowed his head, as if he was in shame, and answered, "I shall not have to do a great deal of acting, Ma'am. I feel as though I am mentally incompetent indeed."

"I'm sorry. I did not intend to hurt your feelings, William. I'm merely suggesting what we think will be best for you at this time."

"Yes, Ma'am. I understand, and I will act appropriately if I am approached or questioned by anyone. May I ask a couple of additional questions before I take my leave, please?"

"Certainly. Ask all the questions you please. This is an opportunity for us to learn more about each other, that is why we are here, and I am quite pleased with all that we have learned about each other this morning. What additional questions do you have?"

"You mentioned your late husband, are all the other husbands off fighting in this war that you speak of? Is that why I never seem to see any young men hereabouts?"

"My late husband Thomas, and my son Arthur, and Agatha's husband Bernard, were all killed while fighting in this war more than two years ago. Elizabeth and Sarah have not married yet. Does that answer your question, William?"

"I'm truly sorry for your losses. I shouldn't have asked such an insensitive question, Ma'am, and for that, I apologize."

"Your question was innocent enough, William. You have offended no one. Is there anything else?"

"Yes, Ma'am, I'm curious... it seems that whenever I'm in your presence you always seem to have a pistol within close reach, like you do right now. Is there a logical reason for such a thing? Do you fear me, or look upon me as a threat for some reason?"

"The pistol has merely been a prudent precaution. We knew so little about you that our apprehensions were stirred initially. Unfortunately, the world we live in seems to have an over-abundance of dreadfully evil people, and we had no idea of your character or Christian beliefs until having the opportunity to learn more about you. If the pistol makes you uncomfortable, I'm confident that we know enough about you now that we can disperse with such unnecessary precautions."

"Thank you, Ma'am. I regret not knowing much about myself, but I do know enough about myself that I can swear an oath to you that I pose no threat to you or anyone here. You have each been angels of mercy, and I can only thank you from the bottom of my heart for all you have done. I have but one more question, but I feel as though my ignorant questions are becoming a nuisance. I can save it for another time, if you prefer."

"Please don't hesitate to ask your questions. You've been a nuisance to no one, except for the morning you attempted to walk on a shattered leg."

"Again, I would like to apologize for my stupidity in attempting to do such a thing. I obviously wasn't thinking very clearly that morning."

"And please allow me to apologize once more for my unnecessary display of temper that morning. For me to react the way that I did shows clear evidence that I wasn't thinking very clearly at the time either. My words were cruel, and uncalled for, and for that, I ask your forgiveness."

"I was deserving of the scolding I received, Ma'am."

"You said that you had another question?"

"Yes Ma'am, I see that there is a piano here in your parlor, yet I never seem to hear any music. I was simply wondering why it's never played."

"The piano was once played by my mother, Eleanor. She was an expert pianist. She passed away more than nine years ago. No one here plays the piano, so it has sat here quietly in the parlor for years, I'm sorry to say. It had always been my intention to provide Elizabeth and Sarah with piano lessons, but the war has precluded any such intentions. The war has precluded a lot of enjoyments in our lives, unfortunately."

"I see. Thank you, Ma'am."

"Do you play the piano, William?"

"Me? I shouldn't think so, Ma'am. I certainly have no such recollection. Again, I sincerely appreciate everything that you and your family have done for me here, and I'm most thankful for your taking the time to answer my questions. Before leaving, I would like to take this opportunity to say one very important thing to you and your family, if you would be so kind as to permit me."

"Of course."

"No words could ever properly convey the gratitude I have for the kind attention you have shown me here. I have every confidence that I would be dead now, if it were not for you and your family. Now that I know your names, I will keep you in my prayers, individually, and as a family. God bless you, and thank you."

"You have a very touching way of expressing yourself, William, and you are sincerely welcome."

"Ezra, if you will be so kind as to help me back to my room, please."

Ezra assisted William back to his room as the womenfolk sat there in perfect awe of their first impressions of William's politeness. Abigail felt a need to discuss their guest between themselves. Thinking it best that William not hear what they were saying, Abigail asked, "Elizabeth, please close the door to the kitchen so that William cannot hear us. Now that we all know a little more about him, I would like to go around the room and have each of you share your thoughts concerning our new guest. My opinion of him has changed considerably, and I would like to hear your opinions as well. Agatha, would you please start?"

Fanning herself with a palm fan, Agatha exclaimed, "Oh, my... I almost don't know where to begin. I suppose that my thoughts are, that he seems innocent enough to me now. I think I may have seriously misjudged him initially. He is an extremely well-spoken young man, obviously well-educated, and quite charming, really. I thoroughly enjoyed hearing him read from the Bible, and I hope he can do a lot of that sort of thing while he is healing. I no longer see any inkling of a threat in his presence here whatsoever."

Sarah immediately spoke up and asked Agatha, "You mean to say that you no longer want to kill him, bury him in the woods behind the barn, and be done with him, Aunt Agatha?"

"Sarah! I demand that you apologize to your aunt for your rudeness right now!"

"I'm sorry, Aunt Agatha. Please forgive me."

Agatha responded, "Sarah's ridicule was well founded. My remarks about how we should have dealt with the man when he was first brought here were cruel and unchristian. I was frightened and confused at the time. I'm ashamed of the things that I said then, and I'm indeed happy that the man is showing such a remarkable recovery."

"I'm sorry that I lashed out at you, Aunt Agatha. I had no call to say what I did."

Regaining control of the conversation, Abigail asked her other daughter, "Elizabeth, what are your thoughts, dear?"

"I knew from the very beginning that he posed no sort of threat to us. He seems to be a proper gentleman, and he is healing splendidly. I adore listening to him when he reads, he has such a pleasant voice that I find it very comforting. Yankee or not, he seems to have the heart of a southern gentleman, and

I agree with Agatha, I think he's quite charming. I even feel a twinge of sorrow in knowing that he will heal someday and leave Montgomery Farm."

"Judging by the uniform that he was wearing when he was brought here, he's certainly not a southern gentleman, Elizabeth. However, I must admit, by the accent of his voice, neither does he sound like a Yankee. His true origin remains a mystery to us. Sarah, dear, what are your thoughts?"

"Like Elizabeth and Agatha, I think he's a perfect gentleman. I enjoy having his presence here in our home. It's comforting to have a young man in the house for a change... especially one as handsome and charming as William. I think he's just adorable and I like him a lot. He's so stunningly handsome that he even takes my breath away sometimes!"

"Sarah! Temper your emotions, daughter!"

"I'm sorry, Mother, but that's the way I feel. I can't help it. How about you, Mother? You haven't voiced your opinion yet. How do you see our guest now?"

"I'm beginning to see him as a Christian gentleman, also. I'm intrigued by him, really. He's a charming young man, indeed, but we need to keep a prudent vigil over our emotions. We need to remember that he's done nothing to earn our endearment other than talk to us politely. Many a fair young lady has been wooed into a false sense of enchantment by a silver-tongued, villainous ogre. Evildoers can sometimes be quite clever and charming with their lies in order to take what they want. He's still a Yankee, and as such, he might awaken from this gentle man that we know today as William, and become a dreadful Yankee scoundrel again. It could happen at any time, and we must remain alert, and be on continuous guard for such a happenstance."

"Yes, Mother."

Despite Sarah's brazen words, she had best expressed the sentiments of all the ladies there in Montgomery House, even Abigail's. As for William, he was entirely truthful when he had expressed his gratitude for all that had been done for him, but his mind remained so confused and befuddled over his circumstances that he was very ill at ease in not being able to recall his own identity or his past. He was intelligent enough to know that everyone had to have an origin and a purpose in life, and he was disconcerted greatly by not knowing anything of his own purpose or his past. As for his potential of being an evildoer, nothing could have been farther from the truth.

Later that morning, Abigail brought clothes to his room. She handed him the clothes and said, "Here, William, see if these will suffice. If they fit you, I have many more in the attic, and you are welcome to them. I will wait here, outside of your room, and if alterations are required, my daughters and I will tend to the task before supper this evening."

"Thank you, Ma'am."

As Abigail stood outside of William's room with her back against the closed door she heard him struggling somewhat inside, and turned her head toward the door to ask, "Is everything alright in there, William?" From inside, William replied, "I'm sorry, Ma'am, but I'm having a great deal of trouble in here. My efforts to dress myself are comical. I may require some assistance in getting my broken leg into the undergarment and trousers. Is Ezra available to assist me?"

"Ezra has ridden into town with Agatha and Elizabeth. Are you wearing your new undergarment now?"

"No, Ma'am. I'm wearing nothing at present. I'm having a great deal of difficulty getting it onto my bad leg. My arm is not long enough to reach the end of my foot, and I can't bend my leg because of the splint. If it's not too wasteful, the right leg of the undergarment needs to be cut off, so that my splint can pass through it freely."

"I have scissors with me, is it necessary that I come inside and assist you?"

"I would be most appreciative if you did, Ma'am, if you could do so without being embarrassed. I'll cover myself as best I can with the corner of my bedsheet."

"Very well then. I'm coming in. Have you covered yourself?"

"Yes, Ma'am."

Abigail assisted him by cutting off the right leg of the undergarment and helping him dress in his undergarment, trousers, and one of the boots. His bad leg was still too painful for him to wear a boot on that foot. The clothes fit him almost perfectly, without any further need to be altered, and in his dressed condition, his self-esteem and dignity began to improve almost immediately. William felt revived by having himself clothed for the first time since awaking, eighteen days previous. His attendance at the family meals contributed even more to his healing—both in body and spirit. In fact, the conversations at mealtime uplifted everyone's spirits, not just William's, and with each new conversation, they learned more about each other. William's remarkable gift of wholesome humor added an element of excitement to their conversations which tended to elevate everyone's outlook on life. As Abigail had told William earlier, Montgomery House had been absent of humor, and William's pleasant levity brought a welcomed measure of joy to the hearts of the family. Unknowingly, they were beginning to form the early precepts of an unmistakable bond together. Odd circumstances and horrible events had brought them together at this place, to be sure, and perhaps the uncertainty of what the future would bring provided an even greater strength to this early bonding. Regardless, uncertainty continued to be the key element that seemed to dominate and rule their daily lives, and the more uncertain things were, the more the occupants of Montgomery House needed each other's ongoing reassurance. Families draw strength from each other, and even without his awareness, William was becoming a resource from which the ladies of Montgomery House could draw strength and moral support.

At the very first family meal together, Abigail asked William if he would feel comfortable in asking for the blessing of the food. The elder Mr. Montgomery was too feeble to offer an appropriate prayer, and William was the only other man in the house. Without hesitation, William agreed, and offered such a splendid prayer that it became customary for him to do so at each meal. At the first prayer, William held his hands out, and for a brief moment the ladies seemed to be unfamiliar with the practice of holding hands during prayer. However, they soon complied, and that too, became a customary practice at Montgomery House thereafter.

After an additional three weeks of healing, William cut his bandages and removed the splints that had held his shattered leg in place. Abigail thought it much too early for him to do such a thing, but William insisted that the splints were causing him much more discomfort than the broken leg. At the breakfast table one morning, William announced, "Miss Abigail, I feel like I am now quite able to attend to some of the menial chores around here that might offer some small expression of the gratitude I have for the way you and your family have cared for me."

"It's not necessary for you to feel like you have to repay us in any way, William. I've told you that before. We would much prefer for you to continue to rest, and allow yourself ample time to heal before pursuing any tasks that would require you to stand or walk on your injured leg."

"I appreciate your concern, Miss Abigail, I really do, but nevertheless, I feel like I am quite capable of working at the woodpile this morning. I can split kindling wood without causing any unnecessary stress to my injury, and I feel like the fresh air would do me well. I have rested for far too long now, and feel like the time has arrived in which I should try to earn a small portion of my keep."

"I shan't attempt to restrain you from doing what you feel is necessary, William, regardless of how stupid I think it might be, but if you re-injure yourself in the commission of such foolishness and fall to the ground in pain, don't expect to receive any sympathy or compassion from me."

"I have already come to realize that I should never expect to receive such personal considerations as sympathy or compassion from you, Abigail."

"Mother! What a cruel thing to say to William!"

"I... I'm sorry for what I said... I didn't mean for that to sound as scornful and belligerent as it probably did. Please forgive me, William."

"I do, Ma'am. I always try very hard to forgive the hurtful things that you are sometimes prone to say to me... I only wish that I was as successful in forgetting your words as I am in forgiving them."

Abigail was ashamed of herself. She had lashed out angrily at William again, and knew that she had unwittingly hurt his feelings. Instead of offering a more sincere apology, she arose from the table quickly and walked up to her bedchamber and closed the door. Sarah knew that William was brokenhearted over Abigail's unsympathetic words. She looked pitifully at him and said, "Mother didn't mean what she said, William."

"I know she didn't, Sarah. Still, I can't help but wonder why she seems to dislike me so much. My God, I'm trying very hard to be nice to her, yet nothing that I say or do seems to please her."

"It's not that she dislikes you. You've become endeared to all of us here at Montgomery House, Mother included. The last few years have been very bitter years for us here. They've been the hardest on Mother, and have caused her to be ill-tempered at times. Between the war, and the living hell that my father put her through, she's had a very difficult life here. Please try to understand that she's been through a lot, William."

"I do, Sarah... I really do. I just thought that your mother would have been proud of me for wanting to contribute to some of the work that's done around here. I can't help but be disappointed in learning otherwise."

"I'm sure that she is indeed proud of you, William, as we all are."

"Your words are comforting, Sarah. Perhaps someday I will be comforted by hearing pleasant words from your mother, at least I pray that will be the case."

The age-old defining characteristic of hurtful words is; once they are spoken, they can never be completely retracted. All of the apologies in the world can never completely erase the hurt from an offended heart. William was so eager to hear pleasing and complimentary words from Abigail that when she spoke hurtful words, they cut into him as surely and deeply as a knife. If the exact same words had been spoken to William by a stranger, they wouldn't have affected him at all. But when the words came from Abigail, they seemed to fall on his ears as a hellish, unwarranted torment. William was unaware that Abigail's painful words were not intended to hurt him—they were only spoken in a vain attempt to ward off her own aggravatingly persistent attraction to him. There was a battle being fought within the depths of Abigail's heart, and because of her success in concealing her emotions, no one knew it but her.

One morning during the third week of William's usage of the crutch to move about, he came into the kitchen and took his usual place at the table after bidding a good morning to Abigail and Agatha. He took immediate notice of the fact that Sarah and Elizabeth were not at the table. He waited patiently for Sarah and Elizabeth to come downstairs until it became apparent that something about this morning was different. He worried that the sisters may have been ill, so he inquired of Abigail as to the reason for their absence.

"Are Sarah and Elizabeth feeling poorly this morning, Abigail?"

"They are both fine, William. But there is a founder's day festival taking place today in the town of Blanchard, and we have a shortage of workmen in our fields today. In fact, it's much worse than just a shortage, it seems that all of our workmen have gone into town for the festival. No one showed up this morning to work, and we will probably have no help here until Monday."

"Have Sarah and Elizabeth gone to the festival?"

"No, Sarah and Elizabeth have both gone to the fields to help Ezra and Vivian pull tobacco today."

"You mean to tell me that Sarah and Elizabeth are out there pulling tobacco? In this heat?"

"It's seldom necessary for them to work in the fields, but today is an exception. Agatha and I would be going to the fields as well, but we have vegetables to preserve today, lest they spoil. The southwest field is in need of pulling or the tobacco will lose a lot of its value at market. Our tobacco is always the first to sell at market, because we take such great care in pulling it at precisely the right time. Even with Sarah and Elizabeth helping Ezra and Vivian, it's doubtful that they will get it all pulled today. At Montgomery Farm, we simply do what we have to do in order to get by each day."

"What will Elizabeth and Sarah eat today?"

"They took some biscuits and some peaches to the fields with them."

William was shocked. He never touched the cup of tea that Abigail had poured for him. Instead, he rose from his chair immediately, grabbed his crutch from the floor, and limped out the door. Abigail didn't know what to think, and dashed out of the door after him, catching him a few feet from the porch.

"Where are you going in such an all-fired hurry, William?"

"I'm going to the fields and pull tobacco, that's where!"

"No you're not! You're not going anywhere on that leg! Come back inside this house right now! I won't hear of you trying to pull tobacco today in the shape your leg is in!"

"I dislike defying you like this, Abigail, but I'm not going to lie around on my lazy ass all day while Sarah and Elizabeth pull tobacco in the hot sun! I won't do it! So you may as well get used to the idea and go back inside without me! You can scold me to your heart's content at the end of the day!"

"How could you possibly expect for your leg to heal properly, when you insist on doing stupid things like this?! I demand that you come back here right now!"

"You can make demands until your face turns blue if you like! I'm going to the fields, and that's all there is to it!"

Abigail could say or do nothing to deter William from going to the fields. As she watched him limping down the hillside toward the tobacco fields she yelled out at him one final time.

"You've got the hardest head of any person I have ever known in my entire life, William!" In the distance she heard him faintly shout back at her, "That's funny, Abigail, I share the same opinion of you!"

She watched him disappear over the hillside and shook her head in futile frustration. Then, a broad smile crossed her face and as she shook her head, she uttered, "My dear God... that's one determined man, if I do say so! Jesus, help him! Please watch over him today!"

That evening, when Ezra began pulling the tobacco wagons back to the barn, Abigail was greatly relieved when she saw Sarah and Elizabeth riding on the wagon driven by Ezra, and a very tired William riding on the back of the wagon being driven by Vivian. Ezra and Vivian placed the tobacco leaves on drying racks and remained at the drying barn to finish storing their crop. Sarah and Elizabeth were the first to come into the house, and Abigail asked, "Where's William? Isn't he with you?"

"He's gone down to the creek to bathe, Mother."

"Bathe? My, my, my... Go upstairs and wash yourselves, and we'll hold our dinner in the warming oven until William is here to join us. My Lord, after what he's done today, I don't think I could bring myself to start eating without him tonight."

"You should have seen him today, Mother, holding his crutch in one hand and pulling tobacco with the other! Ezra says he works better with one hand than most folks do with two! He's amazing!"

"Yes... I know he is... in more ways than one, bless his heart. Has he been in much pain today as he worked?"

"He kept telling us that he's not been in much pain at all, but by the looks on his face, I'm sure that he was telling us a lie. A couple of times I swear I could see tears in his eyes. All day we tried to get him to come back to the house, but he wouldn't listen to us. He just kept pulling tobacco. We couldn't have finished today without his help. We would have lost a third of the south field crop had it not been for him. I'll bet he's lying down in the creek right about now in the cold water, trying to get the pain in his leg to let up."

"I don't know what to think of him sometimes. When he gets here, I'll pour him a glass of bourbon. That might help with the pain a bit, and he's certainly earned it. God bless him."

"Mother, are you crying?"

"Of course not. You and Elizabeth need to go wash up and put on some clean clothes before Will gets here for supper."

"Mother, you are so crying!"

"Listen to me and do what I said, right now!"

"Yes, Mother."

Although highly frustrated by William's determination to work that day, Abigail could not help but admire the fact that he had the fortitude and courage to do what he thought was right, despite the pain that he experienced in the process. She anticipated that William was going to have a difficult night with his pain, and her heart was overcome with sympathy. William soon joined them, and made a gallant effort to hide the fact that he was still experiencing a great amount of pain. He exerted every effort to display a jovial, cheerful disposition so as to avoid Abigail's wrathful criticism, but Abigail knew he was in a great deal of pain. She could see the pain in his eyes and read it on his face. She poured him a generous portion of bourbon, and the family enjoyed a pleasant meal together. Owing to everyone's hard labors of the day, the family retired to their bedchambers early that evening.

In the middle of the night, Abigail had come into the kitchen and walked to William's door to listen, hoping that she would hear some sound that would reassure her that he was sleeping peacefully, and free of pain. Instead, she heard the disturbing sounds of soft moaning coming from inside. She listened at the door for a moment or two longer and went back into the kitchen. Soon, she returned to William's door, and knocked.

"William, may I come in?"

"What?"

"May I come in?"

"Oh... Yes Ma'am, of course. Is something wrong, Abigail?"

"I've brought you another glass of bourbon with some elixir in it, and a cool, dampened towel to lie across your leg. Hopefully, this will offer you enough relief so that you can rest better."

"How did you know that I was hurting tonight? I've made every effort to keep it hidden from you."

"You have made a gallant effort to hide it from me, William, but I'm more observant than you might think I am. You were moaning quite loudly in your sleep a little while ago. Here, drink this."

"Thank you, Abigail. I'm sorry if I disturbed you. Should I light the lamp?"

"I'd rather you didn't, William. I'm not dressed appropriately, and I would not want you to see me like this. I think the light of the moon outside will be quite sufficient for us to see."

William drank the bourbon and handed the glass back to Abigail. In the darkness of the room, only faint shadows were distinguishable. William could not see the tears of sympathy that appeared on Abigail's cheek.

"Where is most of your pain coming from, William, is it in the leg wound itself?"

"No, Abigail. Most all of the pain is in my lower leg and foot, well below the wound. It feels like my leg is on fire."

"Your neck must feel like it's on fire as well. I noticed at the supper table that you have been badly burned by the sun today. I brought a cool towel for that as well."

"Thank you, Abigail... that's very thoughtful of you."

"I'm so sorry that you're suffering like this, William. Would you permit me to rub your leg and foot with this cool cloth and see if that helps reduce the pain?"

"It grieves me to know that I'm disturbing your sleep like this, Abigail. You need your rest, and..."

"I'm fine, William. Lie back and close your eyes. After what you've been through today, you need the rest more than I do. Is this helping you any at all?"

"God Almighty, yes. But what about you, Abigail? I shan't be able to sleep, knowing that you are out of your own bed and fussing over me like this. Please go back up to your room and try to get some sleep, I'll be fine now."

"Always concerned with everyone else's welfare more so than your own, aren't you, William?"

Abigail softly rubbed William's leg and foot for more than a half hour. In the darkness, even in his pain, William wanted to reach over and hold Abigail's hand, but he clearly recognized that such a thing would be entirely improper. Instead, he simply said, "I'm feeling much better now, Abigail. I think the bourbon is also helping. Please go to your room and try to get some rest."

"Very well... I'll leave your door open and leave mine opened as well. If you need me during the night, just call out to me, and I'll hear you."

"Thank you, Abigail, I will."

"If your leg still pains you as much in the morning, I'll send Ezra to fetch Doctor Michaels."

"Thank you, Abigail, but I don't think that will be necessary. And thank you for not reminding me that I brought all of this additional pain on myself by going to the fields today. I fully expected you to rake me over the coals for doing what I did today."

"I shan't ridicule you about that, William. Your motives were most honorable. As much as I would like to take a stick and beat you over your hard head sometimes, I can only admire you for your courage in doing what you thought was right. You had Elizabeth and Sarah's welfare in mind. As cold as my heart must seem to you sometimes, how could I ridicule you for that? Goodnight, and God bless you. I hope you sleep peacefully for the rest of the night."

"Abigail?"

"Yes?"

"Nothing... Thank you again, and may God bless you as well."

Abigail was greatly touched by the sacrifice that William had made that day. She had never known a man who would have done such a thing. When she went back upstairs to her room, she offered a special prayer for William, and spent the next hour listening closely for any sound of distress emitting from downstairs. Hearing none, she eventually faded off to sleep.

○ ○ ○

Abigail continued to provide tender care for the healing of young William's scalp and leg. Every other day, she would wash the wounds with sulfur and warm water, removing any scab tissue that was loose. It was still too early for her to remove the stitches that held his scalp together, but as time went on she successfully removed the stitches from his leg injury, and knew that the time would soon arrive for the stitches on his head to be removed. William had come to treasure these tender moments when Abigail tended to his wound. It was an opportunity for him to experience her loving touch, enjoy being close to her, and it was also a time in which they could share quiet conversation together. When Abigail would touch his head in the process of tending to his wound, William would close his eyes and pretend that she was touching him for the purpose of conveying her love. William lived for the conveyance of such tender moments, yet he was without a clue that Abigail relished these touches as much as he.

William knew that his head injury had almost completely healed, and he began to dread the day that Abigail's comforting attendance would no longer be necessary. What William did not know however, was that Abigail had come to treasure these private times with him as much as he did. Still stubbornly reluctant to do or say anything that would have allowed William to know the true extent of her growing enchantment, she was cautious to an extreme in the manner in which she touched him, talked to him, or even looked at him. She viewed her emotional attachment to William as a weakness, unbefitting a woman who was supposed to be the leader of her family. She was supposed to have sufficient inner strength to ignore these types of sentimental shortcomings and rise above them... but she was slowly learning that she did not have the strength to ignore William. She nevertheless resolved herself to pretend not to be as susceptible as she really was. William had come to mean much more to Abigail than simply that of a random man in need of medical attention, or Samaritan kindness. She had never been exposed to a man who possessed such warmth of personality and innocent tenderness before. She could clearly see now that William was like no other man she had ever known. Her heart was crying out to her in an effort to convince her that William was a man worthy of her adoration. Yet her lessons in life regarding men had taught her that men were a breed not to be trusted. They had taught her that men were deceitful and untrustworthy, cunning and promiscuous, and that the instincts of thievery and adultery were inbred in all men. Her heart was drawing her closer and closer to William with each new day, and she did not trust her heart. She loved her sister and her daughters dearly, and had made many sacrifices during her life for the benefit of her family. There was no room in her life for the presence of a man, and William was just another man. He would heal completely someday, probably regain his memory, tire of his surroundings and his unfruitful flirtations there at Montgomery Farm, and disappear soon to become nothing more than an oblique and anonymous memory of the past. He might even regain his memory and go off to fight alongside his northern comrades again. Either way, it made no difference to her—or so she tried to tell herself.

Still and all, during the times when she tended to his wounds, she felt something magical happening to her each time she touched him. The sessions in which she would attend him were never performed in haste. If a family member would have questioned the excessive amount of time that she was taking with William, she would have rationalized, and defended her intentions as being no more than a sincere effort to provide the most competent and complete attention possible. But in truth, Abigail was being helplessly drawn to William and she treasured every moment they were together. Regardless of her overwhelming adoration of William, she was insistent that these irrepressible feelings be concealed, kept to herself, and held well under strict control. She was frightened—not by William, but by her own recognition of what was happening to her.

The Dawning Of A Brand New Day

"This is my commandment, That ye love one another,
as I have loved you." John 15:12

The days at Montgomery Farm quickly passed into weeks, and each new day and week found young William's health and fitness improving with remarkable new stamina, and his injuries were offering him much less pain. Although he still walked with a noticeable limp, after just three weeks of walking with the assistance of a crutch, he was able to discard the crutch altogether, and walk without any assistance at all. Even with Abigail's continual pleadings for him to go about his recovery at a slower pace, he assisted in helping Ezra cut firewood and helped Sarah and Elizabeth in the milking of the cows. He also began taking exclusive care of the chickens, as well as performing other chores around the farm that required a limited amount of walking or heavy lifting. Every chore that William accomplished was one less chore that the ladies had to attend to. William knew this, and such knowledge provided him with the motivation to do more.

Fall and winter would be upon them soon, and the entire family, as well as two migrant farmhands, joined in the preparation of the land for the spring crop of tobacco, corn, melons, and vegetables. Old tobacco stalks were pulled from the ground and burned, and the tobacco fields were tilled so that they could sit dormant over the upcoming winter months. Potatoes were harvested from the ground and stored in the cellar and firewood was laid in for the winter. Young William was soon fit enough to attend to most any of the chores with the exception of tilling the soil, with Ezra and the mules managing that task quite capably without the need of William's assistance. His leg still pained him immensely during the times that he would attempt to do too much work, or attempt to lift and carry heavy items, but nevertheless, his mending was commencing quite nicely. It was on the second day of August that William lay on the corner of his bed while Abigail sat in a chair next to his bed, and attended to cleansing the wound on his head and painstakingly removing the stitches. The morning sunlight shined through the window and allowed Abigail to see perfectly as she proceeded with her delicate cleaning. William had been at Montgomery Farm for more than two and a half months. With a warm, dampened cloth, Abigail gently washed the scar in his scalp, and with meticulous care, she was removing the last of the stitches. The stitches could have been removed safely two weeks earlier, but Abigail had delayed their removal, in hopes of prolonging the sessions when she attended him. William's head was on her knee as she worked, and because he was facing away from her, he could not see the adorable smile of pride and tenderness on Abigail's face as she attended to his wound. In fact, if she thought that William could have seen her smile, she would have made every effort to conceal it from him.

"Am I hurting you in any way when I do this, William?"

"No, Abigail, it doesn't hurt at all. You have the touch of a goddess, I swear you do."

"Good. Lie very still, and I'll be finished shortly."

When she was nearly finished with the cleaning and the removal of the stitches, Abigail said, "I think this is most likely the final time that it will be necessary for me to attend to the wound on your head, William. There is only the faintest remnant of a scab that remains, and it has healed so perfectly that it can barely be seen in the thickness of your hair. One would almost have to part your hair in order to see any trace of a scar. I think you will be quite capable of tending to yourself after today."

"I suppose that I should be happy about that, shouldn't I, Abigail?"

"Well, yes, of course you should be as happy about that as I am. Why on earth would you *not* be happy about that, William?"

"I should think that my reasons would be quite obvious to you, Abigail. I shall miss your caring attention and the quiet moments that we spend together like this when you're attending my wound. I've come to treasure your attention. I shan't begin to tell you how comforting it is for me just to feel the touch of your hand on my head..."

"I sense that you are preparing to journey far into the realm of inappropriate remarks again, William."

"Yes, Abigail, I suppose that you would most likely interpret my true thoughts as being inappropriate. You seem to judge all of my honest words to you as being inappropriate, I'm sorry to say."

"Then please, William, for my sake, have pity on me and keep such words to yourself. They only tend to upset me. Would you be so kind as to spare me on this otherwise beautiful morning?"

"My Lord, but you make life terribly difficult for me sometimes, Abigail... I would give anything if you would only allow me to express myself... truthfully..."

"Please, William?"

"Very well, I will keep my words to myself, Miss Abigail... but only for your sake. I have become rather adept at keeping my words to myself, unfortunately, and I will continue to do so."

"Thank you for being so considerate. I have work to attend to in the kitchen. You may return to help Ezra in the fields if you would please, William. You've healed very nicely, and I'm really quite proud of that. It's not been that long ago that we all thought you were on your death bed, in your final hours. I can't tell you how elated everyone is over your remarkable healing."

"Yes, Ma'am. Thank you for caring for me as you have. I would suppose that with the healing of my wounds, I will be expected to move into the barn now, and sleep among the other farmhands there."

"What...?"

"I'm a farmhand, Abigail. That's all I am. That's probably all I'll ever be, and now that my wounds have healed, I would suppose that my rightful place is in the barn, with the other farmhands, don't you think?"

Aggravatingly stubborn as always, Abigail marshalled up her trademark obstinacy and her emotional wall of defense, offering a rather cold and impersonal response to William's question. Almost flippantly, she said, "If you would prefer to sleep in a barn rather than in the house... then you are certainly free to do so. You have my blessing. It doesn't matter to me where you choose to sleep at night." Abigail was bluffing, but her detached remarks fell on William's sensitive ears as if they represented the unsympathetic, bitter truth.

"Very well, Abigail, if you'll be so kind as to loan me a blanket until such time as I could afford to purchase one, I'll start spending my nights in the barn, with all of the other laborers."

"**NO**! I mean... please don't do that. You may continue to stay in the chambermaid room, if you would prefer. You may consider it your permanent room for as long as you stay here at Montgomery Farm."

"Thank you, that's very gracious of you, indeed, but it's not a matter of what *I* would prefer, Abigail. You are the head of the household here, and I'm merely trying to determine what *your* preference would be. Do you prefer for me to remain in the house, or would you rather that I move to the barn?"

"I shan't drop to my knees and beg you to stay in the house, if that's what you're asking of me, William, but yes, I think the family would prefer that you remain in the house. Your presence and your conversation during our family meals has become a delight to Agatha and my daughters, and I'm sure they would prefer for that to continue... if you don't mind. I shan't begin to tell you how delighted they are to share conversation with an educated person such as yourself. Such a thing has been a rarity here at Montgomery House in recent years."

"I'm flattered beyond words to know that Agatha and your daughters somehow find my presence in the house to be delightful, but how about you, Abigail? Does my presence at Montgomery House please or delight you in any small way at all?"

"Make your own choice, William! It doesn't matter to me one way or the other! I have work to attend to in the kitchen, and I don't have the time to frolic and play children's games with you this morning! You have a choice to make today. If you want to borrow a blanket so you can sleep in the barn, then you are more than welcome to do so. If you wish to continue taking your meals with the family, then you are welcome to do that as well. Please return to your duties in the fields with Ezra and spend your nights wherever you damn well please!"

"Thank you, Ma'am, I will do just as you say."

As William left the house to resume his daily labors in the fields, Abigail hurriedly went inside to the parlor to mend some clothes. But she was so flustered and aggravated with herself that she temporarily forgot what she had walked into the parlor to do. Instead, she just stood there, confounded by the sudden predicament she had found herself in. She was ashamed of the fact that she had always scorned William when he had attempted to say pleasant and complimentary things to her, thinking it best that she maintain the strictest of matriarchal images for the benefit of setting a prim and proper example for her sister and her daughters. She was embarrassed and ashamed of the fact that she had just used profanity when expressing herself to William—an imperfection of Christian etiquette that was highly uncharacteristic of her. She was well aware of the fact that this strange young man had been attempting to pluck at her heart-strings, and outwardly, she cared not to acknowledge such foolish and personally offensive music. At least that was the outward image that she struggled to project. But in the depths of her heart, the opposite was true. Even as much as she feared her own vulnerability to William's gratifying charm, when he paid her compliments or said pleasing things to her, she almost melted with satisfaction within. She often wondered what William would say to her if she allowed him to speak his mind without her imposing any of her encumbering restrictions. She had consistently put forth a great deal of effort to ignore the fact that William was in love with her, but her most gallant efforts were focused on denying the fact that she loved him.

Abigail spent the remainder of the day, as she worked, praying that William would choose to continue abiding in the house with the family, yet she was stubbornly defiant enough that she didn't want William to know just how much his presence in the house really pleased her. She found herself looking out of the window at William several times throughout the course of the day as he worked in the fields with Ezra and the other workmen. She was beside herself with anxiety over the matter of where William would choose to spend his nights, and regretful that she had lacked the courage to tell him just how precious he had become to her. Just the thought of knowing that William was sleeping in the same house was immensely comforting to her, and she did not want to entertain the possibility that he might prefer sleeping in the barn with the transient laborers. She regretted her coarse display of temper that day, and wished that she had spoken to William with kinder words. She greatly lamented the fact that she so often spoke to him in such scathing and depersonalizing manners. The harsh words that she had spoken to William that morning unpleasantly echoed in her ears throughout the afternoon, *"It doesn't matter to me...you can spend your nights wherever you damn well please!"*

After their evening meal, Abigail was alone in the kitchen, washing the tea kettle and the last of the dishes while the other ladies had adjourned to the parlor to tend to their evening knitting and sewing duties. William had gone into the small bedchamber, and Abigail could hear him rummaging around inside as if he was tidying up his room. She glanced toward William's bedchamber door a multitude of times as she worked in the kitchen, still held in a state of apprehension as to where he would choose to spend his nights. She thought to herself, *"William is not stupid enough to prefer sleeping in a barn. His room here is small, but it offers a good, clean condition that could never be found in the barn, for heaven's sake, and he's welcome to stay here as long as he wishes, but only under **my** terms. **I'm** the head of the family, and **I** make the rules here!"* The evening sun was just beginning to set over the western horizon and it would soon be dark enough inside the house to light the oil lamps. Out of the corner of her eye, she watched in anguished disillusionment as William quietly emerged from the small bedchamber carrying a few clothes which were wrapped up tightly in a blanket. He looked into the kitchen at Abigail with mournfully saddened eyes and simply said, "Goodnight, Abigail. Thank you for that wonderful meal this evening and thank you for the loan of this blanket."

Disappointed almost to the point of not being able to speak, Abigail somehow found strength, and answered almost as though she was uninterested in what he had just said, "You're welcome. Goodnight, William." In her heart she was thinking, *"Damn it all anyway! I can be just as stubborn and hardheaded as he can be! I'll not allow any man alive to weaken me! I'll never let a man see me crawl before him! As far as I'm concerned, he can spend his nights at the bottom of the well if he wants to! My dear Lord... what on earth have I just done?"*

Sadly disheartened, William had walked through the back door on his way to the barn as Abigail remained in the kitchen, washing the tea kettle and fuming over William's apparent decision. Her lips began to quiver, and there were soon tears welling up in her eyes. Her heart was breaking into pieces, and her desperation was intensifying by the moment. Her incessant stubbornness had finally come into direct conflict with her heart, and she had to do something quickly in order to rectify the shattering circumstances that had suddenly developed. In a moment of sheer unbridled panic over a situation that was completely of her own making, Abigail swallowed her foolish pride for once, and quickly rushed outside to catch him. He was halfway to the barn when Abigail ran up to him and grabbed him by the arm, turning him around to face her. In a final desperate attempt to save face and conceal her true emotions, with a fiery and defensive voice, she rather sarcastically asserted, "And just where are you going, William?!"

"Well, I'm going to my new home in the barn, with the other workmen, I suppose, Abigail. We talked about this earlier today after you so kindly removed the stitches from my head, remember?"

"Land sakes alive! This kind of behavior is utterly insane! Have you completely lost your mind or something?!"

"No, I don't think so..."

"So, William, you mean to tell me that you've decided that you would prefer to sleep in the barn with the insects, the spiders, the mice, and the snakes, not to mention the odorous snoring men, than to sleep in the comfort of a warm, clean bed in the house?"

"No, that's not what I would prefer at all, Abigail. I've simply decided that it would be more comfortable for me to sleep in the barn with the insects, the spiders, the mice, the snakes, and the odorous snoring men, than to sleep in any house where my presence is not wanted."

"This is absolutely absurd! I told you this morning that your presence in the house is wanted! Are you deaf?! Did you not hear me when I said that?!"

"I heard you quite well this morning, Abigail. You made it perfectly clear to me that your daughters and Agatha are delighted by my presence in the house. You also made it perfectly clear to me that my presence or absence in the house was of no concern to you whatsoever. You said that it didn't matter to you where I spent my nights. You said, *...spend your nights wherever* *you damn well please!* Don't you remember your own hurtful words, Abigail? I certainly do!"

"And just why would you possibly care more about what I think than what everyone else in the house thinks?!"

"You know the answer to that as well as I do. It's because I care more about what you think than what anyone else in the house thinks, that's why, and I refuse to stay there, knowing that my presence or absence is of no concern to you."

"Lord have mercy, you can be the most cantankerous and hardheaded man in the world sometimes! I've never known anyone like you! And just what must I do to convince you that I desire your continued presence in our house, William? What is it that you expect of me? Are you expecting me to drop to my knees to beg and plead with you to stay in the house? Is that what you want of me?"

"No, Abigail, I don't want that at all. I would only ask that you simply give me a kind word once in a while, maybe just a smile now and then, and tell me that you prefer my presence in the house, if you honestly and truly feel that way in your heart."

"Very well, then! [*long pause*] William, **I prefer** that you remain in our house... Is that good enough? Is that what you wanted to hear?

"Why don't you stop trying to act like such a cold-hearted fuddy-duddy for just a moment and tell me the truth for a change, Abigail? Does my presence in the house matter to you at all? Does my being there bring you any small amount of satisfaction at all?"

Stubbornly obdurate, and shouting rebelliously, Abigail screamed out at the top of her voice, **"Yes! My God, yes! Your presence in the house pleases me to death! It delights the hell out of me! I treasure your blessed presence in our house!"** After a short pause, her tears began to flow in earnest and she broke down miserably in front of William, sobbing terribly and hiding her face in her apron. William put a sympathetic hand on her shoulder, but she reached up quickly and brushed it away. She composed herself momentarily, dried her eyes with her apron, and asked, "Was that sufficient? Was that what you wanted to hear me say, or do you expect even more of me?"

"My Lord, you've said all that I needed to hear. Even in your vindictive tone of voice, yes, Abigail, that's exactly what I wanted to hear you say. That's all that I've ever wanted to hear you say. Whether you actually meant it or not, thank you for saying it. It may be the kindest words that you've ever shouted at me."

Abigail began crying again, and in a broken voice, she asked, "My dear God... William... Why must you persist in tormenting me like this? I swear to you, my life is difficult enough as it is."

"I know you've had a difficult life, and I have never intended that I should be a torment to you, Abigail. It's always been my fondest desire that I would bring some measure of satisfaction to you... that my presence would bring you happiness, not torment."

"I need to go. I have work to attend to in the kitchen. Are you coming back to the house, or not?"

"Yes, Abigail, I'm coming back to the house. But while we're alone like we are, I must apologize for causing you to cry like this... that was never my intention. I merely wanted you to be honest with me for once, that's all that I've ever wanted."

"I'm not crying... much... your stubbornness over the issue has upset me... a little... maybe... that's all, but I've regained my composure now, and I'm going back to the kitchen. I have work to do. Are you coming?"

"Yes, Abigail, I'll be right behind you."

They walked rather briskly back to the house, but when they got there, rather than going inside, Abigail turned to face William again. Even in the dim light of evening, it was obvious that she had something else to say. "May we speak with one another frankly for just a moment before going inside, William?"

"Yes, Abigail?"

"If we are to abide happily in the same household, might we take this opportunity to convey our personal needs and expectations to each other, in order to better understand each other, and be more respectful of each other's feelings?"

"Certainly. And just how would you suggest for us to convey these personal needs and expectations to each other?"

"I would simply suggest that we merely tell each other what our expectations are... clearly and honestly. So there can be no misunderstanding between us after tonight."

"That sounds very reasonable to me, Abigail, and it's probably long overdue."

"Thank you. Now, please, tell me what you expect of me, William."

"I would much rather for you to begin, Abigail, and I will follow. Please tell me exactly what you expect of me."

"Very well... To begin with, your work and your management of the other workmen here at Montgomery Farm far surpasses any expectations I would ever have of a workman. I have never known a more capable farm worker than you, and I highly commend you for that."

"Thank you, but I'm waiting to hear your expectations."

"Very well. First and foremost, I expect for you to be more considerate of my feelings, and keep your emboldened comments to yourself. Secondly, I expect for you to restrain yourself from toying with my emotions and upsetting me like you did tonight. Thirdly, I expect for you to be more understanding of my need to conduct myself as a proper lady, worthy of being the leader of my family. Fourthly, I expect for you to cease staring at me so much when we have our family meals. Your stares make me uncomfortable. Fifthly, I expect for you to regard me as the leader of my family, and not a weak and desperate woman who is desirous of any support from a man, nor desires anything that a man has to offer. And lastly, I expect for you to start looking out for yourself more. It frustrates me to see you turning down food until you're sure that everyone else has had all they want... getting everyone's chair for them when they go to sit down or stand up... always choosing the smallest portions of meat until you are sure everyone else has had their fill! I expect you to pay better attention to your own needs and less to everyone else's. Those are the things that I expect of you, William."

"I see. You've opened my eyes, Abigail, and I thank you. I didn't realize that I have been making you uncomfortable by staring at you. I'm sorry, and I'll try very hard not to do that in the future. I fully understand your expectations now, Abigail, and I will make every effort to govern myself accordingly. You have my promise to that effect."

"Thank you. Now, what are the things that you expect of me, William? I want you to be just as truthful with me as I was with you, and tell me everything."

"You want me to be truthful?"

"I want nothing less than the full truth."

"Very well. I expect for you to swallow your foolish pride and tell me if there is ever anything I can do that would bring more happiness into your life... that's the only thing that I would ever expect of you."

"Dammit William! That's not fair for you to say that to me!"

"Why?"

"Because you let me ramble on like a selfish idiot, listing all of my expectations, that's why! Be honest with me and tell me **all** the things you expect of me!"

"Does it really surprise you to know that your happiness means so much to me? I have no expectations beyond that which I have already told you, Abigail, I swear it."

Abigail was furious—mostly with herself. The night had been a disaster, and everything that had gone wrong had been a result of Abigail's stubbornness and fiery temper. She turned quickly to go into the house as William said, "Please don't start crying again, Abigail..."

"Just go to your room and tend to your own business! This is **my** home! No man can tell me what to do here! I'll cry as much as I want to!"

"Very well. Goodnight, Abigail."

126

○   ○   ○

Abigail was frustrated immensely by William's ability to entice her into saying things that she preferred to keep to herself, and aside from her pugnaciously obdurate temper, she was relieved beyond measure to learn that William would indeed, continue to abide in the house. His presence afforded them all with a sense of security and comfort, and Abigail knew in her heart that if William had chosen to sleep in the barn that night, she would have humiliated herself even further, if it had been necessary, and willingly dropped to her knees to beg him to stay. In Abigail's opinion, William's presence was the best thing that had ever happened to Montgomery House, and the thoughts of him moving into a barn were repulsive to her. In her bedchamber that night she could not seem to focus her thoughts on anything but William. '*Who is this man, William? And why does he seem to have such dominion over my every thought? Lord, what am I to make of all this? Is it proper that I should find myself falling in love with a man who doesn't even know his own name? Tell me what I should do, Lord, for I'm not sure that I can continue to act as though he doesn't exist.*' William had discovered a diminutive fracture in the stone wall which Abigail Montgomery had so belligerently constructed around her heart, and he seemed determined to breech the wall until he could clearly see the true woman who was hiding within.

During the following days, Abigail's anger and frustration slowly mended. She knew that William had manipulated her with his kindness in order to get her to become a more humble person, but she didn't resent him for it. She spoke to William quite pleasantly after that night, but only when it was necessary, stubbornly refusing to believe that William was becoming a part of her very heart and soul. Abigail was losing her battle to ward off his affections, and her vulnerability had become an embarrassment to her. Disregarding her tenacious resolve to ignore William's persistence, she found life to be surprisingly more pleasant for all involved during the following days as she began being more congenial to him, especially during mealtimes. She was beginning to realize that her frustrations did not result from the attempts of William to talk lovingly to her. Instead, her frustrations lied solely within her vain attempts to disregard his pleasing words and act as though he had no power over her. In her heart, she knew otherwise.

O O O

Four weeks later, in the early predawn hours of the twentieth day of August, the family slumbered quietly in their beds, completely oblivious of what was about to occur. A remarkable event was about to happen—one that would change the very complexion of life within the walls of Montgomery House. In fact, the event that was about to occur would have seemed so extraordinary to the residents there as to have been impossible for anyone to foresee. Twenty-five minutes earlier, the clock in the parlor had completed striking the hour of five, and dawn was still more than an hour away. It was the final minutes before the family would normally begin to arise and start another one of their usual work days. However, this particular day was the Sabbath, and it was customary at Montgomery House for the occupants there to sleep at least an hour later in the mornings than they normally would on a weekday. This morning would prove to be much different than just another of the Sabbath mornings at Montgomery House, though—much different.

In the quiet darkness of her bedchamber, Abigail Montgomery had already awakened once, probably out of habit, but came to the realization that it was the Sabbath and closed her eyes again to enjoy the soft comfort of her bed for a few more minutes before arising to start her day. It was a Sabbath morning luxury that Abigail and the other ladies absolutely treasured. The serene quietness that morning was suddenly transcended by the marvelous and mysterious sound of piano music, as it flowed pleasantly upstairs from the parlor below. Almost simultaneously, all of the ladies who slumbered upstairs awakened from their sleep and rose up in their beds to assure themselves that the sweet sound of music was not a melodious phantasm, nor some kind of a dream. What they were hearing was real. They sat upright there in their beds almost breathless, absorbing the strange and wonderful sound of music. The walls of Montgomery House had heard no such music from within for nearly ten years. When the ladies each realized that the beautiful music was not a dream, they quickly donned their robes, and gathered together in the dark hallway outside of their bedchambers. Agatha held a single candle lamp in her hand as the women stood there in astonishment and listened to the music flowing up the stairway from the parlor. Abigail simply looked at the others, and whispered, "My dear Lord! Would you just listen to that?"

Breathlessly, Sarah asked, "But who could possibly be playing such wonderful music here in our house?"

Abigail whispered loudly, "William! My dear God, it must be William! It has to be William! There's no one else in the house but William!"

"Isn't it beautiful, Mother, just beautiful?!"

"Yes it is, Sarah. I believe it's the music of the Polish composer, Frederic Chopin. I think that I remember it from a symphony I attended in Richmond with Uncle Nolan and Aunt Clara before the war. Walk quietly, and let's all go downstairs to the parlor."

Elizabeth grabbed her mother by the arm and asked, "Should I fetch the pistol, Mother, in case it's an intruder?"

"That won't be necessary, Elizabeth. No intruder ever played the piano like that! I swear that it must be William! It's got to be him! Let us go downstairs and see for ourselves!"

The group of robed ladies descended the stairway and gathered themselves in the parlor, a few feet behind William as he played. The parlor was dimly illuminated with the soft glow of a single oil lamp which sat atop the piano. William's eyes were closed in concentration, and he was deeply engrossed as he played, and unaware of the flabbergasted group of awestruck ladies who stood closely behind him. Agatha placed her candle on the table as the group of astonished listeners stood there in perfect awe. William played the piano flawlessly, and the music flowed as the most delightful sound that had been heard there at Montgomery House in nearly a decade. When his recital was completed, his delighted listeners all applauded joyously. They were so consumed by the joy of the moment that they were completely oblivious of the fact that they were still dressed in their bed robes. William turned in his chair to face them, and as he did, he himself was momentarily held spellbound. It was the first time that he had seen the ladies of Montgomery House dressed in bed gowns and with their hair down. Having never seen such a beautiful sight, he silently gasped with delight, but quickly contained himself and stood, bowed politely before them, and said, "Good morning, ladies. I'm sorry to awaken you at such an early hour on the Sabbath."

Abigail, still utterly astonished by William's music, said, "Nonsense, William! What a superbly delightful way to be awakened! My Lord, you play the piano so beautifully that... I'm almost speechless!"

"Thank you, Abigail, but I must admit that I'm just as surprised as everyone else must be. I had no idea that I could play the piano, even as modest as my playing is."

"Modest?! Ha! Your playing is absolutely flawless and beautiful, William! It's magnificent!"

"Thank you, Sarah. I've been awake for an hour or so, and I took the liberty this morning of starting a fire in the stove, but I was afraid to make the tea this morning for fear of ruining it. I would like for one of you to instruct me on how the tea is made, and perhaps if this ever happens again, I can have a cup of hot tea prepared for you."

"How in God's amazing world did you ever determine that you had the ability to play the piano?"

"I'm not sure, Elizabeth. I was in my bed this morning, and I couldn't sleep. Somehow, I felt a strange compulsion to go to the piano, and so I did. I lit the lamp here and sat down, raised the cover, and... when I placed my fingers on the keys, it felt oddly familiar to me for some unknown reason... like my fingers knew exactly what they were supposed to do. I just closed my eyes and let my fingers do their will... I can't explain it, I truly cannot."

"It was the most beautiful music we've heard here since before our mother passed away! I always thought that Mother's playing was grand enough, but yours... yours is absolutely superb! Surely you've had a great deal of training."

"Thank you, Agatha, but I cannot recall any such training."

"Can you play other types of songs as well?"

"I think so. I may have to practice a bit, but I think so."

In a sudden moment of mental clarity, Abigail recognized the fact that they were all standing there before William with their hair down and dressed only in their bed robes, and in a condition of such awkwardness, she buttoned the top of her robe and offered, "Let us all go to our rooms and dress appropriately for the day. William, would you please continue to play? Your wonderful music brings a certain pleasure to us that we have not experienced here in many years."

"I would consider it an honor to play for you, Abigail. What would you like for me to play?"

"My word, William, it does not matter at all. Just play whatever comes to your mind, please. I'll put the tea on to boil before going upstairs. Thank you for the wonderful music and thank you again for starting the fire this morning. I haven't felt this enlivened in years."

Abigail went into the kitchen to prepare the tea as the other ladies went upstairs to dress and William continued to play his delightful music. As she walked past William to return to her room, Abigail paused, and took the opportunity to once again tell William how much she had appreciated his music.

"Thank you again for the wonderful music this morning,

William. You have brought such a warm delight to my heart that I could never find the words to properly express myself."

"Be careful, Abigail, you need to exercise caution."

"What on earth do you mean?"

"Your words are becoming dangerously close to being highly complementary. If you're not careful, you might accidently say something of an *'emboldened'* nature. I would dislike having to scold you for making an emboldened comment on the Sabbath. At Montgomery House, it's mandatory that one's actual feelings be kept to oneself, and not spoken aloud. Didn't you know that?"

"There's no question that I deserved that for the way I have behaved sometimes, William. I have been making a sincere effort to be a more pleasant person, I really have. It's my fondest desire that you will play for us often. Would you, please?"

"I shall play for you as often as you wish. Might I have your permission just this once to make one small comment of a *slightly emboldened* nature?"

"Slightly emboldened? Oh my Lord... William. I cannot help but be fearful of what you might say..."

"Please, Abigail? There's no one here but you and I, and I feel overwhelmingly compelled to say something to you. May I please have your permission to do so? Just this once?"

"Very well, William. I must tell you once more, though, that I'm sorely afraid of what you might say to me, but you seem determined to say it... After your delightful music, I suppose the least that I can do is to listen to what you have to say."

"Thank you... It's just that... Since I first saw you, I've always thought you to be the most beautiful woman that I've ever seen. To see you with your hair down like this leaves me without sufficient words to describe your beauty... I'm in perfect awe of your loveliness, and even weakened by it."

"My Lord, William... That's much, much more than just *slightly emboldened...*"

"I understand, and you don't have to scold me or raise your voice or anything. I said what my heart demanded that I say, and all I ask is that you know in your heart that I meant every word I said. I'm going back to the piano now."

"Thank you. If you'll excuse me now, I'll be back down to make some tea and prepare our breakfast shortly. Is there anything special that I could prepare for you today? Anything at all?"

"Everything that you prepare is always special to me, Abigail."

Abigail turned to walk upstairs, but only took a couple of steps, and stopped. She paused for a moment or two and stood there motionless, like a statue, facing away from William with her head slightly bowed, and then turned to face him again. William's compliments regarding her beauty, along with his wonderful music, had evidently warmed her heart to such an extent that she felt compelled to say something. The expression on her face was both apologetic and heartfelt, and was made all the more sincere by the presence of a tear on her cheek. Swallowing a lump in her throat, she asked, "William?"

"Yes, Abigail?"

"Might I have your permission to say something *slightly emboldened* to you for a change?"

"Really? Oh my Lord, yes!"

"Four weeks ago, on the evening that you were so stubbornly intent on sleeping in the barn with our migrant laborers, do you remember that particular evening?"

"Yes, of course I do. I'll never forget it. What about it?"

"I behaved very poorly that night, not unlike a spoiled child who just had their candy taken from them. I told you that evening that your presence in Montgomery House pleases me. Despite the unpleasant and ugly way that I expressed myself to you that evening, and the fact that I was very angry with myself at the time, my words to you that night were truthful, and I wish to say them to you again, now, without shouting at you, with no spitefulness or anger in my voice or my heart, and without having to be asked to say them. Your presence here in Montgomery House does please me, William... more so than I've ever been pleased before..."

"My dear Lord... I hardly know what to say, Abigail. Hearing you say that in such a meaningful manner has been an answer to my prayers. You've taken my breath away..."

"I should have told you this long before now, and I regret that I haven't. I'll be back downstairs in a few moments."

"Abigail..."

"I must go now."

Once Abigail was upstairs and out of William's sight, she produced the most prolific smile imaginable. Her smile was partially attributed to William's delightful music, of course, but a good portion of her smile was a direct result of William's compliments. Her smile was also brought about by a sense of relief that she felt in her heart for having been honest with William for once, and giving him a tiny provocative sampling of her true feelings. As the family's leader and matriarch, Abigail had never thought of herself as being beautiful, despite the undeniable fact that she was. Knowing that William perceived her as being beautiful created a special kind of warmth in her heart that she had never experienced before. This new warmth came upon her as such a pleasing and unfamiliar surprise that she was unsure of whether she should accept it or reject it. She decided that it was such a pleasant feeling that she would cautiously accept it. She was completely unaware of the fact that she couldn't have rejected it, even if she had wanted to.

Abigail had always assumed that if she allowed William to speak his heart to her, she would feel ashamed of herself for permitting such a thing. She was only now beginning to recognize that there was no shame in being truthful, yet she knew that if such truthfulness was not harnessed and controlled, it could easily lead to more compromising relations between her and William. After all, they were abiding under the same roof, in a house co-occupied by her sister and her young daughters. She was not ready to submit herself to what may later prove to be errant impulses. These odd sensations were originating in her heart, and she did not trust her heart. Thusly, she would persevere to keep a tight rein on her emotions.

As Abigail had requested, William did play the piano often, in fact he seldom declined a request to play. Perhaps the most inspirational and uplifting of their music, would be when the family stood together as William played a selection of hymns, with the ladies and the elderly Mr. Montgomery raising their voices in joyful tribute to God. The elderly Phillip Montgomery was one of William's most dedicated listeners. Regardless of where he was in the house at the time, when William would start to play the piano, Mr. Montgomery would immediately make his way to the parlor and take a seat on the bench beside William. Even in his old age, he had a keen love of music, and he joyously sat there at William's side each time William would play. Hearing William play so beautifully reminded Mr. Montgomery of when his daughter, Abigail's mother, played the piano for the family. Seeing her grandfather sit so contentedly with William as he played was a sight that brought much satisfaction and warmth to Abigail, and everyone else at Montgomery House. Abigail knew that there were few visiting men who wanted to take the time to be congenial to Mr. Montgomery because of his feeble mind. William was an exception, and treated Mr. Montgomery with the utmost respect and dignity. Mr. Montgomery was so enthused with William's piano music that he even joined in to sing on several occasions. It delighted everyone when Mr. Montgomery would sing at the top of his voice, *"Ohhhh... Jimmy crack corn and I don't care..."*

Given the extent of their burdensome farm work, it was unavoidable that Ezra and William would become very fond of each other during the pursuits of their daily tasks together. Ezra couldn't help but feel regret over the fact that he had once volunteered to kill the young man. Perhaps a great deal of his admiration toward William was due to his conscience troubling him for his original willingness to take William's life when he had been a wounded soldier. Nevertheless, he was extremely happy that he had not been asked to do such a horrible thing, and the two soon became more than just casual friends. They worked in the fields with one another every day, and they came to depend on one another. They oft times sang together in the fields as they worked. With such a close association, it was inevitable that they would become such close friends. William's personality was so warm and cheerful, that Ezra and Vivian were soon regarded by him as more of a brother and sister. There was nothing they wouldn't do for one another.

At the breakfast table one morning, William unknowingly bore a sullen expression on his face which had not gone unnoticed by the family. Abigail initially said nothing, but when they had finished their breakfast, her curiosity overcame her, and as William was rising to leave for a day of labor in the fields, she asked, "William, is there anything you would like to talk to us about?"

"I don't understand, Miss Abigail."

"It's just that you seem as though you have something on your mind this morning, and I was wondering if it was something you wanted to talk about."

"I'm sorry, I wasn't aware that it was so obvious..."

"Well, I'm afraid that it is. Would you mind telling us about it, or is it something that you would rather discuss in private?"

"At the risk of sounding like an imbecile, may I speak freely for a moment?"

"Of course you may. Please sit back down and tell us what has you in such a melancholy mood this morning."

"I'm just very confused about myself, Abigail."

"What are you so confused about, William?"

"Well, Abigail, it's just that, thanks to your family's kindness and generosity, I have healed quite well now. I've taken advantage of your hospitality here at Montgomery Farm to such a great extent... and Lord knows that I've stayed here far longer than I should have, and I..."

"Please don't be afraid to tell us what is troubling you, William."

"I have mended well enough that I should consider leaving, and going to find my rightful place in this world, yet to my knowledge, I have no home to go to. I have tried my best to recall who I am, where I'm from, and where I belong, but my efforts have been in vain."

"William... you poor soul..."

"I should try to find my home, but I wouldn't even know which direction to start looking. I know that I have been a great burden to you here, and as much as I would like to relieve you of that burden, I have no idea where I could go if I were to leave Montgomery Farm."

"William, I'm quite certain that I speak for everyone here when I say that we would like for you to consider Montgomery Farm your home, for as long as you wish to stay here. We would like for you to think of yourself as belonging here with us, and think of us as your family. As for your being a burden to us, that's utterly ridiculous. You've been a burden to no one. On the contrary, you've been a blessing." Nods of approval came from everyone seated there as Abigail spoke her words of reassurance to William. Her words fell upon William's ears as being among the most pleasantly comforting words that Abigail Montgomery had ever spoken to him. Obviously deeply touched, William said, "Thank you, Abigail, thank you all."

The ladies all gathered at the window to watch William as he walked toward the barn, and their hearts were filled with sympathetic understanding. Abigail stifled a tear before it left her eye and told her sister and her daughters, "We need to keep William in our prayers, and ask God to comfort him."

As the days and weeks turned into months, William became a familiar fixture to the visitors at Montgomery Farm, and he had even taken on the responsibility of supervising the other farm workers and laying out their daily schedules. He was enthralled in the operation of the farm, and dedicated to contribute to its success. William had found something overwhelmingly addictive in the planting of crops and derived much satisfaction in watching them grow to maturity. There were precious few days in which he did not work from daylight until dark. After five and a half months of recovery, Abigail called William to the back porch early one afternoon for some brief conversation. Abigail was appreciative of William's obvious dedication to his work there. In fact, she had become so dependent on his ability to keep the farm operative that she wanted to offer him a monetary incentive to remain there. Farm workers were notorious for arriving one day, collecting their wages, and disappearing the next, and she did not want to risk finding William gone one morning in search of greener pastures.

"Ezra said that you wanted to see me, Abigail?"

"Yes, William, you and I have never discussed the subject of your wages yet, and I feel like it's several months overdue for us to do so. I meant to say something to you after breakfast this morning but you rushed out so quickly..."

"Wages? What on earth do you mean?"

"I'm speaking about the amount of money and the manner in which you should be compensated for your labors here at Montgomery Farm."

"I have neither asked for, nor do I expect to receive any wages, Abigail. Your generosity, your kindness, and your friendship have been such an immense compensation that I am still greatly indebted to you and your family."

"Nonsense! This cannot be. I've watched you for many months now, and you work harder here than anyone else ever has. I've even seen you grimace in pain as you worked when your leg was healing, yet, you continued to work without complaining and you always seem to find the time to play the piano for us, even on the days when you must surely be exhausted from your labors. You are entitled to due compensation for such gallant efforts. It's only fair."

"I play the piano for you simply because it pleasures me to know that you enjoy listening to me. As for the work that I do here, suppose I were to tell you that I would be deeply hurt by being offered such a thing as wages after all that you and your family have already done for me, Abigail?"

"It wasn't my intention to offend you, or hurt your feelings in any way, William, I just wanted to..."

"Then, can we dismiss the issue as though it never happened?"

"Think about what you are saying first, William. You have needs. We all have needs. There are things that you need that can only be obtained with money. I'm just trying to determine what kind of emolument would be fair and appropriate, that's all."

"Everything that I need is right here on Montgomery Farm. When I asked you for a razor two weeks ago, you presented me with a razor. When I asked you for a new pair of boots last month, you sent Ezra to town to buy me a new pair of boots. You prepare my meals and wash my clothes, and whether or not you know it, you have given me a reason to look forward to each new day. Why can't we just leave things as they are?"

"But your efforts and your labors here at Montgomery Farm have almost doubled our normal income from the sale of our crops, even in time of war... We can afford to pay you, and we should pay you. It's only fair."

"I'm delighted that the farm is producing so well, but..."

"You have taken so much on your shoulders, that it relieves me of most all of the outside work that I have been burdened with in years past. Your presence here has been such a blessing for me that I do not feel as though the few things that you have asked for has been sufficient compensation for all that you are doing here."

"Then perhaps you could compensate me by continuing to give me an occasional smile, and a pleasant word or two at the end of the day, would that be asking too much of you?"

"I have indeed been trying to be more congenial and cheerful, but even that is very poor compensation for all you have done, William."

"In my opinion, your kindness and an occasional cheerful word is worth much more to me than all the money in the world."

"My dear Lord, William..."

"Please, Abigail, consider how grateful I am to be here. You've provided me with a home here. You feed me. I even sense that I'm among people who care for me here at Montgomery Farm. My Lord, Abigail, that means everything in the world to me. I have no one else! You and the others are the only family that I have, and the only family I'll ever want. I'm very happy here. If you are happy with my work, can't we just leave things the way they are?"

"I just want what's best for you, William, that's all."

"Then let me be the judge of what's best for me. If I accepted wages, I would be just another hired hand, Abigail, and that's not what I want to be. If I thought for a moment that I could never mean any more to you than just another hired hand, I would leave Montgomery Farm this very instant."

"I'm almost speechless... I hardly know what to say. Your senses are correct... you *are* cared for here at Montgomery House... very much. No one here regards you as just another hired hand, I can assure you of that."

"Even you?"

"Especially me. I don't know what it is, exactly, but there is something very special about you, very special indeed. I've never known anyone quite like you, William, and I hope that you believe me when I say that."

"And at the risk of being scolded for another one of my emboldened comments, I've often looked into your eyes during the times that you smile at me across the kitchen table and thought the same thing about you, Abigail, you are someone special to me... very special."

"Lord help me... William, I... I feel like I'm..."

"What, Abigail?"

"It's nothing, William. Forgive me. Well... uhhh... I won't keep you from your work any longer, William. If you should change your mind about the issue of wages or think of anything else you might need, please tell me."

"Thank you, Abigail, I will. And thank you for your kind words. They give me an encouraging comfort that I could never describe."

Abigail went inside and hastily closed the door behind her. Standing with her back against the door, she took a deep breath and tried to consider all that was happening to her. She had developed the deepest of feelings for William, feelings that she had always thought to be a temporary infatuation—something that would diminish in time. Such was not the case, as her adoration for William was developing stronger within her with the passing of each new day, and her attempts to hold her feelings at bay were failing miserably. She felt a desperate need to talk to someone about these overpowering feelings that were beginning to consume her, yet there was no one with whom she could share her innermost thoughts. Even her sister, Agatha, as close as they were, was no one that she could share her deepest private emotions with, and she surely couldn't share her secret emotions with her young daughters, who were already enjoying their own immature fascination with William. She felt the strongest need to discuss her feelings directly with William, but knew that she lacked the courage to do so. Consequently, with no one to talk to, she would keep such emotions contained within her, and try her best to ignore them. Nevertheless, she walked quickly to the parlor window, parted the curtain a few inches, and watched William as he worked. *"Who is this marvelous man? Is this really what it feels like when a woman is in love? Why have I never experienced such wonderment in my life before? Is it because I have never known William before? Lord have mercy, am I really in love with William?"*

Due to her present station in life, and her responsibilities as the family leader, Abigail had almost completely avowed herself to living the rest of her life as an abstemious widowed spinster, despite her young age, accepting such a fate as her destiny in life. Even when she had been a married woman, she had thought that the parts of her heart that were responsible for cultivating romantic sentiments were either dead, or so badly damaged that they would never be capable of feeling such sensations of fervency. In her opinion, love had always been an emotion intended to be experienced by other women—not her. Her marriage had been a tragic marriage of happenstance and ordeal, and never a marriage of love and affection. In her youth, she had heard other young ladies describing what it was like to be in love, and thought that they had all been victims of their own ridiculous fantasies. She had never known what it was like to feel any type of sincere love for a man. Yet, somehow, as if a wondrous miracle was beginning to occur in her life at a time when she least expected it, these unfamiliar romantic impulses were beginning to come to life for the very first time, and produce emotions of a higher magnitude than she had ever experienced before. They were warm, good feelings, feelings that reminded her that she was still a young woman, both in body and spirit despite her station in life. Yet they were also feelings that she felt were best hidden from everyone else. She had found herself thinking of William often, as she worked in the kitchen, as she worked with her daughters doing the laundry, and she held visions of him in her mind as she lay in her bed at night. Almost by coincidence, an astonishing young man with no name had come into her home, and as if by some superlative feat of magic, he had also gained a remarkable entry into her heart. In the privacy of her bedchamber that night, she closed her eyes, folded her hands, and asked, *"Dear God, thank you for bringing William into my life. I fear that I am losing my struggle to resist him. I love him with all my heart, Lord, and I cannot help myself. I wish to give my heart to him, Lord, but he already owns it. I only ask for your divine guidance. Please tell me what to do, Lord, and please grant me the wisdom to understand these strange new urges that have crept into my life. If it is your will that I embrace these urges, please grant me the courage to do so. Please continue to shower your blessings on William. He is a good man, Lord. Comfort him, Lord, protect him in his labors, and let him be made aware that he is loved... by me. Help me to guard my words, that I may never say cruel and disrespectful things to him again. Please bless our family, oh God, and bring this terrible war to an end. Amen."*

Work has a splendid way of bringing a close family even closer together, and with each new work day, William felt more like he was a valued member of the family, and not just the stammering, feeble-minded, convalescing guest that he pretended to be when visitors would arrive at Montgomery Farm. His contributions to the overall performance of the farm made him proud, as if he was repaying a small portion of the tremendous debt that he owed to Abigail Montgomery and her family. In just a few short months after William began handling all farm matters, the Farm was producing an enviable profit, such as it had never produced before. A portion of the farm's success was rightly attributed to the superb weather that year, but most of the success was a direct result of the organizational skills and dedicated labors of William. He seemed to enjoy the challenges and hard work associated with raising their crops, and the more he learned, the more successful he became at the task. Yes, William had achieved much satisfaction his work there, yet nothing provided him with more contentment than the communal time which he shared with the family at mealtime. His lighthearted nature and keen sense of humor made mealtime an event that the entire family looked forward to.

The unabashed and open adoration felt by Elizabeth and Sarah toward William also continued to grow as well, and private conversation between the sisters regarding William began to diminish accordingly. Each of them were well aware of the other's growing infatuation with William, and rather than bicker childishly between themselves over their romantic competitiveness, they wisely agreed not to address the issue with each other for fear of arguing. Neither Elizabeth nor Sarah were even vaguely aware of the extent that their mother, Abigail, had come to love and adore William. She had been successful in keeping her adoration well hidden from her daughters, and everyone else for that matter. Even though she continued to make an effort to conceal and even deny her deep sentiments toward William, she could not hide nor deny them to herself. Given a choice in the matter, she would have gladly stepped aside, for the benefit of allowing her daughters to enjoy their immature and giddily youthful fascination with William. To that self-sacrificing end, she had so earnestly dedicated herself. But the overpowering love she felt for William was beginning to weaken her resolve and lower her armor of defense.

If there was ever any doubt in William's confused mind that he had transpired into becoming an integrally important part of the family, it was completely eradicated on the twenty-third day of November that year when Abigail Montgomery called for an urgent family conference in the parlor. As William was occupied with the chore of splitting and stacking firewood near the back porch, Abigail went outside and called out to him as he worked.

"William! Could you come here for a moment, please?"

"Yes, Abigail, what is it?"

"William, we are about to have one of our important private family conferences, and we would like for you to come inside and join us if you can leave your work for a few moments."

"You want me to attend your *private* family conference,

Abigail? If it's a private family conference why would I be invited to attend?"

"I shan't play games with you, William, by denying the fact that we regard you as an important part of our family now... and you should know that without being told. You mean much more to us than we could ever express. We depend on you, we trust you, we even adore you, and we would like for you to be present inside."

"I am deeply honored to think that I am adored, and that I would be considered to be some part of the family. I feel that I am unworthy of..."

Interrupting William as tears began to form in her eyes, Abigail said, "I have a rather grievous announcement to make this morning, William, and I feel as though I may require your emotional support in order to get through this..."

"Abigail! You are crying, dear! Is something wrong? Please tell me."

"I need you desperately now, William, and I would rather for you to come inside with the rest of us. I wish only to say this once, and as yet, I have told no one."

"Of course... You appear weakened, Abigail, take my arm and let me help you inside."

William had no trouble recognizing the extent of Abigail's distress. He had long since developed the ability to read Abigail's eyes and facial expressions, perhaps better than anyone else could. The two of them often looked across the table at each other during their meals, yet each of them would turn to look elsewhere when they saw the other looking back at them. But her eyes reflected something markedly different this morning, something very disturbing. Once everyone was seated at the parlor table, William brought a glass of water to Abigail and seated himself beside her. With great difficulty in her broken voice, and with tears in her eyes, Abigail took a deep breath and addressed the family who was poised apprehensively to hear what she was about to say.

"It grieves me to be the bearer of such sad news this morning, but Grandfather Montgomery has passed away in his sleep sometime last night... God bless him..."

Gasps were heard from around the room, as Abigail continued, "I was shocked when I found him. He seemed so chipper and full of life last evening. He's upstairs at present, in his bedchamber, just as I found him. When he did not come down for breakfast this morning, I went up to his room to wake him and found that he had quietly passed on. William, would you please summon Ezra and Vivian? I would appreciate it if you would assist Ezra in building a coffin this morning and digging a grave in the family cemetery. I will come out shortly and show you the exact location where he is to be buried, next to my mother. She was his only daughter, and they loved each other dearly."

"Yes, Abigail, of course I will. I hardly know what to say. I am so sorry for you and Agatha and everyone here..."

"Thank you, William. I would like... I..." Abigail's grief overcame her, and she quietly sobbed for a moment, as did her daughters and Agatha.

"Abigail, is there anything I can get for you?"

"Thank you, William, but no. Elizabeth, when Vivian gets here, would you and Sarah please assist Vivian and I in dressing Grandfather for his interment?"

"Yes, Mother, we will."

"Agatha, would you please prepare a table on the side porch where it's cool? We'll put Grandfather's body there for today, and bury him in the morning. We will have neighbors that will want to view Grandfather's body before he is buried. I will have Ezra carry word to the surrounding farms this afternoon. I want Grandfather to look his best when he is seen by our neighbors. When Grandfather was a younger man, and in possession of his mind, he was a proud man. I would like him to appear as such when our neighbors come to pay their final respects. For as long as I have known, he has been a member of the Blanchard Masonic Order, and they will be here to assist in his burial rites, I'm sure.

I would like for him to be wearing his Masonic apron when our guests arrive to view his body."

"Yes, Abigail, of course."

"William, before we leave the parlor, would you please offer a prayer for Grandfather's passing? It was my intention to offer a prayer myself, but I don't feel like I'm... very capable at the moment."

William stood, and with his hand tenderly and sympathetically resting on Abigail's shoulder, he prayed, and as he prayed, Abigail reached up and held his hand tightly.

"Almighty Father, we stand here before you this morning with saddened hearts. We take comfort, Father, in knowing that Phillip Montgomery is in Your hands now, and his soul is in the place that You have prepared for him... a place where he can be at peace, unburdened by his frail earthly body. We give his soul to you, Father, and in grand Masonic tradition, we ask pardon for his sins, comfort for his soul, and Your eternal blessing. Allow him to enter Your Kingdom with honor, for his labors on this earth have been just and righteous. Please ease our sorrow, Father. Touch our hearts and provide us with the assurance that he is at home with You now. We ask this in the precious name of Jesus, Amen."

Abigail squeezed William's hand even tighter, and tearfully said, "Thank you, William. May I speak with you in private for a moment before you go to help Ezra?"

"Certainly."

When the others had left the room, Abigail said, "Thank you for the beautiful prayer, William, I found your words both touching and comforting, as I always do."

"My heart is breaking for you, Abigail, and I will truly miss Mr. Montgomery. He was a pleasant man, always smiling and cheerful. His innocent smiles always brought a smile to my own face."

"Most people nowadays have regarded him as a pathetic idiot, because of his feeble mind, and didn't want to waste their time talking to him. But he was once a strong, intelligent man, with admirable qualities. Other than me, I've never known anyone but you, who would take the time to have conversations with him. I've heard you speaking to him on many occasions, and you were always respectful and compassionate. He thought very highly of you, and I thank you from the bottom of my heart for helping to make this last eight months of his life pleasant for him."

"He helped make the last eight months pleasant for me, Abigail, and I was simply returning his kindness. I can't believe how much I came to love him in just eight months, and it's hard for me to accept the fact that he's really gone from us now. It seems unreal... I expect to see him walk around the corner and say good morning at any moment... It saddens me to know that we'll not hear his voice again..."

"I shan't begin to tell you how delighted he was during the times when he sat beside you as you played the piano."

"I enjoyed playing for him. I loved hearing him sing so joyfully, and as I said, I will miss him greatly."

"Tell me something please, William, are you a Mason?"

"A Mason? Me? Not that I'm aware of, Abigail. Why do you ask?"

"In your prayer for Grandfather, you quoted a passage of the Masonic burial rites prayer perfectly. I've heard it before, many times, and you quoted it perfectly, word for word."

"I did? Perhaps it was just a coincidence."

"Perhaps so, but I can't help but feel differently. It's not important, I suppose. There will be a number of people visiting here for Grandfather's burial, and I want to remind you to act the part of an incompetent person tomorrow. Also, I have taken notice of the fact that you no longer seem to be favoring your right leg. Could you please act as though your leg was still quite painful, at least while we have visitors among us?"

"If you think it's necessary for me to do such a thing, of course I will."

"I do not want us to take any unnecessary chances, that's all. Your presence has been such a blessing here at Montgomery House that I don't want us to risk having hooded visitors come in and take you from us during the night."

"Nor do I, Abigail."

"And from the bottom of my heart, I want to thank you, William."

"For what, pray tell?"

"For being William. For being the person that you are. For being a rock for me to lean on when I need you the most. For always being so unselfish, and placing the needs of others above your own. And, for bringing happiness into our lives here at Montgomery House..."

"I don't deserve any of those kind words, but thank you for saying them, Abigail. I'm very touched. I'll be at the barn, helping Ezra build the coffin. We'll be back to the house to carry Grandfather Montgomery's body downstairs as soon as we are finished with the coffin, and if you feel up to it then, you can show Ezra and me exactly where you want us to dig the grave. If you need me for anything just send Sarah or Elizabeth to fetch me and I'll come quickly... alright?"

"I will."

"Do you need anything before I go?"

"I'll be fine now."

And so the family went about the sad task of preparing for the interment of Phillip Montgomery's body. Ezra carried word to several neighboring farms as well as the Masonic Lodge in Blanchard, and on the following morning there were more than three dozen people at the graveside when a church deacon and William lowered the coffin into the ground. Eight Masons also stood at graveside as Mr. Montgomery's body was lowered. Without being obvious, William studied the hand movements and language expressed by the Masons who were present, and couldn't help but feel that they were more than just slightly familiar to him. *"Perhaps I am a Mason,"* he thought to himself.

Abigail and the family had prepared a large amount of food to feed the attendees, and while a throng of friends and neighbors gathered at the house, William went to the barn, and kept himself out of sight as much as possible. William was uncomfortable while he was in the presence of the inquisitive stares of all the visiting mourners. Such uneasiness was understandable in lieu of the consequences, should his identity as a soldier be discovered. Perhaps he was feeling overanxious because of Abigail's words of caution. He was uncertain in his circumstances there at Montgomery Farm, not knowing for sure who he was, his real name, or his real identity. He knew that there was most likely a valid reason to pretend that he was mentally incompetent, and he resolved himself to continue to live behind the disguise of such a person. When anyone outside of the family would say anything to him or ask him a question, he convincingly answered with incoherent mumbles.

○   ○   ○

William had reached a strange point in his recovery. With the passing of each new day, he began to care less about who he really was. He was quite satisfied with being William, and reluctant to learn that he had ever been anyone else. His only source of discontentment lied within his yearning to be closer to Abigail than simply living in the same house with her. His heart cried out for her, yet he knew that his situation demanded that he comply with Abigail's request to keep his feelings to himself. After all, she was the head of the family, and William was little more than a man in hiding, a man without a home, and a man without a name.

○   ○   ○

Weeks later, at the well one day, William spoke briefly with Elizabeth as she was drawing water. It was his hope that Elizabeth could enlighten him, and solve one of the mysterious questions that lingered in his mind.

"Elizabeth, if I were to ask you a question, will you give me an honest answer, please?"

"Of course I will, you know that."

"I'm beginning to have faint recollections of when I was brought here as a wounded soldier that are discomforting to me. I'd rather not ask your mother about it just yet, and I know that you can explain it to me, and be honest in your explanation. I can faintly remember being covered with a bedsheet, and hearing talk about the war..."

"Oh, my Lord! It was not my idea, William, I swear to you! It was Sarah's idea! I would have never looked under there if Sarah hadn't raised the..."

"What are you talking about, Elizabeth? I merely want to ask you a question about the war."

"The war? That's the event that you want me to be honest about?"

"Yes."

"Oh, thank you, God."

"What did you think my question was about?"

"It's nothing, William, ask your question, and I will try to answer you."

"You're trembling, Elizabeth. What question could I have possibly asked you that would cause you to tremble so?"

"It's nothing of importance, William. Please just ask your question, and I'll give you an honest answer."

"Very well. This war that everyone speaks about..."

"What about it?"

"When I was brought here as a wounded soldier and placed under a bedsheet, was I a soldier for a different army than that of your father and your brother? Was I a soldier in the enemy's army?"

"You wore a different uniform than that of my father or my brother, that's all. You are not an enemy, William, of that I can assure you."

"I suspected as much. That would explain why your mother had a pistol with her most of the time when I was first brought here... she was afraid of me, wasn't she?"

"We didn't know you then as we know you now, William."

"Nor I you, Elizabeth."

"This wretched war has pitted son against father and brother against brother. Since meeting you, I now have come to realize that there is no good side or bad side. There is no right side or wrong side. When men cannot resolve their differences by negotiation, there is only death, and I feel as though there have been many good men to perish in this war... on both sides, while the politicians fatten their purses with blood money. I thank God every day that you have been spared and that you are here with us."

"I was a soldier of the Northern Union that people talk about, the Yankees, wasn't I?"

"Yes, but we've all been telling people that you were a wounded Confederate soldier, and that you were left here in our care. We tell them that your body has practically healed but your mind remains badly damaged. People have believed us thus far."

"I'm glad that they have. You have not lied, Elizabeth, my mind does remain badly damaged. And I have fear for what I might discover about myself, should I ever recover my memory."

"Why would you fear such a thing?"

"Because I don't know who I really am. Am I an evil person? Am I a tyrant, an insensitive and heartless creature? I don't know, and I am so contented here at Montgomery Farm that if I find out who I really am, it can only come as a bitter disappointment to me."

"Then why not shed your fears, and simply enjoy your fate as it is right now? You are among people who love you now, people who will help you to conquer your fears."

"My fears do not preclude me from being happy today, Elizabeth, they only rob me of the assurance that I can be happy tomorrow."

"Then try to take comfort in the happiness that you have today. None of us know what tomorrow may bring, William - only God knows. Just put your trust in God, and know in your heart that you are loved here... by all of us."

"I do trust in God, Elizabeth, and I do sense that I am loved here. This is my only family here, but I feel like it's all the family that I would ever want. Thank you for talking to me. Your words have been comforting."

As Elizabeth and William talked at the well, Abigail called from the back porch to summon them to yet another family conference. The purpose of the conference appeared to be of a lighthearted nature this time, as Abigail had not been crying, and she appeared to be most joyous and contented in disposition. Once everyone was inside and assembled there in the parlor, Abigail revealed the nature and purpose of the latest family conference. As she reached over and held Agatha's hand, she announced to the family, "Everyone knows that James Brighton has visited here many times to speak with Agatha. It's been no secret that he has actively been courting her, and now there has been a remarkable development in their relationship. I think it would be best if I let Agatha tell you the rest in her own words."

Still holding her sister's hand, Agatha blushed, and said, "Well, as Abigail just told you, James and I have been seeing each other frequently for over the last two months, and as you all know, last Saturday afternoon he came here to Montgomery Farm for tea. We had our tea on the side porch, and during our tea, he asked for my hand in marriage. I told him then, that I would give him my decision in a week. I have studied over the possibility and prayed over the situation, and when he came this morning for my answer, I told him that I would marry him."

William suddenly felt sickened in the pit of his stomach upon hearing Agatha announce her betrothal, yet tried his best to conceal his bitter disappointment. He tried to convince himself that he had no interest whatsoever in Agatha's decision, but there were ulterior concerns, uninvolving Agatha, which weighed heavily on William's heart.

The group arose to their feet and the womenfolk all rushed to Agatha to bestow their congratulatory warm kisses and best wishes while William simply stood stoically by, smiled a broad but insincere smile, and produced a short but unenthusiastic round of applause. When Agatha looked at William, he reluctantly stopped applauding and gave her a symbolic hug and a kiss. Abigail was the only one to take notice of the fact that William lacked the genuine enthusiasm displayed by everyone else. William was even anguished over Agatha's decision, but said nothing that would detract from her glowing joy or the merriment of her sister and her nieces. Abigail continued to study William's demeanor inquisitively. "*Why is William acting so oddly about this,*" she wondered. His reaction to Agatha's betrothal had not been what she had expected of him. In fact, William's subdued reaction had puzzled Abigail to such a great extent that she silently promised herself that she would discuss the issue with him at the earliest opportunity. Agatha went on to further announce, "James and I will be married on Saturday afternoon at his church, and on Monday, I will begin moving my things into his home at Blairmount. I shall miss you all immensely, but with my living only a short forty-minute buggy ride away, I hope to visit you here and see my wonderful family often."

Heartfelt congratulations continued to be extended to Agatha as Abigail brought forth an old bottle of port from the cellar and handed it to William, to be opened in celebration of the occasion. In hopes that she could enliven William's paucity of enthusiasm, Abigail asked him if he would present an appropriate toast for the occasion. William's heart was not in concurrence with such a thing as a toast, but he seldom denied a request from Abigail, and thusly forced himself to comply. With everyone's glasses filled, William raised his glass and even though his heart was far from being in harmony with the occasion, he submitted to Abigail's request, and presented a seemingly appropriate toast.

"May God bless you, Agatha, and your forthcoming husband, James, as well. May your hearts be filled with wonderful, warm spirits just as our glasses are now filled with the spirits of this wonderful wine, and may you both flourish in your newfound life together for as long as the sun continues to circle the earth.

May you cherish each other all the days of your life, and may your hearts beat as one, for now, and forever more."

It was the first time that Abigail's daughters, Sarah and Elizabeth, had tasted the stimulating spirits of wine. They relished in the joy of being treated as adults, and treasured the fulfilling warmth that the wine had brought to them. Although they drank precious little in quantity, the wine had succeeded in making them feel more like the mature women that they really were. Giddy laughter prevailed between the women as William drank his wine rather quickly and slipped silently dejected out of the rear door. William's quiet exit from the parlor had gone unnoticed by all but Abigail. Abigail had watched him closely when he left, and her curiosity over William's unusual behavior became tantamount in her mind.

William had left the merriment of the house, and returned to the chores that awaited him outside. His thoughts remained disturbingly troubled though. He was not quite as sentimentally or romantically attached to Agatha as he was to the other womenfolk there at Montgomery House, but he was still concerned over the decision that she had made, and thought that James Brighton was an ill-conceived choice as a husband for Agatha. William was deeply in love with Abigail, and the possibility that Abigail might someday choose a man such as James Brighton to marry cut into his soul like a knife. He knew that Brighton was a very wealthy man, and he wondered if wealth was a required prerequisite in order for a man to be considered eligible for marriage among the ladyfolk at Montgomery House. If so, he felt that his love for Abigail was doomed to die a miserable death. His poverty had never been a concern to him before, but Agatha's sudden betrothal had created a firestorm of desperation in his heart.

Later that day, on his way from the henhouse with a basket of eggs, Abigail saw him from the back porch and immediately took notice of the fact that he still maintained a distinctly sullen and worried expression upon his face. She had acquired the ability to read William's face and eyes just as well as he could read hers. Abigail was beside herself with curiosity as to why William had reacted so strangely to Agatha's betrothal. She eagerly awaited him there on the porch so that she could intercept him as he drew closer.

"I must tell you, William, the words that you spoke in tribute of Agatha's betrothal this afternoon were marvelously eloquent. Thank you so much. Your warm words touched the hearts of everyone there."

"I'll be truthful with you, my warm words were insincere, Abigail. They had no meaning and they certainly didn't come from my heart, and for my deception, I sincerely apologize. I offered the toast only as an appeasement for you and Agatha."

"Land sakes alive! Whatever in the world has brought you to say something like that?! You've caught me completely by surprise! Is there something troubling you, William?"

"Oh, it's nothing much, Abigail. I'll get over it, I'm sure. Can we not overlook my offensive comments just this once?"

"No, we cannot. If something is troubling you, I would like to know what it is. I can clearly see that whatever it might be, it's very unsettling to you. Please talk to me."

"It's probably nothing, Abigail, I'm just more than a little disappointed to hear about Agatha's decision to marry James Brighton, that's all. All of this came as a complete surprise to me. I knew that they have spent a few evenings on the porch together, but I never suspected that anything this serious had developed between them."

"Oh? My Lord, William! Am I to assume that you have romantic interests in Agatha that I don't know about? Are you in love with Agatha and envious of Brighton?"

"Mercy no! Of course I'm not in love with Agatha! And I'm not jealous of Brighton, either! I'm not envious of any man alive... much less, Brighton."

"Then why would such a thing as Agatha's marriage to Brighton cause you any great concern, pray tell?"

"Agatha is what, thirty years old, maybe?"

"She's thirty-one years old, a year younger than I."

"And James Brighton must be at least fifty, I would assume."

"He's fifty-two years old."

"That's precisely my point, Abigail. Twenty-one years separate them! Twenty-one years! He's old enough to be her father, for heaven's sake!"

"And so, what if that's true? Why is the difference in their ages such a significant thing to you, if you're not in love with Agatha?"

"It's absolutely none of my business, but I would feel much better about their marriage if they were closer to the same age. I'll admit, I've not felt nearly as close to Agatha as I have to you and Elizabeth and Sarah, but I still want what's best for her. I've grown to love every member of your family dearly, and she's a part of your family, and I think she deserves someone much better than James Brighton."

"You must realize, William, that the war has claimed most of our younger men here in the south, at least in our region it has. Would you deny Agatha the joy and happiness of marriage simply because there are no suitors in the vicinity nearer her own age?"

"No, of course not. I would simply feel better about things if she had a wider range of men to choose from, that's all. As I said, I have a great deal of love for everyone here in the family, and I suppose I just want what's best for everyone. The scarcity of eligible men notwithstanding, I can't help but feel that there is someone out there nearer her own age that would have made a much better husband for her."

"And what causes you to think that Brighton won't make an absolutely perfect husband for Agatha?"

"You heard her in there telling everyone the details about how Brighton has been courting her, how he proposed to her, and how she thought long and hard about it, and even prayed about it..."

"Yes, I heard all of that, and so what is your concern?"

"Tell me, Abigail, while you were listening to her give everyone that gloriously happy oration of her wonderful marriage plans, did you even once hear her mention the word, *love* anywhere in her account of their courtship or betrothal? Did you?"

"No, but..."

"Then perhaps you can understand my concern. I may be archaic and just a sentimental fool in my way of thinking, but I thought marriages were supposed to be based on mutual love for one another. Am I wrong in feeling that way?"

"Not everyone is willing to reveal their deepest feelings publicly, William, especially when it comes to declaring one's love for another."

"Publicly? Publicly? My God, Abigail, this is her family here! If she can't profess her love in the presence of her family, who can she profess it to? I think she failed to profess her love because there is no love, and to think she would marry someone like James Brighton and not even be in love with him, sickens me."

"I can't believe that this has had such a devastating emotional effect on you, William."

"Well, it has! I'm sorry to say!"

"Did you study her face closely when she made the announcement, William? Did you look closely at her eyes as you made your eloquent toast?"

"No, not really. Why?"

"When you go back inside, look closely at her face. She's bubbling over with happiness, William, and we should all be happy for her. As her family, we should give her the benefit of assuming that her decision was based on love, even though she didn't specifically mention the word."

"Perhaps you're right, Abigail... perhaps I should be happy for her. Perhaps I'm over-reacting, and being nothing more than a sentimental fool. Perhaps love is something that's not as important as I perceive it to be... I don't know..."

"It would break her heart if she thought that you disapproved of Brighton. She thinks the world of you, William, and puts a great deal of credence in your opinion of things, as we all do."

"And how about you, Abigail? If you were her, would you have selected the likes of James Brighton for marriage, simply because he's wealthy? And if so, would you be bubbling over with happiness about it?"

"I cannot answer that. I am not her, I am me. Everyone is different, William. No two people are exactly alike in the way they think."

"Then tell me this, if you were to marry again, would you simply resort to accepting the best offer available at the time, the wealthiest of your suitors, or would you earnestly search for a person that you truly loved with all of your heart, regardless of his financial wellbeing?"

"I can't answer that either. I don't know what I would do..."

"For the love of God, Abigail, taking the best offer available at the time is the way that we go about selling our tobacco and our corn and our wheat—and it's certainly not the method that should be used to select a lifelong companion! Should love not be the determining factor in a marriage? I'm sorry, but that's the way I feel about something as important as marriage..."

"You really are greatly upset about this, aren't you?!"

"Yes... I am! And you haven't answered my question yet... Would you simply take the best marriage offer available, or would you seek out a man who you truly loved?"

"I've never even considered remarrying. If I ever did remarry, I can't say what I would do at the time. I'm thirty-two years old, William. I gave birth to Elizabeth when I was only fourteen years old, and Sarah when I was barely sixteen. The next year I had a son. I was so young when I had my children that my daughters are more like sisters to me. I'm content to be here with my daughters, I've dedicated my life to *their* happiness, not mine, and I can't imagine myself ever being married again. I sometimes feel as though marriage is something that is meant for other women—not me. It would take a very special person to ever give me pause to consider marriage again, I can assure you of that."

"Oh? And just what kind of special person would it take for you to consider marriage? What special qualities would a man have to possess in order for you to open your heart and consider being a young woman again—the woman that God intended for you to be?"

"That is a terribly personal question, William."

"Then how about this question; are you content with being the woman you are now, or do you sometimes feel that there is something vitally important that is missing in your life? Tell me the truth, Abigail."

"I feel at peace when I'm in your presence, like I could talk to you about almost anything in the world, but I'm not comfortable with discussing my deepest feelings right now, nor my future plans regarding the possibility of marriage, William. Please understand."

"Forgive me, Abigail. I did not mean to pry into your deepest feelings... Although, that's really not true at all. I was indeed attempting to know and understand your deepest feelings, and I should be ashamed of myself, for I have no right to do such a thing. I shall try to keep a tighter rein on my inquisitive thoughts as well as my stupid emboldened comments and questions. You've warned me about such behavior before, and I should have taken better heed of your warnings."

"Oh my God, William... Jesus help me..."

"What is it, Abigail? What's wrong?"

"Lord help me, but I think I've suddenly come to understand the true nature of your concern in this whole matter. Jesus help me... but it's not really Agatha's decision to wed James Brighton that has you so terribly upset, is it?"

"Well..."

"Is it?"

"I... don't know if I should answer that, Abigail."

"Please answer me truthfully, William!"

"I'm just... just..."

"Please!"

"No, Abigail, I suppose you're right, I'm not really all that concerned with Agatha's decision to marry Brighton. In truth, if that's what she really wants to do with her life, then I'm not very concerned about her at all, I suppose."

"Lord have mercy... Now I know why you are in such a panic over this... You're concerned over the possibility that I'll make a similar decision for myself, aren't you?"

"Well..."

"Look at me in the eye, and be honest with me, William, please. I must know!"

"No, Abigail, I'm not simply concerned that you'll make a similar decision... It would be more accurate to say that I'm absolutely terrified of that possibility! I'm frightened to my core! Just the thought of it sickens me and sends a chill up my spine!"

"Why?"

"Dammit, Abigail, you already know why, without my having to tell you!"

"Your fears are unfounded! I swear they are! You may dismiss it from your mind, William! That will never happen with me, I can promise you that! Besides, no man in his right mind would ever want to be married to a cantankerous, ill-tempered, and... arrogant woman such as I am."

"I think you should have added '*hardheaded*' to your list of attributes, Abigail."

"Thank you for your candor and outspokenness, William, and I shall gladly add that to my list attributes, because it's true."

"Despite all of your greatest efforts sometimes, you're not really any of those things, Abigail! I can assure you of that! You try very hard to be sometimes, and perhaps you've even fooled a of lot people in the past. But you've never fooled me... even for a minute. Behind that mask of sternness and determination that you wear there is a very kind heart inside, and I would wager my life that it's a very loving and tender heart that you have so cleverly hidden away from everyone's sight."

"Please don't do this to me, William. Please come inside so we can rejoin the family. This is a very special day for Agatha..."

"Abigail... My Lord, I just..."

"Please trust that I would never permit wealth to influence my heart, and dismiss the issue from your mind... please? I am deeply touched that you would be so concerned for my wellbeing and happiness, but your concern is unwarranted. Please believe me... God help me, but I don't even deserve your concern."

"What I feel for you runs a lot deeper than just concern, Abigail!"

"Please let me say this, and then I must go inside—my feelings for you also run deeper than mere concern, much deeper. But I need time to consider everything that's happening to me, William... I'm confused, and I beg you to please give me time..."

"My Lord, there is not another woman in the world like you, Abigail. I swear to the Almighty above there's not. I just..."

"Forgive me, but I must go inside. Please bring the eggs in, William, I feel like baking a cake today in celebration of Agatha's future happiness. This is a special day for Agatha, and I need to be inside with her and the family."

"My undisciplined words have caused you to cry again, haven't they, Abigail?"

"No! Well... maybe... Your words have touched me very deeply, William. It's unfamiliar for me to know that someone cares about my welfare and my future, as you so obviously do. I'm grateful for your concern, but I must step inside now and have time to gather my senses. Please understand, and bring the eggs in, William."

Once she was inside, Abigail practically ran through the merriment in the parlor and up the stairway. She went quickly into her bedchamber and shut the door behind her. In the privacy therein, she fell face-down on her bed and once again released her tears to run their ugly course. The dreadful sound of her sobbing was muffled, and rendered inaudible by the bed covers as she turned herself loose into the depths of her regret. She scorned herself. She had just shunned the perfect opportunity to be completely truthful and honest with William, and tell him how she felt about him in her heart. She could have simply said, *"I love you, William,"* but she didn't. She could have revealed her true emotions then and there, and brought her love for William into the light of day where she could have rejoiced in it, but she did not. She had come dangerously close to being honest and open with him, but her courage had vanished quickly when William began asking his compelling questions. She had the discomforting feeling that William somehow had the ability to look inside her heart and see a clear image of the torrent of emotion that was building within her. She dried her eyes, tidied her appearance somewhat, and went back downstairs to join in the family celebration. She tried not to look at William in the eyes for fear that he might have observed the true extent of her distress. Nevertheless, she was keenly aware of the fact that William was watching her as she feigned joyousness for her sister's betrothal, and she thusly remained vigilant in her efforts to present a jolly and exuberant aura about her. William was soon asked to play the piano for the occasion, and he readily complied. Despite his eloquent, lighthearted music, his heart was not into his playing. With William's back to Abigail as he played, she could not take her eyes off of him. She was hopelessly in love with him, yet remained steadfast in her conviction to keep her feelings hidden from sight. Abigail had demonstrated tremendous strength of character during her entire life, rising to accept each new challenge that had befallen her. The act of denying her love for William was proving to be the most difficult thing she had ever done, and she was nearing a breaking point.

Abigail was indeed happy that her sister seemed to be so content with the decision she had made to marry Brighton. But she found it disconcerting that in the depths of her heart, she agreed with William in regards to the seemingly imperfect match of her sister and James Brighton. In Abigail's opinion, James Brighton was in no way handsome, and even bordered on obesity. He was a poor conversationalist, and in most respects, even boring. He lacked the intriguing talent for humor that William so often displayed—a humor that had enlivened spirits so much there at Montgomery Farm. The only thing even remotely attractive about Brighton was his prominence in the community and his enormous wealth, and she prayed that her sister was not marrying him for such a shameful and dishonorable reason as that.

Amidst the gaiety as William played the piano, in her heart, Abigail made a solemn vow to herself; If such an opportunity to be honest with William ever presented itself again, she would set aside her foolish dignity and bear her heart and soul to him. Her dignity had gained her precious little in life, other than being an asset to her position of authority as the leader of the family. More than anything, she longed for happiness, and was only now beginning to realize that she had been rejecting happiness. All of her life she had been denied the opportunity to relish in the joys of love and womanhood. She knew that William was offering his heart to her on a platter, and she had been rejecting it. It was well past the time for things to change, and she knew it. She had an overwhelming urge to interrupt the piano music and beckon William to the porch, where she could reveal her true feelings then and there, but felt that this was neither the time nor the place for such a thing. Instead, she would wait. Such a release of her restrained emotions would represent a tremendously important step in her life, and she wanted to be certain before taking such a step.

As William played the piano and everyone sang a cheerful song, Abigail continued to stare at William from behind. In a stark moment of self-confession, Abigail spoke to herself aloud, without realizing that she had done so. Her voice was drowned out by the music and the singing, yet the surrounding merriment did not detract from the significance of her soft words... *"God help me, but I do love you, William... I really do. Forgive me for not having the courage to tell you as much. I will someday... I swear it!"*

O   O   O

James Brighton and Agatha Martin were married in an elaborate ceremony at Brighton's church near his Blairmount Estate amidst a crowd of more than a hundred guests and well-wishers. Tensions and unrest in the region caused by the war dictated that it would be much safer for him if William remained there on Montgomery Farm rather than to expose himself to the huge crowd of people. Brighton was a man with important political affiliations, and there would likely be guests in attendance with politically suspicious natures. Abigail and her daughters attended of course, and upon their return home, they gave William a full account of everything that had taken place. Given his predisposed disapproval of the marriage, it was prudent and best for all involved that he not attend the wedding anyway.

O   O   O

The week following Agatha's wedding, William and Ezra moved a wagonload of clothes and other items belonging to Agatha to her opulent new home at Blairmount. Of the seven bedchambers on the second floor of Montgomery House, four were now vacant. Abigail had entertained the possibility of offering one of the large upstairs bedchambers to Will, but decided that such an offering could potentially be perceived as being inappropriate and even forwardly brazen on her part—possibly even misunderstood as an invitation for misconduct. After all, the lady's bedchambers were all on the second floor and it would have been less than proper for a man, unrelated to the family by blood or marriage, to be offered a bedchamber in such proximity to the single and eligible ladies there. As much as Abigail wanted to offer William better sleeping accommodations, she thought it best not to. While the family members continued to feign happiness over Agatha's marriage, her presence there at Montgomery House was clearly missed once she had departed. At the breakfast table on the morning following the wedding, at one time or another, everyone had looked upon the empty chair where Agatha used to sit and felt a twinge of sadness over her absence. Each time that William would offer a prayer for God to bless their food, he always included the sincere postscript to his prayer, "*...and God, please bless Agatha. Keep her safe, healthy, and happy. Amen.*"

The World Changes Overnight

"And the peace of God, which passeth all understanding,
shall keep your hearts and minds through Christ Jesus."
Philippians 4:7

The passing weeks and months found more and more travelers making their way along the old road that ran less than a quarter mile to the east of the farm. The road was clearly visible from the front porch of Montgomery House. A large portion of the passing travelers had been military in composition, as the road was a well-used travel way for all north-south journeyers passing through that part of central Virginia. Processions of horse-drawn artillery were a common sight from the front porch of Montgomery House. In the most recent weeks, passing troops had become mostly that of Union forces, and seemed to be an indication that the tide of supremacy had shifted in the war, that perhaps the northern forces had assumed an advantage over the southern forces. Word had come to Montgomery Farm a year earlier that Vicksburg had fallen to the North. In the grand scheme of things, no one knew for sure exactly what was happening at any given time because it always seemed that news of the war was aggravatingly slow in arriving at Montgomery Farm, or anywhere else for that matter. There had been many occasions when the troops had stopped to water their horses at the creek there on Montgomery Farm. When they did stop to water their horses, bits of information regarding the war were often obtained. On one such occasion, Ezra had been plowing a field that was adjacent to the creek, and had taken time away from turning the soil to converse with a group of passing Union soldiers. Leaving his mules in the field, still hitched to the plow, Ezra ran excitingly toward the house, screaming "Miss Abigail" at the top of his lungs. Everyone knew that Ezra was the bearer of important news and quickly gathered on the rear porch. Will was working in the southwest fields at the time, unaware of such excitement.

"**Miss Abigail! Miss Abigail!**"

Quickly stuffing a dish towel into the pocket of her apron, Abigail asked, "What is it, Ezra?! What in the world are you so excited about?!"

"General Lee done gone and surrendered the South... day before yesterday, Miss Abigail!"

"What?! Surrendered the South? You mean the war is over? Are you quite certain?"

"Yes, Ma'am. A bunch of them Union soldiers done told me so!"

"Where did all this supposedly take place?"

"Somewhere east of here, Miss Abigail, in a place called Appomattox."

"Appomattox? **Good Lord**! I know the place! Agatha and I were born near Appomattox! Our family went to church in Appomattox when I was just a young girl!"

"What does all this mean, Miss Abigail?"

"I don't know, Ezra. If Lee has really surrendered, I suppose it means that the war really is over, but I'm not sure of what we should expect at this time. I can't believe the South has fallen. I need for you to run down to the southwest field and carry word to William immediately. Tell him to come to us as quickly as possible!"

"Yes, Ma'am, Miss Abigail!"

This news came as a devastating blow to most southerners, especially the people who had lost loved ones during the conflict. They were wrought with the desperate feeling that their husbands, sons, and brothers had given their lives for no reason. Their willingness to die for a cause they believed in, while honorable, brought little consolation to those relatives and friends who would remained to face an uncertain and potentially threatening future in the South. Every passerby bore the same news; ***The war was over! The South has fallen!***

There had been many southerners who, while distraught over the outcome, were not extremely surprised. They had seen many signs during the preceding months that the ending and the defeat was inevitable, yet the more devout southern sympathizers were reluctant to admit it. Many had known in the depths of their heart that a northern victory was on the near horizon, and Abigail Montgomery had been one of them.

It was later that day when James Brighton and Agatha arrived from Blairmount to shed some more light on the current situation. They brought news from Blairmount verifying that General Robert Lee had surrendered to General Ulysses Grant in Appomattox, Virginia, and a general armistice had been declared. Other Confederate Generals all over the South were surrendering as well, and large numbers of disheartened southern troops were breaking rank and going home. The South had truly fallen for good. Jefferson Davis had abandoned the Confederacy, packed his belongings, and fled Danville, and the general population was in a state of utter confusion. Davis and his administration had gone into hiding somewhere in North Carolina for fear of being hanged as traitors if they were caught. Rumors that the Union Army would return in force to seek horrible retribution were running rampant throughout the south. Some residents even fled their homes to seek secluded refuge in the nearby mountains. Widespread panic ensued, and the only positive thing that transpired in the immediate aftermath of the war was the return home for a few battle weary southern soldiers in the region. Surviving soldiers were finally going home, albeit with the anxiety and uncertainty of what they would find when they got there. Despite the defeat, Southern soldiers were being received in their home towns as heroes, albeit penniless and defeated heroes.

A week after receiving word that General Lee had surrendered, James Brighton and Agatha visited Montgomery Farm again to bring the family word that the President of the United States, Abraham Lincoln had fallen to an assassin's bullet. This news only added to the chaos and uncertainty that permeated the region, and there were but few southerners who received news of the president's murder with any joy. With the death of President Lincoln, Andrew Johnson had assumed the presidency, and little was known about the man or his ability to lead the nation compassionately through its time of healing. Everyone thirsted for news, but the news was always excruciatingly slow to arrive. When word did come, it was usually filled with gloomy speculation that the South should be expectant of horrible retribution.

Confederate soldiers traveling back to their homes were relegated to travel by the only means available—walking, or seeking rides upon one of the many passing supply wagons. Some veterans had the money to travel by rail, but most were penniless. Many of them abandoned or sold their rifles and uniforms for fear of being shot by patrolling Union forces. Rather than feed the horde of enlisted soldiers, the Union army soon dismissed large numbers of their veterans, who also traveled afoot to their respective homelands. It was not unusual for fights to take place between passing veterans of the blue and the grey. But as the days continued to pass, fighting between veterans became less and less frequent. Most every man who passed by Montgomery Farm had been a soldier for one side or the other, and was eagerly on their way back to their homes and the beloved families who awaited them there.

With the official ending of the war, the coming months found William slowly beginning to emerge from his deceptive role as a mentally incompetent veteran to that of a stable, yet still somewhat confused, young man. William proved to be highly competent in managing the operation of the farm. In less than five months after the end of the war, it became evident that William's incredible ability to manage the farm would not only permit the Montgomery family to maintain the farm's profitability, William would continue to improve upon it significantly. He planted the crops in a slightly different manner than they had ever been planted before, and he learned how to better manage the cultivation of the crops and rotate the planting of different crops in order to maximize their yield. His managing of the farm operation had become so efficient and successful, that Abigail had given him exclusive responsibility in the handling of all farm-related matters. It was a tremendous burden lifted from her shoulders, and a role which William thrived in.

In the fields one day, as Abigail and her daughters were delivering water to the workers, William posed a question to Abigail that momentarily gave her pause for very serious and disconcerting thought. William took a long drink of water and asked, "Abigail, I've noticed that there is what appears to be an open grave or a hole of some sort in the woods just behind the barn. It's obviously been there for a number of months. Is that hole there for some sort of a purpose?"

"Uhhh... Oh, my Lord!" Abigail immediately turned pale, having forgotten that she had once instructed Ezra to dig a grave for the wounded soldier that everyone had thought would die. The question served to remind her that William's survival had been a miracle. The question also prompted her to consider what her life at Montgomery Farm would have been like without the presence of William. She gathered herself together and answered, "No, William, it's just a hole, that's all. It serves no useful purpose at all, thank God."

"Are you alright, Abigail? You look as though you are about to become faint!"

"Yes... I'm fine, thank you."

"May I cover the hole over before one of the horses or cows steps in it and breaks a leg? It's rather deep."

"Yes, please do, William. My Lord, yes, by all means!"

"Abigail... I'm concerned about you. Now you look as though you are about to cry."

"Nonsense! I'm just fine, thank you."

Abigail walked quickly back to the house, and even broke into a run during the final steps. Inside, she went up to her bedchamber, closed the door, and as she had done so many times before, she again thanked God for having spared William's life. His innocent question regarding the hole in the ground had jostled her memory, and reminded her that William's survival of his wounds was nothing less than a gift from God. William's presence at Montgomery House had become the most important element in Abigail's life, yet the misery of having to hide her love for him had become a source of constant irritation. She lived her life in the same house as the three people that she loved most in this world, yet in her heart, her loneliness was beginning to suffocate her.

Initially, William could not understand why Abigail had appeared to have been so shaken by his simple question, but he nevertheless dismissed it from his mind. That afternoon, he and Ezra walked into the woods with shovels and filled the hole, and Ezra confided in him, by telling him the true original purpose of the hole. Ezra's explanation instilled William with a gruesome reckoning of his own mortality. It was the first time he had given any serious consideration to just how close he had come to dying when he had been brought there to recover. It was a moment of sobering realization for him, but he nonetheless used the opportunity to introduce some lightheartedness into an otherwise macabre task. Such was the humorous nature of William. Ezra looked at William as he added another shovelful of dirt to the hole and said, "We all thought you was gonna die fo sure, Mister Will. You was bad off then, I swear you was. I dug this here grave for you back when you was all busted up and almost dead."

"Well, Ezra, I shan't begin to tell you how comforting it is for me to be able to assist you in covering this hole up... it's especially comforting for me to know that I'm not in it."

"Yes Sir, Mister Will. It gives me comfort, too! It truly does!"

"Let's not ever tell Miss Abigail that I found out it was supposed to be my grave, alright?"

"Yes Sir, Mister Will. Ole Ezra ain't never gonna breath a word about it to nobody."

Will never mentioned the grave to Abigail again after that day, yet he found a strange sense of contentment in knowing by her initial reaction, that she was happy for him to cover over the unused grave, and even more happy to know that he was not to be occupying it anytime soon. Her reaction had been one of many such subtle indications that gave William hope that her feelings for him perhaps ran much deeper on the inside than they appeared outwardly. Nevertheless, Abigail continued to keep her deepest sentiments well-hidden within the depths of her heart.

In the spring, their annual crops were planted, pastures turned green again, and spring violets in the pastures bloomed abundantly in their full glory. If one took the time to admire the landscape surrounding Montgomery Farm, one could hardly tell that there had ever been a war. Other than the occasional veteran that came to the door looking for work or food, there were few visitors who dropped by during this period. Times were tough, and southern commerce had been practically destroyed by the war. It would take time for economic conditions to recover, and in the meantime, folks simply did the best they could with what the aftermath of the war had left behind for them.

Everyone who remained in that portion of Virginia was occupied with their own dutiful chores of planting their crops, rebuilding their homes, and picking up the pieces of their traumatized lives. Many shattered families moved away, so that they could live closer to other family members or loved ones. There was not a home, and not a family in the region that had not been scathed in some manner or another by the cruel realities of war. With the blockades removed from the James River, and the shipping channels in the Chesapeake Bay restored, coffee beans were soon available again, and it became a highly favored beverage there at Montgomery Farm, both in the mornings and evenings. On the day that the first sack of coffee beans was purchased and brought back to Montgomery Farm, the event was treated as a grand celebration. Every family member sat in the kitchen, anxiously watching with glorious anticipation as the coffee brewed. The wonderful aroma was savored as the kettle began to boil. It had been three long years since there had been coffee or sugar in the house, and it truly was a cause for gaiety and festiveness.

William's presence in the house had necessitated many changes in the customary daily habits of the womenfolk abiding at Montgomery House. Abigail insisted that the women keep themselves presentable, and dressed with dignity and modesty in mind anytime William was in the house. William had become an accepted family member, and given the fact that his presence was so familiar in their home, there were occasions in which Abigail had to remind her daughters to button the tops of their bed robes so as not to inadvertently expose their bosoms. Nor would she allow her or her daughters to parade about barefooted, or expose any part of their legs above the ankles. William was an accepted member of the family to be sure, but he was also a man.

In the years prior to William's arrival at Montgomery House, Abigail had exercised the liberty of talking freely with her daughters, anytime she wanted to, openly and candidly, regardless of the topic of their conversation. Many young ladies in the community of Blanchard that were two or three years younger than Elizabeth and Sarah were already married and had children, and yet Elizabeth and Sarah had remained somewhat ignorant of many of life's enchanting secrets, especially those secrets which related to men. Given the natural curiosity of Elizabeth, and Sarah's relentless inquisitiveness, the subject of 'men' had been a frequent topic of conversation between Abigail and her daughters, discussed at liberty, with much candor, and often with much giddiness and laughter between the young ladies and Abigail. The themes of many of their conversations were often based on Abigail bestowing her young daughters with knowledge concerning the opposite sex. Their topics ranged from, *"why do some men lose their hair and go bald, and others don't?"* to *"why did God give men testicles... what purpose do they serve, and do they cause the man discomfort when he walks?"* On several occasions, Abigail would retrieve her medical book, *Dr. Thaddeus Welch—Compendium Of Human Anatomy,* from her chest of drawers and use it to further educate her daughters in the complexities and intricacies of the human body. It was innocent yet essential education passed down from a loving mother to her curious and inquisitive daughters, but with Will's presence in the house now, such topics could only be discussed in the privacy of their upstairs bedchambers, or when Will was at his daily labors in the fields. Such subjects could never be discussed in the presence of a man. Will's presence in the house had not preempted these necessary *'female'* consultations, his presence had only created a need for the ladies to be more selective as to when and where these subjects were discussed.

Will's presence in the house had tremendously elevated everyone's dispositions, enlivened their conversations at the breakfast and supper tables, and provided an air of comforting satisfaction within the family that would have been difficult for any of them to define or explain. Will's inclination to introduce levity and lightheartedness in the household was an attribute that gained him even more favor among the ladies there. His occasional humor was a pleasant escape from the doldrums of constant labor, and such levity had been long absent at Montgomery Farm. His presence in the house was not viewed as an inconvenience—it was viewed as a blessing by everyone there. Even the simple act of holding hands at mealtime as Will offered the morning and evening blessing of the food, was an act that seemed to bind the family closer together than they had ever been before Will's arrival.

Will's pleasant personality and warm character had given Abigail considerable pause for thought when she contemplated her station in life. She had always known that her deceased husband, Thomas, had been a terribly abusive scoundrel in life—a circumstance that had hardened Abigail's heart toward men. It was only now, as she assessed the wonderfully honorable qualities in William's character, that she came to realize just how despicable Thomas had really been. She had once thought that all men were probably alike in most every respect, but since coming to know William as she had, she knew that was not true. William was someone of exceptional character, and no one knew that better than Abigail Montgomery.

Abigail was by her nature, a very resourceful and industrious woman. There was very few periods during the course of a day in which she was not engaged in doing something productive for the family, such as cooking, cleaning, churning butter, putting up preserves, or washing clothes. On one particular morning however, her mind was much too deep in detached thought to allow her to concentrate properly on her many domestic responsibilities. Her mind was in the mood to wander, and she was in the mood to permit it. She stood at the parlor window, gazing outside, and became deeply lost in her thoughts. Sarah and Elizabeth had been busy washing laundry that morning, and were now upstairs changing the bedsheets in their bedchambers, and as usual, Will was at labor with the workmen in the fields. She took a sip of coffee and looked at the piano there in the parlor. She thought of the many years that the piano had sat silently dormant there until William had brought it back to life. She and her family treasured William's music, and she was beginning to come to terms with just how much she had come to treasure William himself. There were qualities within William's character that she had never seen in a man before—qualities that were irresistibly attracting, yet at the same time, mysteriously inspiring. Although she would never admit it to another living soul, Abigail was deeply in love with William and had been for months now. She had no idea of how she could best deal with the fact that he was now dominating her every thought. She trusted William more than she had ever trusted any man in her life, yet her feelings of love for this man were so new to her that she dared not to reveal them to a soul.

Abigail took the final sips of coffee from her cup as she gazed outside at the clothesline where the family laundry was hanging to dry in the warmth of the morning sun. She smiled contentedly at what she saw. There on the clothesline, amidst an elaborate array of snow-white bustles, corsets, and various bleached women's undergarments, was a single pair of men's work trousers and a man's work shirt. She smiled even wider, chuckled musingly to herself, and contemplated how well the clothesline now portrayed their lives at Montgomery Farm. She thought... a single, solitary man, a magnificent man, a man previously unknown to them, had come into their home... and had somehow magically made his way into their hearts. But he had not come alone, for with him, he had brought cheerfulness, indescribable warmth, and the ever-present comfort of masculine companionship. It seemed odd to Abigail, that something as inoculant, inanimate, and as simple as the sight of a clothesline would warm her heart and bring a tear of joy to her eye, but it did. Her heart truly belonged to William, yet she had relegated herself to keeping her love a secret. She would have given anything for the ability to read William's thoughts, to know his innermost sentiments... yet because of her propensity to censor his attempts to talk openly with her, in her heart, she felt that a miracle such as that would most likely never happen.

In an old trunk in the attic, Sarah had discovered a wrapped bundle of assorted sheet music, which she presented to William. The family thought that it would be of assistance to William as he played. Everyone, including William, became quite perplexed to find that he could not read a single word of the music notes. Even though he seemed to be able to play any song at his heart's desire, he had evidently learned to play without the assistance of sheet music. Even the most intricate and difficult songs of the classics came naturally to him, and he continued to render the most beautiful of music for the family. On the Sabbath, they sang hymns together, and most weeknights found the women gathered nearby the piano to hear William's splendid renditions of the classics as they tended to their quilting and sewing.

Three or four times a month, during the warmest months of the summer, William and Ezra would take a wagonload of tobacco into the nearby town of Blanchard. There, the tobacco would be graded and weighed, inspected closely by buyers, and sold at auction to the highest bidding purchaser. Montgomery Farm tobacco was regarded as the highest quality tobacco sold in Central Virginia. Its quality was the standard by which the other farms in the area were measured. The money collected from the sale of the crop would be carried back to Abigail for her to deposit at a later time in the bank. With the reopening of northern markets, demand for tobacco had soared even higher, and crop prices also rose accordingly. Many farmers failed to make a profit from selling only their annual vegetable or wheat crops, but tobacco was still in extremely high demand throughout the country, and most tobacco farms that were well managed prospered during this time. Montgomery Farm was no exception, and most of the credit for such success was attributed to the long, hard labors, and management capabilities of William. His mind continued to endure the harassment and uncertainty of his own origin, yet he constantly kept himself occupied with tasks that would contribute to the success of the Farm. Despite his attempts to keep his mind focused exclusively on his arduous labors, there was a battle taking place within his mind. He felt as though he had arrived at a time when it may have become possible for him to find more contentment in his life if he left Montgomery Farm, and went to seek his peace of mind elsewhere. He struggled within himself to find an answer, for his torment over Abigail's apparent romantic disinterest in him had become a source of constant agony... one that was eating away at his very heart and soul. He knew that she had warm feelings for him, she had even told him as much, but William longed for something much more tangible and meaningful than warm feelings. He was beginning to think there would never be any hope for Abigail's feelings to mature into love, and his hopelessness was leading him into despair. He wanted to discuss his emotional unrest with Abigail, but he lacked the courage to do so. Abigail had taken due notice of the fact that Will had not been displaying his usual gaiety or lighthearted humor at the family meal tables. She knew that something was disturbing him, and deep in her heart, she even suspected that she knew what was tormenting him, but the perfect opportunity to privately inquire of him had not presented itself. She looked across the table at the sad expression on Will's face, and thought to herself, *"My Lord, Will... what's troubling you so? Are you aware of how very deeply I adore you? Are you aware that when you are hurting like this, I am hurting too? I can't go on like this, Will. I'm ready to tell you how much I love you if you will only let me... I swear I am."*

On a tepid and very rainy Monday morning, too wet to work in the tobacco fields, Will had given all of the workmen the day off. Handling wet tobacco leaves was a risky business, to be avoided whenever possible. Workmen could be subject to violent sickness and headaches if they handled wet tobacco leaves with their bare hands. The strange illness was called, *"tobacco poisoning,"* and occurred when the wetness of the tobacco leaves was absorbed into the skin of the hands or arms. Due to the rain, the workmen had all gone into the town of Blanchard to spend the day, and in their absence, all was quiet and peaceful at Montgomery Farm.

On this rare day of idleness and tranquil quietness on Montgomery Farm, William stood there on the back porch, leaning against a porch post, and gazed out across the property, looking at the many acres of crops in the fields below. The falling rain made a satisfying sound on the metal roof of the porch. His emotions were in a state of bewilderment. He was extremely proud of the crops that he had planted, and how efficiently the farm was now operating, but he was agonizing deeply within his heart at the same time. William's very existence there at Montgomery Farm had regressed into a state of discontentment, and he was fighting a very serious battle within his heart. Abigail approached him on the back porch as he stood there watching the rain. Her body was unavoidably tingling with that special feeling of warmth that she always acquired whenever she was in his presence... a sensation that she perpetually treasured, yet had always managed to keep well hidden from everyone else, especially William. Abigail and William had reached a critical juncture in their lives, and it was high time for things to change. The time in which to be completely truthful with one another had finally arrived for Abigail and William. Abigail struggled briefly with the screen door as she attempted to carry a cup of coffee in each hand to the porch. Through the screen wire of the door she announced, "I've brought a cup of coffee out here for you, Will."

"Oh! Thank you, Abigail. That was very thoughtful of you. Here, let me help you with the door."

"Thank you, Will. As you can see, I've brought a cup of coffee for myself as well. I was hoping that we could sit here and have our coffee together and talk for a while this morning. It seems that with all the work there is to be done around here nowadays, that you and I seldom have the opportunity to talk, and you've been managing things around here so well without my interference that we don't even talk much about the farm work anymore."

"I enjoy the farm work, Abigail. It helps me to keep my mind occupied, lest I sometimes find myself dwelling on some of the more unpleasant thoughts in life. I agree, things have been rather busy lately."

"Would you mind if we take advantage of this rare opportunity and speak with each other for a few minutes?"

"I would like that very much, Abigail. This seems to be the perfect morning for coffee... and I suppose it's also a perfect morning for conversation, as well. Should I go inside and ask Sarah and Elizabeth to come out to the porch and join us?"

"No, please... I would rather that you didn't, Will. Sarah and Elizabeth are scrubbing the floors in the upstairs bedchambers, and they will be quite busy for the next couple of hours. Besides, I would much rather it was just you and I this morning. We never seem to have any time to talk when it's just you and I like this."

"I agree, and I appreciate you taking the time out of your busy day to talk to me."

Abigail's heart began to beat strongly. She was well aware that there would never be a better opportunity for her to tell Will that she was in love with him. She had foolishly let many opportunities slip away from her, and was more determined than ever before... to reveal her true feelings to him once and for all. She continued having casual conversation in an effort to build up her nerve.

"Elizabeth and Sarah picked four buckets of blackberries yesterday, and I thought we would put up some preserves this afternoon, and perhaps we could even make a pie for you. Would you like that?"

"I adore your blackberry preserves and your pies. It would be difficult for me to choose which one is my favorite."

"Would you be agreeable to play the piano for us tonight, Will?"

"Of course I will, Abigail, you know that."

"So, tell me what's on your mind on this rainy Monday morning, Will. You looked like you were lost somewhere, deep in thought when I came out on the porch just now."

"Oh... I don't know, Abigail. I was just standing here thinking about nothing particularly important, I suppose. My thoughts nowadays can sometimes be a torment to me, so I try to discipline myself in regards to where I allow my thoughts to carry me."

"You seem to be very deep in thought about something this morning. Please come over here and sit here beside me on the porch swing. Would you care to bring me into your confidence and share your thoughts with me on this rainy Monday morning, Will?"

"It's funny, I've been here at Montgomery Farm for thirteen months now, and I've never sat in this swing before now."

"Why not?"

"Oh, I don't know... I always felt like it was something that was reserved for the ladies of the house and their suitors, I suppose."

"Then let's pretend that I'm a lady of the house and you are my suitor. Tell me what's on your mind, Will."

William sat down beside Abigail, took a sip of coffee, and answered, "I would like that very much, Abigail, but my thoughts right now would be very difficult for me to put into words, much less share them. Besides, my thoughts have been known to get me in trouble on occasion. I'm sure you know that better than anybody else."

"I'm not sure that I understand what you mean by that. I would love to hear your thoughts this morning if you would only share them with me. Perhaps I could even be persuaded to share a few thoughts of my own. I haven't shared as many of my own thoughts with you as I should have, and I would like nothing more than to change that this morning."

"Abigail... I just... I don't know, never mind. I'm confused right now... about a lot of things, that's all."

"You haven't seemed to be yourself the last few days. I know that there is something weighing very heavy on your mind, isn't there? I can tell."

"Yes, I suppose there really is something that's weighing heavy on my mind."

"Won't you please talk to me and tell me what's got you so deep in melancholy thought this morning?"

"Yes... yes I will... It's hard for me to put this into words, but for some reason..."

"What?"

"I'll be honest with you, Abigail, for the first time since I've been here, I'm beginning to feel like the time has arrived that I should be giving serious thought to moving on soon... going somewhere else... I just don't know... I think it would be best for me, and I think it would be best for you and your family if I just left and went somewhere far away from here."

Abigail was stunned breathless at William's comment, but gasped an immediate response, "Oh, my God Will! No! Please don't say anything like that!"

"I know that I can't very well leave here right now with all the work that has to be done, and I would never leave you without finding someone to replace me, but when the crops are harvested this fall, and the farm work slows down..."

"Dear Jesus! I don't know what to say, Will. I... I just know for certain that there is no one on this earth who could ever replace you. No one!"

"Practically anyone could replace me, Abigail and it wouldn't be very difficult to find a farm manager. Men are returning home from the war, and some of 'em will be looking for work soon. I would certainly assist you in finding someone before I leave. Besides, I couldn't bring myself to leave without knowing that someone trustworthy was here to carry on in my place."

"No man alive could ever fill your shoes here, I swear to you Will!"

"I wish that I could believe that, Abigail."

"I fear that this will come as devastating news for Elizabeth and Sarah. They are both deeply in love with you, but I would suppose that their love for you has been so girlishly obvious that you probably already know that."

"Yes, I know they're in love with me, Abigail, and in truth, that is one of the reasons that are compelling me to leave Montgomery Farm. My present situation here is breaking my heart. I once found contentment in my work here, and slept well at night, but my heart is so heavy now that there seems to be no contentment for me. I can't help it. Believe it or not, I really do have feelings, Abigail, feelings that are becoming unbearably painful for me to live with, and I just can't go on like this much longer."

"Do you have no love in your heart for Elizabeth or Sarah? Is that it, Will?"

"Of course, I have a very deep love for them... both of them. Under different circumstances, if they were a few years older, and I was a few years younger, I would be proud to ask for either of their hands in marriage. I have grown to love them so much that I would gladly give my life for either of them."

"If that be the case, why would you feel like you have to leave them and go elsewhere? That doesn't make any sense to me, Will."

"My love for Sarah and Elizabeth is a different kind of love than any kind of romantic love. I'm afraid you wouldn't understand, Abigail. Nobody would, so I think it would be best if we just changed the subject of our conversation."

"How do you know that I wouldn't understand, unless you tell me, and give me the opportunity to understand? It's only fair, Will. It's heartbreaking for me to think that you would be so unhappy here as to consider leaving us without telling me the source of your discontent."

"I... I... I'm just miserable here, Abigail..."

"Talk to me, Will! Give me a chance to help you through whatever is troubling you! I came out here this morning with the intention of being completely truthful with you for the first time since you've been here, and I want you to be truthful with me as well."

"Since I was first brought here, you've made it rather difficult for me to speak to you openly and truthfully. Most of the times that I've attempted to do so, you've either walked away from me just as I was about to be completely honest with you or you have threatened me. You've maintained a very stringent control over what I'm permitted to say to you and what I'm not permitted to say."

"I shan't even begin to argue with you on that point. I have been entirely too controlling and restrictive in that respect... not because I didn't want to hear what you had to say, but because I was afraid of the things that you might say. That's been a terrible mistake on my part, I can see that now. The truth is, I have longed to hear your thoughts... your true thoughts, all of them, and I long to hear them now more than ever. Please confide in me Will while we have this opportunity to be alone like this."

"Very well. You've asked me, so I'm going to tell you. The simple truth of the matter is that I do love Elizabeth and Sarah very deeply, just like I said, but..."

"But what?"

"Abigail... The simple truth of the matter is, that I love them as if they were my own sweet daughters. And God help me, but I love their stubborn, hardheaded, cantankerous mother more than anyone's mind could possibly fathom. I'm in love with you, Abigail, so much that it hurts, and don't you dare tell me that you are surprised to hear me come out and say that."

Abigail set her coffee cup on the porch, spilling it and breaking the cup in the process, and quickly buried her face in her hands, saying, "My dear God, Will..." and her tears began to flow as William went on to say, "You fed me soup when I first woke up that day last year, and when I looked up into your eyes, I saw an angel looking down on me... and well... I fell in love with you that very second, and I've been in love with you ever since. I still see an angel every time I look at you. That was thirteen months ago, and my love for you just keeps growing... every day it seems to grow, and there's nothing I can do that will ever change the way I feel about you inside—nothing!"

"Dear God... What a stupid fool I've been... I've waited too long to tell you..."

"For just a moment, can you imagine what it must feel like to love someone so deeply that you would willingly surrender your life for them, and the best that you ever had to look forward to was an occasional kind word and nothing else... never an adoring word... Never a hug... Never a kiss... Never a warm embrace or even as much as hearing a simple, '*I love you*...' I could never describe how much it hurts me, Abigail. Sometimes I feel like there is a knife being twisted in my heart."

"My dear God, Will, what have I done? How could I have been so cruel and foolish? I am so ashamed of myself for the way I have tried to ignore you."

"I'm sorry for taking such bold liberties as to talk to you so bluntly like this, Abigail, I know it's upsetting for you to hear this, and it's breaking my heart to see you cry like this, but you asked me what was on my mind, and for once, I'm going to be completely truthful with you."

"I've been so stupid..."

"I mean to show you no disrespect, Abigail, but my heart will not permit me to remain here and cause any additional heartache for you or your daughters. God knows you have already endured enough heartache to last a lifetime, and I'll not add to it. As soon as the crops are harvested this fall... I think it would be best for everyone here if I move on."

"And you honestly think that running away from me will solve anything? What is it that you fear so much Will?"

"I fear that Elizabeth and Sarah would hate me, and I fear that they would possibly even hate you as well, if they only knew how deeply I'm in love with you."

"Your fears are unfounded. I know my daughters better than anyone, Will, and that's simply not true. They would never hate either of us!"

"I just don't want to be the source of anyone's discontentment, Abigail, especially the very people I love most in this life. As much as I cherish you, I just can't stay here much longer under these circumstances."

"I told you a while ago that my reason for coming out on the porch this morning was to be truthful with you. Truthfulness between us has been long overdue, and I have no one to blame for that but myself. You've always been truthful to me, or at least you've tried to be. I am the one who has been untruthful, and I wish to correct that by making a confession to you."

"Confession? What confession?"

"I'm hopelessly in love with you, Will, I swear I am."

"What?"

"I think back about my life before you came here and I realize that I had no life. You are my life, Will, and I love you with every ounce of my being!"

"My God… do you know how long I've waited to hear you say that?"

"Yes! Too long! And it's all my fault! Listen Will, it's true that Elizabeth and Sarah both love you, but I know that their love is a childish and an immature kind of love that is common to fickle young women of their age. I refuse to believe that anyone in the world is capable of loving you more deeply than me, and my love for you is not a childish fantasy, it's as sincere and as real as any love that a woman has ever felt for a man. I love you with all my heart and soul, Will, I really do."

"Lord have mercy… I just… don't quite know what to say. Those were the most wonderful words I have ever heard spoken. Are you really being truthful with me, Abigail?"

"I cannot continue to lie to myself, or deny the love I have for you, Will. I said that I love you because it's true, and my words are coming from the bottom of my heart."

"If that's true, then please tell me why you have continually prohibited me from saying anything complimentary or affectionate to you? I've wanted to tell you that I was in love you for more than a year now. Why have you not allowed me to express my love to you? And why have you not told me how you feel about me before now?"

"Because I've been a stupid fool, Will, that's why! I've been afraid to listen to my heart because it's never spoken to me before. I've never felt this way about a man before, and I didn't trust myself. I fell in love with you the day I shaved you last year, and was too stupid to tell you. I've loved you for more than thirteen months now, and my love for you is too deep to allow me to go on pretending that it doesn't exist. I feel like I have wasted the last thirteen months of my life and your life too, by trying to hide something that's too big and too important to hide. Just being able to tell you how much I love you has lifted a tremendous weight from my shoulders. I almost feel as though I have been reborn now that I've finally told you how I feel."

"Then what am I to do, Abigail? What are any of us to do? Things couldn't be any more complicated between us than they are here at Montgomery Farm."

"Leaving me is not the answer. If you should leave, I would worry myself to death about you. I simply can't bear the thought, Will."

"I only know that if I stay here much longer, living in the same house and under the same roof as the woman I love, and forbidden to express my love, I feel like my heart will soon burn to ashes."

"And if you should leave here, my heart shall also burn to ashes. I would rather be dead than to see you leave! I couldn't bear it! Would you consider that, Will? Please?"

"My Lord, Abigail... I just... I just... don't know what to do. Sometimes I even fear for my own sanity when I'm alone in my room at night. I go to bed at night thinking about you... I wake up thinking about you... I even dream about what it would be like to hold you by my side. Knowing that you are upstairs in the same house, and I can't go to you... I just can't go on like this, Abigail."

"And the real tragedy is that I lay in my room each night with the same desire to be with you. My heart aches to be with you! Living the last thirteen months in my stupid self-imposed loneliness has been a torment to my heart as well as yours."

"Oh, Abigail... My sweet, sweet Abigail..."

"Tell me truthfully, is it intimacy that you long for, Will? Is a longing for intimacy responsible for such unhappiness and discontentment in your life?"

"I only long for one thing in life, Abigail, and that's the fulfillment of the love that I have for you! Fulfillment without intimacy is impossible! It doesn't exist! If you want to know the truth of it, Abigail, yes, I crave touching you, and I crave kissing you! I crave being touched by you, and being kissed by you! Dammit, I even dream about what it would be like to feel your hair in my face at night and your breast against my cheek! I crave what it would be like to feel your breath against my chest! I love you enough to die for you, Abigail Montgomery, and I've never even so much as kissed you on the cheek, and it's eating away at my very soul!

There was a long pause as William gathered his thoughts together and regained his composure. Abigail sobbed a moment or two longer and reached over to hold William's hand.

"I'm sorry that I raised my voice like that, Abigail. My Lord, I surely wouldn't want Sarah and Elizabeth to hear me talking like this."

"They're upstairs. They can't hear us on the porch here, Will."

"Anyway, that's how I feel inside, Abigail. I've been ranting away just like some kind of crazy lunatic, haven't I? If I didn't hurt so bad inside, I might even find myself to be amusingly humorous."

"Nothing about this is humorous to me, Will. I understand your hurt, I really do, because I've been feeling just as much hurt as you."

"Lord have mercy, I can't believe the disrespectful things that I just said to you, Abigail. Can you ever forgive me? It's almost like I have stored all my feelings inside for thirteen months and then suddenly released them all at once and dumped them all in your lap—which is exactly what I just did. I'm so sorry to embarrass you like this."

"I'm not embarrassed, Will, I'm deeply touched. We are only

being honest and truthful with each other, and it's high time that we were. It's the human nature of a man and woman in love to crave being intimate with each other. You're right, intimacy is the fulfillment of love. Craving intimacy is nothing for either of us to be ashamed of, Will. It's only shameful when it's done with adulterous intentions or committed for the sake of sinful lust and betrayal, and without love."

"My Lord, what would Elizabeth or Sarah say if they could hear us talking now? It would break their heart."

"You and I have hearts, too, Will. Should we continue to ignore our own feelings? I think we've done that long enough, and I'm not going to do it anymore! Like you, I'm nearly at my wit's end. My desire to be touched and kissed by you is every bit as strong as yours, perhaps even stronger!"

"I've revealed the secrets of my soul to you just now, Abigail. I thought it would come as an appeasement to me if I was completely honest with you for a change, but I find that I am only complicating matters and further agonizing both myself *and* you."

"You are not agonizing me, Will, I swear you're not."

"Your beautiful, beautiful face is covered with tears, Abigail. They were not there until I started taking bold liberties with my words. You came out here on the porch to enjoy your coffee this morning, and look what I've done to you. I should be ashamed of myself."

"I didn't come out here on the porch to enjoy my coffee or look out at the rain, or simply pass the time of day with you. Believe it or not, I came out on the porch this morning to finally tell you how deeply I love you, something I wish I had done thirteen months ago."

"It breaks my heart every time I see tears on your cheek, Abigail."

"I see tears on your cheeks as well."

Will quickly wiped his tears away, rose to his feet, and offered, "I deeply apologize for everything that I just said. I'm truly sorry. Thank you for the coffee, Abigail. I'm going to the barn. Even though it's too wet to work in the fields today, I have harnesses in the barn that I can mend while it's raining outside."

Abigail grabbed William by the arm and pleaded, "No, Will! Please don't leave me here in such a miserable state as this! Talk to me, Will, so that we can better understand each other... Please? Sarah and Elizabeth are upstairs, and we're alone here. We've learned so much about each other's feelings already this morning! Please talk to me some more!"

"I'm not sure of what else I could say that I haven't already said, Abigail."

"Then tell me something Will, if our craving for intimacy and fulfillment was appeased, could you be happy here at Montgomery Farm? Would you be willing to reconsider leaving me? Would you stay with me then?"

"Wait a minute, Abigail! I hope you don't have such a low opinion of me that you think that I would stoop to using my presence here at Montgomery Farm as if it was bargaining material to blackmail you into doing something that your heart is opposed to. I love you far too much to take advantage of you in such a disgraceful way. I'd sooner cut off an arm than to..."

"Listen to me, Will, my heart is in perfect alignment with yours, I swear it is. We're in love, Will. There should be no yearnings between us that go unappeased. People in love should be able to appease one another's yearnings. Don't you know that?"

"How could my yearnings possibly be appeased, given our current circumstances here? I'm afraid to even ask for you to let me kiss you, for fear of your rejecting me or our being seen together. And what would Elizabeth and Sarah say if they knew that I was so deeply in love with their mother? I'm tormented, Abigail, and there seems to be nothing I can do about it."

"You may dismiss any fears that you might have regarding my rejecting you. I've tried rejecting you for thirteen months now, and it's purchased only agony for both of us. Denying my love for you has been the most stupid mistake of my life. My heart will no longer permit me to do such a cruel and heartless thing to you... or me."

"Abigail... you truly are the most beautiful woman in the world, I swear to the Lord above you are..."

"I believe that difficulties such as these are best solved one at a time, approaching the most important difficulty first. Sarah and Elizabeth are young and fanciful, but they are my daughters, and we love each other. If I told them that I love you as deeply and sincerely as I do, they would understand. God has blessed us all when he sent you here, and these difficulties that you're talking about can all be resolved, but they can't be resolved by running away from them, Will. Running away is not the answer. Putting additional miles between you and me is not the answer, Will! We need closeness! I need you more than I have ever needed anyone or anything in my life!"

"I'm not much of a prize, Abigail. I have no dignity, I have no confidence, I don't even know my correct name. I just know that I love you with all my heart, and I always will."

"I love you, too, Will, deeper than you may ever know. As far as you being a prize is concerned, I'm in a much better position to judge that than you are, and you are indeed the prize that I have prayed for all my life."

"Abigail... my wonderful sweet Abigail... My God, I would give anything in the world if I could only kiss you."

"Then come with me to the barn, Will, where we can be together without fear of being seen by anyone. If you have harnesses to mend, I can help you, and we can kiss there to our heart's content."

"It's raining too hard, Abigail, you would get wet walking to the barn. Anyhow, I lied about the harnesses. I mended them all yesterday."

"We can still go to the barn. It's not raining so hard, and we can walk quickly. Besides, I would rather get soaking wet than to wait a moment longer. I need your kisses as badly as you need mine, Will, and perhaps even more! We've waited far too long for this, and I wish not to wait another minute! Take my hand and come with me, darling, quickly!"

A very lovesick William and Abigail started walking to the barn at a normal pace. They walked faster and faster and soon broke into a run. It was as though they had just been liberated to begin a new life together—and in fact, they had. In the barn, the rain continued to pour relentlessly. The metal roof echoed the melody of the rain as the lovers sought shelter inside. Once they were in the barn and alone together, William and Abigail became lost in an immediate flurry of impassioned touching and kissing. Will's fingers gently caressed the delicate features of Abigail's face... her lips... her neck... her hands... Such spontaneous release of emotion was a dream come true for both of them. It was a delight that far surpassed what either of them could have possibly expected, and such tender exchanges between them had been long overdue in coming. It was as though a deluge of emotion had been suddenly released and allowed to run its own course. Between kisses, Abigail looked deeply into William's eyes and spoke lovingly to him.

"I love you Will, I swear by all that's Holy, I do!"

"My God, Abigail... your skin is so soft and smooth... It's like heaven for me to touch you like this. I've spent the last thirteen months of my life praying for this very moment."

"I can see the house through the opening in the doorway. We are completely alone here together. It's just you and me here, Will. Let's pretend that the rest of the world doesn't exist for a while. You and I are finally free to be ourselves here, dear. Our moment has arrived. Please... Follow your heart, Will. Allow yourself to do what your heart tells you to do, and I'll do the same!"

For several vehement minutes the rain continued to pellet the metal roof, and the awestruck lovers who had become lost in the hay inside perceived the relentless pattering as nothing less than music made by the grandest of nature's symphony orchestras. Another forty minutes passed, and the rain began to subside until it represented no more than a gentle drizzle. After submitting themselves to their deepest desires, Will respectfully lowered Abigail's dress and re-buttoned his trousers. They were both still profoundly mesmerized as Abigail assisted him by pulling his suspenders back over his shoulders, then kissing him again. Their first bonding as lovers, although an unfamiliar and unceremonious exercise in desperation, had at least provided them both with a merciful and pacifying measure of appeasement. For William and Abigail, it was but a splendid sampling of the wondrous opportunities that awaited them as lovers. Will assisted Abigail to her feet, respectfully held her undergarment open so that she could step into it, brushed the hay from her dress, and looked deeply into her eyes. As they each pulled pieces of hay from one another's hair, William said, "My dear sweet, Abigail. I'm not sure how this all happened so quickly like it did... but I feel like I just helped myself to something which I was not entitled to, and took something very precious away from you... I'm sorry if..."

"Don't you dare apologize for what we just did! What we just did was something wonderful and beautiful, and I'll entertain no suggestion to the contrary! You've taken nothing from me, my darling, except that which I freely gave. I'd gladly do it again, ten thousand times, if I thought it brought you a single moment of delight."

"My Lord, but I do love you, Abigail, I swear I do."

"And I love you, darling, from the depths of my heart, and I always will. I want you to listen to me for a moment, darling. Let's work on life's little difficulties together, one at a time. With God's blessing, I feel as though there are no difficulties on this earth which you and I cannot rise above, as long as we have each other."

"I feel the same way, Abigail."

"I will come to your bedchamber tonight... after midnight... when I'm sure that Sarah and Elizabeth are both asleep, and..."

"Abigail... I can't ask you to do such a thing. If we were to be discovered..."

"You didn't ask me to come to your bedchamber—I told you

that I was coming. My heart demands that I come to you, and when I do, I'll be discrete. Men are not the only ones who long for companionship and intimacy, Will. You won't understand me when I say this, but I've never had a man in my life, even when I was married. I've never had anyone that I could give my heart to, NEVER! Then one day, God sent you here."

"I know God brought me here, Abigail."

"He sent you to me, Will, I know He did! I've been so desirous of your affections that I have cried myself to sleep, many nights. It's hard for me to express myself without embarrassing us both, but, I have intimate needs too, Will, needs that I can no longer ignore now that I know we're in love. I'm only human, Will, and my physical needs as a woman cannot be appeased as easily or as quickly as yours, darling. I'll come to your bedchamber tonight for my appeasement, alright?"

"Abigail... it was never my intention to humiliate you by making love to you in a barn like this. I know that my behavior here in the barn has not been very gentlemanly or romantic."

"It wasn't your behavior, Will, it was *our* behavior, and it was brought on by waiting too long to appease ourselves. I only have my own stubbornness and stupidity to blame for that. Try to think of our behavior just now as a declaration of love... a very precious declaration of love."

"I do, Abigail, I really do, but I can't help feeling ashamed of myself for having been so open and outspoken with you this morning. You deserve much better than that, and you certainly deserve much better than me."

"How can you possibly say that? You're the man I love, Will. And it's about time that we were open and honest with each other. If you hadn't said something first this morning, I may have never had the courage to say anything. Think about it for a moment... Where would we be right now as lovers if we had never opened our hearts to each other this morning?"

"You're right, Abigail, we would be nowhere, which is precisely where I felt like I was an hour ago."

"See? I thank God for allowing us to finally be honest with each other. Up to now, I've been the world's biggest fool! Now that we each know how the other feels, we've been relieved of the burden of holding our feelings inside. It's not necessary for us to hold any of our feelings back from each other ever again. We've already conquered our first difficulty together... you and me."

"Yes, Abigail, we have indeed."

"All that I'm asking of you now, is that you withhold any hasty decisions about leaving Montgomery Farm for a few days. Wait to see how you feel about things after we have been together tonight."

"I don't need to wait until after tonight, Abigail, I'd rather die than ever leave your side, I swear it."

"What you and I just did here was something very wonderful— something that should only be shared between people who love each other deeply. We can make tonight something even more special, for both of us. Please, let me come to you tonight, won't you? Please, Will?"

"Abigail... My Lord, yes. I would do anything for you. Would you be willing to do something very special for me tonight if I asked you to? It may seem unimportant to you, and it may even seem like the silly request of a lunatic, but I swear to you, it would mean everything in the world to me if you would do it."

"I'll do anything you ask, Will... absolutely anything."

"You will probably laugh at me when I ask you this..."

"I shan't laugh, Will, what is it?"

"Well... would you be willing to let your hair down for me when you come to me tonight?"

"What...? That's your special request? All you want for me to do is let my...?"

Upon hearing Will's humble request to let her hair down, Abigail was taken aback and overcome with emotion again. Will's modest request had caused Abigail's guilt over the months that she had shunned him to come crashing in on her. Her eyes glossed over and welled up with tears again as she answered, "Yes... my God, yes..." She took Will by the hands and went down to her knees to look up at him. On bended knees, she continued to sob pitifully as she looked up and into his eyes.

"What are you doing, Abigail? Why are you on your knees like this, darling? What's the matter? Did I say something wrong when I asked you to let your hair down for me? Please stop crying and talk to me, tell me what I did."

Several moments passed before Abigail could gather her words and speak. With quivering lips and a terribly broken voice, she said, "From the bottom of my heart, Will, I'm asking for your forgiveness for all the times that I have spited you, all the times I have tried to ignore how much I love you, all the times I have talked so cruelly to you. You've given me so very much and always asked for so little in return..."

"Please get up Abigail, it's not necessary for you to..."

"I must finish saying this, Will!"

Will pulled her up to her feet, and said, "Then say it to me standing up, and looking me in the eye. I'll not permit you to kneel shamefully before me like you've committed some great sin against me or something."

"The most important thing in my life is that you forgive me for the way I have treated you. My foolishness had almost driven you away from me, and I would rather die this very moment than for that to happen."

"I forgive you, Abigail. The past is the past, and it's over now. Let's forget about the past and start anew, darling, and just treasure every moment that we're together from here on. Can you and I do that?"

"Yes, Will, we can do that. And when the time is right, I'll tell Elizabeth and Sarah about our love. Please don't worry in the meantime. They'll understand, Will, I know they will. I just need to find the proper time to tell them, and I will."

"I'll leave that to your judgment, darling."

"I'll come to you tonight, dear, and I promise you that my hair will be down."

"Please don't start crying again, darling."

"I can't help myself, Will. I've never been as happy in my entire life as I am right now. I've never known that such happiness even existed, and I want to be with you forever."

"I know nothing of my life before coming to Montgomery Farm, but I do know that I've never been this happy either."

"I would suppose that Sarah and Elizabeth should be finished scrubbing the bedchamber floors anytime now. While it's still raining, would you please sit on the porch with me again? I can fix us another cup of coffee, if you like, and I think I might even know where there is a piece of pie hidden away."

"Abigail, I would enjoy nothing on this earth more than having another cup of coffee with the woman I love."

Fifteen minutes before the stroke of midnight hour that night, on the fifteenth day of July, the oblique dark shadow of a small woman descended the creaky wooden stairway at Montgomery House, tiptoed silently through the parlor and kitchen, and quickly disappeared into the small bedchamber near the back door. A faint metallic click signified the locking of the door. In the darkness there, the woman's only garment, a bed robe, fell silently to the floor as she entered her awaiting lover's bed and became lost in the warmth of his eager embrace. It was as though thirteen long months of thirsting for ultimate fulfillment and an end to their loneliness had been completely obtained and satisfied in one wondrous night of glorious romance. In the ebb of such romantic release, Abigail wept, and whispered softly to William, "I am so truly sorry, Will..."

"For what could you possibly be sorry, darling?"

"I'm so very sorry that I didn't come to you months ago. I desperately wanted to, and I even sensed that you wanted me to, but I didn't. I was too stupid. Please forgive me. I've been a fool for denying my love for you, and I shall never do it again."

"I love you, Abigail, and you've done nothing that requires my forgiveness... Being with you without having my words censored is, well... it's just liberating. I could never describe how wonderful it is to be with you like this, finally..."

"My Lord, Will, I can hardly breathe, my heart is pounding so…"

"Are you ill, Abigail? Do you need fresh air?"

"Mercy no! I just need to savor the wonderment of all that is happening to me for a while longer. Land sakes, Will… I've never known such…"

"Such what?"

"I don't know, Will, I can't find the words…"

"Can't you even try, darling?"

"You're a man, Will. It's nothing that you would understand, just kiss me, darling, and make this night last forever. I don't want to waste a single second of this wonderful night in slumber!"

"Nor do I, darling, but if you don't try to get a little sleep, I'm afraid tomorrow may be a very difficult day for you."

"I don't care about tomorrow, Will. I only care about now, and this magnificent love that you have brought into my life… My Lord, Will, I'm thirty-two years old, and I've only now come to realize what I've missed in my life. I wish I could have met you years ago. I feel like every second of my life before meeting you has been wasted."

"You have two wonderful daughters, a sister who loves you, and you have me, Abigail. Your life to this point has not been wasted. As for mine, I just don't know about any life that I had before meeting you. None of that is very important anyway. We've come together now—and from this day forward we shall have each other."

"Kiss me again, Will… I want a thousand kisses before the sun rises."

○   ○   ○

When the clock in the parlor announced that it was five-thirty in the morning, the two lovers sighed mournfully, knowing that the hour had arrived for them to part. Will kissed Abigail once more, dressed himself, and slipped silently out of the back door to go to the barn. Abigail donned her robe and tiptoed quietly upstairs to her bedchamber to dress herself. Their hearts remained joyfully infused with the wonderment of their newly celebrated love.

An hour later that morning, dawn found Will cheerfully helping Ezra hitch the mules to the wagon while Abigail was busily preparing breakfast in the kitchen. Will's heart was swollen magnificently with the manifest of love. It seemed as though it was the beginning of another normal working day for everyone at Montgomery House—everyone with the exception of Will and Abigail, of course. They had been together in Will's room for five and a half magnificent hours, and their love had left them both in a state of dazed mental detachment. Without being aware of their own demeanors, they were as capricious as school children. Under the curious eyes of Ezra, Will whistled joyfully as they hitched the mules and prepared them for a day in the fields. Ezra had no idea what had come over William that would have caused him to be so unusually cheerful. He only knew that whatever it was had been uplifting and good. Ezra removed his hat, scratched his head, and said, "I don't know what you's been drinking, Mr. Will, but whatever it is, I'd sho like to have me a couple gallons!"

"It's called happiness, Ezra, and it doesn't come in a bottle."

○ ○ ○

In the kitchen, Abigail engaged in girlish singing as she practically danced around the kitchen in pursuit of her chores to put a meal on the breakfast table. Seeming to be none the worse for lack of sleep, Abigail was busily preparing biscuits and gleefully singing aloud as Elizabeth and Sarah walked down the stairway and toward the kitchen together. They paused briefly in the parlor to hear the melodious singing of their mother.

"Oh... Praise the rising of the morning's sun...
Praise all the flowers, praise them one by one...
Praise this new day that God has given...

Praise the blessings that make life worth living...
Oh, praise the mornings, praise them every one...
Look around and see what God has done!"

Sarah and Elizabeth looked dumbfound at each other, then looked back at their mother and cautiously walked into the kitchen, unsure of what had brought on such gleefulness in her demeanor. Sarah was the first to take notice of her mother's peculiar difference in appearance when she stepped up to bestow her customary morning kiss.

"Mother! My Lord! What's come over you this morning?"

"Whatever on earth are you talking about, Sarah? There's nothing come over me that I am aware of."

"Your cheeks are terribly red, and there are little red places all over your neck as well, and you were singing the *'Morning Glory'* song when we walked in! I've never heard you sing in the mornings like this before, and Elizabeth and I have never heard you sing in such a loud and glorious voice before! It's such a delight to hear you sing like this, but... I can't help but worry about you. Are you delirious, Mother? Have you come down with the fever or something?"

"Of course I'm not delirious and I don't have the fever. Is there some reason that I should not sing this morning? Is there some new law that forbids us from singing or being joyous in our own house? Heaven forbid! As for my face and neck, it's nothing, Sarah. I scrubbed my neck and face this morning, and I can only suppose that I scrubbed much too vigorously. I shall be more careful in the future, dear, I promise."

"I don't understand any of this, you're usually very ill-tempered and cross in the mornings, Mother, but look at you now..."

"I am not usually ill-tempered and cross in the mornings!"

"Elizabeth, look at Mother's face!"

"Sarah is right, Mother! Your singing was so loud and glorious that we even heard you upstairs, and your face looks like you have scrubbed it with sand or something. And your neck...

there's little round rashes all over the side of your neck. Does it hurt very much?"

"It doesn't hurt at all. Please just dismiss it from your mind. As I said, I'll be more careful in the future. Elizabeth, please pour the coffee. Sarah, please go to the back porch and summon Will for breakfast. He's at the barn, helping Ezra hitch up the mules."

"Yes, Mother."

When Will arrived at the house, instead of going directly inside, he opened the door and yelled inside to the ladies, "Hurry and come here everyone! Please! You've got to see this to believe it!"

Abigail and her daughters ran quickly to the porch to see what Will was so excited about. Will pointed to the east, where the sun was just beginning to peek through a scattering of grey-white clouds, casting bright orange beams of sunshine majestically toward the earth. It was a splendorous sight to behold, at least for Abigail and William it was. Restraining himself from wanting to hold Abigail in his arms, William said, "Isn't that the most beautiful sunrise you've ever seen?"

Abigail swooned over the sight, and said, "Oh! I believe it really is the most beautiful sunrise I've ever seen! Thank you so much for showing it to us, Will! We would have missed it, had it not been for you!"

Sarah and Elizabeth also agreed that it was a beautiful sunrise, but they failed to appreciate it with the same sense of grandeur as William and Abigail. For Will and Abigail, it was their first sunrise to be viewed together as lovers, and was made all the more magnificent by their newly declared love, yet commensurately devalued in beauty because they could not embrace one another while enjoying the spectacle. Sarah and Elizabeth were the first to go back into the house, and as Will and Abigail turned to walk back inside, Abigail whispered, "I love you so much, Will, that I almost feel faint." Will quietly reciprocated, "I love you, too, and you'll never know how happy I am now." They wanted to say more to each other, much more, but under the restricting circumstances, they couldn't. Abigail was hopeful that the glorious sunrise had diverted her curious daughters' attention from the red rash on her face and neck, and that it would not be a topic of conversation at the breakfast table.

Once Will and Abigail came into the house, the four of them were soon seated at the table. They joined hands and bowed their heads while Will asked a blessing for the food.

"Lord, we thank you for this food, and we thank you for the wonderful hands that prepared it. We thank you for all the enormous blessings that you have brought into our lives. Please forgive us when we fail you, and please continue to bless us, Lord, and we ask that you bless Agatha as well. Amen"

With that, the family immediately began enjoying their breakfast. Still annoyingly curious about her mother's odd condition, and seeking another opinion, Sarah asked, "Will, what do you think of Mother's face and neck this morning?"

"Oh... What do I think? Well, I think it's a very beautiful face and neck this morning. Of course I always think that same thing every morning... uhhh... about all of your lovely faces."

"I'm speaking of the red rashes that Mother has on her cheeks and her neck. Do you think she may be coming down with something contagious, like the fever?"

"Well, uhhh, I don't know. Let's ask her. Can you tell us how you feel this morning, Abigail?"

"I feel magnificently and superlatively splendid! In fact, I haven't felt this good in years, Will. Thank you so much for asking, that was very kind and thoughtful of you."

"Well then, it's probably nothing to be concerned with, Sarah. She sure seems alright to me. In fact, she seems a lot better than alright. Would you pass the preserves please, Elizabeth?"

"I still think it must be something contagious. Your face is starting to turn a little red too, Will! Oh my Lord! There's a few rashes on your neck, too, I swear there is!"

"Abigail, I think I'll take these biscuits with me and eat them down at the barn as I work, if you don't mind."

"I do mind! Don't you dare walk out on me right now! I mean... uhhh... I went to a lot of trouble to prepare this meal, and I would prefer that you stay here and enjoy it with the rest of us. Would you please do that as a special favor for me, Will?"

"Yes, Ma'am, I surely will."

Still inquisitive, and even aggravatingly relentless in her attempts to make sense of the morning's events, Sarah asked, "Why does everyone seem to be acting so odd this morning?"

Defensively, Abigail asserted, "No one is acting odd this morning, Sarah, except for you. Please eat your breakfast, dear, and let us enjoy being together on this beautiful morning that God has given us."

"You're even being extremely pleasant to Will this morning, Mother... if that in itself isn't an oddity, I don't know what is."

"I'm being pleasant to Will this morning simply because he is deserving of our pleasantness... and I have been errantly cold and unsympathetic in the way that I have treated him in the past. I'm merely trying to make amends for my previous shortcomings."

"Any way you look at it, this has been a very strange morning, Mother. Don't you think so, Will?"

"I believe it would be in the best interest of all concerned if I reserved comment, thank you."

Feeling as though it was time to put an end to her daughter's persistent and prying questions, Abigail said, "For the last time, let's all eat our breakfast and just be thankful for this wonderful day that God has given us. I don't want to hear any more of this talk about the rashes on my face or the ones on Will's neck, or the fact that I'm in such a good mood. I'll be more careful the next time I scrub my face. I've learned my lesson, in that respect, and..."

"I know, Mother, it's just that..."

"Sarah! Dismiss it! Now!"

"Alright, Mother, I'll not say another word."

Abigail exercised the only appropriate means of stifling Sarah's inquisitiveness when she had raised her voice. It may have seemed rude, but it was certainly effective. Will and Abigail were both terribly embarrassed, yet nonetheless thankful that Sarah and Elizabeth seemed to remain ignorant as to the true source of Abigail's red face and neck and Will's involuntary blushing. As they continued to eat their breakfast, Abigail and Will looked into one another's eyes lovingly, when Will was suddenly struck with an amazing epiphany. He swallowed a mouthful of food, almost choking in the process, and proclaimed, "Oh, my Lord!"

Abigail quickly looked at Will and asked, "What is it, Will? Is something wrong?"

"I don't know... For some unknown reason, as I was sitting here, I just remembered that I might have been twenty-seven years old when I was first brought here last year. I was carried to an upstairs room here, I think. I swear I can remember men in blue uniforms carrying me up some stairs... soldiers, I think."

"It's true, Will, you were carried upstairs by soldiers when you were first brought here. You weren't moved downstairs to the chambermaid room until the eighth day you were here."

"My birthday is July the seventeenth, and I think I may have been born in Ohio someplace, but I'm not sure. Excuse me, please, I need to step outside for some fresh air for a moment."

Will quickly rushed outside as Elizabeth asked, "Mother, what's happening to Will? Do you think he is going to get his memory back now?"

"I don't know, Elizabeth. You and Sarah stay here and tend to the dishes. I'll go outside and see if he needs anything."

Will sat in the sprawling shade of an ancient elm tree near the back porch, put his face in his hands, and tried to make some sense out of what was happening to him. Abigail sat down beside him and reached over to hold his hand.

"Will, please tell me what's happening to you. I'm worried to death about you."

"I don't know, Abigail. It's nothing to be concerned with, I suppose. I just suddenly remembered that my birthday was on the seventeenth day of July. I was twenty-seven years old when

I could last remember, so I must be twenty-eight or twenty-nine years old now. I can faintly remember being carried up a stairway by some soldiers."

"Do you remember the year in which you were born?"

"Yes, it was1837, I think… I'm almost certain of that."

"That would mean that you are twenty-eight years old now, and will be twenty-nine this Thursday, Will… day after tomorrow. That means there is only three years and four months that separate us in age."

"I could not love you less if fifty years and four months separated us in age."

"Can you remember anything else, dear, anything at all?"

"Ohio came into my mind for some reason, but I'm not sure why. For a moment, I thought I might have been born there, but I don't think that's the case… no, I'm sure that I wasn't born there… I'm not sure where I was born."

"Have you remembered your true name?"

"No, and I don't care to remember my true name. I'm quite happy in being Will, and it even scares me to think that I could have ever been anyone else."

"Perhaps you shouldn't go into the fields today. It's going to be terribly hot again today. I would die if anything happened to you, Will, I swear I would. Maybe you should go back inside and spend the rest of the day in bed."

"No, I'll be alright, I'm sure of it. I've got a lot of work to do today, and I'll be just fine. While we're alone here like this, though, I would like to apologize for the redness I caused to your face and neck last night. I didn't realize that the rough stubble of my beard could do such a thing as that, and I'm deeply sorry."

"I refuse to accept any apologies for anything that happened last night. I wouldn't trade the events of yesterday and last night for anything in the world, Will. I do regret the fact that I made those marks on your neck, I suppose we both got a little carried away with ourselves, but the freedom to share our love with each other has brought me happiness beyond description."

"Me too. I love you, Abigail."

"I do think that I would have died a thousand deaths if you had left me, Will."

"For the first time since being brought here, I feel like my life has been fulfilled. Until the time is right for us to speak with Sarah and Elizabeth—I will exercise more caution in the way I rub my beard against your cheeks."

"And I promise you that I will make every effort to never deprive either of us of the intimacy and closeness that we need. I... I... despise having to tell you this, Will..."

"Despise having to tell me what, Abigail?"

"I would really like to come to you again this Thursday night, on your birthday, but it makes me heartsick to have to tell you that I must refrain from intimacy for the next six days..."

"Why, Abby? Are you ill?"

"It's not an illness, Will, it's a physical curse, common to all women, not just me, and the horrid nature of the curse is that it occurs regularly every month. For the next six days, I must not have intimacy. It breaks my heart to have to tell you this. We've only just begun to experience the wonders of intimacy, and for me to present you with this kind of news so soon... I'm very sorry, Will, I have no control over the matter."

"If you can't control this curse, then why apologize? Six days is not so terribly long to wait. I waited thirteen months for last night, six days will pass quickly."

"I had waited all my life for last night..."

"Would it be an invasion of your privacy if I asked you a question about this curse?"

"I love you, Will, and I shan't keep anything private from you."

"Does this curse preclude us from kissing, or holding each other in our arms?"

"No, of course it doesn't."

"Could you come to me a couple of times during that six days just to be by my side and kiss me?"

"Yes, darling, yes I can."

"Does this curse in any way preclude you from letting your hair down for me?"

"Ha! Nothing on this earth will preclude me from letting my hair down for you, darling, nothing! I will come to you on your birthday, Thursday, if you'll have me."

"That's just day after tomorrow. I can wait that long, and I promise you that I will exercise greater caution in rubbing my beard against your face and neck."

"And I promise that I will try to restrain myself from making marks on your neck. Are you sure that you are up to working in the fields today?"

"I'm certain, thank you. You have a wonderful sparkle in your eyes this morning that I have never seen before, Abigail. It makes you seem even more beautiful to me, and I never thought that would be possible."

"Oh, my! If there truly is any kind of sparkle in my eyes this morning it's because you put it there yesterday. I'm happier at this moment than I have ever been in my life."

"Ezra is at the barn with the mules now. I hate to leave you, Abigail, but I must go and help him. If I had my way about it, I would pick you up in my arms and carry you off to a place where we could spend the entire day together."

"And if I had my way about it... I'd gladly let you, although, I really should get back to the kitchen. I have the oddest sensation that Sarah and Elizabeth are in there right now, talking about my red face and neck."

"I never realized before this morning just how inquisitive Sarah and Elizabeth can be sometimes."

"You don't know the half of it, Will. Sometimes they can even be sneaky and conniving... especially when they put their heads together. But the Lord only knows how I do love them."

"While we're alone like this, I really would like to kiss you before I go to the fields."

"And I would like to kiss you, Will, but I'm afraid we're not alone, dear. Unless I'm mistaken, Sarah and Elizabeth are probably at the kitchen window right now, watching every move we make. We'll catch up on our kisses Thursday night, I promise, alright?"

O   O   O

Abigail's motherly intuition was correct. Her daughters were in fact standing at the kitchen window watching them. To Elizabeth and Sarah, the events of the morning had been quite bizarre when compared to most other mornings there at Montgomery House. Their mother's joyous behavior had seemed extraordinarily jubilant, and in stark contrast to her normal demeanor, and as a result, Elizabeth and Sarah's curiosity had been greatly aroused.

"What are they doing now, Elizabeth?"

"See for yourself, Sarah. They're sitting under the elm tree together."

"I can't see anything, you're hogging the entire window for yourself."

"There, I'll share it with you. Can you see now?"

"Yes, thank you. Oh my goodness! I think they're holding hands, Elizabeth! Yes! Mother is holding Will's hand!"

"Mother may be trying to comfort and console Will. When he left the table he seemed upset about getting some of his memory back. I hope he's not ill or anything."

"If I didn't know better, it almost looks like two lovers sitting there under the elm tree, doesn't it, Elizabeth?"

"Ha! Ha! Our mother and Will, lovers? Impossible!"

"If Will is twenty-eight years old, then Mother is only a very few years older than him, Elizabeth. They're practically the same age, and stranger things than that have happened."

"I refuse to believe it. You're imagining things, Sarah."

"Oh, my Lord, Elizabeth! It's all starting to make sense to me now!"

"What in the world are you talking about, Sarah? What's making sense to you?"

"Mother's red face and neck, that's what!"

"What about it?"

"Will's beard! It all makes sense now! I'll wager that they have been kissing a lot last night, and her face and neck have been scratched by Will's beard!"

"When could Mother have had the time to kiss Will? For heaven's sake, she went to her bedchamber even before you and I went to sleep."

"She could have easily sneaked out after we went to bed."

"Mercy sakes, Sarah! You have the most vividly devious imagination of anyone I have ever known! You should be ashamed of yourself for saying such a thing as that about our mother! I can imagine Aunt Agatha sneaking down to Will's bedchamber for a bunch of kissing if she still lived with us, but Mother—never in a hundred years!"

"I'm not imagining things, Elizabeth! Did you take notice of how congenial and polite Mother was to Will at the breakfast table this morning? She's never talked that pleasantly to him before this morning!"

"Yes, but... she explained that. She was simply making amends for the harsh way she had treated him when he was first brought here. Besides, how else would you explain Mother being so impersonal to Will one day and then suddenly endeared to him so much that she would kiss him the next? Your suspicions are a victim of your sinful imagination, and nothing else, I tell you."

"I don't know... Mother treated him so sweetly this morning that maybe they just fell in love last night or something. But I do know without any doubt that Will and Mother are lovers and they have been kissing each other! I'm absolutely sure of it!"

"And just how would you explain the red places on Will's neck? Mother has no beard! Your outrageous theory is both ridiculous and incredible, and you should be ashamed of yourself!"

"The red places on Will's neck looked more like bite marks of some kind to me. They were moon shaped. I'll wager that Mother..."

"I refuse to believe that our mother would ever bite Will or any other man on the neck! Mother is a saintly woman, and…"

"Back to the dishes! Hurry! Will is walking toward the barn and Mother's walking back toward the house!"

An Honorable Man,
Or A Caller From Hell?

"And we know that we are of God, and the whole world lieth in wickedness." 1 John 5:19

The harvesting of Montgomery Farm's large annual crop of tobacco was proving to be more than the family could manage by themselves that year. To supplement their farm labor, the family often employed passing men to help them during the busiest times of the planting and harvest seasons. A few transient war veterans were soon hired to augment the farm's available manpower because of the growing necessity to keep up with all of the work that was to be done there at Montgomery Farm. Will was managing all aspects of the farm now, and at Abigail's request, he had also taken on the responsibility of all the hiring of men, as he had a certain innate ability to judge the character and qualities of men to a much greater degree than Abigail. Abigail was predisposed to be suspicious and distrustful of all men, other than Will of course. As the family matriarch, she was inclined to be over-protective of the farm, and especially over-protective of the women who resided thereon. Abigail was the family leader of course, but she seemed to be making fewer and fewer decisions regarding the operation of the farm or anything else for that matter. In Abigail's new freedom under Will's protection, she basked in the glory of not having to make decisions, and trusted Will's pronouncements in all farm related matters. It was inevitable that William would eventually emerge from his role as a farm manager into the esteemed position of being the recognized leader of the family household, yet such was being accomplished in slow progression.

As far as the hiring of farm labor was concerned, it was important that they did not employ thieves or men of questionable moral character. A thief could have easily robbed the toolshed of many precious tools during the course of a single night, and such a theft would have required Will to leave his important farm work behind, in order that he might go in pursuit of the crook. Also, men of low moral character or men prone to licentious behavior could have presented a possible threat to the ladies residing there, and Will would most certainly not permit such a thing.

These transient veteran farm workers were allowed to sleep on cots in the barn at night, furnished with a blanket, and they were served two meals a day, which would either be brought to them at the barn, or the meals would be delivered to them where they worked in the fields. These meals usually consisted of biscuits or cornbread, beef or pork, potatoes and beans, and were delivered in shallow metal plates or pans. When Will needed to employ additional farm workmen, he would post a sign in a visible location at the side of the road, which simply stated,

"FARM WORKERS NEEDED"

William also had some ulterior motives that guided him in the selection of the men who would work there on Montgomery Farm. Most all of the men that he selected were between the ages of eighteen and twenty-five. Having very few local suitors to pay proper tribute to Sarah and Elizabeth, Will wanted to expose the sisters to the fact that there were other men, besides himself, who were perhaps more deserving of their immature girlish fixations. He held high hopes that a distracting romance would spark, resulting in the sisters somewhat losing their childish infatuation for him and thus diverting their attentions elsewhere. Without conspiring between themselves, Abigail saw what was happening and believed that when her daughter's interests were drawn away from Will somewhat, the perfect opportunity would present itself for her to tell Sarah and Elizabeth about her and Will's love without hurting their feelings.

Will and Abigail continued to find only brief moments during the course of their busy days in which they could talk privately, and during their secret nighttime coalitions, their talking had to be kept to whispers for fear of being heard outside of Will's bedchamber. Abigail was the love of William's life, and he and Abigail both longed for the day that they could be free to announce their love to the world. Three long weeks of hiding their love from the family and living their romance only in the secrecy of night was terribly restraining.

On a brisk early fall morning, the family was gathered at the breakfast table. Laughter dominated their conversation that morning, and the family was in a particularly jovial mood, despite the numerous labors that awaited them that day. As Will was finishing his breakfast, Abigail walked to the cupboard and returned with a piece of pie for Will.

"Here's a little surprise for you to enjoy with your coffee this morning, Will."

Will was pleasantly surprised upon seeing the pie, and having been lulled into an involuntary sense of candor and openness, he accidently responded, "My Lord! This is a surprise indeed! I don't quite know what to say! I love you, Abby!"

The very instant that the words had left his mouth, Will knew that he had committed a serious blunder in front of Elizabeth and Sarah. He and Abigail were both anxious for the family to know about their love for each other, but the family breakfast table was not the proper time or place to make such a bold announcement. Abigail had intended to talk with Sarah and Elizabeth privately and individually, when the time was right. In a desperate last-minute effort to conceal his spontaneous blunder, Will quickly added, "...and I also love you, Sarah and you, Elizabeth, and I really do love your delicious pecan pies, Abigail!"

Slightly red-faced and embarrassed, Abigail smiled graciously, looked at William, and simply said, "It's not a pecan pie, Will, its cherry... and our family here loves you, too."

Sarah and Elizabeth looked at each other with flushed faces for a moment, as if they were unsure of what they had just heard William say. Sarah and Elizabeth tried not to make their astonishment evident as they looked at each other and silently pondered over what they had just heard William say. *"Did William just call our mother, Abby? Did my ears deceive me, or did I just hear William tell Mother that he loved her? Perhaps he didn't mean it in the romantic sense."* In Sarah's mind, she conjectured, *"I thought so! Mother and Will really are lovers! I knew it all the time!"* And Elizabeth's assessment of Will's statement was, *"Will is such a sweet person. He just told us all that he loved us. Wasn't that precious of him?"* Before leaving for the fields, Will had a brief moment in which he could speak to Abigail alone.

"I am so sorry, Abigail. I love you so much that it just naturally slipped out while I was talking, I wasn't thinking... and I just forgot to safeguard my words for a moment. Please forgive me, dear."

"Don't apologize. It just happened, and I can't tell you how much I adored hearing you say it aloud. I almost wish that I had gone ahead and announced our love at the breakfast table, but there will come a better time, and for our sake, I think it should come sooner than later."

"Do you think I let the cat out of the bag?"

"I think Sarah and Elizabeth are starting to have their suspicions, especially Sarah. She's the sneakiest one of the two. Don't worry, Will, I'll tell them soon enough."

"In the meantime, perhaps it would help matters some if you found some reason to scold me in front of them for something at suppertime this evening. Perhaps that would relieve them of their suspicions."

"No! It's hard enough for me to keep myself from proclaiming my love for you aloud! I shall never pretend to scold you! I could not force myself to do that."

Inspired by a new sense of urgency, William began devoting his efforts toward gently encouraging Sarah and Elizabeth to direct a portion of their romantic interests elsewhere. Try as he did to draw the sister's attention to some of the young farm workmen, his efforts proved to be in vain... that is, until the arrival of a certain young war veteran from Maryland by the name of Timothy O'Donnell.

Timothy O'Donnell was a handsome young man of twenty-two years, who was journeying back to his home state of Maryland after serving with the North Carolina Infantry of the Confederacy. He was obviously a northern citizen who apparently had southern sympathies and convictions, and would have been called a *"Copperhead"* by his northern neighbors. He also had relatives living in Raleigh and Charleston who had been deeply embedded in the hierarchy of the confederacy. He needed funds to finance his return to his home in Baltimore, and happened upon Montgomery Farm at just the right time. Just like many of the workmen there, O'Donnell had been originally drawn to Montgomery Farm by the sign that William had posted on the road. Working at the farm for two or three weeks would offer an expedient way for him to earn enough money for meals as he traveled home.

Sarah and Elizabeth both seemed to be enamored with the handsome young man, and Will took every available opportunity to see that they were placed in situations where they could see more of each other. O'Donnell was well spoken, and in the young eyes of Elizabeth and Sarah, he had the charm of a debonair swashbuckling cavalier. When water needed to be carried to the workmen, Will would cunningly summon either Elizabeth or Sarah to attend to the chore. When the meals were carried to the workmen in the fields, Will would always see to it that Sarah and Elizabeth brought the meals. Conversations between

O'Donnell and the ladies increased, and it soon became evident that something more than just a subtle interest was developing between them. Will took clandestine notice of the fact that the sisters were spending more and more time in the presence of young Timothy, and less time swooning over him. This revelation came as a great relief to Will, relieving him of the anxieties of having his love for the sister's mother exposed and brought to the forefront.

Will was proud of Abigail in every respect. He was proud of the way she had raised her daughters during her five years without the support of a husband. He was proud of the moral values and Christian principles that she had instilled in her daughters, and he was proud of the strength and determination that Abby had displayed in keeping Montgomery Farm alive and productive during such a turbulent and terrible war. William was also very proud of the love that he had for Abigail, and eager for the day to arrive when he could proclaim his sentiments to the world. Concealing their mutual love had become an ever-increasing burden to both of them.

To encourage the progression of a potential romance between Abigail's daughters and Timothy O'Donnell, Will invited Timothy to join them for dinner on a Tuesday evening. Immediately after O'Donnell had come to the house for dinner, Will was able to back away somewhat and allow nature to discover and run its own course. There had been somewhat of a rivalry between Elizabeth and Sarah for the young man's attention for the first two or three days, but after the night that O'Donnell had come to dinner, Elizabeth had suddenly and unexpectedly relented to Sarah's more energetic exuberance, and took a more passive stance toward her sister's overwhelming attraction to young Timothy. Elizabeth's disenchantment with young O'Donnell had arisen so abruptly, that William and Abigail did not fail to take notice, yet they refrained from making inquiry as to why Elizabeth had suddenly turned such a cold shoulder to O'Donnell.

Abigail was keenly aware of Will's surreptitious exploits in playing cupid, yet the two had never discussed the issue nor conspired between themselves in any way. Abigail knew that Will's intentions were honorable, intending only to find suitable candidates as suitors for her daughters, and even though she remained silent, she was in full agreement. Abigail's surreptitious romantic visits to be with Will were now regularly performed on an *every-other-night* basis, and on these nights, the couple was afraid to have discussion any louder than faint whispers for fear of being heard and discovered together by another family member. In fact, there were many occasions in which they found themselves very frustrated because of the limited amount of time in which they could enjoy meaningful private conversation together in a normal tone of voice. It was one of many such annoyances that would vanish from their lives once their love was announced.

In the tobacco drying barn, across the field behind the house, Will was busy hanging racks of tobacco leaves to cure in the overhanging rafters when Abigail walked in to assist him. As Will was perched high on a ladder, Abigail and Ezra would hand him the racks of tobacco leaves from the wagon. When Ezra would leave with the empty wagon, it would be the first opportunity in which Abigail and William would have an ample opportunity to discuss Sarah's newfound enchantment with young Timothy O'Donnell. Once Ezra had taken the empty wagon back to the fields to be reloaded by the workmen, Will looked outside long enough to make sure that he and Abby were alone, and asked, "Tell me, Abigail, what do you think about Sarah's infatuation with this Timothy O'Donnell fellow?"

"I'm delighted for her. She's absolutely stricken by him, and he seems like he's a fine young man to me. He's well-spoken and polite, and charmingly handsome. Sarah is almost eighteen years old now, and I think she is quite capable of choosing the man that she someday hopes to marry without any guidance or interference from me. How about you, Will, what do you think about their blossoming relationship, after all, you're the one who made it all possible?"

"Me? I didn't do very much. I just saw to it that they would meet, and sort of arranged for them to have opportunities to see and talk to each other now and then, that's all. Nature began taking its own course after that without any need for my encouragement."

"Nature has a marvelous way of taking its own course sometimes, doesn't it, dear?"

"Maybe... I suppose... I don't know..."

"You seem worried, Will, what's wrong?"

"I love Sarah as if she was my own daughter, Abby, and I'm not so sure that allowing nature to take its own course with them is such a good idea. It certainly helped Sarah come to realize that there was at least one man in the world besides me, and I feel greatly relieved because of that, but..."

"But what?"

"I hope she's wise enough not to get herself into any kind of trouble with him. We have only known O'Donnell for less than a month, and he seems like an honorable sort, but..."

"But what?"

"I've seen the way they are looking at each other nowadays when she brings water to the fields, and... I'm praying that a marriage proposal comes along before she ends up... you know..."

"Before she ends up getting herself pregnant?"

"Yes, exactly. That possibility scares me to death, Abby."

"Sarah hasn't confided in me about any intentions of having intimacy with O'Donnell, and I'm absolutely certain that they've not gone that far in their relationship yet."

"And you honestly think Sarah would confide in you if she was intent on having intimacy with O'Donnell?"

"I'm certain that she would confide in me before she did anything like that. I've always encouraged my daughters to be open and honest with me, even in regards to personal issues like that, and I've raised them to save themselves for marriage."

"I suppose that I just have a suspicious nature, Abigail. When I fell in love with you, I discovered that the urge to do that sort of thing can be so powerful that nothing else seems to matter."

"When could they possibly have had the opportunity for intimacy, Will? You've been supervising Timothy in the fields, and I've been keeping a close eye on Sarah most of the time."

"Most of the time? Something like that could take place in a very few minutes under the right conditions. That morning that you and I first went to the big barn together, we were only in there for about thirty or forty minutes, and look what we were able to accomplish in that short amount of time, Abby. You're here with me now... and do you know for sure where Sarah is at this very moment?"

"Of course I do, she's down in the west field, carrying water to the workmen."

"O'Donnell is in the west field too. How do we know they haven't sneaked off into the woods together?"

"Because I've raised Sarah better than to do such a thing, Will, and you're making a mountain out of a mole hill, darling."

"I can't help worrying, Abby. I wouldn't worry if I didn't love her."

"Will! You called me Abby, again! I've noticed that you've been calling me Abby a lot the last few days. You've even called me Abby in front of Sarah and Elizabeth a time or two."

"I'm sorry, Abigail. All that I'm saying is that I do know how powerful those urges can be, and I can't help but recall the old saying that where there is a will, there is a way..."

"Put your fears to rest, Will. Timothy O'Donnell came to the house and proposed to Sarah this morning at the well, and they've asked us for our blessing to be married."

"Really!?"

"Yes, really. And like I said, they've asked for our blessing."

"Our blessing? They've asked for my blessing as well as yours?"

"Yes, of course."

"But why in the world would they ask me for my blessing? I'm not Sarah's father."

"Whether or not you realize it, you're the closest thing to a father that Sarah has ever had. Everyone here at Montgomery Farm considers you the head of our household now. Sarah still loves you, Will, only now she loves Timothy in a much different way, thank the Lord. She now sees you as being more of the father that she never had, and she wants your blessing to get married."

"If that's what she wants, of course she can have my blessing. I'm extremely touched, and very proud that I would be considered the man of the house... it kinda brings a special kind of warmth to me..."

"The reason that I'm telling you all of this, is because Timothy O'Donnell will be coming to the porch this evening after supper to ask you for Sarah's hand in marriage. I wanted to forewarn you, so you could be prepared. Will? What's the matter?"

"You'll probably think that I've lost my mind, but this isn't going to be easy for me, Abby... giving Sarah away like that. It sort of puts a lump in my throat just to think about it. I've never had such an uneasy feeling as this before."

"You really do love her like a daughter, don't you, Will?"

"I love them both like daughters, Abby."

"And they both love you as well. They practically worship the ground you walk on. I've never talked with you about this, but their father was a cruel and heartless man, incapable of loving them as daughters. Yours is the first fatherly love they have ever known."

"And how about Elizabeth? How does she see me now?"

"As I said, she loves you dearly, Will, but I think she has some idea now that you and I are in love, and respects that, as I knew she would."

"How could she possibly know about our love?"

"I'm not sure. Perhaps we gave ourselves away at the breakfast table the other morning, when you said, *I love you, Abby.* I think it must be written on our faces or something. I'm sure that it's reflected in the way that I talk to you nowadays, and I can't help that. I feel like it's time for me to talk to her this evening and clarify things between her and I. I think the time has finally arrived that I should tell her and Sarah both about you and me, if it would be alright with you."

"I just don't want to cause anyone any unnecessary heartache, Abby. And I especially don't want to be the cause of any dissention between you and Elizabeth. I love you all too much to let anything like that happen. Not too many weeks ago I was prepared to leave Montgomery Farm, so that I wouldn't cause any unnecessary heartache between you and your daughters."

"My heartaches would have only just begun if you had left. I know now that such a thing would kill me, and I thank God every day that you didn't leave."

"Me too, Abby. You're Elizabeth's mother, and if you think the time is right to talk to her, then fine, you certainly have my approval to do so."

"I will talk to both of them tonight. I'm weary of hiding our love from the family. Sooner or later we're bound to be discovered anyway, and I would much rather announce our love than have it discovered accidently."

"I live for those precious times that we get to spend together. As much as I treasure them, they always seem to end too quickly, though."

"I agree, Will. I cherish sleeping in your arms like I do, but I never seem to be fully relaxed. I'm always aware of the time so that I won't oversleep and be there when Sarah and Elizabeth come downstairs in the morning. I want to go ahead and announce our love, so that you can move upstairs with me, where you belong, and we can sleep as late in the mornings as we wish."

"I agree wholeheartedly. And along that same line of thinking... Abby, do you think that... I mean... what with Sarah planning to get married now and all... Have you ever given any kind of consideration to..."

"To what, Will?"

"What I'm trying to say is, do you think there might come a day that it would be possible for... uhhh... you and me to maybe be married?"

"Why, Will! That sounded a lot like some sort of awkward attempt at making a marriage proposal. Did I misunderstand you?"

"I can't hide the way I feel about you, Abby. Even though I have nothing of any value to offer you, I love you, and I know that I always will. I want to spend every moment of the rest of my life with you, and I was just wondering if, I mean..."

"Before you say any more, Will, allow me to say that I have every intention of marrying you... I always have. You and I have already declared our love before the eyes of God, declaring our love before the eyes of man is merely a formality, and yes, Will... I will gladly marry you."

"Could I steal a kiss or two while we're alone like this, Abby?"

"Wait a moment, I haven't finished what I was saying."

"I'm sorry, Abby."

"I would like to address this idiotic impression you have that you don't have anything of value to offer me."

"But I don't have anything, Abby."

"You've already given me your heart, Will. What greater gift... what greater acknowledgment of love, could any man alive ever give to a woman? Any woman who demanded more of a man than his heart would not be worthy of his love."

"Lord have mercy, but I do love to hear you talk sweet to me like that. It makes my knees weak. May I kiss you now, Abby?"

"Yes... please do. I will always treasure your kisses, and when we are married, I want you to promise me that you'll give me thousands of them."

"When we're married, I'll give you tens of thousands of them... I promise."

By mutual agreement, Abby and Will decided that it would be advisable if they would forego any further romantic midnight visits until such time as they were married. Abby thought it would be too risky to continue, lest their intimate encounters be discovered by her overly inquisitive daughters. It was nearly impossible to ascend or descend the wooden staircase without alerting everyone in the house who was not asleep at the time. Because of her small stature, Abby made much less noise on the stairway than anyone else, but they still thought it was best that they practice restraint until after they were married. Will understood, and was in perfect agreement. Besides, if things went according to their plans, they could hopefully be wed within a month.

O   O   O

Early on the evening that Will had proposed, Abby knocked on Elizabeth's bedchamber door after dinner and quietly asked, "Elizabeth, may I come in, dear?"

"Yes, Mother, please do."

"Elizabeth, would it be alright with you if we talked for a few minutes, just you and I?"

"Of course it's alright, is something wrong, Mother?"

"No, darling, there's nothing in the world wrong. I would just like to talk to you for a little while. How do you feel about the fact that your little sister will soon be a married woman?"

"I'm extremely happy for her, Mother. Timothy O'Donnell seems like he'll make a suitable husband for Sarah, I suppose, and I pray that they will have a long and happy life together."

"I couldn't help but notice that you backed away from Timothy O'Donnell, and allowed your sister to pursue her own relationship with him. That was very gallant and generous of you."

"I wasn't really being gallant or generous, Mother. I backed away from O'Donnell because I saw him in a different light than Sarah, that's all."

"Oh? What do you mean?"

"I don't know exactly, I can't explain it. I'll admit, I was somewhat infatuated with him at first, but that night he had dinner with us..."

"What about it?"

"I don't know, Mother. I looked into his eyes and I just didn't like what I saw. He doesn't look people in the eye when he speaks to them, and I was uncomfortable in his presence. The look that I saw in his eyes seemed to be repugnant and even sinister to me. Nevertheless, I'm just glad that Sarah finds some appealing qualities in him and she seems to be very happy now."

"I have every confidence that Sarah will be happy—it's you that I am asking about, Elizabeth. Are you happy?"

"Of course I am. As the eldest daughter, I'm a little disappointed that Sarah should marry before me, yes, but not so disappointed that I would let it detract from my being happy for her. Besides, I'm in no hurry to marry."

"I love you, Elizabeth. Your time will come soon enough, I promise you. Do you have any suitors that I don't know about?"

"Joseph Greer, maybe. He's been showing a lot of interest in me these last few weeks. And George Curtis has been looking in my direction at church a lot."

"Do either of them appeal to you?"

"Yes, they do, Mother. I like both of them a lot."

"Romantically?"

"Perhaps... but it's much too early to tell about such a thing."

"Are there any other possible suitors?"

"Yes... one. Reverend Stephens' son, Michael, has invited me to come to their home for a special dinner and Bible reading. He is the object of most of my attention at present."

"And Will?"

"I love Will deeply Mother, as we all do, but Will's romantic interests lie elsewhere, and as I eluded to, my romantic interests seem to be drawing me in the direction of Michael Stephens."

"Are your interests in him becoming serious?"

"It's way too early for me to become serious, Mother, as I said, I'm in no hurry to marry. As far as Will's romantic interests are concerned, is there anything that you would like to tell me, Mother? I sense that you are about to burst if you don't."

"Oh my Lord, Elizabeth! You already know, don't you?!"

"I think so, but I would much rather hear it in your own sweet words, without my having to guess."

"Elizabeth, I must be truthful with you. I haven't let it show, and I've never really mentioned this to anyone before, but the truth of the matter is, I've been lonely for the companionship of a good man for a long time... forever it seems."

"I'm sorry, Mother. I know how hard it must have been for you to raise two daughters, without the support of a man. Father was so much of an abusive scoundrel, that Sarah and I understood your reasons for wanting nothing to do with him."

"You understood?"

"Of course we did. He betrayed you every chance he got, and I was always very understanding of what he put you through. He touched me inappropriately when I was a child, and you came to my rescue and chased him away with a gun. I remember you gathering Sarah and I in your arms and taking us into your bedchamber where you could protect us. I never blamed you for not loving Father. I hate to talk about the dead, but I didn't like him very much either. God help me, but I even disliked my own father."

"My dear God, Elizabeth, I wasn't aware that you were old enough to remember what he attempted to do to you that day. I'm truly sorry that you have been burdened with such horrid memories."

"My memories are wonderful. My memories are of a mother who made sacrifices for her daughters... a mother who dedicated her life to her children, and a mother who gave every ounce of her love to her daughters. I love you, Mother, and I could never repay all that I owe you. But the time is well past due for you to share your love with someone else, and I can think of no one more deserving than Will."

Elizabeth's touching oration was all it took to launch Abby into a sobbing stupor of tears. They hugged and wept together until Abby finally regained a portion of her composure and asked,

"How did you know that Will and I are in love? For almost four weeks now, we've made every effort to keep our love hidden."

"My darling sister, Sarah, planted the seed in my mind with her suspicious nature. I didn't believe it at first—I don't know why, I was just blind I suppose. But then, I started to notice little things, and of course all the while Sarah was emphatic that you and Will were lovers."

"It's true, Elizabeth, Will and I love each other with every ounce of our hearts and souls."

"I didn't understand at first. You never seemed to display any sort of affection toward him until the last few weeks. At times a few months ago, you've even been downright rude to him, and I just don't understand how you can be in love with someone and treat them in such a manner."

"It's all because I've been a stupid fool. I know that I've been rude to him in the past, and I deeply regret it. It's a scar on my heart that I'll probably carry to my grave. I've kept my true feelings well hidden, even from Will. We only confided in each other for the first time about three and a half weeks ago. I cannot hide the way I feel about him any longer, Elizabeth, I just can't."

"You really do love him, don't you?"

"Yes, Elizabeth, I do. I love him with all my heart. I never thought it would be possible for me to love any man as much as I love Will."

"Then why make attempts to keep it hidden away? Why not announce it to the world, and rejoice?"

"That's exactly what we intend to do, but I wanted to tell you and Sarah first, in private."

"I'm so happy for you and Will that I could scream!"

"Tell me Elizabeth, what made Sarah so cock-sure that Will and I are in love? As I said, we've made every effort to keep our love hidden until now."

"Oh, Mother, if what Sarah told me is true, it's too embarrassing for me to talk about. Perhaps you'd better ask Sarah."

"Please tell me, Elizabeth, I'm asking you, dear."

"Mother, it's so hard for me…"

"Please?"

"It has something to do with Sarah going into the kitchen in the middle of the night about two weeks ago to get a drink of water. She heard noises coming from Will's room and went to his door to listen. Sarah would kill me if she knew that I was telling you this, Mother!"

"Oh, my Lord!

"Sarah sneaked back upstairs and peeked into your bedchamber and found your bed empty. When she told me the next morning, I thought she was lying to me, and I refused to believe her, but now…"

"I'm so ashamed of myself, Elizabeth!"

"Mother, if your love for Will is as powerful as you say it is, then please don't be ashamed. Love is nothing to be ashamed of, I can assure you of that."

"I'm not ashamed of my love for Will, I'm ashamed that I haven't set a better example for my daughters, that's all. I just don't want you to think poorly of me, Elizabeth."

"Knowing that you and Will love each other, how could I possibly think poorly of you? Perhaps there will come a day when I will experience such a powerful force in my own life. Anyhow, like I said, I am extremely happy for you and Will. What are your plans, can you share them with me?"

"He proposed to me and asked me to marry him this morning."

"And… what did you say?"

"I told him that I would be proud to marry him, but I wanted to talk to my special friend first."

"Oh? I wasn't aware that you had a special friend, who might that be?"

"You, Elizabeth."

"Oh, Mother… may I hug you?"

Abigail and Elizabeth hugged and kissed each other. They wept in joy for a moment or two, until Elizabeth dried her eyes and asked, "When will you and Will be married?"

"We haven't discussed a particular date yet, but I'm hopeful that it will occur very soon. I would marry him ten seconds from now if I thought it possible."

"Will you tell me as soon as you know the date?"

"Besides Will and I, you will be the first to know, I promise you."

"Now that your love for Will is finally out in the open, may I ask you one other question, Mother?"

"Yes, darling. You may ask me anything your heart desires."

"About three or four weeks ago… the morning that your face and neck were all red, was that caused by Will's beard?"

"Oh, my Lord, I'm blushing again."

"Well, was it? Be truthful with me, Mother."

"Yes, but how did you know?"

"Sarah said that it was probably caused by you and him kissing. She also said that you must have bitten Will on his neck several times, did you, Mother?"

"Elizabeth please, darling, allow me just a little privacy. Will and I love each other, can we not leave it at that?"

"Yes Mother, of course we can. Besides, by your blushing, you have already answered my question anyway. I cannot believe that Sarah is a year and a half younger than me, and yet she seems to know so much more about everything than I do."

"Sarah doesn't know nearly as much about everything as she thinks she does, and no one on this earth is sweeter than you, Elizabeth, and don't you ever forget that."

"Thank you, Mother, and God bless you."

"Speaking of Sarah, I think I'll walk down the hall and have a little talk with your sister now."

"Oh! Mother please don't mention that I said anything about the noises she heard coming from Will's room that night, Please! I promised her that I wouldn't say anything… but you somehow managed to pry it out of me."

"I won't say a thing, darling. It will be our little secret. I just want to tell her about mine and Will's intention to marry. I suppose that what I'd really like to do is to bend her sneaky little behind over my knee and spank the living daylights out of her, but she's much too mature and much too sweet for anything like that."

○ ○ ○

Abby did talk to Sarah afterwards, and she never mentioned a word of what Elizabeth had told her. Sarah was equally as excited for her mother, but not nearly as surprised to hear the news as Elizabeth had been. Sarah was indeed happy for Abby and Will, but her young mind was so preoccupied with thoughts of Timothy O'Donnell and their upcoming marriage that it was impossible for her to fully comprehend anything else.

At the breakfast table the next morning, discussion between the womenfolk and Will was immensely light-hearted and pleasant, but became seriously emotional long enough for Will to say a few words.

"Your mother has told me that she has announced our intentions to marry, and I would like to add a few words of my own, if you would permit me to do such a thing."

"Sure, Will..."

"I love your mother more than I could ever express with feeble words alone. As Abby's daughters, I want you both to know that I love you as if you were my own flesh and blood, and I always will. Since I was first brought here as a wounded soldier, I have had but one painful regret that I've had to live with, and that was in not having the freedom to speak from the depths of my heart when expressing how I feel about the people whom I love most in this world. Your mother and I have both been tormented by our reluctance to be truthful when it comes to expressing our love. We have both learned an important lesson in life, and have agreed to establish a new rule here at Montgomery House—We will never again hesitate to be truthful in expressing our love to each other. I love each of you... dearly."

All tensions and stress had been extricated from the family.

Sarah and Elizabeth discussed the arrangements for Sarah's upcoming wedding, and Abby and Will changed their usual seating arrangement at the table so that they could now sit side by side instead of across from one another. Even though Will treasured being able to sit beside Abby, the arrangement lasted but a few moments when they both came to realize that they could not look into one another's eyes when sitting side-by-side. Will wasted but little time moving back to his former place at the table. Will had just taken a sip of coffee when he looked as if he had just seen a ghost. Abby took immediate notice and asked, "Will? Is everything alright, Will?"

"Yes... of course, everything is wonderful. I just had a strange, disturbing thought cross my mind, though, that's all."

"Have you regained more of your memory, dear?"

"No, it's nothing like that, Abby."

"Can you share it with us, dear?"

"Yes... It just occurred to me that if we are to be married... I have no surname to give you. How can we possibly be married if I have no surname to give you?"

Elizabeth asked, "Are you comfortable with your first name, Will?"

"Yes, of course I am, Elizabeth... it's the only name that I know."

"Mother gave you that name, why couldn't she simply give you a surname as well?"

"No!" Sarah interjected. "Wives don't get to choose their husband's surname. Something like that would be unlucky. Elizabeth and I should invent a surname for Will. Would that be alright with you, Will?"

"Well, I don't know, I suppose so, if it's alright with your mother. Abby, what do you think?"

"I'm in agreement, as long as it's not something that is terribly difficult for people to spell or pronounce."

Elizabeth spoke up to suggest, "Then how about if Sarah and I start naming surnames, and when we get to one that you both like, that will be that? Are you in agreement, Will?"

232

"Well, yes, Elizabeth, I suppose so..."

"Mother?"

"This seems awfully strange and unnatural that we should be doing something like this, but I suppose I am in agreement. It certainly seems to be an appropriate remedy to our dilemma."

"Good. Sarah, you go first."

"Alright, how about something simple, like Smith?"

"Smith and Jones are much too common," Abby said.

For the next fifteen or twenty minutes Sarah and Elizabeth tossed out one surname after another, yet to Abby and Will, none seemed appealing or befitting. It seemed as though their efforts would be in vain, until finally...

"Samuels?"

"Wait a minute. What about it, Abby? Does '*Samuels*' sound like a good name to you?"

"I think it sounds too much like a Hebrew name to me. I would prefer something else."

"Alright then, how about Collins?"

"That's not bad. What do you think, Abby?"

"William Collins... Abigail Collins... Mr. and Mrs. Collins... hmmm..."

"Well, what do you say, Abby?"

"I like it. I like it a lot. The name has a nice sound to it and I think it will work just fine."

Elizabeth looked puzzled for a moment, and then asked, "I can't help but wonder if it's legal under the law for us to be doing something like this?"

Will swallowed a sip of coffee and quickly spoke up, saying, "It can be made to be perfectly legal at any time we choose, simply by petitioning the court for a writ of '*legalis nomen*,' under Article 107 of the uniform code of law of the Commonwealth of Virginia. In paragraph three, I believe, the law states that such a declaration is official and binding, not from the date of filing, but from the actual date of said declaration. That document can be executed at any time, even after we're married. Once the writ is approved by the magistrate and registered by the court, it becomes official and is legally binding, hence and forever more. It can all be accomplished in a matter of an hour or less, and only requires two witnesses, one of which must be an officer of the court. It's really quite simple."

The entire family sat there in wonderment over Will's amazing comments. Abby gathered her senses, and asked, "Have you spoken with an attorney and looked into this already, Will?"

"Why no, Abby, I haven't..."

"Then how is it that you seem to be able to quote the letter of the law so adroitly? And how did you come to learn those Latin words?"

"Uhhh... I haven't the faintest idea, Abby... I truly don't know. It's something that I just sort of know, for some reason."

Abby, still amazed and somewhat puzzled about Will's spontaneous quoting of the law, shrugged it off and said, "Perhaps we can speak to Lawrence Brumfield, our family's attorney, next time we see him. He will give us the proper legal direction, that is, if it's alright with you, darling."

"Of course it's alright."

The anonymous young wounded soldier, who had been carried to Montgomery Farm nearly fifteen months earlier, finally had a full name, even though it was absent of a middle name, and had been conceived almost as an amusement or a parlor game, at the family's breakfast table. Such an arbitrary selection of a name would have seemed a trivial and inconsequential matter to most people, but to William Collins it was much more than just a frivolous and arbitrary exercise in vanity. It was a serious bestowment of permanent identity, and such an identity had been long overdue. As the group finished their coffee and sat in idle chatter, Ezra came bursting in through the back door, catching his breath and calling out to Will.

"Mister Will! Mister Will! Come quick... there's a dead man in the barn!"

"A dead man?! What happened, Ezra?"

"I don't know, Mr. Will, but there's plenty of blood!"

"Will hurried to get his boots on, and said, "Abby, please fetch the pistol for me... Hurry!"

Abby ran into the parlor to get the pistol as Sarah sprang to her feet and shouted at Ezra, "Oh, my God! It's not Timothy, is it?!"

"His face is in the hay, Miss Sarah, I don't know who it is, but whoever it is, he's wearing Confederate trousers."

Sarah quickly walked toward the door, saying, "I must go to him immediately!"

Will grabbed her by both arms and said, "No! Stay here, Sarah! I'll let you know something just as soon as I know. Stay here with your mother where it's safe."

"I've got to go to him, Will, I swear I do!"

"**I said, no**! Not until I satisfy myself that it's safe down there! I apologize for raising my voice at you, Sarah, but your safety is the most important thing to me right now! Stay here with your mother and sister where it's safe! Abby, will you and Elizabeth watch over Sarah? I'll send word back just as soon as I know what's going on."

"Yes, Will... Be careful!"

As Abby and Elizabeth tried to restrain and console Sarah, Will ran to the barn with Ezra and they were soon standing over the body of one of the young farm workers who had recently come there looking for work. Will took a deep breath and turned the young man's body over to reveal his face. Will immediately recognized the young man's body as being that of Robert Marshall, and not Timothy O'Donnell.

"Ezra, run back up to the house and tell Sarah that the dead man is not Timothy."

"Yes Sir, Mr. Will."

While Ezra was gone, Will searched around the inside of the barn and loft to assure himself that there were no assailants hiding there about. Then, he inspected the body of the young dead man and determined that the man had been stabbed one time in the left center of his upper chest. Death must have been almost instantaneous. The assassin had either been very lucky with the thrust of his knife, or he knew exactly where the best location was to kill a man quickly. Will searched around the barn, looking for clues as to how this tragedy could have happened, but found nothing definitive. He searched through the dead man's pockets, but they were all empty. Ezra soon returned from the house, and Will quizzed him for information, asking, "Where are the other workmen, Ezra?"

"They left here before daylight to pull tobacco down by the creek in the west bottom... right where you told me to send 'em this morning."

"Don't tell anybody what's going on up here, but I want you to take a horse and ride down there. I want you to bring Timothy O'Donnell back up here so I can talk to him. Make haste, Ezra!"

"Yes Sir, Mr. Will."

Will was puzzled as to why anyone would want to kill the young man, Robert Marshall. He had only known the young man for a very few days, but his impression had been that the man was of a gentle nature, and not one who was prone to violence. But war has a way of changing people, and creating desperate men, and during such a conflict, it was possible for anyone to become violent. He searched through the man's pockets again, but again found nothing, and in Will's mind, the mystery of the man's death only deepened. Hearing the rapid approach of a horse in front of the barn, he stepped outside to find that Ezra and Timothy O'Donnell had just arrived from the distant tobacco field. Will brought Timothy into the barn, and asked, "Timothy, do you know anything about this dead man here?"

"Damn! He really is dead, isn't he? I just know that he told us that his name is Robert Marshall. He was alive an hour and a half ago when me and the others went down to the field to pull tobacco."

"Do you know why anyone would want to kill him?"

"No. He never caused anybody any trouble that I know of."

"Do you know why he didn't go to the field with everyone else this morning?"

"I thought they were coming along right behind us."

"They?"

"That new fellow, Shelton Lewis was with him here in the barn when the rest of us walked to the field to work. I thought they were coming along right behind us, but neither one of them ever showed up down in the field. I suppose now I know why."

"Ezra, ride on into Blanchard and fetch the sheriff, please. Tell him what's happened here."

"Yes Sir, Mr. Will."

"Timothy, before the sheriff gets here, is there anything else you can tell me about Robert Marshall? Did he own anything of any value?"

"He's got a bone-handled pocket knife and a fancy pocket watch that his father gave him. The watch is gold, and has got some kind of jewels in it that Robert said was valuable. His father told him to sell it if he ever needed the money to get home, but Robert said that he would never part with the watch. He said it meant too much to him because his father gave it to him. That's why he was working here, to get the money to travel back to his home. That's why most of us are working here."

"Well, there's no watch or pocket knife in any of his pockets now. What about Shelton Lewis? What do you know about him?"

"Not very much, he just hired on yesterday. He is a dislikeable sort of fellow, and I've been told that he likes to drink and gamble a lot, but that's about all that I know."

"I want you to go back to the field to work, but first I want you to go up to the house and see Sarah. She's been worried sick about you, and if you hurry, she's most likely got a bunch of kisses waiting for you."

"Yes Sir, Mister Will. But before I go, you should know that Shelton Lewis has a pistol. I saw it in his pocket when he came here looking for work yesterday. I can only assume that he didn't use it to kill Robert this morning because he didn't want to make any noise here at the barn. I'm sorry this happened. If you need me for anything I'll be down in the creek bottom with the rest of the men after I see Sarah."

"How about taking charge of the men until Ezra gets back with the sheriff?"

"Yes Sir, I'll be glad to."

"And whatever you do, don't mention to Sarah or Abby that Shelton has a gun. I don't want them to worry about such a thing when I leave here to go after the sorry scoundrel."

"No, Sir, I won't say a thing."

Will walked over to the road to look for tracks, and it didn't take long for him to discover a set of fresh footprints heading north on the muddy road. It had just rained the evening before, and the tracks were quite evident. The stride length of the tracks were spaced widely apart, which was an indication that the fleeing man was running away on foot. Once he had ascertained the direction of the tracks William walked back to the house where Abby was waiting for him on the porch.

"Abby, I've sent Ezra to fetch the sheriff. When he gets here, I feel certain that the sheriff will want me to go with him to identify the man who did this. Would you mind throwing a couple of biscuits and a jar of water into a bag for me?"

"I'd be happy to, but do you really think it's going to be necessary for you to go along with the sheriff?"

"A man's been murdered here, Abby. It's my duty to do what I can to help the sheriff apprehend this guy. My personal involvement is something that would be expected among our workmen. I could never let them see me backing away from such a responsibility."

"I know, Will. I'm just concerned with your welfare, that's all."

"Before the sheriff gets here, it may be a good idea for you to tell me again what my new surname is. In all the confusion this morning, I've forgotten it already. Is it Carter?"

"No, Will, its Collins, darling."

"If that's my name now, I suppose it would probably be a good idea if I memorized it."

Even as Will spoke to Abby, his mind was attuned to the puzzling circumstances of the murder. A multitude of unanswered questions hung in his mind. *"Why would a man murder someone and not steal a horse to make good his escape? Why would a man kill another man for a watch and a pocket knife? Why would he run straight for the road, where he knew everyone would be looking for his tracks?"* Even though the circumstances were not making sense to him, he finished the cup of coffee that Abby had brought out to him and said, "I see that Ezra and the sheriff are riding up to the barn now, Abby. I need to go."

"I'll hurry and put some food in a bag for you, dear."

"You might want to throw some extra biscuits in the bag for the sheriff, too."

As Will had anticipated, the sheriff was by himself, and asked him to join in the pursuit of the murderer. Just as Will was giving the Sheriff all of the information that he had been able to obtain, the sheriff's deputy rode up and they loaded Robert Marshall's body onto a horse for the deputy to take back to Blanchard, where an inquest would be held in the magistrate's office. Will and the sheriff left the farm on horseback, following the fresh tracks in the muddy road.

They followed the tracks for less than a mile and a half when Will stopped his horse and asked the Sheriff, "Sheriff, if you don't mind me asking, doesn't this whole thing seem sort of odd to you?"

"Doesn't what seem odd?"

"The tracks we're following. It seems like the culprit is going out of his way to leave clear tracks behind him. Look there, he could have easily walked three feet to the left and he would have been walking on much firmer ground. It would have been almost impossible for us to pick up his tracks on that hard ground. Instead, it looks like he walked over here in the mud to be sure to leave good tracks behind. He's going out of his way to make sure that we have good tracks to follow, or at least it looks that way to me."

"Now that you mention it, it does sort of appear that way, doesn't it?"

"Tell me this, Sheriff, why would a fleeing murderer go to so much trouble to leave tracks that were so easy to follow... unless he wanted us to follow him for some reason?"

"That doesn't make any sense to me either, William."

"And why would he flee on foot, instead of stealing one of my horses? If he had taken one of my horses, he could have been six or eight miles from here by now. And he could have cut across country several times to throw us off even more."

"That doesn't make no sense either."

"I don't know, Sheriff, now that I think about it, maybe it does make sense. Maybe it makes all the sense in the world..."

"What do you mean, William? If you got something hangin' in your craw, why don't you just go ahead and spit it out?"

"Tell me something, Sheriff, do you have any enemies?"

"Lord have mercy, William, I'm a sheriff, and I've put a lot of bad men in jail, of course I have enemies. More than I would want to count, really."

"Do you have any enemies that would like to see you dead?"

"Ha! A bunch, I suppose..."

"Has anyone threatened you recently?"

"Eight or nine days ago, I put a drunkard in jail for getting drunk and breaking a couple of windows in the shoe store in Blanchard and stealing a pair of boots. When I opened the cell the next morning to bring him breakfast, the man was dead. Dr. Michaels said that the man died from consuming too much alcohol spirits, and his heart had stopped. When his two sons came to get their father's body, one of them told me that he'd send me to hell before I ever got a chance to arrest another harmless drunkard."

"And how long ago did the man threaten you?"

"About eight or nine days ago. You think that maybe he's wanting to make good on his threat?"

"I don't know, Sheriff, but I don't like this at all. The hair is starting to stand up on the back of my neck. I would wager that one of those sons came to my farm and hired on just so he could kill one of my workmen for the sole purpose of luring you into an ambush when you came after him... at least there's a high possibility of such a thing. He knew you'd be coming after him. If he's got a brother, there may even be two of 'em waiting ahead. With me being with you like this, they're likely to try to kill us both. They surely wouldn't want me to get away and sound an alarm. No, I think it's very likely that there's two men waiting ahead someplace for us, and they intend to kill us both."

"It seems like an outrageous scheme... but it's also a very possible scheme. It's pretty damned vindictive of a person to kill an innocent man just to get me off some place where they can kill me."

"There may be another reason as well, Sheriff... Robert Marshall had a valuable watch, and it was missing from his pocket when we found his body."

"People have been killed for much less, I suppose."

"Stop. Let's don't go any further just yet, Sheriff. If it is an ambush, they're probably waiting for us just ahead somewhere. There's no houses near here. They could do their dirty work and be gone from here before anyone ever saw them. They've most likely got horses with 'em ahead. I don't want to get any closer to 'em on horseback, lest the horses start whinnying back and forth and tip them off that we're here."

"You sound like you might have an idea in mind."

"If we don't show up by dark, they'll probably camp there for the night and wait for us to arrive in the morning. They know we'll be coming after 'em sooner or later, they just don't know exactly when we'll be coming. We could wait here for an hour or two, until it gets dark, then, ease ahead on foot in the dark. We may even be able to spot their campfire tonight, if they're stupid enough to make one. Let's dismount and sit over there in those trees and rest for an hour or two."

"Are you some kind of a lawman, William?"

"A lawman? Me? No, of course I'm not. Why do you ask such a question?"

"You sound like you've done this type of thing before, that's all."

"No, Sheriff, I've never pursued a murderer before, I can assure you of that. I suppose that I just have a suspicious nature and a desire to keep on living for a while longer, that's all."

"Where are you from originally, William?"

"Originally, Ohio."

"My wife has got relatives in Ohio. What town are you from?"

"Town? Uhhh, Cleveland."

"Her relatives live in Canton."

"Never been there."

Will and the Sheriff waited patiently until the sun set in the west. The sheriff was even afforded the opportunity to take a short nap, with Will sitting nearby in amazement that any human could snore as loud as the sheriff. Once it was dark, Will woke the sheriff, and the two slowly eased their horses ahead. Barely fifteen minutes had transpired when the glimmer of a distant campfire came into view.

"Do you think that's them ahead, William?"

"I would place a wager on it. Who else would be way out here in the middle of the night? Let's tie our horses here, before they start whinnying, and quietly walk up there on foot. Try not to make any noise, and let's see how close we can get to 'em."

Will and the sheriff moved slowly ahead until they had sneaked within thirty yards of the suspected murderers. The sheriff carried a double barrel shotgun as well as a pistol. Will was armed only with a pistol... a circumstance which made him even more uncomfortable. When they had crept an additional ten yards or so, the sheriff yelled out at the top of his lungs, "**Put them hands up in the air and stand up! Now!**"

The frightened scoundrels were caught with such surprise that they offered no resistance other than to shout back, "Don't shoot! Please don't shoot!"

"Put the shackles on 'em, William! If you men even look like you're gonna move, I'll cut you plumb in two pieces with this here shotgun!"

"We ain't done nothing!"

"William, does either of these here men look like the man you hired to work on the farm?"

"The short one here is the one, Shelton Lewis."

"I ain't done nothing!"

"Let me see what you have in your pocket, Lewis. Where'd you get this watch, Shelton? And where'd you get this pocket knife? And look here what I found, sheriff. He had this knife in his boot and this looks like blood up here on the hilt."

"Shelton Lewis ain't his real name, William. This here one is Cecil Hodges. That one over there is his brother, Milton."

"Are they the ones who threatened you, sheriff?"

"Yer damn right they are!"

"If you'll keep your gun on them, I'll saddle their horses and help you take them back to Blanchard."

Will gathered up two rifles and two pistols from the camp, and brought his and the sheriff's horses back to where they could secure the murderers horses to their own for the duration of the trip back to town. Progress in the dark was awkward and slow, but in the early hours of the morning, the sheriff and Will managed to finally put the murderous brothers into a cell at the back of the courthouse. There was the faintest glow of a sunrise on the eastern horizon when Will climbed wearily back on his saddle.

"You're one mighty fine lawman, William... I don't believe I ever caught your last name."

"It's Collins."

"Well, you're one mighty fine lawman, William Collins."

"Not really, Sheriff. I'm just glad I could help out a little. My workmen on the farm would have expected me to do as much, and I didn't have much choice in the matter."

"Whether you know it or not, you saved my life, William, and

243

I'll not be forgetting it anytime soon. If it hadn't been for you, I would have most likely rode right into their trap. My wife would have been a widow and my children orphans. Come see me if you ever need anything, and I mean that.... Anything at all."

"I will, Sheriff. Thank you."

"When these boys go to trial, I'll be a needing you to come back into Blanchard and testify before the court."

"I will, Sheriff. You can count on it."

It was nearly nine o'clock in the morning by the time that Will rode back onto Montgomery Farm land. Ezra was busy with the workmen pulling tobacco. As a courtesy, Will rode over and explained to all of the workmen everything that had happened. By the time he rode up to the house, a very apprehensive Abby, Sarah, and Elizabeth ran out to greet him.

"We were worried sick about you! When you didn't come home last night, we didn't know what to think! We thought you had been shot or something! We were about to send Ezra out to look for you! Why have you been gone so long!?"

"Please stop worrying over me... all of you. Settle down. I'm fine. It just took a lot longer than I expected, that's all, but the sheriff and I apprehended the men responsible for the crime and they are locked up in the Blanchard jail now."

"Thank God you're safe, and home with us now!"

"I'm just as sorry as I can be, Abby, but I can't stay very long. I've got to ride back into Blanchard now. I'll be back just as soon as I can. Goodbye ladies."

"**Wait**! You're leaving again already? Why do you have to ride back into Blanchard, Will? Didn't you just come from there?"

"Yes I did, Abby, but you see, I came home to Montgomery Farm hoping that I might find some nice friendly folks here that were willing to fix me something to eat, but all I've found here was a bunch of crying, fidgety women. I've got to go back to Blanchard to get something to eat. I'm about to starve to death!"

Jokingly outraged, Abby laughed and shouted, "Will Collins, if you don't turn your horse in the pasture right now and get your cantankerous bones up to the house, I'm going to find a switch and you won't be able to sit down at the table for a week!"

"Mercy! I'll be right along behind you, Abby!"

"You make very good decisions, Will Collins, once you know the rules and the consequences!"

"Ha! And you have a very colorful way of explaining the consequences, Abby!"

"I love you, Will!"

"And I love you, Abby. I'll be up to the house shortly, darling."

Will chuckled, led his horse down to the pasture, and was still chuckling when he took the saddle off and turned his mare into the pasture. He relished the joking exchanges between him and Abby, and as he had told his loving family, he was quite anxious to savor a meal at the family table. This had been Will's first overnight absence from Montgomery Farm since being brought there as a wounded soldier, more than fourteen months earlier, and he was not very fond of any duty or chore that took him away from his precious loved ones for even as much as an hour.

The Gentle Snows Of Winter

"Likewise, you who are younger, be subject to the elders. Clothe yourselves, all of you, with humility toward one another, for "God opposes the proud but gives grace to the humble." 1 Peter 5:5

On the twelfth day of December Sarah Montgomery and Timothy O'Donnell were married in a gala ceremony that took place there in the front lawn and veranda of Montgomery House. At Sarah's request, William Collins gave the bride away. Will and Abby donated sufficient money for the newlyweds to travel back to Baltimore, as well as five hundred dollars to help them begin their new life together. Immediately following the ceremony, Timothy and Sarah left Montgomery Farm as husband and wife and traveled to the town of Blanchard. Ezra rode along with them to bring the family carriage back to Montgomery Farm. From Blanchard, the newlyweds would travel to Richmond by coach. From Richmond, they planned to travel by railroad to Washington, and then finally to Maryland where Timothy would introduce his new bride to his mother and father. Their plans sounded wonderful to the family. The ceremony had been an uplifting event for the post-war community surrounding Montgomery Farm, but the ceremony that the community would longest remember had occurred the day before, in the Blanchard Episcopal Church. In that ceremony, Abigail Margaret

Montgomery became Mrs. Abigail Margaret Collins. Sheriff Homer Bellisle had stood beside William, and Elizabeth, Sarah, and Agatha stood beside Abigail. William and Abigail were now husband and wife, and the event marked the beginning of their legal life together as Mr. and Mrs. William Collins.

Six weeks after the confusion of having two weddings in the family only a day apart, Will stood at the kitchen window while watching a gentle snow fall upon the land. He used his handkerchief to wipe the condensation from the window pane so he could see outside. He and Abigail had become well-settled into their life there as man and wife, and the warmth of their love for each other only continued to grow deeper. Will had risen early on that particular day, well before dawn, and started a fire in the kitchen stove. With Abby still upstairs in their bed, Will made a pot of coffee as best he could, and was waiting for it to finish boiling. Elizabeth soon arrived in the kitchen, kissed her stepfather on the cheek, and asked, "Good morning, Will. Is Mother still in her bed?"

"Good morning, Lizzy. Yes, but she will probably be down in just a few minutes. If I didn't know better, I would think that she is growing lazy during these dreary winter months. I think she was just starting to stir as I was getting dressed."

"Correct me if I'm mistaken, but did my wonderful stepfather just call me, *Lizzy*?"

"It was an accident, Elizabeth, I'm sorry. I seem to be notoriously guilty of unwittingly assigning nicknames to those whom I love the most. Please forgive me, I meant no disrespect."

"I'm not offended by the name at all. I've never been called, Lizzy before, and I kind of like it... No, the more I think about it, I like it a lot, especially when I hear it from you!"

"Well then, would you mind if I started calling you Lizzy?"

"No, I think I would even treasure hearing you call me Lizzy. You have such a pleasant voice that I would probably adore hearing you call me any name of your choosing."

"Very well, 'Lizzy' it is, then."

"And for that, you get another kiss this morning."

"My! This is my lucky day indeed! Thank you, Lizzy."

"What are you thinking about as you look out at the falling snow this morning, Will?"

Will poured himself a cup of coffee, took a sip, and answered, "A curious observation just entered my mind, Lizzy."

"Oh? And what might that be, Will?"

"I've just taken notice of the fact that coffee always seems to taste much better when you or Abby makes it. I wonder why that is?"

"It's because the coffee hasn't finished boiling yet, Will, give it time. You were about to tell me about the thoughts that are going through your mind this morning, please continue."

"Oh... many things are going through my mind this morning, I suppose."

"Like what, Will?"

"I'm just in a lazy mood myself today, what with the snow falling outside and all. On mornings such as this my mind has a tendency to wander about, like a dog turned loose from its leash. It just runs all over the place, and I seldom know where it's going, how long it will stay there, or where on earth it may end up."

"That sounds rather interesting. Could you share some of your thoughts with me?"

Just then, Abby walked into the kitchen and said, "Yes, Will, please share your thoughts with us. I'd like to hear them as well."

"Good morning, Abby."

"Good morning, darling, good morning, Elizabeth. Please go ahead and share your thoughts with us."

"Wait a moment, Mother. You should know that Will has endowed me with a new name. He's started addressing me as, Lizzy."

"How sweet! May I start calling you Lizzy as well, sometimes?"

"Certainly!"

"Well how about it, Will, won't you share your thoughts with my darling Lizzy and I this morning?"

"Well, one of my thoughts was that... I was just wondering if Sarah and Timothy made the journey up to Maryland without any great difficulty."

Elizabeth spoke up in response to Will's remark, "I'm sure they have made it to Maryland long before now. They probably got there just two or three days after departing here, at the very latest. Why would you wonder about such a thing?"

"I don't know. I've just got an uncomfortable feeling that has crept into my mind. It's probably nothing."

Elizabeth looked to be puzzled and concerned by Will's flippant remark, and asked for a clarification. "What do you mean, you've got an uncomfortable feeling, Will? Can you tell Mother and I about it?"

"Like I said, I don't know... I'm sure it's probably nothing. Most likely, it's because I miss her so much."

Elizabeth thought about Sarah for a moment or two and offered, "I never knew how much I would miss her until she was actually gone. We used to talk so much when we were doing our chores around the house. The silence is sometimes deafening."

"I know," Abby added, "There was certainly not as much silence when Sarah was in the house."

Elizabeth went on to say, "I'm afraid that I didn't appreciate her when she was here as much as I should have. She aggravated me occasionally with her frankness, but now I find myself missing her rascally ways. She was an extra measure of sunshine in our lives, and always has been."

William considered what Lizzy had just said, then added a comment of his own, "Then perhaps the rest of us need to shine just a little brighter for each other in her absence."

"What an excellent thought, Will."

As Abby poured everyone a cup of coffee, she asked, "I'm sure that's not all that you were thinking about Will. What else are you thinking about as you watch Montgomery Farm getting covered with this beautiful snow?"

"I suppose that I was thinking about how happy I am that I

stacked a bunch of dry firewood on the porch yesterday before it started to snow. And I can't help but feel happy knowing there is half an apple pie in the cupboard. That in itself is enough to make any man happy. Sitting here with the two most beautiful ladies in the county and seeing them with hair their down is a treat as well!"

"Ha! And, what else are you thinking about? Please keep on..."

"Oh, I was thinking about how quiet and peaceful it is here in the wintertime, watching the snow fall. The workmen have all gone home, there's no work to be done in the fields, and the snow makes everything seem so clean and fresh. God has been good to us here. We laid in a good crop this year, and we are enjoying good health. But I suppose my main thought as I look out of the window here this morning is that I'm so fortunate to be here. I have the best wife and the best stepdaughter in the world, and the prettiest ones too, I might add. And I'm quite positive that I am not deserving of all the many blessings that God has brought to me."

Abby walked to the window where Will stood, held his hand, and looked lovingly into his eyes as she said, "Our lives have been blessed beyond measure by your being here with us, Will."

"Mother? Do I see redness on your cheeks and neck this morning?"

"We'll discuss this when we are not in the presence of your stepfather, if you don't mind. He embarrasses rather easily and so do I."

"Don't argue between yourselves, ladies, I'm trying to enjoy the sublime quietness of this beautiful morning."

Abby walked over to Elizabeth, kissed her on the forehead, and said, "Lizzy my dear, I suppose we really should let your stepfather enjoy the quietness while he can. Things may not be so quiet around here when August arrives."

William was puzzled by Abby's comment, and asked, "What's going to happen here in August that will be so disruptive to the quietness, Abby?"

Elizabeth's face lit up with immediate astonishment, as she excitingly shouted, "Mother! Are you insinuating what I think you are? Are you being truthful?"

"I would never lie to you, Elizabeth."

"Oh! I can't believe it! This is wonderful!"

More perplexed than ever, Will begged for an explanation, "Will one of you please tell me what's going on?"

"I love you, Mother! This is a miracle!"

"Lizzy? Abby? Why are you both crying? Would one of you please share your little secret with me? Perhaps I can start crying, too. Perhaps the three of us can weep ourselves into a stupor together. Wouldn't that be a delightful way for us to spend this beautiful morning?"

Abby arose from her chair, walked over to Will, stood on her tiptoes, and whispered in his ear, "You and I are going to have a baby, Mr. Collins. What do you have to say about that?"

"What!? A baby? Lord have mercy... I can't believe it! I'm going to be a father? Lizzy, would you please fetch me the small bottle of brandy from the parlor, please?"

"Are you not happy about my announcement, Will?"

"Of course I'm happy, Abby! I'm elated! I just didn't expect... Lizzy, would you please pour me half a cup of coffee and finish filling the cup with brandy if you will."

"Please share your thoughts with Lizzy and me now, Will. Tell us what you think about the fact that we're going to have a baby."

"Just a few minutes ago I said that I didn't deserve all the blessings that have come into my life, and now... I find that I have been blessed yet again, in a way I could never have imagined. I love you both. You are my family, and you are my reason for living."

Will and Abby had never discussed the possibility of her becoming pregnant. Because it had been seventeen years since Abigail had last given birth, they had both assumed that such a pregnancy would have been so unlikely as to be assumed impossible. The news came to Will as an amazement, yet a very blessed amazement. He and Abby were beside themselves with joy, and Elizabeth gleefully celebrated along with them.

On a bitter cold January morning, Will saddled his horse and rode the nine-mile journey into Blanchard to attend the trial of the brothers, Cecil and Milton Hodges. Will and the sheriff both gave their testimony, and a deputy sheriff who had overheard Milton Hodges' original threat against the life of the sheriff, also gave his testimony. The watch and the knife were displayed as evidence, and in the small courtroom there was barely enough room to hold the crowd of spectators, many of whom had to remain standing. The jury returned after deliberating for less than ten minutes and presented their verdict of guilty. With the somberness and solemnity expected of his position, the judge, with one raised eyebrow, sternly said, "Milton Hodges and Cecil Hodges, having been found guilty of the crime of murder by a jury of your countrymen, it is the order of this court that on the fifteenth day of February, at precisely the noon hour, you are to be remanded to the custody of the sheriff, and taken to a place designated by this court, and there, hanged by the neck until you are dead. May God have mercy on your evil souls."

With that, the judge banged his gavel on the bench and the brothers were led away by the sheriff and his deputy. The brothers shouted profanities at the courtroom of spectators as they were led down the stairway to the cells in the basement below. Their fate having been determined, the courtroom soon emptied and the crowd dispersed. Will visited briefly with Sheriff Homer Bellisle in his office and arrived back at Montgomery Farm just after noon.

On the fifteenth day of February, in a misty light rain, as the judge had ordered, the two brothers were led up the steps of a scaffold behind the courthouse and the court's sentence was carried out. Even though the execution was attended by a throng of several dozen onlookers standing under their umbrellas, Will was not among the many spectators. He had more precious and important things to do than to watch two men die, and felt that there was nothing to be gained by witnessing such a thing. The thought crossed Will's mind that, one life had been needlessly taken, and now two were being taken in recompense. Was that justice? Knowing the circumstances and the heinous nature of the crime as he did, Will determined that, *"Yes... it probably was."*

As for the young man that the brothers had murdered, little was known beyond the fact that his name was Robert Marshall. It was thought that he was from someplace in Pennsylvania, but no one knew for certain. Therefore, there were no letters of notification sent to his family. It was known that his father had given him a valuable watch, but beyond that, no one knew if he had a wife, a mother, children, or any remaining family. He became another of the many thousands of young men who simply left to go off to war, and never came home again. His family, if in fact he had one, were most likely left with the impression that he had lost his life in battle, and perhaps that was best, because in truth, he really had been another casualty of war.

Throughout the winter, the numbers of passing veterans along the roadway became fewer and fewer until there were no more. Tensions eased somewhat in the south when it became apparent that Yankee retribution would not come in the form of troops storming in to burn everything in sight as they had done in Atlanta. Instead, retribution would arrive in the form of Carpetbaggers; northerners with money, arriving as buzzards to feast on the helplessness of distraught southerners. Manipulating the law in a manner which would allow them to steal homes, land, and businesses, these carpetbaggers successfully ruined the lives of many of the widows and orphans that had been left behind by the ravages of war. Some affluent southern veterans banded together secretly to administer their own form of justice to an occasional carpetbagger. One such scoundrel was found hanging from an oak tree on the outskirts of town after he paid the mortgage and back taxes on a property east of Blanchard, and evicted a widow with four children into the street to fend for themselves. The written letter of the law was in the favor of the carpetbagger, and they relentlessly used it to their evil advantage. Desperate people do desperate things, and war has always had the unscrupulous and uncanny capability of manufacturing desperate people.

Over the course of the winter, Josh and George, the two wayward sons of Ezra and Vivian, returned home from the north, having found that life in the north for a black man was not as pleasant and wondrous as they had been led to believe by their so-called 'Northern Liberators.' The year and a half that they had spent in Washington had been a harsh existence of wandering about the streets with hundreds of other liberated slaves looking for food and work. They scorned themselves for ever having left the security of Montgomery Farm and the warmth and love of their family, and were most happy to be back home with their mother and father. It was as though the prodigal sons had returned home for Ezra and Vivian, and they rejoiced in their happiness as a family reunited. Will immediately hired Josh and George at the same rate of pay that he was paying the other laborers—a circumstance which caused two of the white laborers to quit. With Will's moral conviction, there would be no disparity or injustice committed on family property as long as he was running things at Montgomery Farm. In Will's opinion, equal work meant equal pay, and his opinion among the workmen at Montgomery Farm was non-negotiable.

It was in the later days of February that Abby received a letter from her very distraught daughter, Sarah. She opened the letter one afternoon as Ezra had returned from Blanchard with the mail and some fencing wire. Abby said as she opened the letter, "This is wonderful! I've been dying to hear from my sweet Sarah! I'm so excited I can hardly stand it!"

But Will and Lizzy could clearly see that the expression on Abby's face had quickly gone from joy to somberness, and then from somberness, to outright distress as she read Sarah's letter. By the time she finished reading, she was in tears.

"What's the matter, Abby?"

"My God, Mother? What is it?"

Then the tears started to intensify, as she handed the letter to Will, buried her face in her hands, and asked him to read it. Will took the letter from her, pulled in a deep breath, but paused briefly before reading aloud. There was no doubt in his heart that what he was about to read would be disturbing. He could tell as much by Abigail's reaction to the letter. Nevertheless, he bolstered up the courage, cleared his throat, and read aloud, as Abigail and Elizabeth held hands.

February 8th, 1867
Sarah O'Donnell
Bishop Landing
Baltimore, Maryland

My Dearest Mother, Elizabeth, and Will
It is dreadfully delinquent of me to have waited so long to write, but in truth, I was hoping for some form of good news to share with you, and there seems to be no such good news in my life at present.

My husband, Timothy, whom I promised to love forever, has become my worst enemy. He is an incurable drunkard who amuses himself by beating me. The beatings are getting progressively worse, and I fear that if I don't soon leave this place, I will surely die at his hands. His father is also an incorrigible creature, and I have no one to turn to here in this place. If you are reading this letter, it is because I was able to drop it from my window to a boy in the street. I have no money to return home, and I am not permitted to leave the house. I beg you to do something, anything to contribute to my relief. Please don't write, as I am not permitted to receive mail and to receive a letter would probably cause another beating. I don't know where to turn for help except to my family. God bless each of you. Whatever happens, please remember that I love each of you with all my heart and soul.

I remain,
Sarah Montgomery

Elizabeth screamed out, "Oh my God, I tried to tell her! I knew he was an evil man! I knew it! But Sarah wouldn't listen to me! It's all my fault for not trying harder!" In tears, Abby added, "It's no one's fault, dear, Sarah has always been a very strong minded soul when she has her heart set on something."

Will's jaws tightened with intense fury as he looked at the letter and read it a second time, silently. Turning the horrible letter face down on the table, Will said, "Lizzy, listen carefully... I want you to summon Ezra for me, please, and have him saddle up the big roan mare with the white face, as quickly as possible and bring her and one other horse to me... that big gelding with the chestnut mane."

"What are you going to do, Will?"

"**Do it now!** Please Lizzy! There's not a moment to waste!"

"Alright... sure, Will."

"Abby, please pack me some food and a few clothes in a bag, darling, and I'll need two blankets as well, and my pistol from the upstairs wardrobe."

"You're going to go get her, aren't you, Will?"

"I've no choice in the matter, Abby. I'm the one who introduced her to that O'Donnell bastard. I'm the very one who coaxed them into getting married, and now my foolish and selfish actions have come back to torment me. I've never felt more like a lowly serpent in my life than I do right now. I gave one of my daughters to the devil…"

"You had her best interest at heart, Will."

"Did I, Abby? I don't think so. I think I had my own selfish interests at heart. I would gladly give my life for any member of my family, and look what I've done to our sweet Sarah! Jesus help me, I've given her to the devil himself! How could I have done such a thing?"

"My Lord, Will, don't blame yourself for what's happened. Timothy O'Donnell had us all fooled. He seemed so…"

"Please pack my things as quickly as possible, Abby. I don't have time to sit around and discuss this."

"It will be dark in three hours, Will. Shouldn't you wait until morning to leave?"

"**No**! I will ride all day and all night if I have to. I will not allow myself to be delayed so that Sarah can endure any more beatings at the hand of this fiend. I feel like my heart's been torn from my body, and I shan't rest until Sarah is home safe and sound with her mother and sister again. My God, the bastard might be beating her right at this very moment! **Hurry, Abby**!"

"I understand, Will. I'll get your things together."

Will was terribly distressed over Sarah's predicament, and grievously overcome with guilt. He quickly changed his clothes, and while making hasty preparations to depart, Will's normally compassionate eyes had transformed into blazing embers of hatred, and yet became teary each time he paused to think of Sarah's desperate situation. Within forty minutes of having read the horrible letter, Will was at the back porch, ready to climb onto his horse. Abby and Elizabeth walked outside with him as Ezra stood there holding Will's horse and one other.

"I put some biscuits and some dried beef and a few apples in your saddlebags, and two jars of water, Will."

"Thank you, Abby. Ezra, I want you to watch over these two wonderful ladies while I'm gone. I'm holding you responsible. Guard them with your life, and allow no harm to befall them."

"Yes Sir. You can count on me, Mister Will."

Abigail took William by the hand and placed an envelope in his hand."

"Will, I want you to take this envelope with you, please."

"What is it, Abby?"

"There's a hundred dollars in there."

"I think I already have all the money I'll need, Abby."

"Take it just in case, Will. Aren't you going to take a couple of horses along for Sarah?"

"No. I can ride faster this way, and buy a couple of horses and a saddle for Sarah when I get there. Elizabeth, I'm sorry I raised my voice at you earlier. Please forgive me, dear."

"I understand, Will. Please take care of yourself and bring my little sister home to us."

Will kissed Abby and Lizzy goodbye and climbed on his horse. From his saddle, he looked down upon them momentarily and said, "I want you to know that whatever happens, I love you both dearly. When I return, our beloved Sarah will be with me. Of that, I give you my solemn oath."

"Will, please don't kill O'Donnell! We'd die if anything happens to you! And don't punish yourself for what's happened to Sarah—it's not your fault!"

"I'll be home as soon as I can. I love you both."

"God go with you, Will!"

Will rode as quickly as he could into the town of Blanchard. There, he had a short meeting with his good friend, Sheriff Homer Bellisle. From the sheriff, Will received a letter of introduction that was also taken across the street and signed by Judge Albright, and could be used for identification purposes, should the need arise. It would also be useful in assuring him safe passage through pickets and roadblocks if any were encountered along the way. As Will climbed onto his saddle to depart, Sheriff Bellisle said, "My badge don't carry any weight up in Baltimore, Will, but if you want me to come along with you, I will. I can be ready in twenty minutes."

"No, Homer. I appreciate the offer, but this is something that I should best handle alone."

"Be careful up there, Will, and don't let your anger overcome your better judgment. It won't do anyone any good if you bring Sarah home and end up getting yourself locked up for killing a man in Baltimore. Just remember, if you kill him, they're bound to come here looking for you, and there ain't a thing that me or anybody else could do to protect you."

Just as quickly as he had tucked his letter of introduction into his coat pocket and finished hearing Bellisle's warning, Will wasted no time, and hastened northward on the road to Lynchburg and Washington to get to Sarah and bring her back to Montgomery Farm as quickly as possible. With a purpose-driven fire still burning in his eyes, and hatred in his heart, he pressed on into the darkness of twilight. He was a man on a mission of mercy, and a man who carried the tremendous burden of guilt on his shoulders. He would not rest until he had liberated his darling Sarah, and every mile of the way found him deep in prayer that he would arrive in time to free Sarah from the clutches of danger before her horrid circumstances escalated to a point where her life was in jeopardy. *"Please protect her, dear God, and allow me to bring her back to a place where she is loved and cherished."*

Mile after mile, Will pressed onward. Oblique visions of Sarah scurried in and out of his mind as he rode. He could envision her smiling face as she carried a bucket of water from the well to the house, and he could see her face light up with delight as it had each time she had said good morning to him. His stomach wrenched into a knot when he considered what the filthy hands of O'Donnell were doing to Sarah. And each time those horrid thoughts entered his mind, he prayed. *"God Almighty, please protect her! Please grant her the peace of mind in knowing that I'm coming for her, Lord, and please grant me the strength to do what I have to do."*

Infuriated By Rage - Guided By Love

"A man of wrath stirs up strife, and one given to anger causes much transgression." Proverbs 29:22

"Dearly beloved, avenge not yourselves, but rather give place unto wrath: for it is written, Vengeance is mine; I will repay, saith the Lord." Romans 12:19

The journey from Blanchard to Baltimore would have normally taken as much as five days by horseback or coach at a leisurely pace. But William Collins wasn't traveling at a leisurely pace. Pushing his horses almost to the limits of their endurance, Will made the journey in less than four days, arriving in Baltimore just before noon hour on a Sunday. He had rested his horses every three or four hours during the journey and changed the saddle onto the extra horse every few hours so as not to exhaust either horse. But the horses and Will were both nearly spent when they finally entered the cobblestone streets of Baltimore. He had very little trouble getting directions to the street called *Bishop Landing*, but it was with great difficulty, and only after knocking on several doors, that he was finally able to find an elderly gentleman who pointed out the O'Donnell residence to him. He looked at the house for several moments, with the ominous knowledge that his darling Sarah was living a life of hell in an otherwise innocent and peaceful appearing house. At half past one o'clock in the afternoon he found a livery stable nearby where he was able to purchase three extra horses and a suitable saddle for Sarah. He would not ride his weary horses on the return trip, but would lead them along with the other horses without the burden of carrying a passenger. Then, he led his horses to Bishop Landing, which was on a hill overlooking the Baltimore waterfront and harbor. He tied his horses to a pasture fence across the street from what he was told to be the O'Donnell residence and walked up to the door of the house. He listened for a moment or two but heard nothing from inside. Taking a deep breath, and making sure that his pistol was in his coat pocket, he knocked on the door. In a very few moments, the door swung open and Will found himself once again standing face to face with Timothy O'Donnell, the young man whom he had once thought to be virtuous and kind, and an excellent choice for a husband for Sarah. Greatly surprised, O'Donnell gasped and said, "Mister Will! This is a surprise!"

"Really?"

"What on earth are you doing here in Baltimore?"

"At the moment, I'm walking into your house and closing the door, and I have little doubt that you are indeed surprised to see me. I also have little doubt that you know why I'm here."

Will locked the door from inside and put the key in his vest pocket. O'Donnell stepped backward, in front of Will, and into the parlor. He was still quite stunned by Will's sudden and unannounced arrival, and even more stunned by Will's emboldened entry into his house. His words of surprise were not deceiving William. He could tell by the look on O'Donnell's face that O'Donnell knew exactly why Will was there. He had *'fear for his life'* written all over his deceitful face.

"Is something wrong, Mister Will?"

Will listened closely to try to ascertain whether or not anyone else besides the two of them was there in the house. He looked around, and seeing no one else, he asked, "Where's your father and mother?"

"They've taken holiday, they're in Pennsylvania at the present time to attend the President's inauguration tomorrow. Might I ask what this is all about and why you are here?"

Will did not answer. Taking his pistol from his coat pocket, Will grabbed O'Donnell by his shirt and held his gun a few inches from his face. Then, he demanded, "Don't waste my time by asking your stupid questions! You know exactly why I'm here! Now, where is Sarah?"

"You can't barge into my house like this!"

"I've already barged into your house! Don't tell me what I can and cannot do! Now tell me where Sarah is! Otherwise, I'll kill you where you stand and go to search for her myself!"

"She's upstairs lying down. Why do you need to see her? What's this all about?"

"Take me up to see her."

"It's not convenient for anyone to see her today. She's not feeling well. She's ill. Could you come back tomorrow?"

"Oh... you'd like that, wouldn't you? That would give you more than an ample opportunity to arm yourself, wouldn't it? That way, when I returned, you could simply open the door and shoot me, couldn't you? Take me to see her. Now! Delay me any longer and I'll put a shot in your guts... right here and now!"

"Alright. Just don't shoot me... Please!"

O'Donnell walked up the stairs with Will right behind him. When they reached the top step, O'Donnell made a desperate attempt to whirl around quickly and kick Will in the face, but Will had been expecting such a thing. He dodged the kick and gave O'Donnell a solid thrashing on the side of his face with the barrel of the pistol, knocking him to the floor at the top of the stairway. After the third or fourth blow, Will simply helped him back on his feet and asked, "Is that enough, or do you want more?"

O'Donnell fell to the floor again, and said, "No more... please!" He turned his head to the side and spat two teeth on the floor, then begged, "Please don't hit me any more..."

"If you only knew how very little it would take for me to send you straight to hell... Get back on your feet and take me to her! Which room is she in?"

O'Donnell held the side of his bloody face with one hand, pulled another tooth from his bloody mouth so he could speak, and with the other hand, he pointed to a closed door halfway down a narrow hallway and said, "She's in that room... the second door..."

"Get on your feet and open the door!"

"I can't. It's locked. The key is downstairs in the parlor."

"You have my Sarah locked in a room, like an animal?"

"You don't understand! It was necessary! She acts like a damned animal, so I've had to treat her like one! It's for her own good!"

"Open the door!"

"I told you, it's locked, and the key is downstairs!"

"Very well, then I'll open it."

Not wanting to waste any more time, Will kicked the door open, and for the first time in four months, he was looking into the wonderful eyes of his darling Sarah again. Will was horrified when he saw the distressed and very badly battered Sarah. She was completely naked, and crouched in a corner. When she saw Will, she quickly stood, and tried her best to cover her breasts and pubic area with her hands. Will was sickened at the sight of Sarah's bruises, yet maintained his composure so as not to lose control of the situation. All of the horrors that he had imagined while on the trail to Baltimore were true, and even worse than he had imagined. With his foot in the small of O'Donnell's back, Will kicked him into the room where the miserable aggressor fell flat on the floor, still spitting blood from his mouth.

"Thank God you've come for me, Will!" Sarah immediately started to come to Will, but he held his hand up and motioned for her to stop. He could ill afford to take his mind off of O'Donnell long enough to receive Sarah in his arms. He knew that he must stay focused on O'Donnell. "Is there a lavatory anywhere in this house, Sarah?"

"Yes, there's one at the end of the hall. God bless you for coming, Will!"

"Where are your clothes?"

"They're down the hall in his father's room. I'm not permitted to have clothes. They took my clothes so that I wouldn't flee during the night."

"They?"

"Timothy and that bastard of a father he has."

Sarah again reached forward to embrace Will, but he cut their embrace short, and said, "We've no time for joyous reunions right now, Sarah. We've more urgent things to tend to first. Pay attention and listen to me closely, and do exactly as I say. Grab a few clothes to wear and a few to bring along with you and go to the lavatory. Wash the blood from your face and hair as best you can, and dress yourself. Do you have a bonnet?"

"Yes."

"Bring it with you. Bring only what clothes you can wear or stuff in a saddlebag, and wear dark colored garments, nothing bright or colorful. I have no saddle for you but a man's saddle, so you must dress with the understanding that you will be riding astride. After you have cleaned yourself and dressed, go downstairs to the front door and wait for me there. Do you understand?"

"Yes, Will."

"Do it now, Sarah... as quickly as you can, dear!"

With the door to the room closed once again, Will directed some straight talk toward Timothy O'Donnell.

"You took a vow before God to love and cherish her, and instead you chose to beat her and mistreat her? You miserable stinking, cowardly bastard!"

"And she took a vow before God to honor and obey! She doesn't know the meaning of the words! Her behavior has been horrible! You had no call to knock my teeth out! You have no idea of what she's put me and my family through!"

"Perhaps not, but I've certainly got a good idea of what you've put her through!"

"She never does anything that I tell her to do! I was only trying to correct her disgusting behavior. That's all! Women are supposed to be submissive to their husbands! All she does is spit and bite! Any husband in my place would have done the same thing!"

"I trusted you with my stepdaughter's life, Timothy O'Donnell! I even gave you my blessing! And look what you've done to her! She's suffered the last beating at your filthy hands!"

"Take her and go, then! I don't want her anymore! I'll be happy to be shed of her! My father was right, I should have known better than to marry a mangy, flea-bitten bitch from Virginia!"

O'Donnell's spiteful words infuriated Will to an even higher degree. Hearing this despicable creature call Sarah a *bitch*, put the fury of hell in Will's heart again, and he had to exert every effort in order to restrain himself from taking O'Donnell's miserable life.

"I will take her and go, of that you can be sure. Tell me, what is the purpose for the bindings that I see tied to the bedposts? Did you restrain her with these ropes?"

"Only at night... sometimes, when her behavior was the worst. You cannot begin to imagine her outrageous defiance and disobedience! She would even spit on me! I swear it! Do you hear me?! That mangy bitch spit on me and my father, and bit me on the hand whenever I tried to touch her! Look at my hand! See where she bit me?! What else was I to do but restrain her?!"

"Lay down on the bed."

"What? Why? What are you going to do to me?"

"Get up from the floor and lay down on the bed, or I will shoot you where you sit and carry your nuts back to Montgomery Farm in a sack to be fed to my hounds!"

Horrified by Will's threats, O'Donnell did as he was told, pleading for mercy the entire time. He knew Will to be a man of his word, and he had no doubt that Will was not in the mood to be defied or trifled with. Will bound him to the bed, using the same rope bindings that O'Donnell had used to restrain Sarah.

"What are you going to do to me? Don't hurt me! Please don't hurt me! I just did what I had to do! God please help me!"

"Shut up! You're making me sick, you coward! After what you've done to Sarah, God won't hear your screams for mercy, and neither will I!"

Will took his knife and cut every single garment from O'Donnell's body, with O'Donnell screaming and crying the whole while. O'Donnell lay prostrate and naked before him, shivering with fright. Will heard Sarah as she walked by the door on her way downstairs. When he was sure that she was downstairs and waiting for him at the front door, he put his pistol back in his pocket and gave O'Donnell his full attention. Sarah heard O'Donnell's screams and whimpers from downstairs, but remained at the door as Will had instructed, finally covering her ears so as not to hear O'Donnell's pleas for mercy. When he was finished, Will looked at O'Donnell as he lied there whimpering and said, "The only reason that I didn't kill you was because I was just as guilty of her abuse as you, by giving her to you in the first place."

Will cleaned the blood from his hands and walked downstairs, lightly kissed Sarah on her bruised cheek, and said, "Listen closely to me, dear. I have a horse waiting for you across the street. There will be no talking between us until we have reached the outskirts of Baltimore. We can talk then. We will ride quickly, but not fast enough to draw attention to ourselves. It will be dark soon, but we will have a good moon for traveling tonight. Move quickly when I unlock the door, but don't run or do anything that might draw any attention to us. Keep your bonnet drawn, so that your face cannot be seen. I don't want to have to shoot any neighbors for interfering with our departure unless it's absolutely necessary. Did any of the neighbors attempt to come to your aid?"

"No one has come to my aid but you, Will."

"Surely they must have heard your screams. No matter. If they do attempt to interfere with our departure, I'll kill every damned one of them. I have water and some food for you in my saddlebags, but we shan't be stopping to rest the horses for at least three or four hours. We'll eat something after we have arrived at the Potomac River. Are you up to this my dear?"

"Yes, Will, I'm up to anything it takes to get away from this horrible place."

"Hold my hand and let us leave this filthy place behind us."

Once they had crossed the street and mounted their horses, they rode through the streets of Baltimore on the noisy cobblestone roads and on into the night. By noon hour the next day, they had crossed the Potomac River below Great Falls on a ferry just northwest of Washington, and were once again on Virginia soil. When on the Virginia side of the river, Will began to breathe easier, confident that their escape from Baltimore had been a success. Even in his confidence, instead of traveling on the road that led directly south, Will turned west, and traveled on a southwesterly road for the benefit of eluding and confusing any possible pursuers.

O   O   O

Will had not slept for more than a few hours since leaving Montgomery Farm. He was exhausted, and knew that Sarah was terribly fatigued as well. By the end of the second day, they stopped at an inn on the Shenandoah River, near the town of Front Royal, Virginia for some much needed rest and a hot meal. The inn served them a hearty stew of beef and vegetables, a tankard of ale, and a pudding. All the rooms were taken, but the innkeeper agreed to let them sleep in the barn without compensation. He had graciously offered to let Sarah sleep on a small cot in his attic, but neither Sarah nor William, were willing to entertain the concept of being separated that night. It was beginning to rain, and although it had turned miserably cold outside, the shelter of the barn offered a much better prospect than sleeping somewhere along the roadside outdoors. Even as cold as it was, at least they would remain dry in the barn. In their haste to leave the city of Baltimore behind them, there had been very few words exchanged between them. Now, with full stomachs and the prospects of spending a restful night in the barn, they could share some long overdue conversation. Even as weary as they were, both of them had questions that needed to be answered. Will tended to the horses once more, then joined Sarah in the barn. Kissing her hand, he apologetically asked, "Sarah, darling, can you ever forgive me for introducing you to such a devious character as O'Donnell? My guilt over the matter is a heavy burden for me to bear."

"Nothing that happened was your fault, Will. Timothy O'Donnell had us all fooled. Fooling people is what he does best. He's an expert liar, just like his father and his mother. They are all evil people, and someday they will all burn in hell for the things they've done to people... not just to me, but everyone they came in contact with."

"Does his father know that you were beaten?"

"Oh, yes! His father was present several times when I would be beaten. His father even taught him how to strike me on the bottoms of my feet with a stick. He said it would cause me more pain when I was beaten on my feet. He was right, Will, my Lord how that did hurt. His father said that beating me would make me a more submissive wife and that I would eventually be obedient, but they underestimated me. As badly as it hurt when I was beaten, I would never consent to being treated like a dog. I'd spit in their eye first, and that's precisely what I did, many times."

"What was it about your behavior that angered them to such a great extent that they wanted to beat you?"

"When we had first arrived in Baltimore, his father and mother wanted me to work for them in the family dry goods store, which I gladly agreed to do. His father said that my face was *convincingly innocent*, and that people would naturally trust me. Immediately, they started teaching me the many different ways there are to cheat people out of money. I stood by the principles I had been taught when Mother raised me, and refused to cheat people, that's all. I told them that the Holy Bible says, *'Thou shalt not steal,'* and that's when I got my first beating, on my very first day in Baltimore. The beatings continued daily, but I still refused to steal. I've never stolen from anyone in my life, and I never will!"

"My Lord, Sarah... this is killing me to hear this..."

"Then, when I refused him his husbandly privileges in our bed, I was tied to the bed and raped. Thank God it's all over now."

"I feel that I can never make this up to you, Sarah."

"There's nothing that you or anyone else could have done to prevent this. You've rescued me from that place. That's all that matters to me now."

"Had I paid closer attention, I might have been able to gain a better assessment of his character, and relieved you of the miseries you have endured for the last three and half months."

"If you had said anything disapproving about him, I wouldn't have listened to you at the time. I thought he was a kind and gentle man, and I thought that I loved him. I was blind to anything and everything else. I think that I may have married O'Donnell out of a feeling of desperation, and it was the most foolish mistake I have ever made."

"That breaks my heart, Sarah... I fear that I will always feel responsible for everything that happened to you."

"Believe me when I say that you were in no way responsible. It was all of my own doing. I thank God that you came for me, Will. I prayed constantly that you would come for me, and you did. That's all that matters to me now, and that's all that should matter to you."

"I can't tell you in mere words, how happy I am to see you again, Sarah, and how anxious I am to take you home with me. Your mother and sister will be delirious with joy to have you in their arms again!"

"Tell me Will, are Mother and Elizabeth doing well?"

"They have missed you terribly, as we all have, but yes, they are both doing very well indeed. Wait till you see for yourself just how well your mother is doing. She glows like a candle in the night now, and you will see why she glows so brightly when you see her swollen belly. She's with child, Sarah... she's going to bear us a child in August."

"No! My mother is with child? Honest?"

"Yep. And you can be assured that your mother and Elizabeth are going to be mighty happy to see you again."

"And I shall be happy to see her and Elizabeth. You know, Will, I don't know if Mother has ever told you this, but there had always been something terribly lacking there at Montgomery Farm until you arrived. You have enriched our lives beyond measure."

"Being there with you and Abby and Elizabeth is the only life I've ever really known. Having you home again will be an answer to all our prayers."

"Would you do a special favor for me, Will?"

"If I can, I would do anything in the world for you, what is it that you want me to do?"

"Would you please not tell Elizabeth and Mother how badly I was mistreated in Baltimore?"

"Sarah, honey, your face is still badly bruised. Your left eye is still almost swollen shut. I'm afraid that all they have to do is look at you, and they'll know how badly you were treated."

"I know, Will, it's just that I would prefer that no one knows that I was bound to a bed and raped by them."

"Them? What do you mean, *them*?"

"Please, Will... things happened that are too horrible to repeat. Please love me enough to honor my need for privacy in that respect."

"Of course I will, Sarah." A torrent of hatred again flushed into Will when Sarah had used the word "*them*" in reference to her being raped. His initial impulse was to return to Baltimore, await the reappearance of O'Donnell's evil parents, and kill the whole lot of them. However, Will had the wisdom to control such urges, knowing the long arm of Baltimore law could easily reach into Virginia and snatch him from his family. His anger subsided somewhat, and he continued to listen to Sarah as she softly wept.

"I could never explain the humiliation of such a thing to Mother or Elizabeth. It was a horrible ordeal, and I only wish to go home to my family and forget that it ever happened. Had you not seen the bindings on the bedposts, I would have shielded you from the burden of such awful knowledge."

"I don't want to be shielded from anything in your life, Sarah—your burden is my burden, and it always will be."

"I just don't want people to feel sorry for me every time they look upon me. I wish there was some way that I could go home and just not have to talk to anyone about the filthy things that O'Donnell and his father did to me. It was a nightmare, and I want to forget about it as soon as I can. If Mother and Elizabeth want to talk about it, I'm afraid it'll only succeed in causing me to relive it all over again."

"I'll tell you what; when we get home, I'll go into the house first, while you wait outside, and explain things to your mother and sister so that they will not ask offensive questions. If you don't want to talk about it, you won't have to. They will understand after I talk to them, and I'm sure they will be respectful of your wishes."

"Thank you. Would you mind telling me what you did with Timothy O'Donnell before we left Baltimore, Will?"

"It's best if we put that sort of thing out of our minds and didn't discuss it, Sarah."

"Did you kill him, Will? You didn't, did you?"

"Sarah please, let's not discuss such trifle."

"All that I'm asking is for you to tell me whether you killed him or not. God forbid that you should be persecuted by the law for anything that you did back there in order to free me."

"No, I didn't kill him, Sarah. He may wish he was dead for a few weeks or a couple of months. But he'll live for many more years to regret what he did to you, I can assure you of that."

"Thank you for telling me, and thank you for not killing him. I'll ask no more questions about him. I love you, Will."

"I love you too, Sarah."

"Do you think it will take a long time for me to get divorced from O'Donnell?"

"No, it won't take very long at all. First of all, you've been married to him for less than four months. Section thirty-four of the uniform code of the Commonwealth of Virginia, article twenty, I believe, allows for expedient annulments in cases of bodily abuse. We won't have to petition for a divorce, we only have to petition for something called a '*nuntium ad destitutionem.*' In paragraph two, it says... my Lord, ...what am I saying?"

"Good gracious, Will! That's the second time that I've heard you quoting the law in such avid fluency. How is it that you have come to learn all of those details about the law and all of those mysterious Latin words?"

"Mercy... I don't know. I just don't know. It just came into my mind out of nowhere for some reason, and I just blurted it out."

"Do you think you were a barrister at one time, before coming to Montgomery Farm, Will?"

"I don't know what I was, Sarah. Lord help me, but I'm so befuddled about myself sometimes that I'm afraid I don't even know for sure what I am right now."

"Don't say that, Will. I know what you are right now, you're the most wonderful man that I've ever known."

"Let's get some rest, Sarah. We have a long day ahead of us tomorrow. Is one blanket going to be enough for you? You can have mine too, if you're cold."

"I'll be fine with one blanket Will, thank you."

"Goodnight, Sarah."

"Goodnight, Will."

o   o   o

Will had stunned himself when he had involuntarily recited certain parts of the Uniform Code of Law of the Commonwealth of Virginia. He wondered why he would have been so familiar with such an odd and multifarious subject as law. Only a well-schooled attorney would have been familiar with such a thing. He lay there in the hay that night trying to recall bits and pieces of his distant past until he finally ceased his fruitless efforts and fell asleep. His sleep was short lived, however. Waking up in the middle of the night, he was terribly cold, and began shivering profusely. He suddenly realized that if he, himself, was so cold, surely Sarah must be intolerably miserable. He took his blanket and spread it over Sarah as she slept, and then went to the corner of the barn where he could sit and wait for daybreak. He scorned himself for not making more adequate preparations. He should have brought more blankets, but he didn't know that they would be forced to sleep outdoors one night. It was not yet the second week of March, and he should have known that the possibility of cold, harsh weather from the north still loomed as a threat. Nevertheless, he remained in the corner of the barn, shivering, but content in knowing that Sarah was warm, sleeping peacefully, and away from danger.

As the night went on, Will continued shivering so violently that his teeth were chattering, and it was impossible for him to sleep. He could never remember being as cold. In the frigid stillness of the night, Sarah came to him, took him by the hand, and led him back to the pile of hay. She lay beside him in the comforting thickness of the hay, covered them over with the two blankets, and snuggled lovingly with her head on his chest. Softly, she said, "My Lord, Will, your hands are as cold as ice. You should have said something."

"I had no idea that it was going to be this cold tonight. I should have made better arrangements for us. I'm sorry that I didn't bring extra blankets for us."

"Are you warmer here beside me now, Will?"

"Much warmer, Sarah, thank you."

"I feel an intense need to be close to you tonight, Will."

"I feel the same need, darling. After reading your letter, I worried myself sick about you all the while I traveled up to Baltimore."

"May I ask you a question before we go to sleep, and will you be completely honest with me?"

"Of course I will. I love you too much to ever lie to you, Sarah."

"If you and Mother had never met and fallen in love and gotten married, do you think that you would have ever had any romantic feelings toward me?"

"Sarah, honey, your mother and I are both certain that God brought us together. Your mother and I did meet, and we did fall in love, and we did get married... and even now, I cannot help but have the warmest of feelings for you. I love you, Sarah. I always have, and I know that I always will. Your mother once told me that love is nothing to be ashamed of, and I believe her. I shall never be ashamed of the love that I have for you and Elizabeth and your mother... never. The love that I have for your mother is the very lifeblood that flows through my veins, and always will be. The love that I have for you is very different from the love that I have for your mother, but it's every bit as strong, and every bit as deep. Am I making any sense in what I'm saying?"

"Yes... I understand perfectly, Will."

"I suppose that I should love you as any stepfather would love his stepdaughter, but I can't. My love for you is so powerful that I think of you and Elizabeth as my very own daughters... and I can't help it."

"You've brought a joy to my heart that I could never explain. I would give anything in the world if I could step back in time and erase the last four months of my life and the stupid errors I have committed when I left Montgomery Farm, Will."

"We all have errors in our past that we would like to erase, Sarah. Fortunately, for me, I cannot remember very many of mine. But, it serves no useful purpose to dwell in the past. God expects us to look forward—that's why He created us with our eyes in the front of our head, and not in the back. Look to the past only long enough to learn from your mistakes, then, look forward, my dear. Every moment that we dwell in the past only steals precious time from the present."

"I gave my purity to an evil man... If only I could have given it to someone of virtue... someone with a kind heart and gentle nature... someone who loved me."

"Losing your purity is not the end of the world, Sarah. In your heart, you need to look upon it as the beginning of a new chapter in your life. You're very young, and very beautiful, and you have your whole life to look forward to. Somewhere in this world, there is a perfect gentleman waiting just for you. He's out there somewhere, and probably frantically searching for you at this very moment, and I would wager that he's a handsome rascal with a lot of love to give you. When we get home, you really should talk to your mother. She's the most wonderful woman I've ever known, and she can help you get through this difficult period."

"I will talk to Mother. But I must be honest with you, Will, you have given me great comfort in sharing your words with me just now. I've never met anyone like you, Will. I love you more than you may ever know."

"Things will look much brighter to you when we get home, and you are once again in the arms of your mother and Elizabeth. Don't hesitate to talk to your mother when we get home. She loves you, Sarah."

"I know she does, Will, and I love her and Elizabeth as well."

"Let's get some sleep, dear. We have many miles to cross between here and Montgomery Farm, and there's two very anxious ladies waiting down in Rockingham County who are just dying to see you again."

"May I hold you closely as we sleep?"

"You may hold me as closely as you like, darling. Sarah? Are you crying, dear?"

"I can't help it, Will. I'm so happy to be going home, and it feels so good to be in your arms like this. I feel like... for the first time in my life, I actually have a father who loves me. I feel protected here with you, like no one could harm me when I'm with you."

"You are protected, Sarah. I would give my life to protect you. I hope you know that."

"I do, and I love you, Will. I shall always love you."

After having a hot breakfast at the inn, Will and Sarah were on their way home, on the final leg of their journey, bypassing Charlottesville and Lynchburg. Sarah became increasingly excited with the encouraging prospects of seeing her mother and sister again, and even more excited when she began to recognize familiar landmarks along the roadway. She had learned an important lesson in life, and had paid a great price for having gained that knowledge. She could see clearly now that she had never married Timothy O'Donnell out of love in the first place. She had married him solely because she had succumbed to her immature and almost insatiable yearning for male companionship, and in such a vulnerable state of mind she had quickly fallen victim to his lies and his deceitful words of love. She married him because she felt an impulse of desperation, and he was handily available to take advantage of her desolation. Timothy O'Donnell was cruel, selfish, and demanding, and didn't know the meaning of the word, '*love.*' Sarah was correct when she had told Will that Timothy was just like his father. Sarah and Timothy's relationship became volatile from the moment they had departed Montgomery Farm, but he had never struck her until they arrived in Baltimore and his evil parents were introduced into their affiliation, and they were well away from the protective arms of William Collins. Sarah had learned the true horrors of the words, *fear* and *evil*, and could only now begin to fully understand the true meaning of the word, *love*. In Sarah's young eyes, God had only created one perfect man, and the man's name was William Collins.

o   o   o

Everything disastrous that had occurred in Sarah's brief marriage was in the past now, and Will vowed that he would never allow anything such as the evilment of Timothy O'Donnell to befall her again. He bore a tremendous sense of guilt for having encouraged her association with O'Donnell, and felt as though he would carry the scars of that guilt to his grave. Will loved Sarah as only a true father could, and the ordeal that she had endured at O'Donnell's wicked hands had instilled William with the grandest sense of the responsibility of guardianship. He would do anything to protect his precious family and to make amends for the act of not paying proper attention to Sarah's welfare. While Sarah bore no permanent scars from her ungodly nightmare, Will, on the other hand, had been scarred quite deeply.

o   o   o

It was approaching three o'clock on the afternoon of March thirtieth when a very weary Will and Sarah rode their horses onto Montgomery Farm property and saw a ribbon of inviting white smoke rising from the chimney of the house on the hill in the distance.

"Look, Sarah! Do you see what I see? There it is! There's Montgomery House! Can you see it?! How does it look to you, young lady?"

"It's beautiful, Will, just beautiful! My God... I'm home! I can't believe I'm really home!"

"I can almost smell your Mother's coffee and biscuits from here!"

"Me too, Will! Thank Jesus we're home! I've been gone for nearly four months, and it warms my soul to see my home again!"

"I've only been away for nine and a half days, yet it seems like an eternity! I can only imagine how you must feel, Sarah!"

278

○ ○ ○

Ezra and his two sons, Josh and George, were the first to take notice of Will and Sarah's approach from the north. They met them at the barn to take charge of their horses, and unintentionally looked upon Sarah's badly bruised face with stunned disbelief at what they saw. Taking a deep breath to control his emotions, Ezra said, "Welcome home, Miss Sarah, welcome home, Mister Will!"

"It's good to be home, Ezra! Will you and your sons kindly take care of our horses for us, please?"

"Yes Sir, Mister Will."

"The saddles need to be oiled before they are put away and Sarah's horse and these other two are new horses. They need to be stabled for a couple of days before they are turned out to pasture with the other horses."

"Don't you worry about a thing, Mister Will, we'll take care of everything. You and Miss Sarah just leave everything to us. I 'spect Miss Abigail and Miss Elizabeth is gonna be mighty glad to see you all! They been a lookin' at yonder road a hundred times a day, just a waitin' to see ya'll a coming!"

"Thank you, Ezra."

Neither Ezra nor his sons said anything in regards to Sarah's bruised and battered appearance, but their astonished eyes had forespoken the fact that they had taken due notice thereof. Will took Sarah by the hand and walked to the side of the house, where he asked her to sit outside on the porch until he had the opportunity to go inside and prepare her mother and her sister for what they were about to see. After leaving Sarah on the side porch, he went to the rear porch, and walked directly into the kitchen. Abby and Lizzy were busily preoccupied with preparing dinner, when they looked around to see Will and shouted in unison, "**Will!**"

"It's so good to see my wonderful family again!"

Abby and Lizzy quickly set aside what they were doing, wiped their hands on their aprons, and ran to embrace Will.

"Did you not find our Sarah, Will?"

"Yes, I did find her, Abby... I did indeed."

"Why is she not with you? I thought you were going to bring her home to us. Don't tell me she decided to stay with O'Donnell after the way he's treated her?"

"No... no. Settle down for a moment and listen to me, both of you. Sarah is outside on the side porch, but I wanted the opportunity to talk to both of you before she comes inside."

"Why? Is she alright?"

"As we expected in reading her letter, Sarah has been badly mistreated. Her face is bruised considerably, and more than anything, she is in need of tender affection from her mother and her sister."

"Oh dear God!"

"When she comes inside and removes her bonnet, please try to refrain from undue emotion, for Sarah's sake."

"My God, Will..."

"She's in dire need of a long, hot bath, and she's very tired. Now listen closely... Her injuries will heal quickly, so please don't let her see you looking horrified at the sight of her bruised face. She limps a little when she walks because she was severely beaten on the bottom of her feet, but her feet will also heal quickly now that she's home."

"God love her... we'll give her the best of care..."

"Try to act as normal as possible, and whatever you do, don't question her about the details of the ordeal she's been through. She doesn't want to talk about any of the specifics. I'll tell you both everything you need to know about it tonight, when Sarah is in her bed asleep."

"Alright, Will... anything you say."

"Like I said, she needs your love and understanding now more than she ever has."

"Please bring my baby inside to us, Will. I can't wait another minute!"

Will brought Sarah into the house, and Sarah simply removed

her bonnet, looked up at her mother and sister, and shyly said, "Hello Mother, hello Elizabeth."

Abby and Elizabeth instantly surrounded her with love and affection, not to mention hundreds of tender kisses, and despite Will's forewarning, the three women sobbed to such an extent that Will had to leave the room so that they would not see the abundant tears that were beginning to form in his own eyes. It was a sweet reunion that would have warmed the coldest of hearts. Sarah had always been notoriously mischievous, brazenly outspoken at times, and seemed somewhat unruly and even impishly naughty when compared to her older and more reserved sister, Elizabeth. But under the childish façade of capriciousness, her heart was tender and pure, and she never deserved being exposed to the vileness of the O'Donnell family as she had been.

Abby and Lizzy temporarily ceased their preparations for dinner and instead, prepared a tub of hot water in Sarah's upstairs bedchamber where she could have the luxury of a proper bath. Lizzy attended to treating the many facial injuries of her sister and assisted her in bathing and washing her hair while Abby resumed her efforts to prepare a meal. Will helped Abby in the kitchen, and they talked about all that had transpired that day.

"Thank you for bringing her home to us, Will. I thank God every day for your presence here in our lives. I don't know how we would ever manage things around here if it wasn't for you."

"I was the sole cause of Sarah's nightmare by introducing her to that devilish bastard. I could never have reconciled with myself had I not gone to bring her home when I did, and even now I feel as though my heart may never be rid of the guilt I bear."

"As you told us to do, Elizabeth and I have talked very little with Sarah about what was done to her in Baltimore. We are trying to keep our conversations as lighthearted and merriful as possible. Sarah is soaking her bruised feet in warm water now while Lizzy is brushing her hair and treating her like a princess. We won't talk about any of the details unless Sarah brings it up."

"That's good, Abby. I think that will be best for everyone, especially Sarah."

"Elizabeth and I don't need to hear the horrible details, we can see by her bruises what was done. The bottoms of both her feet are nearly black from being bruised so badly. I think that you are right, the sooner we can put this behind us, the sooner we can all mend. I just have one question at the forefront of my mind that desperately needs to be answered, Will, and no one can answer it but you."

"What is it?"

"Did you kill O'Donnell?"

"It's strange that you would ask me that, Abby, Sarah asked me the same question on the way home one night."

"Well, did you kill him?"

"Why do you ask such a question, Abby? Do you see a murderer when you look upon me? Have you no faith in me?"

"I have every faith in the world in you, Will, but I saw the rage in your eyes when you read Sarah's letter that afternoon. Such rage was still in your eyes when you rode away from Montgomery Farm. I don't want to wake up one day and find that you have been taken by the law to face a vengeful Yankee court in Baltimore."

"I'll be honest with you, I left Montgomery Farm with every intention of killing him. I will admit that I thought about it long and hard, and came very close, but no, I didn't kill him, Abby. I probably should have, and like I said, I wanted to, but I didn't. Instead of killing him, I tied him to the same bed where he had restrained our sweet Sarah, gave him as many or more bruises as I thought Sarah had received, untied him, and went on my way, that's all. As for his male attributes... well... it will be weeks or even months before he feels like fondling with himself or raping another helpless woman, I can assure you of that."

"I'm glad that you didn't kill him, Will. It gives me great peace of mind. Thank you for telling me."

"On Monday, I plan to take Sarah to the Magistrate's office

in Blanchard and present a petition for an annulment. I want to take care of that while the bruises on her face and arms are still clearly visible. I want the magistrate to see what O'Donnell did to her with his own eyes. Once she is shed of the shameful O'Donnell name, I think it will be possible for her to attend to living the rest of her life as a normal and happy young woman."

"God bless you for all you've done, Will."

"Sarah has deep regrets for having been deceived into giving her virginity to a fiend like O'Donnell. Will you talk to her, Abby, and try to help her put that sort of thing behind her? I tried to comfort her in that respect, but it's awkward for me to talk to her about such tender and personal things as that. It's hard for me to even listen to her talk about such things without my choking up and becoming tearful. Would you talk to her for both of us?"

"Of course I will. I suppose the next suitor that comes to Montgomery House to call on her will have a difficult time satisfying the expectations of her stepfather."

"I don't even want to think about her having suitors for a good long while. But you're right, the next time there is a suitor, he's going to have a very difficult time getting my approval, and an even more difficult time if he tries to deceive me. I learned a horrible lesson at Sarah's expense... one that I'll never forget. I might add that I will be equally as protective of Elizabeth. As I have often told you, I love them both dearly. Their happiness means so much to me... I've told you before that I would gladly give my life for you or your daughters, and I meant every word of it."

"I love you with every ounce of my being, Will Collins."

"I want you to do something important for me, Abby, when the right opportunity presents itself."

"I'll do anything for you, Will."

"Without upsetting her, I want you to discretely ask Sarah if she's with child. I didn't talk to her about such a personal thing on the way home, but it's an issue that is weighing heavily on my mind."

"Elizabeth and I have already inquired of her about that very thing when we were preparing her bath. She doesn't think she is pregnant, but will not know for certain until her next cycle."

"I'm not familiar with what a cycle is, but when you know for sure, one way or the other, will you please tell me so that I can cease worrying?"

"Yes."

"It's an issue that is eating away at the very fiber of my soul, and I shan't rest until I know the answer. Surrendering her virginity to an insensitive bastard such as O'Donnell is heartbreaking in itself, but to think that she may be carrying the horrible seed of an O'Donnell child inside of her is almost more than I can bear."

"If she is carrying his child, we will erase the father's name from our minds and memories and raise the child lovingly, as if it were our own."

"Of course we will, Abby."

The coming weeks found the family deeply involved with the spring preparation of their land, the planting of crops, and all of the associated chores necessary to keep the farm operating and profitable. As Will and Abby had both predicted, Sarah's bruises soon healed and her spirits became much more elevated with the passing of each new day. Ever present in the forefront of Will's mind had been the threatening possibility that Sarah was carrying the seed of Timothy O'Donnell, or perhaps even his father's child in her womb. During the coming weeks, his apprehensions were put to rest, and he received reassuring confirmation through Abby's personal private moments with her daughter that she was not with child.

An annulment petition was presented, filed, and approved by the Rockingham County Magistrate, and a summons of notification was sent to Baltimore for Timothy O'Donnell to appear at the Blanchard Town Office of the magistrate to present an argument if he wished to contest the annulment proceedings. The magistrate, having been well acquainted with

Sarah before her marriage, had become visibly ill when Sarah removed her bonnet and displayed her bruises. O'Donnell never answered by letter or personal appearance, and on the sixth day of May, the magistrate declared the annulment official. When Will had initially presented the petition to the magistrate, the magistrate was unaware that such an expedient annulment was legally possible until Will quoted the section and article number under the uniform code of Virginia law where such a proceeding was recorded. The law allowed that a marriage shorter in duration than six months could be annulled within thirty days of notifying the spouse, if there was evidence of physical abuse involved. The occurrence once again left Will and the family baffled as to why he was so familiar with the laws of the Commonwealth of Virginia. Aside from their puzzlement over the issue, the family was pleased to have this difficult period finally put behind them.

During the same period of time that Will had submitted the petition for the annulment of Sarah's marriage, he had also filed a writ of *legalis nomen* for the legal name entitlement of William Collins with the same court magistrate. It was approved and filed at the courthouse the same day as the annulment, and the name of William Collins was now the legal identity that Will would use thereafter.

It was Will's normal daily routine to arise from bed before Abby, usually just a short time before dawn. Once he had dressed, he would slip silently out of the bedchamber, leaving Abby to sleep peacefully for another hour or more. He would walk to the chicken house, open the door, and feed the chickens crushed corn from a storage bin in the barn. Then he would busy himself with whatever chores needed to be done, feed the mules and horses, and walk back to the henhouse. There, he would gather the eggs, and walk back to the house when all of his chores had been completed. Usually, by the first sign of dawn, Lizzy and Sarah would have a fire going in the stove and Abby would be there to put a pot of coffee on to boil and begin the task of making the biscuits. Once Lizzy and Sarah had started a fire, they would go to the barn to feed and milk the cows. When everything went according to their normal routine, the sun would be starting to rise on the eastern horizon by this time, and the family would sit at the table together to enjoy their morning coffee and discuss their plans for the upcoming day. Enjoying their morning coffee together had become a ritual that everyone looked forward to. It was a jovial time in which the family would discuss their individual plans for the day, and it was also a treasured time for lighthearted family conversation, and a daily reaffirmation of the love they shared between them.

Their daily routine would prove to be different than normal on the morning of the twenty-ninth day of May. Will returned to the house with the eggs as usual, but when he walked into the kitchen, he found Sarah and Lizzy attending to the chore of making the coffee instead of Abby, and the biscuits hadn't even been started yet.

"Good morning, my sweet ladies. Where's your wonderful mother?"

"Good morning! She's still upstairs in your bedchamber. She hasn't come down yet. Sarah and I thought it would be best if we let her sleep for a while longer this morning. She looked unusually weary when she retired last night."

"I also took notice of how weary she seemed last evening. This is mighty nice that you would allow her some extra rest this morning. Would either of you beautiful ladies care to pour an ugly old farmhand a cup of hot coffee?"

Sarah quickly spoke up, "The coffee hasn't boiled yet and Lizzy and I have looked high and low this morning trying to find an ugly old farmhand. There's simply not one to be found anywhere. But if we do find one, you'll be the first to know."

Then Lizzy spoke up to add to the lightheartedness, "But Sarah and I have discovered that there's a tall, handsome farmhand who just delivered eggs to us. Perhaps Sarah and I can find a cup of coffee for him when it boils."

"Ha! If I ever fail to tell you both how much you mean to me, I hope someone takes a gun and shoots me. I love you both dearly."

"We love you too, Will. One of these days Sarah and I will get Mother to teach us how she makes the biscuits so perfectly every time."

"You know, your mother always makes the coffee too, and it always turns out perfectly every time. I hope you two lovely ladies aren't conspiring together this morning, with plans to poison me."

Everyone was in good spirits, yet in the back of everyone's mind, they couldn't avoid feeling a mild concern over Abby's absence. She was usually there every morning to add to the merriment, and her absence there in the kitchen dampened everyone's spirits somewhat. She was entering her seventh month of pregnancy now, how could they not be somewhat concerned? Nearly an hour later, when Abby had still not come down, Will decided to go upstairs and inquire of her. He opened the door to their bedchamber slowly, and saw that Abby was still lying on the bed, her eyes opened, and looking toward the door as he stood there.

"Abby, darling, are you feeling ill this morning?"

"Somewhat, perhaps. I feel strange this morning for some reason, Will, and I find myself with precious little energy as well. I just don't seem to have the strength to get out of the bed, and I've had the most awful stomach cramps this morning."

"You're not preparing to give birth already, are you?"

"No, I don't think it's anything like that, Will, although I should be getting close to that time in another six or seven weeks. I don't know what could be wrong with me, but I feel like it's surely nothing to be overly concerned about. I'll probably be alright in another hour or so."

"May I fetch you anything, a cup of tea or coffee perhaps?"

"No, thank you. I'll be fine. I just want to rest some more, if you don't mind. It's unusual for me to feel this poorly, and I may feel better shortly."

"Sarah and Elizabeth have breakfast ready. Would you like for me to bring yours up here to you, and treat you like the queen you really are for a change?"

"Thank you, darling, but I have no appetite at all, and I'm feeling very odd at my stomach. Perhaps later, dear."

"I'm not going to the fields today until I know that you are feeling better. I will be downstairs in the kitchen. I'm going to leave your door open so we can hear you from downstairs. Will you call for me or one of the girls if you need anything?"

"Yes, darling... I will. Thank you."

About mid-morning, Abby called for Will and asked him if he would summon Vivian. As a midwife, Vivian had been attending to the childbearing needs of expectant women for years, and perhaps she could determine what ailed Abby. Vivian came to her bedside, and lingered at her bedside throughout the remainder of the day. Vivian examined Abby thoroughly, and although she feared the worse, she said nothing which she thought might upset Abby. She had felt no movement from within Abby's belly and feared that Abby and Will's child was dead, yet she kept her suspicions to herself, and suggested that Abby send for Dr. Michaels. Abby felt as though the doctor's presence at this point was unnecessary. Family concerns over Abby's welfare continued to rise with each passing hour. She was normally vivacious and full of energy, and her current illness was met with extreme anxiety throughout the household.

By noon hour the next day, Abby's condition had not changed, except that the intensity and frequency of the cramps had worsened. She asked Vivian to quietly summon Ezra to her bedside. When Ezra arrived, she asked him to ride into Blanchard and fetch the physician, and she asked him to perform another task while he was in Blanchard—to carry word to her family's attorney, Lawrence Brumfield, that she wished for him to pay her a visit there at Montgomery Farm. The physician arrived late that afternoon, and after a long series of examinations, he left Abby's bedside and retired to the parlor to speak with Abby's daughters and William. The somber expression on his face foretold that he had unpleasant news to convey. Will looked into the doctor's eyes, and what he saw brought immediate fear into his trembling body and soul.

"Mr. Collins, it grieves me to be the bearer of unpleasant news, but I fear that the child that your wife carries is no longer a living child. I can hear no heartbeat or detect any movement whatsoever. I'm so very sorry to have to tell you this."

Sarah and Lizzy erupted with distraught sadness, and in tears, they embraced each other as Will accepted the news with equal difficulty, leaned against the parlor table to steady his trembling knees, and asked the physician, "What about Mrs. Collins, Doctor, will she be alright soon?"

"Her body is preparing to pass the child as we speak. In cases of stillborn children, we never know the effects it will have on the mother. These things are difficult to predict with any degree of certainty. Her condition will remain indeterminate until after she gives birth. I wish that I could tell you more, but at this time, I can't."

"How soon will she bring forth the child, Doctor?"

"This evening or tonight, I expect, and I would think no later than tomorrow morning."

"Will you please remain here with her until our baby is brought forth?"

"Of course, I wouldn't think of leaving her at a time like this. I will require the assistance of your midwife, Vivian. She has about as much experience in these matters as I do, and will be of great assistance to me when your wife progresses more into her birthing labors."

"Vivian is in the kitchen preparing some hot water. You may go in and instruct her as you like. I wish to go upstairs and speak to my wife privately for a few minutes, if I may."

"Vivian and I will be upstairs in a half hour or forty-five minutes. Does that give you enough time to speak with her, Mr. Collins?"

It seemed like the longest climb to the top of the stairs that Will had ever made. He was almost delirious with concern as he took in a deep breath and entered the room. He did not want Abby to see him in such a pitiful state of despair, so he dried his tears and put forth his greatest effort to disguise the extent of his deepest concerns. Bringing forth a sympathetic smile, he asked, "Abby, how do you feel, darling?"

"Dr. Michaels says that our child is dead, Will."

"I know. He told me as much downstairs just now."

"I have failed you, Will. As much as I love you, I have failed to deliver you a child. I'm so sorry."

"Lord have mercy, please don't cry. You haven't failed me. You haven't failed at anything. Listen to me, Abby, you are the most precious and important thing in my life. We can try to have another child, if it's God's will. If it's not His will, we still have each other, and we still have Elizabeth and Sarah. We are a family, Abby, and if we never have a child together, we have already been blessed immeasurably. God has brought us together—that in itself has been a miracle."

"You've always told me that you love children, and I wanted so badly to give you children that I cannot help but feel that I have failed you."

"In my heart, I feel like God will send us a child someday... this just wasn't the time, Abby. We need to accept that and go on with our lives."

"I love you, Will Collins. As God looks down on me from above, I swear I do."

William spent the night in a chair at Abby's bedside, and early the next morning, Sarah and Elizabeth brought coffee upstairs to them. Abby took a sip or two of her coffee, and soon felt that she was beginning her birthing labors. The physician was summoned from downstairs, and when he entered the room, Lawrence Brumfield, the family's attorney was with him. Puzzled at the appearance of the attorney, Will asked, "Mr. Brumfield, is there a reason that you are here this morning?"

Abby spoke up quickly to answer Will so that Brumfield would not have to, saying, "He's here because I sent for him, Will. Did you bring the documents that I requested, Mr. Brumfield?"

"Yes, Mrs. Collins, I certainly did."

"Good. Will, Could I please have a moment or two with Mr. Brumfield in private?"

"You're going into your birthing labors! Is something wrong, Abby? What's going on here?"

"Please, Will? Just trust in me, dear."

"Very well, I'll be out in the hallway if you need me."

Abby's peculiar request puzzled Will, but he and everyone else complied with her request, and left the room. Brumfield was in the room with Abby for less than ten minutes when he walked out with his satchel in his hand, bid everyone farewell, and walked down the stairway. Midway down the stairs, he turned back to Will and said, "Mr. Collins, your family will be in my prayers." He soon left the house and rode away, back toward Blanchard. Will and the others walked back into the bedchamber and Will asked, "Can you tell me what that was all about, Abby?"

"I'll tell you later, Will. The pain is becoming much more intense now, and I think the baby is coming at any time now."

"The physician quickly commanded, "Everyone but Vivian please leave the room and go downstairs!"

The next two and a half hours were agonizing for every member of the family. The cries of Abby's physical pain came as a soul-tormenting agony to Will and the sisters as they waited impatiently in the parlor. Finally, The sounds of pain ceased, and Vivian quickly came to the top of the stairs and announced that Abby was fine. Just as quickly, she rushed back inside to assist the doctor. As the doctor had predicted, Abby and Will's baby was stillborn. The tiny child was wrapped in a white linen pillow case and its body was placed in a small coffin that Ezra and Will had constructed, measuring less than thirty inches in length. Tearfully, Sarah and Elizabeth prepared a large kettle of water over a fire behind the house, where the bedsheets carried outside by Vivian could be washed and bleached, and hung out to dry. It was late that afternoon before the physician finally came downstairs and told Will that he could see his beloved Abby.

"Your wife is very weak, Mr. Collins. She passed an unusually large amount of blood. That in itself is not unusual in cases of stillborn births. She needs perfect rest now. Please do not say anything to upset her. I have given her some laudanum to help ease her pain and help her rest. You may go in for ten minutes or so, but please stay no longer than that."

"How long will it take her to recover from this, Doctor?"

"Mr. Collins, I have done everything within my power that I can do. Her recovery is not up to me, she's in God's hands now."

Once again, Will climbed the long stairway. When he walked into the room, he saw Vivian, sitting by Abby's side, wiping her forehead with a cool cloth. Abby's eyes were closed, and she appeared to be resting quietly. Softly, Will asked, "Is she asleep, Vivian?

But before Vivian could return an answer, Abby herself answered, saying, "No, I'm not asleep, Will... I'm just... terribly tired... I was lying here with my eyes closed... thinking about you."

"Does you want me to leave you and Miss Abigail alone, Mr. Will?"

"Just for a few minutes, Vivian. Doctor Michaels told me not to stay longer than a few minutes. I'll keep her forehead dampened until you come back, and I'll only stay for a brief time."

When Vivian had left the room, Will softly said, "I love you, Abigail Collins... more than I love life itself."

"I love you, too, sweetheart... I always will."

"Can I get anything for you, Abby, anything at all?"

"Listen to me for a moment, dear. I need to tell you something very important while I have the energy to talk."

"Please don't force yourself to talk, Abby. Doctor Michaels said that you should rest as much as possible."

"I'll be brief, but I need to tell you this, Will, it's important to me."

"Then take your time, and don't exert yourself, Abby."

"I had Lawrence Brumfield file an amendment to the deed for Montgomery Farm. It's been recorded by now at the courthouse, and everything is official."

"An amendment? What kind of amendment?"

"The deed now carries your name along with mine as the owners of Montgomery Farm. If I should die, you become the sole owner."

"Abby... please, you don't have to talk about this sort of thing now. We'll discuss this later, when you're feeling better. Right now, you need your rest more than anything else."

"No, Will... I need *you* more than anything else. My future is so uncertain... I feel like... I need to tell you a few things, in the event that I should die."

"You're not going to die, Abby! God would not bring us together like this simply to tear us apart! I know He wouldn't! Please don't push yourself, Abby. We can talk about this sort of thing tomorrow or the next day, or even next week."

"Always the optimist, aren't you, Will? I may not have tomorrow or the next day, darling. Promise me that if anything happens to me that you will take care of Sarah and Elizabeth... they love you so much... please promise me."

"Nothing is going to happen to you, Abby!"

"Now is not a good time to be hardheaded, Will... Don't argue with me, please. I lack the strength to argue back with you... Just promise me that you will take care of my daughters if I die."

"Of course I will. I swear it. I'll watch over them until the day that I breathe my last breath. Please say no more, darling. Please rest now."

As if Will's words had given Abby a great deal of reassuring comfort, she was soon immersed in a deep sleep. Vivian returned shortly, and Will went downstairs to the parlor to speak with Elizabeth and Sarah. He knew they were waiting anxiously to receive word about their mother. In fact, they were waiting impatiently at the bottom of the stairs when Will walked down.

"Will! Can we go upstairs and see Mother now?"

"She's asleep now, Sarah. The doctor gave her some medicine to help her rest and she's fallen fast asleep, thank God. She appears to be in a perfect rest. The three of us can go upstairs together in an hour or two and look in on her, but according to Dr. Michaels, we shouldn't do anything to disturb her while she is sleeping. Vivian is up there with her now, and if Abby needs anything, Vivian will summon us."

"Is Mother going to be alright, Will? This isn't something that's terribly serious, is it?"

That single question broke Will's resolve to remain strong for the sisters, and he lapsed into pitiful, involuntary sobs. Sarah and Elizabeth sat down at the parlor table, realizing the extreme seriousness of their mother's condition. Clearing his throat, Will looked down at the floor, and said, "Your mother is very ill. The doctor says that she is in God's hands now. I suppose we all are, and always have been, and always will be."

Elizabeth glanced upward from her chair to look at William. The sister's eyes were still red from crying over the serious illness that had claimed the life of Abigail's baby, and now the strange sickness threatened to claim their mother's life as well. Will poured himself a glass of brandy and took a sip, and then another. Dispensing with taking small sips, Will drank the remaining half-glass of brandy in one big swallow. Sarah and Elizabeth came to him, and the three of them embraced as Will tearfully offered a prayer for God to heal Abby.

"Lord, we humbly come before you... [*long pause*] to ask that you spare Abby's life. If it be thy will, Lord, I would gladly offer my own life in place of her's. I cannot face tomorrow without Abby by my side, Lord... I just can't..."

William could not finish his prayer, so Elizabeth completed it for him, choking down tears of emotion until she finally uttered, "God, please bless our mother... Amen."

Elizabeth and Sarah visited Abby's bedside that evening, but she did not awaken to talk to them. Again, Will spent the night in a chair at Abby's bedside. An oil lamp remained lighted by her bed, but had been turned down to its lowest level of brightness. There was no sleep for Will that night, save for a few very short moments of drifting off from sheer exhaustion. Having achieved no sleep the night before, his body was crying out for rest, yet his heart would not permit it. At about three-thirty in the morning, Will left her bedside long enough to go downstairs for another glass of brandy. Afterwards, he climbed the stairs again and sat back down in his chair at Abby's side. He reached over and swabbed her forehead with a cool, damp cloth, picked her hand up and kissed it, and even though she was oblivious to his words, he spoke softly to her.

"Abby, I know you can't hear me, darling, but I feel compelled to tell you again how much you mean to me. My Lord, Abby, sometimes I wish that you could see yourself through my eyes. You are the most beautiful woman that has ever walked the face of the earth, I swear you are. In a way, it scares me that I don't know who I was before I came here. Yet, regardless of who I was before, I know that my life only began when I met you. I have never been happier than I have been here with you. I know that if it's God's will that He takes you up to heaven, there's nothing that I can do about it. If that should happen, I feel like I wouldn't even want to go on living, except that I have made a promise to you that I would love and watch over Elizabeth and Sarah. My Lord, Abby, I don't think there has ever been a man who has loved a woman as much as I love you, and..."

At a time when Will had assumed that he had no more tears remaining within him, he erupted again into soft sobs. As he softly cried, he felt Abby's hand move... and then...

"Will..."

"Dear Jesus! Did you say something, Abby?"

"Will?"

"Yes, Abby, I'm right here, darling."

"What time is it, Will?"

"Time? I don't know, I don't have my timepiece with me, but

it must be about four o'clock in the morning or so. Do you need anything, Abby?"

"Yes, Will, I need a few things if you don't mind... Is Vivian nearby to assist me?"

"No, Abby, Vivian has gone to her home for some rest. She won't be back until daybreak. Should I go and fetch her?"

"No, dear. I'm sure she needs her rest. Perhaps you can just help me a little, if you would, please."

"I'm so thankful that you can speak to me, just tell me what you need, honey, and I'll do anything I can, but please don't exert yourself unnecessarily."

"I need for you to help me use a chamber pot first and change my compresses. I'm afraid that I lack the strength to attend myself at present."

"Sure. Wait right here and I'll fetch one, Abby."

Will ran quickly to the next bedchamber and woke Elizabeth. Together, they assisted Abby in the performance of her personal needs. Her urine was discolored greatly with blood, but Will was so thankful that Abby was able to speak to him again, that nothing else seemed to matter to him. Will and Elizabeth changed Abby's compresses, cleaned her, and carefully eased her back into her bed, covered her with a light blanket, and Will softly asked, "What else do you need, Abby?"

"Tell me something, Will... our baby... was it, a boy?"

"Yes, darling, it was."

"Has he been buried yet?"

"No, Abby. We plan to attend to that at first light this morning."

"Will you bury him beside my mother and grandfather, in that small space to the east of Mother's grave? Do you know the place I'm talking about?"

"Yes darling, I know exactly where you're talking about, and I'll take care of everything. Do you need anything right now, Abby, anything at all?"

"I know it's early in the morning, and this may sound like an insane request, Will, but I would pay a king's ransom for a cup of hot coffee... if that's not asking too much at this unmerciful hour..."

By this time, Elizabeth was overcome with joy that her mother was showing encouraging signs of early improvement, and with tears on her cheeks again, she looked at her mother and said, "It will be my pleasure to fix you a nice hot cup of coffee, Mother. I'll wake Sarah, and we'll run downstairs and get started immediately."

"Wait, Elizabeth, before you go, I want you to come here and let your mother give her sweet daughter and best friend a kiss."

"What about your husband, Abby? Don't I get a kiss or anything?"

"I'll give you your kisses after Elizabeth has left the room, if you promise not to make my face and neck red."

"A half hour ago, I felt as though my heart was breaking. Seeing you alert and feeling better is about the most precious feeling I could imagine."

"I love you, Will."

"I love you too, Abby. Dr. Michaels is asleep on the settee down in the parlor. Should I go downstairs and wake him so that he can come upstairs and take a look at you?"

"No... thank you. I've seen enough of him to last for a while, and I'm sure that he's seen enough of me to last a good, long time. Let's allow him to sleep a while longer. The only faces I desire to see this morning are the faces of my wonderful husband and my sweet daughters."

Elizabeth hurried down the hall and woke Sarah, and before going downstairs, everyone gathered at Abby's bedside as Will said a prayer of thankfulness for the encouraging improvement in Abby's condition.

Later that morning, Abby and Will's baby was buried in the family cemetery in a simple service attended only by the family, a minister, and Ezra and Vivian. With her Bible in her hand, Abigail had watched the brief burial service from her bedchamber window, after which the minister, Will, and Abby had prayer together in the privacy of her bedchamber. The next day, Will made a temporary grave marker for the infant that was later replaced with one of stone. This simple epitaph for the child was inscribed:

Collins Baby Boy
Of
William and Abigail Collins
Taken at birth to be with God
May 30, 1867

Although Abigail continued to remain bedridden for the next five days, each day she showed small improvements over the day before, and each day found the family's spirits elevated to new heights. As Abigail continued to regain her strength, Will assisted her in taking short walks to contribute to her recovery. At first, they only walked as far as the front and side porches of the house, and as she grew stronger, they walked to the barn, and eventually as far as a hilltop overlooking the crop fields. One night, as Will sat half-asleep in his chair at Abigail's bedside, she reached out to take his hand and beckoned him to join her in their bed.

"Please come to me, Will. I want to know that you are by my side as we sleep. I can't tolerate another moment of your absence."

"Are you sure that my presence in your bed would not be too much of a disturbance to you?"

"I require your presence in order that I may feel comforted, Will. Besides, it's not *my* bed, Will, it's *our* bed."

Normalcy soon returned to their lives there at Montgomery House. Will worked as hard as usual in the fields with the other workmen and Abigail and her daughters tended to their many chores, much as they had done before the tragic loss of Will and Abigail's baby. The farm continued to show a healthy profit, the family enjoyed their weekly visits to church each Sabbath, and peace and harmony abounded once again on Montgomery Farm. Seven weeks later, marital intimacy was also restored within the marriage of William and Abigail, yet from Abigail's perspective, the intimacy shared between them lacked the ultimate fulfillment that had always defined their relationship before... fulfillment that Abigail so desperately desired. She did not want to hurt Will's feelings, because she knew that he loved her more than he loved life itself, but she nevertheless broached the delicate issue in the privacy of their bedchamber late one evening.

"Will, may I hold your hand and speak to you, Darling?"

"Sure, Abby, is something wrong?"

"I want to talk to you from the depths of my heart for a moment, Will, and all I ask of you is that you listen to me with your heart. Will you do that for me, darling?"

"I could never do otherwise. I have always listened to you with my heart. I sense that what you are about to say to me is something of vital importance... isn't it?"

"Yes, darling, it's about you and me, Will, and our physical intimacy... and it's extremely important to me."

"Oh? Is something wrong, Abby? Am I being too rough with you in any way when we...?"

"No, darling, that's not it at all. If anything, the opposite is true. It's just that I feel like you are denying us of that same ultimate fulfillment that we both used to crave. I'm sure that I know your intentions, and while they may seem quite honorable, you are unknowingly robbing us both of that precious sense of fulfillment, like we used to share with each other."

"I think I know what you're about to say, Abby, but just to be sure, perhaps you should go ahead and tell me..."

"Since I lost our child, each time we are intimate with each other, you withdraw yourself at the most critical time, denying me of your life-essence and denying us both the ultimate fulfillment that I think we both need. You handle me as though I was a fragile item that might break, holding tight reign over your passion instead of releasing it to run its natural course. In doing so, Will, I feel like our passion has become subdued, and not nearly as meaningful for either of us."

"I knew that was what you were going to say... and, I suppose I've been expecting you to say something days before now. I love you, Abby, and..."

"You're afraid that I might conceive again, aren't you, Will?"

"No, I'm not simply afraid that you might conceive again, Abby, I'm absolutely frightened to death that you might!"

"Why, what is it that you fear so much?"

"Why? Good Lord, Abby, it's because I almost lost you once, that's why. If you had died, there would have been no one to blame but myself. I don't think I could live with such guilt, Abby. How could a man possibly allow himself to destroy that which he loves above all else?"

"You once told me that you craved fulfillment of the love that you have for me. Have you lost that craving, Will? Have you lost that passion?"

"No, of course not. I crave fulfillment as much if not more than I ever have, but at what cost, Abby? Am I to allow myself to be fulfilled at the cost of your life? Am I somehow supposed to place my selfish desires as being worth more to me than your life? Nothing on this earth is worth more to me than you! Nothing!"

"Oh, Will..."

"I can't face the possibility of losing you, Abby. I'm not strong enough to live without you in my life. I promised you that if something ever happened to you that I would watch over Elizabeth and Sarah, yet I don't know how I could live to fulfill that promise if something happened to you. I don't know what else to do. I feel lost..."

"Listen to me for a moment. God can help us to rise above our fears, Will. He didn't intend for us to live our lives cowering from our fears. He expects us to have faith in Him and conquer our fears. You and I are husband and wife, Will. Can we not resolve ourselves to allow our intimacy to occur naturally, and trust in God that things will work out according to His will?"

"And if you should become pregnant again, what then?"

"If I should conceive again, so be it. We will rejoice! If I should not conceive, it doesn't matter. Either way, God's will be done. You and me together, can face our fears, and we can conquer our fears with God's blessing, Will. We should not live our lives as if we are afraid of where our intimacy will take us."

"I don't know, Abby... perhaps I'm being greedy, because if you were to die, I would have no desire to go on..."

"So you're suggesting that we continue robbing ourselves of complete fulfillment so that we might avoid the risks involved with living our lives to the fullest? What kind of message is that sending to God as to the extent of our faith? What message is that sending to God as to the extent of the love we have for each other? Are we not telling God that we don't trust Him?"

"I love you, Abby... I swear I do."

"Then come to me, Will. Come to me with the faith that we will both trust in God. Come to me unafraid, and come to me as my husband and my lover, and show me how much you love me."

O   O   O

With all of the hard work of harvesting crops and preparing for another winter, the coming months passed quickly and labor-filled for the family. Ezra and Vivian's sons Josh and George had both found wives within the population of emancipated slaves living in the surrounding area of Blanchard and Rockingham County. Having no home of their own in which to live with their new wives, they took temporary residence with their mother and father, Ezra and Vivian, in their small house. As wedding presents, Will and Abigail deeded the brothers ten acres each on a tract of land that adjoined the property owned by Ezra and Vivian, and only a quarter-mile distant from Montgomery Farm. Since the brothers were employed there on the Montgomery Farm, the location would prove to be perfect for them. Ezra and Vivian were elated. Will and Abigail generously donated enough money for the two couples to begin construction of their new homes, and Will donated much of his own time in assisting Josh and George. In addition, Will and Abby had given Ezra and Vivian a contribution of $800 to be used to buy building material for the construction of their church, two and a half miles to the northwest of Montgomery Farm. The Negroes in that community already had a church under construction, but additional funds were needed in order for them to complete the project, and Will and Abby gladly donated the money. It was a gesture appreciated by all of their congregation, but most especially it was appreciated by Ezra and Vivian.

By Christmas, occasional suitors would arrive to visit with Elizabeth and Sarah, under the scrutinizing chaperonage of one very cautious and suspicious William Collins. There were times in which the sisters felt like Will was being over-protective, and his diligence had extended beyond the scope of a stepfather's normal protectiveness. Elizabeth and Sarah remained somewhat tolerant because they knew that Will's intense guardianship was motivated by his deep love for them, and that he only wanted to protect them from the heartbreak of making a poor decision. However, Will's zealousness for watching over '*his girls*,' had become a serious detriment to the sisters ever exercising their own freedom in accepting or rejecting the romantic offerings of inquisitive suitors. Elizabeth and Sarah confided in their mother, voicing their disapproval of Will's overprotectiveness, and afterwards, Abby approached Will. Reluctantly, Will agreed to take a more passive involvement in the sister's romantic concerns, and to Will and Abby's delight, the coming months would reveal that Elizabeth and Sarah were quite capable of making their own choices concerning matters of the heart. They had set their standards high, a circumstance which bore testament to the Christian standards that Abby had instilled in them. In their hearts, they had seen the unambiguous image of the perfect man. They lived under the same roof with the perfect man, and his name was William Collins. They would continue to receive suitors when they came to call upon them, but it would take someone very special to gain admission into their hearts... someone very special indeed. Unwittingly or not, they were comparing the qualities of each of their suitors to the qualities of Will, and were finding that none of their calling suitors were measuring up to their grand expectations. Sarah had learned the consequences of making hasty and irrational decisions when it came to men and matters of the heart, and neither sister would permit such a thing to happen again.

The coming months would also find that despite the fact that full, untethered intimacy had been restored in the private lives of Will and Abby, it appeared that there was not going to be the resulting conception that they were hoping for. Such did not come as an insurmountable disappointment to either of them, for as Abby had told Will, "We will accept what God provides for us, and never question His reasons."

Will had long since recognized their faithful farm worker Ezra, as being among the most trustworthy of men that he knew. The longer he was associated with Ezra and his family, the more he began to recognize that Ezra and Vivian's sons, Josh and George, were equally as trustworthy as Ezra. Vivian and Ezra had raised their children well, and their loyalty to Montgomery Farm was above reproach. Therefore, Ezra and his entire family were held in much higher regard and treated with much greater love and affection than others of their race were treated in the region. Ezra and his family attended a Negro church on the Sabbath, located two miles northwest of Montgomery Farm, and were considered among the most faithful and influential people in the church. This was the church which Abby and Will had donated $800 for the completion of their building project. Theirs was a happy existence there at Montgomery Farm, co-existing among people who held them in the highest of adoration and mutual respect.

Will had taken unavoidable notice of the fact that Josh and George were of a much lighter complexion than their mother and father, Vivian and Ezra, yet he withheld asking Abby any questions about the matter until one evening in March. They sat together on the side porch, having their usual evening conversation. Will posed the question of the brother's light complexion to Abby. Abby seemed embarrassed somewhat by the question, and simply told Will that the father of Josh and George had been a white man, and that Vivian had been raped numerous times by this man over a period of more than seven years. She further told Will that Vivian had once confided in her by revealing that Ezra was incapable of fathering children, yet he had willingly accepted the half-white children as if they had been his own. This revelation stirred Will's curiosity even further, so he posed additional questions to Abby. Not wanting to discuss such a distasteful subject on such a pleasant night, Abby simply begged Will to dismiss the subject from his mind. She had told Will enough to satisfy his immediate curiosity, and he agreeably dismissed the matter. Will and Abby could discuss most any subject between themselves without shame or embarrassment, but Will sensed that there were issues lurking within the history of Montgomery Farm that Abby preferred not to discuss. Given the trust and devotion that Will had for Abby, when he sensed she was uncomfortable in such discussions, he would withhold his prying questions. He simply loved Abby too much to cause her unnecessary distress, and he never doubted that Abby would tell him anything and everything if there ever came a need for him to know.

Through Yonder Woods,
A Lone Rider Comes...

"Return to thine own house, and shew how great things God hath done unto thee." Luke 8:39

O nce more, Christmas was approaching, and in the midst of the perfect harmony that abounded there on Montgomery Farm, everyone seemed to be especially cheerful, and overflowing with the spirit of Christmas. Abby and Will had purchased two new kitchen cook stoves, and had presented them to Josh and George as Christmas presents for their new homes. Everyone had many reasons to be happy and joyous. The war was over, most of the surviving soldiers on both sides had returned home, and practically all of the region's farmers had experienced good harvests that fall. It was also becoming apparent that there would not be an apocalyptic army of vengeful Yankees swooping in from the north to loot and burn southern homes as everyone had feared.

It was the twenty-third day of December, just two days before Christmas, and Will was contemplating what work he could attend to in the barn that day. The weather was far too foul to consider the pursuance of any outdoor labors on this day, as a bitter storm of cold and snowy weather had arrived from the north. Abby and her daughters were upstairs cleaning and dusting the bedchambers, and giddily talking between themselves. Will poured himself a cup of coffee and walked outside to the porch. A light snow, which was mostly rain and sleet, was falling as Will stood there on the rear porch with a cup of coffee and watched as a single rider from the east drew closer to the house. At first, Will studied the rider in order to recognize their identity, but could not comprehend who the person was. He wondered, '*What would bring a visitor to Montgomery Farm on such a foul day as this?*' At a distance, Will soon recognized that the rider was a female, and as she drew closer, Will finally recognized that it was Abby's sister, Agatha. It was strange that she would be approaching as a lone rider, as normally she would have been in a buggy with her husband, James Brighton, and they would have never ventured to travel on such a day as this. It was even stranger that she would be arriving by horseback in such foul weather, instead of in her buggy. When she had drawn close enough, Will walked to her and reached to hold the reins of her horse as she dismounted. She immediately came to Will, put her arms around him, and began a most pitiful exhibition in sobbing her heart out. Even though Agatha had seemed to have been happily married to Brighton for almost two years now, after Sarah's unfortunate involvement with O'Donnell the year before, Will's immediate thoughts were that Brighton had somehow mistreated or abused Agatha, and that she had escaped from Blairmount and come home to Montgomery Farm in order to seek refuge there. However, he was soon to find out that his immediate assumptions were erroneous.

"Agatha, what's the matter, dear?"

It was several moments before Agatha could compose herself and offer a discernable explanation. She raised her head from William's chest and offered, "James is dead, Will... he died last evening."

"My Lord, Agatha! I'm so sorry, dear! How did he die? What happened to him?"

"We were eating our dinner last evening, and he slumped in his chair there at the table and died. The physician was summoned as quickly as possible, and he said that James' heart had failed. Oh, Will!"

"My Lord, Agatha, you poor, sweet dear. Let's get you inside of the house where you can dry yourself by the fire. Abby's upstairs, let's go inside and I'll fetch her. Why didn't you come in your buggy? You're soaking wet and shivering, dear."

"I've never hitched our buggy before... I didn't know how to do it properly, but I've saddled a horse many times. I just wanted to come home to the people I love, as quickly as I could, and horseback was the quickest way. Oh Will, I can't stay in that big house at Blairmount by myself, and James' family hates me. May I stay here with you and Abby?"

"Well of course you may, this is still your home, Agatha, and it always will be. Don't ever forget that. Who is at Blairmount with James?"

"His sister and his eldest son just arrived, and they are there with him now. They have agreed to handle interment arrangements for me. They've never liked me anyway... they've always thought that I married James for his money, which isn't true."

"I'm sure it's not, Agatha. Come inside. Abby needs to help you into some dry clothes before you catch your death of cold. God bless you, you're soaking wet."

Agatha was received with all of the sympathy and understanding that anyone would have expected humanly possible. She melted into the loving arms of her sister and her nieces to receive their condolences. Will was sad for Agatha, but he was not terribly surprised when he heard the news. James had been more than twenty-one years older than Agatha, seriously overweight, and in Will's opinion, James had never had a very healthy appearance about him. Will had thought that their marriage was a terrible mismatch from the very beginning. Agatha, a year younger than her sister, Abby, was as vivacious, energetic, and full of life as Abby. In contrast, James would often tire and breathe heavily at the slightest of chores. Even walking up the stairway at his estate, Agatha had told Will and Sarah that he had to pause to catch his breath halfway up the stairs. Will had never been very understanding of Agatha's motives in marrying Brighton in the first place, other than the slightest possibility that his wealth and prominence had been an attracting factor for Agatha. Agatha was only thirty-two years of age now, and already twice widowed. The family was heartsick for her. In private conversation, Agatha would later confide in her sister, Abby, and reveal to her that James Brighton had really died in their bedchamber, while they were involved in intimate exchange. Knowing that Will had never had a high opinion of Brighton in the first place, Abby thought it best not to mention the horribly embarrassing circumstances of Brighton's demise to another living soul, especially Will.

The following morning, on the eve of Christmas, when the snow and rain had ceased, the family traveled en mass to Blairmount to attend Brighton's funeral and to make preparations to move some of Agatha's personal belongings back to her old room at Montgomery Farm. Agatha had no desire to remain at Blairmount. Instead, she wanted to return to live with her family once more at Montgomery Farm. Agatha had never been happier than when she was at home with her adoring family. With Agatha now in the loving arms of her sister and nieces again, she was welcomed to stay at Montgomery Farm for as long as it took for her heart to mend. At Agatha's request, Brighton's oldest son soon moved into the estate at Blairmount in order to manage the operation of Brighton's farm holdings. It was a task that Agatha was incapable of performing, and in light of the death of her husband, Agatha was happy to be back at Montgomery Farm and among her family again. Brighton's son had reached an agreement with Agatha whereby he would lease Blairmount from her, and thus provide her with a handsome income without the burdens of tending to the operation of the farm. It was an arrangement that best served the needs of everyone involved. Additionally, Agatha was in receipt, and had full control, of Brighton's bank accounts, and was more than financially secure for the rest of her life. Will and Abby never inquired of Agatha as to the grand sum of her wealth, nor did Agatha seem interested in discussing the subject.

At the dinner table one evening, after Agatha had been there at Montgomery Farm for more than two weeks, William reached across the table to take Agatha's hand, and said, "Agatha, we all continue to mourn the loss of your husband, James, and we want you to know that we will keep you in our prayers."

"Thank you, Will. I feel a warm sense of comfort in being here with the people that I love most in this world. There's not another place on earth that I would rather be."

To an unknowing observer, it would have seemed as if time had suddenly reverted back two and a half years, had it not been for the presence of William Collins in the house. Once again, there were four women residing in the house at Montgomery Farm, just as there had been two and a half years prior. The primary difference now, was the fact that William Collins had become the indisputable head of the family—the binding element that protected everyone and held the family together as a single entity. Abby seldom asserted herself as she so often did before, preferring to remain compliant and submissive to Will's wishes. She had never appreciated her burden as being the family's leader in the first place, but had done so out of necessity until Will had mercifully appeared to accept the responsibility. She trusted Will with all of her heart and soul, and would stand behind any decision he made. Before William's arrival there at Montgomery House, Abigail had always made it a family practice to conduct family meetings when it was necessary to make important decisions, thereby listening to everyone's input and opinion before reaching a decision. William had come to admire and respect this open forum when Abby had *ruled the roost,* and therefore continued to use the same approach in most of the important family decisions that were made. It was a formality that made each and every family member feel as though their opinion was valued, and it was.

O   O   O

Agatha Brighton was now the sole owner of the prestigious Blairmount estate, as well as the holder of all of James Brighton's financial assets. And now, she was a widow as well. By everyone's reckoning, she was now considered to be a very wealthy woman, and as a wealthy widow, she was an attractive and potentially vulnerable target in the eyes of society's *'freeloading'* bachelors— men who would aspire to gain immediate wealth by means of marriage. William feared that men would flock to her as flies rush to a cattle pen, and because of James Brighton's popularity in political circles, these amorous scavengers would come from as far away as Richmond, Culpeper, Charlottesville, and Lynchburg. In addition to her wealth, Agatha was also recognized by Virginia society as the young and very beautiful woman she was, as were all the fair ladies there at Montgomery Farm. Will had the uneasy feeling that there would be a never ending parade of suitors that would inevitably attempt to dip their greedy hand in Agatha's purse as soon as a reasonable mourning period had passed. A full year was thought to be a reasonable time for such a mourning period, and hopefully, Will would not have to consider visitation by the region's *'society vultures'* for many months to come. The fact is, Agatha's name was already being whispered in circles of men who gathered at barber shops, hotels, and mercantile establishments as, *'The Charming Widow Brighton.'* Because of Will's deep affection for all of the women abiding there at Montgomery House, he was inherently protective of their wellbeing and better interests. He was not as soulfully attached to Agatha as he was to Abby and her daughters, yet he strived to be equally as protective of her welfare. After all, she was Abby's only sister, and Will considered her to be an integral part of his family, and would continue to regard her as such for as long as she wished to reside there at Montgomery House. Will was aware that the ladies of Montgomery House had endured a history of struggle, yet he remained ignorant of the specific nature of their strife and the extent of their difficulties. The family was abiding in such happiness now, that Abby saw no need to burden Will with knowledge of the family's *'darker'* history.

As Abby's husband, and Sarah and Elizabeth's legal stepfather, Will's presence had become joyously entrenched there at Montgomery House. Will had become the undeniable figurehead of Montgomery Farm; the advisor, the director, the champion, and the protector. The family's acceptance of Will as the leader of the family, and his trusted familiarity among the womenfolk, had gradually relieved the ladies of the bothersome necessity of safeguarding their modesty during every waking moment that they were in Will's presence. William also felt no pretentious requirement to overdress for the sake of modesty in his own home, often coming downstairs for a glass of water at night dressed only in his trousers, barefoot and bare-chested. After all, they were family. The family often enjoyed their morning meal together while the ladies were still attired in their bed robes, and with their hair down in its most gloriously casual condition. For fear of hurting anyone's feelings, Will never made it common knowledge, but he detested the confining buns in which the ladies gathered their hair in order to make themselves more *'publically presentable'* in the eyes of visitors from the world outside of Montgomery Farm. Will reveled in the midst of such relaxed wonderment, proud that his family would regard him with such loving familiarity and enjoy the relaxed comfort to be themselves in his presence. After their morning meal and once Will had left for the crop fields, the ladies would always return to their rooms and dress appropriately for the day.

Once again, spring had arrived at Montgomery Farm, and Will's normal toils spanned from daylight until dark each day but the Sabbath. On most Sabbaths, Will would hitch up the carriage and chauffer the ladies to church in Blanchard, often finding it necessary for him to attend chores when they returned home in the afternoons. Will and Ezra, and Ezra's two sons managed to keep up with most of the work that was to be done, but there was seldom a moment in which anyone found time for leisurely pursuits such as hunting or fishing, coquette or parlor games. As hard as Will was working during this busy season, Abby changed her usual morning routine, and began arising more than an hour before Will in the mornings, affording him a small amount of additional time to rest before waking and coming downstairs to begin his normal workday. Abby would quietly go downstairs to the kitchen, make a fire in the stove, put a pot of coffee on to boil, and begin the process of making their daily biscuits and bread. Abby would leave the door to their bedchamber open when she would leave to go downstairs, and Will would usually sleep soundly for an hour or more, until he smelled the aroma of coffee in the morning air, then he would dress and go downstairs to join Abby and start his day. Such had become typical of the daily activities of farm life there at Montgomery Farm. Agatha had been home with them now for almost four months, and everything seemed to be going perfectly in their lives. Will's wonderful evening piano symphonies were nearly a daily event, their crops were growing well in the fields, and joy and contentment seemed to reign supreme there at Montgomery Farm.

○　○　○

On one particularly cool morning, in the pre-dawn darkness of their bedchamber, Will became aware that Abby had stirred to dress herself and had left their bed to go downstairs, and as usual, he allowed himself to drift pleasantly back to sleep for a short time. What seemed like only moments later, however, he awoke from his sleep partially as he heard the faint sound of their bedchamber door being closed, and soon became aware that Abby was standing at their bedside. He opened his eyes and in the darkness, and saw the shadows of Abby's bed robe as it fell inaudibly to the floor, and watched as she silently entered the bed again. She was warm and unclothed, as she nestled seductively beside him in their bed. Will always slept unclothed under the blanket, and the silky warmth of Abby's body against his was immensely pleasing to him, as it always was. Will's initial inclination was to drift back to sleep with Abby in his arms, however, Abby had not returned to their bed for the purpose of sleeping. Without uttering a word, Abby encouraged Will in his sleep-enhanced state, and they absorbed themselves in an enchanting pre-dawn marital exchange. In the dazzling splendor of the moment, Will moaned satisfyingly and made a cursory effort to re-enter his sleep, managing only to whisper, "I love you, Abby..." It was a brief early morning pleasantry that had ended when Abby kissed him on the cheek, donned her robe, and left the bedchamber to go downstairs. Will continued to lie there in drowsy wonderment, still half-asleep, and seething with delight attributed solely to the spectacular manner in which Abby had just awakened him. Minutes later, he slowly and lethargically slipped into his trousers and boots, donned his shirt, and pulled his suspenders over his shoulders. Feeling his way through the darkness, he walked quietly down the stairs, careful not to awaken the slumbering ladies in their upstairs bedchambers.

When Will walked into the parlor, he could see that there were oil lamps burning in the kitchen, and he could smell the wonderful aroma of coffee in the crisp morning air as well. This had all the earmarks of being another wonderful morning at Montgomery House. In the kitchen, Abby was nearly elbow-deep in dough as she kneaded the day's biscuits and bread. Will was the first to speak when he offered a pleasant, "Good morning sweetheart," and kissed Abby on the cheek as he said, "I love you."

Abby responded, "I love you too, darling." She twitched and contorted her nose and asked, "Darling, would you do me a favor and scratch my nose? My nose itches terribly and my hands are covered with dough."

"I would be glad to scratch your lovely nose this morning. That would be the least that I could do after the sterling manner in which you woke me this morning. How's that?"

"That's wonderful, thank you. And just what sterling manner are you referring to, dear?"

"You know what I'm talking about, you little fox, you."

"Honestly, Will, I haven't a clue as to what you're talking about. I tried my best not to disturb you when I left our bed this morning, so that you could sleep a while longer."

"Sure you did, Abby. Anyhow, I'm very thankful that you came back to bed like you did, and even more thankful for that wonderful surprise........." Will stopped talking in mid-sentence. He said no more, as he watched the color drain from Abby's face. Suddenly, it became devastatingly clear to both of them that an act of transgression had just taken place in their very house, and in their very bed—and it had taken place at the very time that Abby was working so diligently to prepare a meal for her loving family. The sanctity of their marriage had been violated, albeit without the conscious knowledge of Abby or the willful participation of William. Abby quickly washed the dough from her hands, dried them, and sat down at the table with her face buried in her hands. As for Will, he could not utter a sound. He could only stand there, numbed into a stupor of speechlessness. His thoughts ran rampant, as if seeking answers in a hundred different directions. His mind revisited the adulterous act, and he recognized that there had been subtle differences that should have alerted him to the fact that he was making love to someone other than Abby. The subtle differences had seemed more of an oblique pleasure to him than something that would have sounded an alarm. How could he ever justify such behavior to Abby? How could he ever justify such behavior in the eyes of God? And who had the guilty adulteress been? Had Sarah come to him? Elizabeth? Agatha? *"Please God! Tell me that it wasn't Sarah or Elizabeth! I couldn't live with such guilt! **No!** It was Agatha! I know it was!"* Will's initial impulse commanded that he verify that it was Agatha by going directly to the other bedchambers and inquiring as to who the guilty harlot had been, but he knew better than to do such a spontaneous and arbitrarily impulsive thing. Instead, he continued to stand there dumbfound, trying to determine what affect this was going to have on Abby and the future of his family. Will feared that knowledge of such a betrayal would destroy Abby's trust in him. William would have sooner cut off an arm than see Abby hurt in any way. Even though he had intentionally committed no act of betrayal, his conscience was troubling him greatly. He had been seduced, and felt as though he had obtained knowledge in the process of how a woman must feel in her mind and heart when she had been raped. How could he ever face the women of Montgomery House again? How could he face Abby again with a clear conscience?

As he stood there bewildered and dejected, and even trembling in his fear, Abby rose from her chair, kissed him on the cheek, and said, "It was Agatha, Will."

"I know it was, Abby, I know it in my heart and soul. Abby, I swear to you that I would never have done such a thing if I had known that it wasn't you, I swear it. It was dark, and I was still more asleep than awake, I didn't know any different until I came downstairs just now."

"I know with all my heart and soul that Sarah and Elizabeth love you like a father, and they would never have done such a thing. I know that it was Agatha, Will."

"So do I, Abby, I have no doubt. I swear to the Almighty above that I would have never knowingly betrayed you… I just…"

"I know, darling… I know. It's my fault, Will, for not preparing you for such a likelihood. My Lord, Will… I just need a moment or two to comprehend this… my own sister has done this to me…"

"I am so sorry, Abby…"

"I'm the one who should be apologizing, Will, not you. I should have brought you into my confidence and forewarned you of such a possibility months ago. It's always been a closely guarded family secret that Agatha has always suffered from promiscuous urges. She's been that way since she was fifteen years old, and I should have brought you into the confidence of the family and told you as much."

"Abby, I love you with all my heart, and..."

"Please stop apologizing, Will. You've done nothing intentional to betray me, therefore, there should be no guilt on your shoulders. My sister is the one who has disappointed me, not you. Agatha committed the adultery and betrayed me—not you. I should have forewarned you, and I'm very sorry that I didn't. I should have foreseen the possibility of something like this happening someday."

"How should we go about dealing with this, Abby? The whole family will be down here in an hour or so. I cannot live here with this kind of discontentment in the family. Should I go up and ask her to come downstairs so that you and I can confront her, and discuss her behavior?"

"No... please. I'd rather we didn't say anything about it just yet. Please give me a few days to let me think about this."

"Abby... I fear I may never be able to make this up to you..."

"You need offer no further apologies, Will. As I told you, I'm bitterly disappointed, but my disappointment lies entirely with Agatha. The horrified look on your face this morning expresses your innocence far more accurately than any words you may render. I know your heart is virtuous and true, and you committed no act of betrayal."

"I shall never be able to look Agatha in the eye again, Abby. I think we should ask Agatha to pack her clothes and leave Montgomery House."

"And go where, Will? She can't go back to Blairmount."

"I don't care where she goes! She can go to hell as far as I'm concerned! With her wealth, she can go anywhere she wishes! I just don't want her here with our family! She has destroyed any trust that I had in her, she has betrayed and deceived both you and me, and I shan't be able to abide comfortably in our home with any assurance that she will not attempt to repeat her adulterous behavior in the future. After what has happened, I cannot live another day under the same roof as Agatha Brighton!"

"Please listen to me, Will, the guilt of Agatha's transgression lies partially on my shoulders—I am equally to blame. I've been less than completely honest with you in regards to the life that Agatha and I lived prior to your coming here to Montgomery Farm. Please, I beg of you to gather your senses, and grant me a request."

"What request?"

"Before the family comes down for breakfast, allow me to hurry and prepare your meal, so that you can take it to the barn, and not face Agatha just yet. Agatha and Sarah will be leaving this morning with Ezra to go to Blanchard, and they will be gone all day. When they have left, I will come to the barn. There is an unpleasantness from the past which looms over Montgomery Farm, an unpleasantness that I have sought to shield you from. I should have brought you into my confidence when we first gave our hearts to one another, but I was afraid. As much as I dislike burdening you with this knowledge, I know in my heart that the time has come for me to share my pain with you."

"I love you, Abby, and I want to share your pain, such a thing is my responsibility as your husband, and I can do no less."

"Please grant me this request, and I will come to the barn when they have departed for Blanchard. Elizabeth will be occupied with her chores here in the house, and we can talk freely in the barn. If you love me, please trust me."

"I do love you, and I do trust you. I will do as you say, Abby."

O   O   O

It was nearly ten o'clock before Ezra departed with Agatha and Sarah, as William sat in the loft of the barn contemplating all that had happened that morning. Very few minutes had passed when Will heard the barn door open and Abby call his name. He descended the ladder and embraced her, and they sat beside each other on a workman's cot. Holding both of William's hands, Abby poured her heart out to him, and brought him into the confidence of a Montgomery Farm history that made his blood curl. It was heartrending, and filled with evilment, desperation, and horror. Without interrupting her, Will listened to Abby's painful recollections of her childhood marriage to Thomas Montgomery.

"It's my intention to tell you everything, Will, and with your permission, I'll start at the very beginning."

"Please do, Abby."

"Agatha and I were born into a very poor family. For the sake of our family, my birth father encouraged me to seek the hand of Thomas Montgomery in marriage when I was but fourteen years of age, and he was twenty-eight, and as an obedient daughter, I made the sacrifice and complied. I was innocent of men at the time, but Thomas Montgomery, without compassion, cared not that I was frightened, and instead of treating me with any tenderness or love on our first night of marriage, he gave me a brutal introduction as to what I could expect of him in our bedchamber. Our relationship was absent of love, absent of tenderness, and absent of compassion. As time went on, I gave birth to Elizabeth, and she and my little sister, Agatha, represented the only spark of love in my life that enabled me to go on. I soon became pregnant with Sarah, and on the very night that I gave birth to her, Vivian and I could hear the terrible screams for help coming from my little sister's bedchamber. Thomas was raping her, even as I was giving birth. I could not go to her aid, I could only hear her horrible screams for help as they eventually faded into pitiful whimpers. I can sometimes hear her screams in my sleep today... seventeen years later. After I had given birth to Sarah, I obtained a pistol from Thomas' possessions, and ejected him from my bedchamber forever, threatening to kill him if he ever entered my room. I tried to protect Agatha, as best I could, but Thomas was cunning in his wicked promiscuity, and my best efforts could not keep him from her at all times, and she began to recognize that it was less painful for her to comply with his evilness than resist it. She became pregnant before her fourteenth birthday, and when she gave birth, the family deemed it appropriate to give the child to me, as if he was my son. I raised him as my son, and as a brother to Elizabeth and Sarah, in order to spare the family the humiliation of having an unwed mother in their fold. Agatha was deeply scarred by having her son taken from her breast and given to me, but she understood that such a thing was not of my doing, and we often confided in one another. Secretly, she even nursed the child on occasions when we were alone. There were times when Agatha would fall from grace at her own accord, when we had a young workman stay overnight in the barn, or when suitors would begin to call on her. Thomas Montgomery had stolen her virtue, and left her with an exceedingly low opinion of herself. The passing years found Thomas' licentious conduct becoming even more wicked, and there were no boundaries of sexual behavior which he would not cross. Vivian was accosted by him numerous times, and his appetite for evilness only worsened. When Elizabeth was but ten years old I walked into her bedchamber one morning to find Thomas touching her inappropriately. I gathered Elizabeth and Sarah into my arms and took them into my bedchamber. I told Thomas Montgomery that if he ever entered my bedchamber, or ever touched one of my daughters again that I would shoot him on sight and send him straight to hell where he belonged. He laughed, and made a move toward me, but when I pulled the pistol from my apron and pushed it into his face he knew that I would make good my threat. After that, he always looked closely at my apron to see if I carried the pistol, and I always did."

Upon the completion of her lengthy explanation, William sat there in utter astonishment of the horrors that had occurred within the boundaries of Montgomery Farm. He kissed Abby on the cheek and softly offered, "Thank you for telling me this, Abby. I cannot imagine how you found the strength to survive such an ordeal."

"I found my strength through God, Will. He has always given

me the strength that I need to go on. Perhaps this will help you to understand why I've come to trust and love you so deeply, and depend on you as I do."

"It does indeed, Abby. I've told you before that I would give my life for you or your daughters. Knowing now what you have all been through, only strengthens my determination to protect all of you from such foulness. I suppose that I now feel that same instinct to protect Agatha, for some odd reason."

"I have said this before, and I shall say it again; God has blessed us immensely when He sent you here to us."

"No one has been blessed more than me, Abby. Your struggle has pulled at my heartstrings, darling, but there are a few questions that I have, if you would permit me..."

"Please ask any questions you wish. When we leave the barn today, it is my fondest desire that there should be no questions remaining in your heart or your mind."

"Very well... When you became aware of Thomas' dreadful behavior, why did you not pack your belongings and leave him?"

"Where was I to go, Will, with my two babies and my fourteen year-old sister? I was only fifteen years old myself. I lived in the same house as him, yes, but not in the same bedchamber. He was my husband, and I was always obedient to him... outside of the bedchamber. Can you imagine what it was like to be a fifteen year-old girl, frightened and alone, and having to carry a pistol in her apron—in her own home?"

"I can't imagine the nightmare you must have endured, living with a man that would treat you like that... a man whom you didn't love."

"I had always thought that I was expected to remain with him—that it was my duty as his wife, despite his behavior. In my family, when a woman married, she married for life—for better or worse. Besides, I had no idea of what love really was then. I had never experienced the feeling of sincere love in my heart... for any man... until I met you. Living with Thomas caused me to be distrustful of all men. I suppose that I should be ashamed of myself for saying this, but when I received word of his death, I felt a tremendous sense of joy and relief in knowing that he would never return, and God help me, I felt no sorrow or regret."

"You had no relations with your husband after the night that he raped Agatha?"

"The day that you and I first confessed our love for one another and made love in the barn was the first time I had been with a man in seventeen years, Will."

"I have always thought Grandfather Montgomery to be a virtuous and upright man. Where was he when all this foulness was taking place, and why didn't he protect you and Agatha?"

"Grandfather Montgomery was indeed a virtuous man, he was our only protector at the time, but the tobacco business required him to make frequent deliveries of our crop to Richmond and Lynchburg. There was no tobacco exchange in Blanchard then, as there is today. He would be gone for days at a time when he made these deliveries. Thomas was deviously wise and cunning enough to practice his evilment only during these absences."

"I had no idea that Agatha was given to improper behavior. She has always seemed to be the perfect emblem of innocence to me, at least up to the time she married Brighton. If I had only known... Tell me, Abby, how can she sit beside us in church like an innocent little angel, bow her head and pray to God, and then do something like this in our own home?"

"We cannot be critical of her when she prays. I would imagine that she prays often... for forgiveness. When she sits beside us in church, what better place is there for a sinner? I thought she had risen above such behavior when she married Brighton... I can clearly see now that my husband's evil influence over her still lingers on. He was the devil in disguise... an atheist and a demon, and he has damaged her mind."

"I didn't know any of this, but it does answer a lot of questions that have lingered in my mind. But, tell me what we should do about this, Abby. I'm completely at your mercy, and I'll do anything you say."

"Please, say nothing to anyone about this. If word of Agatha's transgressive behavior ever became common knowledge in the community, it could only serve to taint the entire family, and I will allow no such unwarranted shame to fall upon Elizabeth and Sarah. As I told you, Agatha's behavior has always been a closely guarded family secret. She's still my sister, and I still love her dearly, despite the fact that she betrayed me this morning. I do not wish to humiliate her... but when the time comes to talk to her, I shall do it. She cannot help the way she is. Can you bring yourself to do this for me, Will?"

"What's done is done, and it cannot be changed. My biggest concern now is that you believe me when I say that my participation was an act of ignorance, and not an act of betrayal. I would never betray you, Abby."

"I know that with all my heart. Nor will I ever betray you, Will. Betrayals are committed in the heart, darling, not in the bedchamber, and I know your heart is true. Can we somehow dismiss this from our minds, and try to act as though it never happened... for the sake of the family?"

"I'm sorry, Abby, but I'm not capable of forgetting that it ever happened. All that I can promise you is that I will try my best. In the future, I would prefer not to be left alone upstairs at the same time as Agatha. If you leave our bedchamber while I'm still in bed, I'll get up and lock the door behind you. I bear a terrible shame for having derived so much pleasure from her affections this morning... thinking it was you. My Lord, I even told her, *I love you, Abby*, and she never spoke back to me."

"You've no reason to feel any shame or guilt, Will."

"Bringing me into your confidence like this helps me to understand some of the difficulties that you and Agatha have both endured over the years. Believe it or not, it also helps me understand why you always seemed to be so bitter and distrustful towards me when we first met. I'm so sorry, for both you and Agatha."

O O O

At the dinner table that evening, without being obvious with his stares, Will took notice of the fact that Agatha and Abby were almost identical in size, stature, and the length of their hair. This was a characteristic that along with his sleep-enhanced state of mind, had contributed to his unawareness that she had assumed Abby's place in bed that morning. Agatha was most likely the only one who could have successfully staged such a deception. The incident, although behind them now, would never be completely forgotten. Now that Will was aware of Agatha's affliction, and her past, he would make certain that nothing like that ever happened again, and of course, Abby would also keep a vigilant, watchful eye.

Hereafter, William would consider the name of Thomas Montgomery to be synonymous with the name of Satan. He and Abby would make every effort not to mention his name again.

O O O

The ensuing days and weeks found harmony once again returning to Montgomery House. While the predawn incident with Agatha would never be completely forgotten, Will and Abby were successful in disallowing the incident to interfere with their absolute love for one another. It was weeks before Will could look at Agatha without feeling a twinge of guilt, but Abby's remarkable compassion and understanding had worked miracles in helping Will come to terms with what had happened. Will and Abby could both sense that Agatha herself was experiencing some measure of guilt and shame, knowing that she had betrayed her only sister—the very sister who loved her more than any other person on the face of the earth. At mealtime, Agatha seldom looked Abby or Will in the eye, and seemed to cower in her guilt. But as Will had so aptly told Abby, '*What's done is done, and cannot be changed.*'

They Always Come At Night On Horses

"So when they continued asking him, he lifted up himself, and said unto them, He that is without sin among you, let him first cast a stone at her." John 8:7

E ven before the end of the war, throughout the south, secret societies of insidious and malicious vigilantes were formed. Their purported purpose was to administer justice, or malevolent terror, in whatever form their warped and sinister minds deemed appropriate. Their ire was often directed toward the men and families of northern opportunists that had swindled or taken southern land and farms from southern families who were unable to pay their levied taxes or prove exclusive ownership in a court of law. These organizations also held it upon themselves to perpetrate their own idea of punishment to Negros, Italians, and other ethnic groups accused of crimes, whether they had been proven guilty in a legally established court of law or not. These *'self-proclaimed'* vigilantes supposedly justified their actions under some imaginary constitution or a derived code of supreme ethics, but the truth of the matter was that their purposes were more often of a sinister and self-serving nature, fueled by hatred, bigotry, and hypocrisy. They would perform most of their corrupt evilment under the cover of night, a time which struck the greatest fear into the hearts of their intended victims. Their twisted sense of justice often manifested itself in the form of lynchings, beatings, castrations, brandings, and even macabre, permanent disfigurement. There had even been instances where unfortunate victims were burned alive in their houses. These clandestine organizations were a disease to the very Christian humanity that they purportedly represented.

These fiends came at night, the perfect cover for a coward, and wore hoods to conceal their identities, another perfect tactic for a coward. They had confidence in their numbers, and incited each other's anger during rallies, in which they expounded their hatred until it festered into a frenzy of demented behavior. It was an excellent opportunity for an individual with a grudge against someone to drag his neighbor's name through the dirt, thus spreading the fires of contention and hatred even further. Most law-abiding citizens voiced no outspoken opposition to these organizations. In many communities they were afraid to do so because many of the horrid scoundrels were lawmen by day and vigilantes by night. In other instances, they voiced no opposition simply because of their apathy. They were content to leave well enough alone as long as these ruthless organizations brought no harm to them or their families.

Will had been approached by a man after church one Sunday named Herbert Myers, who brazenly solicited Will's membership in such an organization. Will's unexpected response was to ask the man, "What does the Bible say about that kind of behavior? Does the Bible not say, *'Judge not, that ye be judged?'* And tell me this, if you would please, when you die, how will you ever explain your biased and cowardly actions to God Almighty?" The repugnant solicitor turned his back on Will and walked away in disgust. After that, the man never approached Will at church again. In fact, they both went out of their way to avoid one another. Will was unaware that voicing his opposition to such wickedness could have easily marked him as a target for retribution. Nevertheless, it was deeply embedded in Will's character to take a stand for what he thought to be right, and he always did. Many others, who agreed with Will, were too intimidated by these mysterious organizations to take a stand, and they simply hoped that they and their families would never be subject to any form of reprisal.

News pertaining to the atrocious deeds of vigilantes was usually communicated in the small circles of gossip that formed outside of the church when the worship services had ended on the Sabbath, or inside of barber shops and other stores—wherever men would gather. Newspapers reporting such vigilante justice had to exercise caution in their words, so as not to offend these lawless organizations, lest they become a target for reprisal themselves. Accounts printed in the newspapers were often worded in such a manner so as to cause the reader to feel as though justice had been served. These reports were damaging, because they tended to distort the facts and make heroes out of the villains who perpetrated these types of horrible acts. Such corrupt reporting of the news and irresponsible distortion of the truth only served to strengthen public support for their nightmarish activities.

Montgomery Farm seemed to be immune to much of the hatefulness that folks talked about or read about in the newspaper. Montgomery Farm was almost in its own little world, far apart from the deadly disputes and corruptive influences that ailed the southern states during the 'healing' post-war years. There had never been any unrest caused by the vigilantes at Montgomery Farm, that is, until the night of September 7, 1868.

O   O   O

Will and Abby sat at their kitchen table, and under the light of two oil lamps, they were entering records of their daily harvests into their farm ledger. It had been a long, hard day of labor for everyone there at Montgomery Farm. Agatha, Elizabeth, and Sarah had each gone up to their rooms to retire for the night, and Will and Abby were anxious to finish their bookkeeping and adjourn to their own bedchamber. Will was calling out the numbers from the crop registry, and Abby was making the entries into their ledger. But as they sat there, they were interrupted when they heard the dogs barking and the ominous sound of approaching horses outside. Will immediately went to the window to see that a number of hooded riders carrying torches had arrived outside. Will quickly grabbed his rifle and his pistol and despite Abby's panicked pleadings for him not to, he demanded that she run upstairs with the other ladies, and he stepped out on the porch to greet the mysterious visitors. It was evident at the onset that one member who stood out from the rest of the cowardly group, was their leader and spokesman, and despite the presence of his hood, Will recognized the man's voice immediately, but withheld saying anything that would have let the man know that he had been recognized.

Raising his normally soft voice so that he could be heard by the visitors, William asked, "What can I do for you men in the middle of the night like this? At least I assume you are men. It's rather difficult for me to be certain about that because of your humorous looking costumes. For all I know, you could be women, pretending to be men."

"We've not come here tonight to listen to your insults, we've come here to make some inquiries. We represent the Avenging Knights of Justice."

"*The Avenging Knights of Justice,* huh? My, my, I am indeed impressed. Very well then, remove your ridiculous masquerade hoods, extinguish your torches, and come inside. My wife and I will boil some coffee for you and we can sit in my parlor. You may present your inquiries there."

"We'll present our inquiries where we damned well please, Mr. Collins!"

Will unavoidably paused to catch his breath. He was taken aback for a moment and temporarily held speechless, not because of what the cowardly man had just said to him, but because he recognized one of the horses in the group as belonging to his good friend, Sheriff Homer Bellisle. As he looked closer, he recognized

Bellisle's saddle as well. Will was tremendously disappointed that Bellisle would stoop so low as to be a part of such a gutless and hypocritical mob. Ever since Will had ridden with Bellisle to capture the Shelton brothers, he had held Bellisle in the highest esteem, thinking him to be an upright and noble man. Seeing Bellisle in the midst of such evilment gave him pause to reconsider. Will gathered his senses and lashed back at the mob's leader.

"While you are on my property, Sir, you will present your damned inquiries where I damn well please! Do you understand, or shall I pull you from your horse and shout it in your ear?"

"Mr. Collins, around Blanchard, you are thought to be an honorable man, a good citizen, upright and moral, a God-fearing man, and I can assure you that it would not be in your best interest to infuse the wrath of the Knights of Justice."

Will decided to use the occasion as a platform to send a clear message to the ears of his good friend, Homer Bellisle.

"What would your sheriff say if he could see you men now, behaving like the cowardly jackasses that you really are? I happen to be close friends with the sheriff, and I happen to know that he would hold such behavior as yours in the highest disdain. The people of Rockingham County have bequeathed him with the responsibility of administering justice in Blanchard and Rockingham County—not you lowlife snakes! He would be appalled to learn that there were infantile cowards such as yourselves masquerading as emissaries of the law in his county!"

"Enough of this! We've heard enough of your insults! Our inquiries are waiting to be answered!"

"Then go ahead and present your stinking inquiries, and be done with it!"

"There are two male niggers that reside on property belonging to Montgomery Farm, by the names of Josh and George. They work for you, do they not?"

"They do, and what of it?"

"They have each acquired deeds of property here, ten acres each. How did they acquire this property?"

"They acquired the property because I gave it to them, that's how."

"A white man, giving good farmland to a nigger?"

"I'll give my property to whomever I please, regardless of whether it pleases you or not."

"And did you fund the building of a nigger church over by the creek on the Blanchard road?"

"I did. Make your point. My time is too valuable for me to stand here while you spout forth your ignorant babble! You're stupidity is making me ill."

"Consider yourself forewarned, Mr. Collins! Such behavior as giving property to niggers or building nigger churches will not be tolerated in the future. Such goings on could result in your home being burned, and great harm could even befall members of your family."

"As long as we're giving out warnings, let me say this, and I say this with the greatest of sincerity. Listen closely to what I'm about to say. If a member of my family is ever harmed in any way, including Josh and George, even so much as the simplest of bruises, I will hunt down and kill every one of you gutless sons of bitches! I will not stop until I have watched the last ounce of blood flow from your evil veins, and I will cut out your nuts and feed them to my hounds! Now get off of Montgomery Farm property right now! The next time I see a man wearing a hood on my property, I will assume that he has come here to bring harm to my family, and I will kill him on sight! And when I'm finished, I will come and kill you, Herbert Myers. Yes, I recognize your voice, you foul piece of spineless shit! Now you men either get off your horses and fight me like a man right here and now, or get the hell off of my property, otherwise, I'll start killing every man that's still here in twenty seconds! And take this evil stinking bastard, Myers with you!"

"You have been forewarned, Collins!"

"As have you, Myers! And you miserable bastards have fifteen seconds remaining! You've already wasted five!"

The group of twelve cowardly antagonists wasted but little time riding off into the darkness. Will watched from the porch as the lights of their torches grew faint, finally disappearing in the distant woods on the road to Blanchard. In a stark moment of mental sobriety, Will came to the realization that the pistol and rifle that he held in his hands were not loaded or primed. He would have been defenseless if the intruding nightriders had made a move to harm him. His knees became weak, and he softly uttered to himself, *"Lord Jesus... thank you for protecting me in my hour of stupidity..."* He took a deep breath and walked back into the house where he found Abby and the other women huddled in a traumatized group, on the floor of the parlor near a window. The ruckus had been heard upstairs, causing alarm throughout the household. Abby's daughters and her sister had been scared out of their wits, and had rushed downstairs to be with Abby during the melee. They had looked out of the window to see the frightening sight of a dozen hooded men carrying torches and dropped to the floor behind the piano in sheer terror. From the open window above their heads, they had heard Will's every word, and were deathly afraid for his wellbeing until the riders had ridden away in the black of night.

Tension was thick in the air, and Will attempted to add a measure of levity to the moment in hopes of easing the anxieties of the ladies.

"Good evening, ladies. I thought you had all gone to bed. You can all get up from the floor... our visitors have gone now, and there's no longer any danger. It's rather late for a piano recital... perhaps we should all try to get some sleep now, and I'll play a cheery song or two for you in the morning. Would that suit everyone's fancy?"

Abby suggested that Agatha and her daughters go back to their bedchambers so that she and Will could finish putting their entries into the farm ledger. As Will had said, the hour was late, and they had a busy day ahead of them tomorrow. Will again reassured them all that there was nothing to be afraid of, and

Abby and Will were soon alone in the kitchen again, working on their books. Finally regaining her composure, Abby took Will by the hand and said, "I can't believe that you stood up against all those men out there by yourself, Will. There must have been ten or twelve of them out there... maybe more!"

"It was no great act of bravery on my part, Abby, I can assure you of that. I simply had my family to protect. Cowards such as those men feed on the fears of their victims, Abby. Once you let them see that you're afraid of them, then they will never go away... they always come back to feed on your fears again, it's what keeps them alive. Any one of them lack the nerve to do anything by themselves, and even as a group they are without the courage to confront someone who calls them to task. I had no choice but to show them that I was not afraid of them... which wasn't exactly true."

"Tell me something, Will..."

"I'll try."

"How is it that a man who cannot remember his own name or his own past, seems to be the caretaker of so much knowledge and wisdom?"

"It's not knowledge or wisdom that I possess, Abby, more than anything else it's just an instinct to survive and protect my family at any cost."

"That's the first time I have ever heard you raise your voice and curse at anyone like you did."

"I'm sorry you had to hear that, Abby. I deplore such language. Exhibiting a filthy tongue like that is shameful behavior for a man who supposes himself to be a Christian. I was only trying to make a point, and I suppose I got a little too rambunctious with my words. I didn't know until I came inside that my family was here at the window, and could hear what I was saying outside. I'll make every effort to govern myself accordingly in the future."

"I was proud of you, Will, but I was scared to death for your welfare. I thought at any moment they were going to shoot you or take you to the elm tree and hang you. I've never been so frightened in my life. You must ask yourself if there is good judgment in going against powerful men such as that."

"I wasn't concerned with good judgment so much. I was more concerned with letting them know that it wouldn't be in their best interest to ever threaten my family again. As far as their power is concerned, their only power is in the fear that they provoke, and I was determined not to let them see fear in me. They were so surprised that I stood up to defy them that they ran away like scared rabbits, just as I expected them to do. I don't think they will be back anytime soon."

"But suppose they had killed you?"

"They didn't, so let's just forget about it. But let me ask you a question, Abby, there are two banks in Blanchard, are there not?"

"Yes, there's the Second Bank of Blanchard, and the First Bank of Blanchard, where we have our money, why?"

"I want us to move our money out of the First Bank of Blanchard and deposit it in the Second Bank of Blanchard, just as soon as possible."

"Why, Will?"

"I don't feel comfortable with our money in a bank where Herbert Myers is the president and owner. I don't trust him. He was the spokesman and the leader of that mob of idiots out there tonight and I refuse to allow the scoundrel to watch over our money. He's nothing more than a carpetbagger, who came here from New Jersey to exploit people for his own financial gain. He's destroyed a lot of lives since he has been here, and I will not permit him to destroy ours."

"Anything you say, Will. I'll see that our money is moved when Agatha and I go to town on Wednesday. As you can see by our bank ledger, we have a sizeable amount on deposit there, and if you would feel safer moving it to another bank, I can do it on Wednesday."

"I would feel much better about things if you would do it first thing in the morning, Abby. Can you make a special trip to town and take care of that?"

"Agatha and I will go to town immediately following breakfast, and I'll take care of it."

"Thank you, Abby."

"I can finish making these entries in the ledger if you want to go on up to bed. I know you must be tired."

"Agatha is up there. Right now, I'm more afraid of her than I am those men who came here tonight. I think I'll wait for you, Abby."

"Are you really afraid of her, Will?"

"Of course I'm not. I was only joking with you. She's your sister, and as such, she will always have a special place in my heart."

o   o   o

If there had ever been any question in anyone's mind as to Will's ability to assert himself as the head of the household at Montgomery House, all questions were answered that night. Several positive things resulted from Will's actions that night. The Avenging Knights of Justice came to recognize that further attempts to terrorize William Collins would be in vain. Abby moved every penny of their money from Herbert Meyers' bank and into the Second Bank of Blanchard the very next morning. In addition, Sheriff Homer Bellisle never rode with any vigilantes again, and within two months, membership in the clandestine group of cowards dwindled to such a small number that they eventually had to disband altogether. Exactly how much of the group's membership loss could have been attributed to Will's defiance and his condemning words that night will never be known, but Will's defiance of the fiends that night became common knowledge throughout the community and throughout Rockingham County as well. Homer Bellisle had always thought highly of Will, but after that night, he felt that he was eternally indebted to Will for helping him to remember that he represented the law in Rockingham County, and justice was not intended to be administered by vigilantes.

○ ○ ○

When Abby had moved the family's money from Herbert Myers' bank, his hatred for Will intensified to a fever pitch. Will had exposed him for being the coward that he really was, and his reputation in the community had been severely damaged. Ladies no longer curtsied before him on the streets of Blanchard, and men turned their heads to avoid him. Myers' wife had abandoned him, traveling by rail back to her home in New Jersey. His evilness was being dealt back to him tenfold. In contrast to Myers, William Collins was perceived by the community as being a righteous and brave man... a man who would not compromise his beliefs... a man whom people could look up to and respect. Abby had loved Will from the very beginning, and each new day seemed to find her love for him increasing. Words could not describe the pride that she had when she sat by his side in church.

○ ○ ○

A family is an ever-changing entity. Nothing remains the same forever, and such is especially true in a family. What defines a family, is the love that is shared within, the faith that they have, and how well the family adapts to the changes that are bound to occur. The greater the love, the easier it is for the family to accept the inevitable challenges of change. Such a challenge was about to present itself into the lives of all who resided there at Montgomery House, and it was a challenge that could have easily destroyed a less loving and understanding family. But it was also a challenge that held the potential of bringing a loving family even closer together.

William, Ezra, Josh and George were heavily engaged in the cutting of their winter supply of firewood. It had become an annual family event once the last of the tobacco crop was harvested, for them to work together in cutting and laying in their entire winter supply of firewood. It was an event that usually took nine or ten days of continuous labor to complete. Logs of hickory or oak would be cut into the proper lengths using a two-man crosscut saw, and then stacked onto a wagon to be carried up to their respective houses. All of the womenfolk would join together and carry a meal to the men about midday, and for a brief time, the gathering would then transform into more of a festive picnic. Josh would play a guitar, George would play a mouth harp, Ezra would pound out a rhythm on the bottom of a bucket, and everyone would join in the singing. As tedious and burdensome as the cutting of firewood was, with the gaiety that surrounded the event it had more of a carnival personality about it, and everyone looked forward to participating in the jauntiness. It presented a two-hour diversion from the labors of cutting wood, allowing the menfolk ample time to restore themselves before resuming their work for the afternoon and evening.

About the seventh day of the event, the womenfolk arrived one afternoon with fried chicken, boiled potatoes, freshly squeezed apple cider, and hot biscuits, and the group of thirteen hungry frolickers were soon eating their meal as one big and happy family. Everyone was there, save for Agatha, who was feeling poorly that day and had remained at the house to rest. Abby and Will always sat just a little apart from the others so they could talk. Unlike many married couples who had tired of talking with each other after they had been married for a few months, Will and Abby never tired of one another's company or conversation. It was a tribute to the deep affection they shared for one another. On this particular day, Will could tell that Abby had something on her mind, despite her attempt to conceal the fact from him. It was almost humorous when one of them would try to keep something from the other, because both of them were incapable of concealing their thoughts. Initially, Will tried to ignore the fact that Abby had something on her mind. But the more he talked with her, the more he came to suspect that whatever was on her mind was something important.

"You know, Abby, the ladies in our family have the most heavenly singing voices I have ever heard, and your voice is like an angel singing down from the heavens. But I'll tell you something, I'll be darned if Vivian hasn't got a beautiful voice too. That woman can really raise her voice in song, can't she?"

"Vivian does have a beautiful voice... she always has."

"Alright... I suppose that it's useless for us to keep beating around the bush like this, isn't it?"

"What do you mean, Will?"

"You want to tell me something, don't you, Abby?"

"Yes, Will, I really do. I'm surprised that you can tell."

"I can read you like a book, Abby. You want to tell me something important, now don't you?"

"Yes, but not here. We'll talk about it this evening when you come up to the house, Will."

"Now Abby, you know me well enough to know that I'll worry myself sick about whatever it is until you tell me, so you might as well go ahead and tell me right now and get it over with. Whatever it is, I can clearly see that it's something important."

"It is something important. But trust me, Will, it's not the type of thing that we should talk about here, so close to the others. It's much too personal in nature."

"Can you give me a little hint of what it's about, Abby?"

"Oh, Will, please wait until we're alone."

"Just tell me if it's something good, or something bad. Is that asking too much?"

"It's something good, I suppose, unless you don't like it, then I suppose it's something not quite as good, but I surely don't think it's something bad. I think it's something wonderful, and I pray that you will too."

"Can you give me a little better hint than that? You've accomplished nothing more than raising my curiosity even higher."

"We'll talk later, in private!"

"You're teasing me, Abby! Just tell me if it has anything to do with something that I have done."

"Well... sort of... I mean... indirectly, yes, I suppose it really does have something to do with something that you've done."

"Sort of? Come on, Abby! My curiosity is killing me! I can't stand it! I'll bust wide open if you don't go ahead and tell me!"

"Not here! Please, Will!"

"Alright, anything you say, Abby."

But Will was not the type who could wait very long to hear something that he now deemed as being very important, especially now that he knew the subject had something to do with something he had done. After he and Abby had finished their meal, he asked Ezra if he and his boys could finish up for the day without him. Ezra agreed, and Will quickly and unceremoniously scooped Abby up in his arms, placed her atop his horse, and mounted the horse behind her. Abby was surprised by Will's audaciously bold method of placing her on his horse.

"My goodness, William Collins! I take it you can't wait any longer, can you?"

"I've waited just about as long as I care to wait, Abby. My curiosity is killing me."

"I feel like I've just become a princess, and I've just been put on a horse by a knight in shining armor—my champion."

"I am your champion, Abby, but my armor doesn't shine very bright... in fact, it's kind of dirty in places."

"You've got your opinion, Mr. Collins, and I have mine. Lead on, Sir Collins!"

Together, they chuckled and rode back toward the house, but instead of going to the house, Will turned his horse to the southwest and took them to a quiet place on the creek, near the western boundary of Montgomery Farm property. The autumn leaves were in their most glorious color, and in the distance they could still faintly hear the guitar and the singing of the merry group of woodcutters. They dismounted and sat on a moss-covered log overlooking the creek. Various colored autumn leaves floated gently down the current of the stream, as Will suggested, "Let's talk here, Abby. Would this be a suitable place for you to satisfy my unruly curiosity?"

"This is a beautiful place. I haven't been here for years, and I almost forgot how beautiful it really is here, especially at this time of year. I used to bring Elizabeth and Sarah here when they were children, and let them swim in the water."

"It's a much more beautiful place with you here, Abby. Now, how about telling your curious husband what's on your mind before I bust wide open?"

"It's about Agatha, Will."

"Oh, her again... My Lord, what on earth has she gone and done this time, Abby? She hasn't seduced the pastor has she?"

"Please, Will... What I want to tell you is very important to me, and you're making it terribly difficult with your obscene joking. Agatha doesn't deserve your cruel jokes."

"I know she doesn't, Abby, I'm sorry. Please continue, and I'll try to withhold my unfair ridicule."

"She didn't come to the picnic with the rest of us today."

"I know, Abby, you said she was feeling poorly. Is she alright? My Lord, she's not seriously ill or anything, is she?"

"No, Will... she's not seriously ill, she's pregnant with child."

"Agatha's pregnant? My dear God! How can that be? She's had no suitors that I know of, Abby. As far as I know, she hasn't even sat on the porch swing with anyone."

"Will..."

"She's supposed to be in mourning, for heaven's sake. Did she sneak away during the night some time and get together with a man somehow? Is that what you're trying to tell me? Who did she get with?"

"Will, please be quiet for a moment, and let me finish saying what I want to say."

"Pardon me, please go on..."

"Think about it for a moment, Will... six and a half weeks ago... that morning she got into our bed with you..."

"Dear Jesus above! You mean... I'm the guilty party? Agatha is pregnant with my baby? Oh, my Lord Jesus, Abby!"

"Wait a minute, Will, before you fall completely to pieces over this, let me tell you something first."

"It doesn't seem fair that you and I are trying so hard to have a baby without success, and she sneaks into the room with me one morning for twenty minutes and gets pregnant! My Lord! It's just not fair!"

"Please let me tell you something before you say any more, Will. There's no cause for you to be upset about this!"

"There's no cause for me to be upset, you say?! I think there is plenty of cause for me to be upset! This is very distressing to me, and I can't help it!"

"Please, Will? May I finish?"

"I'm sorry, what do you want to tell me?"

"Will, Agatha and I had a long talk this morning."

"It's about time someone had a long talk with her! I've a good mind to go up and have a little talk with her myself!"

"Please, Will, let me say what I need to say without any more of your disparaging remarks! It's very important to me! Your criticism of her is completely unfounded, and very unfair! She's not a bad person, she really has a heart of gold, whether you realize it or not."

"I'm sorry, Abby. Go ahead, and I'll try to bite my tongue."

"Like I was saying, I had a long talk with Agatha this morning... for more than two hours. What I want more than anything in this world is for Agatha to deliver a healthy baby. I want it to be *our* baby, Will... mine and yours, and so does Agatha."

"You and Agatha both want us to raise the child when it's born? Like it was ours?"

"It would appear as though my ability to conceive has come to an end. I'm desperate to raise a child with you, Will. And because Agatha is such a generous and loving person, God has placed a wonderful opportunity before us to have a child... our very own child."

"Yes, I suppose that's true, but..."

"Consider this, Will; as I've told you before, Agatha was raped when she was but thirteen years of age. As a result, she had a baby. Three years later, when she was married, she was married to her first husband for almost seven years, and she never conceived during that whole time. She had periodic relations with my first husband for more than eight years, and she never conceived. She was married to James Brighton for almost two years, and she never conceived. Now, consider this, Will... she came to your bed for only a brief moment or two, and as a result, she conceived. If that's not a message to us from God, I don't know what is! Agatha and I want everyone to think that the baby is ours... yours and mine. You're the father of this child, Will. Your son or daughter is growing inside of Agatha, even as we speak... your own flesh and blood."

Will paused in conversation as he considered Abby's poignant comment that his son or daughter was growing inside of Agatha at that very moment. He cleared his throat and asked, "How could we possibly go about concealing the fact that she's pregnant and you're not, Abby? Have you and Agatha given that any thought?"

"Yes. Agatha and I want to be sequestered here on Montgomery Farm. We want no visitors here, and neither of us will go anywhere until after the baby is born. If someone arrives that needs to talk to me about something, I will talk to them from an upstairs window and tell them I am ill with child. That will spare Agatha the ridicule of our community, and in about seven and a half months, you and I will have the child that we have longed for."

"So, Agatha has been pregnant ever since sneaking into my bed that morning? She's been with child for a month and a half already?"

"Yes, almost seven weeks. Haven't you noticed?"

"To be quite honest with you, no, I have not. I spend very little time studying over Agatha. I spend very little time studying over any woman but you. I've noticed nothing unusual in her appearance."

"Please give us your blessing to do this, Will."

"You can't hide something like that from Sarah and Elizabeth... or even Vivian, Abby."

"I know, but they are all trustworthy. We can bring them into our confidence. I wouldn't have it any other way, Will, and I know them well enough to know that they will not breathe a word of this to anyone outside of our family."

"I had hoped that Sarah and Elizabeth would never know that Agatha and I had once gotten together. I wouldn't want them to think that I had ever betrayed you in any way whatsoever."

"I can explain that to them by simply telling them the truth, Will. They'll understand. I am so desperate to raise a child with the man I love that I will do anything to make this successful. Please give Agatha and me your consent to go forward with this."

"Every time that I think I already know all the reasons I have to love you, you always surprise me by giving me another. You amaze me, Abby."

"I love you, Will, and Agatha loves us both. You are the father of this child. Please give us your blessing to do this."

"Of course you have my blessing. What kind of a father would I be if I said no? This child will never lack for being loved, I can promise you that!"

"Oh, Will. I often find myself wondering what my life here would be like today if I had never met you. I can't imagine. You've brought so much happiness into our lives here at Montgomery House. You and I have so many blessings to be thankful for."

"I suppose after all things are considered, Agatha's pregnancy really should be regarded as a blessing in disguise. It's true, God works in mysterious ways. It's strange, but..."

"What, Will?"

"It's strange, but since we've been talking, I no longer feel any bitterness toward Agatha for deceiving me that morning. With the prospects of our family having a child, I even feel happy about what happened... It's hard to explain..."

"I understand, because I feel the same way."

"Tell me something, Abby, when you talked with Agatha this morning, did she ever look you in the eye and confess to coming into my room that morning?"

"She started to, but then she broke into tears. As she wept, I told her that I already knew about it, and have known about it all along. She asked me how I found out about it, and I told her the truth, that you had confided in me that very morning. She said something then that really makes me proud that you're my husband."

"Oh? What did she say, Abby?"

"She said that most men would not have told their wives about such a thing. She said that William Collins truly was a remarkably special kind of person. Of course, she didn't have to tell me that, because I already knew that."

"The music back at the picnic has stopped, Abby. I think the men are all preparing to go back to work. I suppose I should go back to the woods and finish helping Ezra and the boys."

"I wish you wouldn't, Will."

"Oh? What would you prefer that I do, Abby?"

"I would really like for you to come up to the house with me while we have some privacy. I would like for you and I to talk things over with Agatha. She's up there now, worried to death about how you would react to this."

"Oh, Abby, I don't know if I can face her just now..."

"She's really a sweet-hearted person, Will, and I think it would help to clear the air if the three of us just sat and talked for a while. It would mean so much to Agatha and me if you would. She's carrying our child for us, Will, can't we go and sit with her and tell her how much we both love her, and appreciate what she's doing for us? Would you be willing to do that for me, Will?"

"Of course I will, Abby. I have to face her again sooner or later anyway. Besides, the more I think about her being pregnant with a child that I have fathered, the happier I am. Sure, let's go to the house and see her. It would be cruel of me not to tell her how elated I am. May I have a kiss before we go?"

Will and Abby went to Agatha's bedchamber and knocked on the door.

"Agatha? It's Will and me, dear, may we come in?"

"Yes, of course you can."

Will was nervously unsure of himself, and had no idea of exactly what he would say to Agatha until he and Abby had walked inside and closed the door behind them. Without being prompted by Abby, once he looked into Agatha's eyes, all apprehension quickly faded away. He and Abby stood at Agatha's bedside, and his soft words flowed fluently from his heart.

"Agatha, dear, I'm so sorry that you are feeling poorly. Is there anything Abby and I can get for you?"

"I'm not feeling so poorly anymore. I feel sickly in the mornings for an hour or so... but, I'll be fine, Will. Thank you for asking."

"Agatha..."

"Yes, Will?"

"Agatha, may I tell you something, while Abby is here with us? I really need to say this, if I may..."

"Of course, Will."

"I... uhhh... I mean... Agatha, it's like this... For a weeks now, I have greatly resented your deceiving me that morning that you came into my bed... but it's important to me that you know that I no longer bear any resentment for what happened that morning. On the contrary... Abby has helped me come to realize that what we did, although sinful as it was at the time, has resulted in a miracle. Abby and I love you, Agatha, and mere words could never express how thankful we are for what you are doing for us."

"What I did that morning was sinful, Will. What you did was sinless. I was the one who betrayed my only sister after all that she has done for me over the years... after all the times that she cared for me and comforted me... after all the times that she had sacrificed her own needs in order to provide for me, I rewarded her by betraying her..."

Agatha broke into the most pitiful spell of sobbing that Abby and Will had ever seen, and with pain in her eyes and heart, Agatha went on to say, "I have begged and pleaded for God to forgive me, and this morning, I have also asked Abigail to forgive me. Would you please forgive me as well?"

"Of course I do, Agatha."

With tears in her eyes, Abby stepped into the conversation to say, "Let us not dwell in the past. Let us look forward, and revel in this glorious promise of a child that we now have. From this point forward, let there be no shame between us and no guilt. As Will said, Agatha, we love you, and we shall always love you."

The three of them talked for over an hour. Agatha cowered in guilt, and acted as though she was grievously ashamed of the fact that she had taken unfair advantage of Will that morning. She also acted as if she was equally ashamed of having done so behind her sister's back. She wept with guilt several times until Will and Abby reassured her that she was loved. With all transgressions forgiven and in the open now, through the process of talking honestly and openly, the three of them became much closer, and for the first time, Will thought that Abby was correct when she had said that her sister really had a kind and generous heart. She had acted solely out of a frantic and spontaneous impulse on that September morning, and the family was now able to come to terms with both the act and the wonderful miracle of the resulting pregnancy. By the end of their discussion, they were able to discuss the issue without embarrassment, and regard it as an extraordinary promise of a forthcoming child for the family.

The most awkward phase of their plan came that evening when Abby met privately in the parlor with Sarah and Elizabeth. The young sisters were shocked, and became livid when they learned that Agatha had entered Will's bed that morning and cleverly deceived him into thinking he was making love with Abby. It was only after much discussion with her daughters that Abby successfully defused their anger and helped the sisters to understand what a blessing Agatha's pregnancy really was. Once

Elizabeth and Sarah overcame their initial shock and anger, Abby called Will and Agatha into the parlor. There was much weeping to begin with, yet there was so much love there in the family that congeniality soon prevailed. The issue was addressed by the entire family until all shame, embarrassment, and guilt between them had been extricated. Everyone was in harmonious family agreement with Abby and Will's desire to raise Agatha's baby as their own. It was the only honorable thing for the family to do in order to save face in the church and the community, and with Will being the baby's father, the family truly would treat the event as the blessing from God that it really was. Before dispersing to begin preparations for their evening meal, they held hands as a family and Will offered a prayer for Agatha and the child she now carried.

"God be with us, guide us, and give us courage. Help us to be more worthy of the many blessings that you bring into our lives daily. Father, with the new life that Agatha now carries, we ask that you shelter mother and child from all harm. We ask that you bring comfort and good health to Agatha, and provide her with the peace of knowing that she and the baby will be in our daily prayers. In the Holy name of Christ we pray, Amen."

O O O

The following months were often filled with confusing circumstances as the family worked in unison to keep Agatha's pregnancy a secret, while at the same time feigning the pregnancy of Abby. On one particular occasion, Abby was at the barn helping Will attend to an infected lesion on the leg of a baby calf when two visiting ladies from the Blanchard church arrived, asking to speak with Abigail. Abby had to remain hidden in the barn until Will could run to the house and tell the visitors that Abby was confined to her bed that day, and was not feeling well, at the time. Neither Abby nor Will favored the idea of being deceitful with their neighbors, but in their present circumstance there at Montgomery Farm, deceit was the lesser of the two evils. There were a few close calls such as that, but by the time the baby's birth drew near, everything had gone precisely according to plan.

Something else happened during the ensuing months as well. Apparently Will and Abby Collins were not the only people who had become dissatisfied with the First Bank of Blanchard's president, Herbert Myers. Will had been disgusted by Myers' involvement and leadership role with the vigilantes, but there were other folks in and around the town of Blanchard who were equally as disgusted. Allegations of fraud and misconduct were soon filed against Myers and a scathing exposé was published in the Blanchard Herald. Soon, many people were withdrawing their money from the First Bank of Blanchard, and moving it to the Second Bank of Blanchard. Meyers' bank had seen a steady decrease in depositors for months, and the bank finally had to close its doors forever. Some people lost their entire savings. Herbert Myers was a ruined man with charges of misconduct and lawsuits pending against him, and rather than accept the blame himself, he blamed all of his failures and misfortunes on William Collins. He was seething with hatred for Will. In truth, Will had not encouraged anyone else to withdraw their money. They had done so of their own accord. Nevertheless, a coward such a Myers needed to attribute his business failures to someone other than himself, so he chose Will, probably because of the way that Will had discredited him in front of his vigilante comrades the night they had attempted to terrorize Montgomery Farm. The Second Bank of Blanchard was owned by an upstanding and honorable man who was worthy of the trust that his depositors had placed in him. He was a deacon in the Methodist church there in Blanchard and a respected high-ranking member of the Blanchard Masonic Institution. Depositors could not have wanted for a more honest and upright man to safeguard their savings.

○　○　○

The following spring, on the morning of April 22, 1869, Vivian was quickly summoned to come to the house in order to assist Abby. Agatha had gone into her birthing labors during the early morning hours. Less than two hours after she began her sincere labor pains, Vivian and Abby were cleaning the afterbirth from a beautiful, healthy baby boy. The family was elated. Sarah and Elizabeth had been allowed to attend and witness as their new brother came into the world and took his first precious breath. It was the first time that either of them had observed the birth of a child. Abby thought it best for her daughters to be there to witness the event and to learn from it. Sarah and Elizabeth were adults now, and they had each bore firsthand witness to the event. Despite the fact that Elizabeth had fainted during the delivery, the birth had otherwise been without difficulty. Agatha nursed the newborn baby for the first three days. Abby was still capable of producing milk from her previous pregnancy, but not to the extent of which Agatha was capable. Nevertheless, Abby shared in this responsibility as best her body would provide. She soon found that the more frequently she nursed the baby, the more milk her body would produce, and after seven weeks, Abby assumed the largest role in nursing the infant. Abby and Will, with Agatha's blessing, named the child Christopher Montgomery Collins. Christopher's birth had worked wonders in bringing the family even closer together as a sovereign unit, joyously defined by the ever-present love that dwelled within the walls of Montgomery House.

On a Thursday morning, during the second week of June, Will was hard at work in the fields with Ezra and his sons, repairing a fence that separated one of their pastures from the crop fields, when he first looked up to take notice of the impending arrival of a lone rider, approaching from the east. Will leaned on his shovel for a moment, wiped the sweat from his brow, and continued to focus his attention on the approaching man. As the rider drew closer,

Will objectionably recognized that the person approaching him was none other than the malicious, Herbert Myers. He wondered why a scoundrel such as Herbert Myers would have business here at Montgomery Farm. When he was close enough to speak, Myers looked down from his horse and condescendingly said, "I figured that I would probably find you here, Mr. Collins. Working in the fields with the rest of your black nigger family, I see."

"If you have business here, go ahead and state it, Myers! Otherwise, get the hell off of my property right now!"

"Oh, I have business here, Mr. Collins, of that you can be damned sure."

"Then state your business and be gone with you!"

Abby sat next to Agatha, on the corner of the bed in her and Will's bedchamber, nursing young Christopher as Sarah and Elizabeth looked on with adoring delight and perhaps imagining themselves as being mothers sometime in the distant future. Christopher had just turned three months old on that day. The four adoring ladies each talked to young Christopher in the sweet language of baby talk, as little Christopher gently and contentedly suckled Abby, seemingly oblivious to all but the business at hand.

"He looks just like Will, doesn't he?"

"He's adorable! Just adorable!"

"Look at his little fingers and hands… isn't he precious?"

"He's as healthy and handsome a child as I have ever laid my eyes on!"

The conversation that they shared among themselves was lighthearted and spirited, yet ended abruptly when they heard two rapid gunshots from outside. Sarah was the first to dash to a window. She saw a lone rider, quickly fleeing to the east, and she also saw Ezra and his sons bending over something on the ground. Abby asked Sarah, "What is it, Sarah? What were the gunshots all about? What do you see?"

"I'm not sure what's going on, Mother. I can see Ezra and George and Josh…"

"What about Will? Do you see him?"

"No, I don't see Will. Wait a minute! Dear God! Will's on the ground! I think he's been shot, Mother! Yes! My God, I can see blood!"

Immediate panic and chaos consumed the ladies of Montgomery House as they hurried downstairs and out onto the front porch. Their gaiety in frolicking with little Christopher had suddenly come to an abrupt end, and transformed into stark terror, as the very foundation of their family, William Collins, lay critically injured and bleeding on the ground.

As Ye Sow—So Shall Thou Reap

"Let all bitterness, and wrath, and anger, and clamour, and evil speaking, be put away from you, with all malice: And be ye kind one to another, tenderhearted, forgiving one another, even as God for Christ's sake hath forgiven you." Ephesians 4:31 - 4:32

Ezra and his faithful sons carried Will as quickly and as gently as they possibly could from the field where he had been shot, up to the house. There, they hastily placed him atop the parlor table while Abby, Agatha, and both daughters worked feverishly in the midst of their grave concern to slow the flow of his precious lifeblood. Abby quickly took off her apron, and used it as a compress while shouting at Elizabeth to fetch a bedsheet and cut it small pieces and strips. William had been shot twice at very close range; once in the lower neck just above his collarbone, and once just above his left ear, grazing the right side of his head. It was the wound to his head that concerned Abby so deeply. With stark terror, she remembered how dangerously close Will had come to dying when he had received an injury to the left side of his head scarcely more than two and a half years earlier. Even as frantically as she attended to Will, she maintained enough self-control to shout out for Ezra, and dispatched him to town to fetch Dr. Michaels and Sheriff Bellisle. Once the flow of blood was successfully

351

halted, Elizabeth asked, "Should we carry him upstairs to your bedchamber, Mother?"

"No! I don't want him moved in any way until the doctor gets here and tells us that it is safe to move him. Fetch a pillow for the back of his head, please, Elizabeth. Sarah, you and Agatha bring some cloths and a pan of warm water, and try to clean some of the blood from the table and floor. I'm going to hold this compress in place on his head until the doctor gets here. I think I've successfully slowed the flow of blood, and I don't want to remove the compress again until Doctor Michaels gets here."

"Are you going to be alright, Mother?"

"We've all got to stay strong for Will. I'll be alright. Go ahead and fetch the pillow, quickly. When you get back, we'll hold prayer as a family."

With one of her frail, trembling hands holding the compress against the side of Will's head and the other holding a like compress against the wound in his neck, when everyone had gathered around Will again, Abby offered a prayer, amidst the sobs and tears of Agatha, Elizabeth, and Sarah.

"Dear Lord, please don't take him from us... please! He means so much to us, Lord! He's all we've got! He has a son, now! Please let him live to see his son grow to manhood! Please!"

Abby wanted desperately to present a more humble and befitting prayer, but her nerves were shattered, and the best that she could do was to call out to the Lord frantically. She felt faint in her knees and in the pit of her stomach, yet she forced herself to hold the compresses tightly against Will's head and neck. Tears flowed from her eyes, and her lips quivered at the gloomy possibilities of Will's condition. Still, she remained steadfast in placing her feelings secondary to those of her beloved husband. Without disgrace, she talked lovingly to Will as he lay there. She was oblivious to the fact that there were others in the room, and talked to him without shame.

"Listen to me, Will... I'm right here with you, darling, we all are... and we need you to fight to stay alive, Will. I'm not strong enough to live in a world without you again. You have a son now, Will... we have a son now! We need you, darling! We need you to fight to stay alive for us! If you never do another thing for me as long as I live, please do this for me Will!"

For the second time in two and a half years, a horrible irony was occurring at Montgomery House. The womenfolk were gathered over the body of an unresponsive and badly wounded William Collins. Perhaps they would never hear those wonderful words, *I love you*, from his lips again. In her mournful desperation, Abigail remembered when Will had spoken those words to her before leaving to go to the fields that very morning, and she wondered if she would ever hear them again. She wondered if she would ever experience his kisses again, or see the smiles of pride on his face as he held little Christopher in his arms. She wondered and she prayed, and with nervous hands, she continued to hold the compresses in place.

Ezra arrived back from Blanchard in an astonishingly short amount of time with both Dr. Michaels and Sheriff Homer Bellisle. Their lathered horses testified as to how quickly they had ridden to arrive there as early as they possibly could. It was also a vivid tribute as to how endeared they were to their good friend, William Collins. The doctor immediately went into the parlor to administer to Will while Homer Bellisle asked questions of Ezra and his sons on the porch. Soon, Bellisle removed his hat and stepped inside the parlor to where the doctor was stitching the wound on Will's neck closed while Abby continued to hold the compress against Will's head. Bellisle stooped down close to Will, and even knowing that Will probably couldn't hear him, he said, "Will, I'm going to make this right... I swear to God Almighty I will." Without saying another word to anyone, he went back outside, mounted his horse, and rode quickly back toward the town of Blanchard with the fire of hell's fury burning in his heart. He was unfaltering in his determination to find Herbert Myers... not to capture him or bring him to justice, but to kill him. As word spread through the town of Blanchard, it soon became apparent just how well William Collins was loved. Many citizens flocked to the porches of Montgomery House to stand in vigil on Will's behalf while others joined the sheriff to go on the hunt. Practically everywhere in Blanchard, there were armed citizens looking for Herbert Myers. They searched his home, his barn, the old bank building, and everywhere else they could think of.

After giving Will a thorough examination, stitching the wound above his ear, and changing his blood-soaked dressings, the doctor declared the flow of blood to be under control and deemed it safe to move Will into the small chambermaid room where he could rest more comfortably... the exact same bedchamber where Will had spent many months recovering almost two and a half years prior. The doctor didn't want Will to be carried up the steep stairway to the second floor, and the closest bed was there in the chambermaid room. Ezra and his sons were summoned from the porch to carry Will into the room as all the womenfolk looked on with the sheer expression of despondency on their faces. They held on to each other for support as the men lifted Will from the parlor table and began carrying him to the chambermaid room. As Will was being carried through the narrow bedchamber door, he astonished everyone by saying, "Careful not to bump my head on the doorpost, men... I don't think I could stand another blow to my head right now."

Abby fainted dead away on the kitchen floor when she heard Will's voice, and for a brief moment, everyone seemed to be in another state of utter chaos and confusion. The baby started crying from the next room, and Agatha rushed off to tend to his needs. Sarah and Elizabeth rushed to Abby's assistance on the kitchen floor as the menfolk and the doctor continued to carry Will to a bed and get him situated there. Then, the doctor hurried back to the kitchen to attend to Abby. Other than having a goodly portion of Will's blood on her arms and cheeks, Abby was fine, and she regained her needed cognizance within a moment or two. She had become so overwhelmed and relieved to hear Will's voice again that she had momentarily fainted into unconsciousness. When all of the mayhem had settled down, Elizabeth and Sarah helped Abby go to Will's side, and sit beside him on the bed. She held Will's hand compassionately as the doctor asked him questions. Agatha held Christopher in her arms and stood at the doorway with Sarah and Elizabeth. The small bedchamber was much too small to admit anyone else into the room. The doctor cleared his throat and asked, "How do you feel, Will?"

"How do I feel? Lord Almighty, I feel as though I have been trampled on by a herd of wild buffaloes, doctor."

"Do you know what day of the week this is, Will?"

"Of course, it's Wednesday, isn't it? At least it was this morning when I woke up."

"Very good. How about the month?"

"It's July. Come on Doctor, I'm just hurting, I'm not delirious. I'm going to be alright now."

"I think so, too, thank God. Are you aware of what happened to you?"

"Yes, I'm aware that I was shot in the head by that rotten scoundrel, Herbert Myers, if that's what you mean."

"He shot you in your neck also. You're mighty lucky to be alive, Will."

"Doctor, let me ask you something, if I may."

"Certainly, what is it?"

"Who are all those people on my back porch and lawn?"

"They're your friends from Blanchard, Will, from the church and from the community. They've come here to pray for you."

"My Lord... Can you please go out and tell them that I'm alright?"

"I would be honored to do just that."

"May I ask you just one more question, Doctor?"

"Of course, what is it?"

"You've seen an awful lot of people during all the years that you've been a doctor, haven't you? I mean running all over the county for so many years like you have, you must have seen just about everybody in two counties at one time or another, haven't you?"

"I certainly have. Why do you ask?"

"In all of your travels, have you ever in all your years, seen a woman more beautiful than my sweet Abigail here, or my lovely girls standing there in the doorway?"

Abby broke into tears again, kissed Will's hand, and told the doctor, "I think my husband will mend quickly now, Doctor."

"I think he will too, Abby, and to answer your question Will, I've only seen one other woman in the whole world who could even hold a candle to your family of beautiful ladies."

"Really? And who might that be, pray tell?"

"My wife, Ruth. Abby, I would appreciate it very much if you would tell Ruth on Sunday that I said that. I need all the help at home that I can get nowadays."

"I'll be sure to tell her, Doctor."

"My head hurts so bad, I feel like it's about to burst, Doctor."

"I'm sure that it does hurt, Will, and I'm afraid it's going to feel that way for at least a couple of days. I'm going to give you something for the pain, but it's going to make you sleep pretty soundly for a while."

"Not just yet, Doctor. Before I do any sleeping, I want to look at my beautiful family for just a while longer."

As Abby had predicted, Will would be healing very quickly. Two days later, he was able to climb the stairs and resume sleeping in his own bedchamber. All seemed to have returned to normal in the household, except that Will was as yet unable to resume his usual farm labors. Ezra and his boys managed to keep up with the work quite capably, allowing Will the necessary time to heal. Will appeared to be healing rapidly, but appearances can sometimes be very deceiving. All had not returned to normalcy in the life of William Collins. In fact, things would never be quite the same again, as they were before he was shot by Myers.

Sheriff Homer Bellisle returned to Montgomery Farm less than a week later to report that Herbert Myers had finally been discovered hiding in the bell tower of a church in Blanchard. A gunfight had erupted, and during the fight Myers had killed one citizen and badly wounded another. His demonstration of resistance was futile, and he soon found himself without any ammunition. He was captured by twelve or fourteen citizens who dragged him out of the church and into the street. Homer Bellisle watched from across the street as the townsmen led Myers toward a barn across the street from the church. Bellisle started to intervene and take Myers into custody, and bring him back to a cell at the courthouse, but he noticed that one of the citizens leading Myers to the barn had a rope in his possession. Bellisle paused briefly, thought about it for a moment or two, and turned to walk slowly back to his office. The integrity of his elected office would not allow him to be a participant in the fate that was about to befall Myers, but his appetite for vengeance would not allow him to intervene. He and his deputy recovered Myers' body later that afternoon, hanging from an overhead beam in the barn, confident in their minds that justice had been served. The fate of Herbert Myers caused no undue wave of sorrow in the town of Blanchard, nor at Montgomery Farm. And as far as justice was concerned, Myers had ironically received his just reward at the hands of the same type of mob that he had so often participated in. His death was poor recompense to the many scores of people that he had hurt during his evil life, but folks thereabouts were at least provided with the assurance that the days of Myers' malevolent influence over the people of Blanchard had come to an end.

In his recovery from the gunshots, Will was undergoing disturbingly strange mental anguishes as he healed. He spent many long hours on the porch of his home as his body mended, and he began seeing strange flashes of light in his peripheral vision, usually accompanied by very minor restorations of memories from his distant past. Will had arrived at a point in his recovery in which he came to recognize that unmistakable segments of his memory were beginning to return to him, and he initially struggled within himself to block the returning images of his past life. He kept telling himself that he was William Collins now, and he did not wish to acquire knowledge that he had ever been anyone else. He was happy as William Collins. These extraneous impulses to accept himself as being anyone other than the man who he wanted to be were very discomforting to him. Even with the strong opposition that he put forth to block his returning memory, it nevertheless began returning to him until he remembered his birth name, his mother and father's name, and a clear vision of the friends and acquaintances whom he had left behind in his previous life as a young man. It was impossible for him to block out these unwanted recollections of his past, and thus he was bequeathed the responsibility of coming to terms with who he really was, where he had come from, and what he had done in his previous life.

Anyone who would have observed William sitting on his porch with his head bowed, trying to chase away the demons that attempted to draw him back into his past, would have assumed that his anguish and torment was rightly attributed to the pain from his gunshot injuries. They would have been wrong in arriving at such a presumptuous conclusion. But such an assumption allowed Will the opportunity to privately search his soul and come to terms with himself without the bother of interfering questions from his inquisitive family members. In the course of a single day, he recalled several years of his previous life, and by late afternoon, on the fifth day of September, a large portion of Will's memory had been restored. Under normal circumstances, a person would have been elated over the return of their memory. William should have shouted out in joyful tribute, but he did not.

Commensurate with the restoration of his memory, there was much unrest within Will's heart caused by the fact that he was keeping the strange and disconcerting return of his memory hidden from his family. Such an important revelation must be shared with them, he concluded, but when? He would reveal this secret to his family eventually, but first he had to arrive at a complete understanding of it in his own heart. With the return of his memory, he had choices to make, and none of them would be easy. He kept the return of his memory a secret from his precious family for two full days before deciding that the day had come in which he should bring his family into his confidence.

In some ways, Will felt that he had been emancipated from the frustrations of not knowing who he was, where he was from, and how he had come to arrive at Montgomery Farm. In other ways, he was disappointed to know the certainty of his past, and the binding implications that came along with rediscovering himself. He would have to reveal his secret to his family, of that, he was certain. To do otherwise, would be a betrayal to the people who loved him the most... and the people whom he loved the most. He wrestled with the idea of revealing his secret to Abby first, and then the family, but decided that it would best be done all at one time, in the presence of every member of the family that he loved so dearly.

Abby had known for more than a day that Will was being pestered by his conscience for some reason. She had asked him on a number of occasions to confide in her, but he stubbornly told her that he had to come to terms with a few things first and make some decisions before discussing the matter. Abby was hurt by the fact that Will did not want to confide in her, but did not press him for fear of causing him undue stress during the time of his healing and recovery. Early one evening, as Will watched Abby nursing young Christopher, he decided that he had completely come to terms with his identity, and would reveal his innermost secrets to his family for the first time. It would be a long overdue introduction. Will sat next to Abby at the foot of their bed, kissed her gently on the cheek, and said, "Abby, when you are finished nursing Christopher, I wish to meet with the family down in the parlor. I have some important things I would like to share with the people that I love most in this life."

Abby knew that this was the moment she had been waiting

for. She had sensed all along that Will had regained a portion of his memory, and simply answered him by saying, "I understand, Will, and I love you."

Abby kept her emotions well contained. Inside, she knew that she had arrived at a critical juncture in her life. She feared that there was a possibility that Will was about to shatter her life by announcing his permanent departure from Montgomery Farm for the purpose of going back to some previous life, yet she loved and trusted him to such a great extent that she would not allow such fears to overcome her. Her anxiety was prompted by the question of which man would emerge the victor in this mysterious battle that had raged within the heart of her husband—Will Collins, or the man to whom she had not yet been introduced.

Once Christopher had been put to bed, the family gathered around the table in the parlor. All but Abby were completely unaware of what Will was about to say, and even Abby had merely been speculating, and paying homage to her feminine intuition. She knew Will far better than anyone else, and her emotions were held suspended in fear of what she was about to hear. Will poured himself a glass of bourbon to steady his nerves, took a few sips, and addressed everyone.

"Before I begin, I just want to start by telling you all how much I truly love each of you. You mean more to me than any feeble words that I could ever express, so with your indulgence, I won't even try."

Concerned with the seriousness in Will's voice and demeanor, Sarah asked, "What's the matter, Will? What's going on?"

"It's my intention to satisfy all of your questions tonight, questions that we have all had in our hearts since I was first brought here. Be patient for a moment longer, Sarah, and I'll answer everything, I swear it. To begin, I wish to announce that my memory, or at least the biggest part of it, has somehow been restored to me, and it's high time that I shared my thoughts as well as my true identity with the family that I love so dearly."

Elizabeth gasped, "Oh, my Lord!" Agatha held Abby's hand tightly, as if she was expecting grievous news, and Sarah turned pale and almost faint with anticipation. Everyone held their breath. Will took another drink of bourbon and continued with his explanation.

"To begin with, I still remember nothing about how I was wounded. There are still a lot of gaps in my memory—gaps that I may never be able to fill. But I'll share everything that I do know about myself with you."

Trembling, Abby softly said, "I love you, Will."

"And I love you, Abby. Please don't be so tense. I have nothing earth-shattering to tell you. I can see the fear in your eyes, and it is unwarranted. My birth name was Eugene Reginald Winston, and before I go any further, let me just say that I much prefer the name of William Collins. William Collins is who I am, and it's who I will always be until the day that I die."

Everyone breathed a short but apprehensive sigh of relief, and sat on the edge of their chairs, waiting to hear more. Will went on to say, "I remember that I was a corporal in the hundred and seventeenth cavalry brigade of Ohio regulars in the Union Army of the United States of America, but I suppose you already knew that. I was born and grew up in Charlottesville, Virginia. I went to Cleveland, Ohio to attend the university there when I was seventeen years old. I studied law there, and acquired a degree to practice law in 1863. I acquired law books from the University of Virginia and studied them vigorously, with the intention of practicing law in Virginia."

Abby asserted, "That would explain how you seem to know so much about the law in Virginia, wouldn't it?"

"Yes, I suppose it would, Abby. Shortly after obtaining my degree to practice law, I enlisted to fight in the war, primarily because I am so opposed to slavery. My heart was with the south on most issues, but I simply could not bring myself to fight for a government that condoned slavery. I'm sorry, but I just couldn't."

"We understand perfectly, Will, there is no need to apologize for your beliefs. Our family has been opposed to slavery for more than twenty years."

"Anyhow, I fought in several battles northwest of here, of which I remember very little, and several battles north of Richmond, and escaped major injury until the morning I was wounded here on Montgomery Farm I suppose. In several battles throughout the state of Virginia, I can remember nothing but the fact that hundreds of men were falling dead around me, but God chose to spare me for some unknown reason..."

"He spared you so that you could come here to us, Will!"

"I think so too, Abby, I honestly do. While I was a soldier, I witnessed the deaths of so many who fought by my side that I fully expected to be killed at any moment. Every day I wondered if this would be the day. God had other plans for me, though. I remember very little about exactly how I was wounded, but I hope that I've given you an adequate explanation as to how I got here and who I am."

Abby kissed Will's hand, and said, "You've told us quite enough to satisfy our curiosity, darling."

"No, I haven't, Abby. There's one more thing that I need to tell you that's very important, and it's eating away at my very soul. You see... in Charlottesville, before I left for the university in Cleveland, I... I..."

"What, Will?"

"I married a young woman there by the name of, Patricia Anne Metcalf." With this news, soft gasps were heard from around the room and a look of horror crossed every face in the parlor. Abby's face became devoid of color, and she inadvertently uttered, "Oh, my God... No! Please, God!"

"Patricia and I had no children... we were only married for a short time before I left to attend the university for my final year of law school. We wrote often to each other, but I only returned to Virginia once during my years at the university, and the last I wrote to her was in August or September of 1863, as best I remember, almost six years ago now. I do have the assurance that the brief marriage of Patricia Anne and I did not produced a child."

Abby looked deeply into Will's eyes, and asked the question that Will knew would be forthcoming, "With this new knowledge of your identity and your previous marriage, what do you plan to do with it, Will?"

"I knew that would be the question foremost in your mind, Abby, and it's been foremost in my mind as well. I've struggled with my conscience for the last two days, and I've made some important decisions regarding what I must do with the rest of my life."

"Please tell us, Will... I feel as though I am about to fall to pieces... I feel as though my world is about to be destroyed."

"Please don't worry, Abby. There's no cause for you to be distressed or feel concerned, I promise you. Let me finish, dear."

"Alright, Will."

"As soon as I'm able to ride, I plan to travel up to Charlottesville and pay a respectful visit to my former wife, Patricia Anne Winston. I owe her at least as much. I will explain everything that happened to me, as best I can, and once I have satisfied myself that she is provided for, I'll return to live the rest of my life with the woman that I love above all, our child, Christopher, my wife's wonderful daughters and sister. I've always detested deceitful behavior, and my heart won't allow me to live the rest of my life in happiness here, while Patricia Anne mourns over a dead husband. I just can't do that to her."

Abby asked the question that was now at the forefront of her mind and her heart, and also foremost in everyone's mind as well, "Suppose she behooves you to stay there with her in Charlottesville? What then? What's to become of us?"

"My home is here with you and my family, Abby... not in Charlottesville. I shouldn't have to tell you that I would rather die than leave you. I've told you that many times, and regaining my memory has done nothing to dissuade me from fulfilling my obligations here. My heart is here with you and my family - not in Charlottesville! Nothing will ever supersede my love for you... nothing! I need for you to trust me now, more than I've ever needed your trust before."

"Why can't you just write her a letter, Will, and tell her everything in a letter? Why is it so important to you that you leave us and go to see her in Charlottesville?"

"Because she lives with my mother and father, Abby. I owe them an explanation as well. They most likely think that their only son is dead, and I can only imagine their heartache. No, I must go there myself, and speak to them all, face-to-face. You once asked me if I was a Mason, and I know now that I am. I need to visit my Masonic Brothers in Charlottesville and inform them of my circumstances. It's strange, but Charlottesville is less than two days distance from here, and yet I never had a clue that I had been born and raised there until a very few days ago."

Abby again looked deeply into Will's eyes, and while holding his hand tightly, said, "I shan't be able to sleep at night until your return."

"As I said, Abby, my life is here, at Montgomery Farm with you and our family, not in Charlottesville. I won't stay there any longer than is absolutely necessary, I promise."

Sarah spoke up after remaining silent for most of the discussion, and asked, "What about your name, Will? Are we to start addressing you as, *Eugene* now?"

"Heaven forbid, Sarah. I'll always be William Collins. With all due respect to my mother and father, any other name is unfamiliar to me now. In my heart, Eugene Winston is dead. He died more than two and a half years ago on the field of battle, when a family of angels took pity on some poor soul named William Collins and brought him into their house, nursed him back to health, and took him into their hearts. That is when William Collins was born, and for as long as I am able to draw a breath on this earth, I will remain William Collins. I say that with all the sincerity that my heart has to offer. I love you all."

Abby trusted Will more than she trusted any other human

on the face of the earth. But the very nature of his impending visit to Charlottesville was causing her a great deal of anxiety. In her mind, despite the extent of her trust in Will, loomed the possibility that he could fall in love with his first wife all over again, especially if she had remained faithful to him for all those years and pleaded with him to stay with her. Abby knew nothing about Patricia Anne, and therefore imagined her to have the beauty of a goddess and the persuasive powers of a seductive demigod. She was horrified at the prospects of Will returning to Charlottesville, and the possibility that he would never be seen by her again dominated her every thought.

In the privacy of their bedchamber that evening, Abby nestled closely to Will. Her innocent curiosity implored her to learn more about this mysterious and beautiful seductress that her husband had been married to. She kissed Will softly, and asked him, "Since regaining so much of your memory, do you find yourself thinking about Patricia Anne very much?"

"Only as much as I would like to inform her that I am alive, and that I wish her well in life."

"What does Patricia Anne look like, Will? Is she beautiful?"

"That's not a fair question, Abby. I haven't seen her for almost six years. I don't know what she looks like today."

"What color is her hair?"

"Light brown, if I remember correctly. A color very similar to the color of yours, only not as long and not nearly as beautiful as yours."

"What color are her eyes?"

"Please, Abby... discussing Patricia Anne will accomplish nothing."

"I must know, Will... I'm only trying to imagine what she looks like. Please tell me. What color are her eyes?"

"Green, I think. It's strange, but I'm not really sure. It's been such a long time, Abby, and yours are the only eyes that I will ever find irresistible."

"Be truthful with me, do you still have any love for her, Will?"

"I can vaguely remember loving her when we were first married, yes, but I no longer know her, Abby. How could I possibly love her? People change, and none of us are the same person that we were six years ago."

"When you last saw her... was she beautiful then? What did she look like then? Describe her to me."

"Are you sure that you want to hear this?"

"I'm positive, please tell me."

"Very well, I'll try... Close your eyes and I'll try my best to describe her to you. Listen carefully. Let's see now, she's terribly obese, with a body shaped very similar to that of James Brighton, only much bigger, bless her heart. She has noticeably more facial hair than most women of her age. There are two large warts on the tip of her nose. Most of her teeth are missing, and the few that remain have become terribly blackened, and, oh yes, she is distinguishable from most other women because of the peculiar fact that she has three breasts, instead of two."

"Three breasts?"

"Yes. That's a peculiarity that most men might find wonderfully appealing, were it not for the fact that her third breast is on her forehead."

"Mercy, Will Collins! You rascal!"

"She's still much better off than her sister, though."

"Oh? And why is that, Will? Does her sister also have three breasts?"

"No, her sister only has two breasts, but her sister's breasts are located on her back, and when people see her, it's very difficult for them to tell whether she's coming or going."

"You can be a mischievous devil when you want to be, William Collins! Anyhow, I'm thankful that you have retained your William Collins sense of humor... I treasure it, and I will miss it terribly every second while you're gone."

"Be truthful with me for a moment. All joking aside, you have grave apprehensions regarding my visit to Charlottesville, don't you, Abby?"

"I would be a liar if I said that I didn't. I'm terribly afraid, Will."

"Afraid of what, Abby? What is it that you fear?"

"I don't want to lose you, Will. The thought is more than I can bear. My life was nothing before I met you, and I would rather die than to lose you."

"Then tell me this, Abby, what must I do to convince you that my love for you is greater than any love there has ever been between a man and a woman?"

"Make your visit as short as possible and come back to me when you've finished your visit, that's all that I ask."

"I would feel a lot better about doing what I know is right, if you would promise not worry about me while I'm gone, Abby."

"I shan't ask you not to go, Will, but don't ask me not to worry while you're gone. Such a thing would be beyond my power."

"Do you remember what you told me when I was so afraid for you to get pregnant again? You said for me not to hold back, but to trust in God. That's all that I'm asking of you now, Abby. I told you that I'm coming back to you. Do you believe in what I say, Abby?"

"I've always believed everything that you've ever said to me, Will... well, almost everything, that is..."

"Almost everything? What do you mean?"

"I believed the part about the obesity, the two warts, and even the rotten teeth, but I'm having more than a little trouble believing that Patricia Anne has three breasts, though."

"Ha! You caught me at my own game! I love you, Abby."

"And I love you, too, Eugene."

"Stop it! Kiss me, Abby, and just know in your heart that I love you."

Although Will's head and neck remained dressed with bandages, four days later he was ready to make his pilgrimage to Charlottesville to see his first wife and his parents. His was not a pilgrimage in which to rediscover himself, it was merely a pilgrimage in which he intended to put to rest any and all apprehensions in the minds of his loved ones, and answer any lingering questions regarding what had become of Corporal Eugene Reginald Winston. William Collins did not want to be another of the many soldiers that had been anonymously consumed by the war and forgotten. He owed his parents and his former wife the courtesy of contributing to their peace of mind and eliminating their sorrow.

On the morning of October twenty-third, Will said his goodbyes to his family in the kitchen and left Montgomery Farm more than an hour before dawn. Abby had outwardly remained as unemotional as possible over his departure until Will was well out of sight and sound. Standing on the rear porch, with a blanket wrapped around her to protect her from the cold air of a late October morning, she bowed her head and wept silently. She tearfully asked God to protect Will, and to deliver him safely to her again. As she stood there on the porch in tears, she felt a soothing arm around her waist and a kiss on her cheek as Sarah asked, "Please come inside Mother. You'll catch your death of cold out here like this. Will is coming back to us, Mother, I know he is."

"Would you go upstairs and bring Christopher down to the kitchen for me, Sarah, darling? I want to hold him. He's all that I've got to remind me of Will until he returns."

"I will, Mother. Try not to grieve yourself unnecessarily. The days will pass quickly, and he will return to us. In the meantime we need to remain strong for each other."

"Do you know that he has been here with us for two and a half years now? It only seems like yesterday that he was lying in his old bed there in the chambermaid room, and he looked up at us with those innocent, blue eyes of his and asked, *What place is this, Ma'am, where am I?* Do you remember that?"

"Yes, Mother, I remember that well. Come inside now, and I'll go upstairs and get Christopher for you."

○ ○ ○

Will was bewildered by the sights that he saw as he rode into Charlottesville on the streets of which he used to have such vivid familiarity. Things had changed considerably since he had last ridden on these cobblestoned streets. There were a countless number of new buildings along the road, and others were in the process of being constructed, and scores more people than he had remembered. It seemed like dozens of men were in the streets wearing the trousers or jackets of decaying old confederate uniforms, an enduring testament to the fact that the war was still fresh in everyone's memory. Even though things had changed considerably, there were still plenty of old landmarks and an adequate number of places with which he was familiar, more than enough to guide him in the proper direction of his childhood home, and the parents and wife whom he had left behind.

Among the many faces which he passed along the narrow streets, he sought recognition of a friend or two from the past, a relative perhaps, or even the recognizable face of a tradesman or social acquaintance. He saw no such faces, until he approached within a hundred feet of his boyhood home. Near his home, he saw a neighbor whom he recognized as being a close family friend. He wanted to stop and talk to the man, but his anxiety in seeing his parents and Patricia Anne again pressed him to go onward, and up to the very door of their home. It was a row house, which sat along the cobblestone street... the very street that he had played in when he was a child. The mere sight of the house brought back scores of memories from his childhood. He tied his horse to the rail there at the front of the house, brushed himself off as best he could, took a deep breath, and knocked on the door. Will's mother and father were relatively young. Both being forty-eight years of age at this time, and it would be good for him to see them again while they were still young enough to be enjoying good health. His father soon answered the door and burst forth an immediate and pronounced look of surprise. His eyes widened with disbelief and his pipe fell from his mouth and came to rest on the porch at Will's feet.

"**Eugene**! My dear God! My son has risen from the grave! Praise God! Is it really you, my son!?"

"Hello, Father. Yes, it's really me. It's so good to see you again, Father!"

"Thank Jesus you're alive! You have war injuries!"

"It's nothing, Father. My injuries are practically healed, and these particular injuries were acquired after the war had ended. I'll tell you all about it later. May I come in and see my wonderful mother and father?"

"This is your home, of course you can come in, but please, wait here for a moment, Eugene, I need to prepare your mother for the homecoming of her son, lest she faint dead away to the world! Praise Jesus, Eugene, but we thought you were dead!"

"Certainly, Father, I understand, but hurry on... I'm anxious to see my mother!"

In a few moments Will heard the voice of his mother inside, screaming at the top of her lungs, and his father and mother very quickly came to the door and literally grabbed him by the arms and pulled him inside. His mother held him in her arms and wept joyously for a few moments before saying, "Let me look at you, my son! You're such a handsome man! Thank God you've come home to us! You've been injured!"

"It's nothing, Mother. I'll tell you and Father all about it in a moment."

Will's surprise arrival was wrought with joyousness! His mother and father were more than anxious to hear all of the details regarding his prolonged absence. Will would gladly answer their questions, but first, Will had a question of his own that was begging to be answered.

"Does Patricia Anne no longer live here with you?"

"No, son. This news may come as a shock to you, Eugene, but you must be told sooner or later. Sit down, Eugene."

"What is it, Father? What's happened to Patricia Anne?"

"When no word came from you after two and a half years, we all assumed that you had been killed. There was even a memorial service for you at the church, and then another at the Masonic Temple. By the third year, Patricia Anne remarried, and moved in with her new husband. She lives on a farm, just west of Charlottesville. They have children, Eugene. Your mother and I are so sorry to be the bearers of such dreadful news, Eugene."

"I understand, Father, and I do not receive the news as being dreadful at all. I would not have expected her to wait that long before remarrying. Three years is a long time to wait to hear from someone. In time of war like that, she only assumed the obvious. There is no shame in what she has done, and I wish to bear her no grief, but I do feel as though I owe her an explanation for my extended absence... I owe all of you an explanation... every one of you!"

Will told his parents what had happened to him regarding his battle injuries, his memory loss, and how he had miraculously regained his memory only seven days earlier.

"You didn't even know your own name for more than two years, Eugene?"

"No, Father, I didn't. My memory has only returned to me within the last week or ten days."

Will's mother spoke up and asked the obvious question, "Mercy sakes, Eugene! If you didn't know your own name, what name have people called you by during that time?"

"Everyone in Rockingham County calls me, William Collins now. It's a name that was manufactured so that I would at least have some identity as I healed. But in my healing years, I must confess to you that I have become more familiar with the name of William Collins than I am with Eugene. I hope that you will understand and forgive me."

"We can understand how that could happen, son, and there is no need to ask forgiveness."

"And while I'm revealing all that has happened to me, I should tell you one other very important thing. It's undoubtedly the most important thing that has ever happened to me in my life."

"What is it, son?"

"Prepare yourselves, but I married last year... under the legal name of William Collins. I have a wife and a son down in Blanchard."

"We have a grandson!? Your father and I have a grandson?!"

"Yes, Mother, you have a beautiful, healthy grandson!"

"Praise Jesus! Please tell us about your wife and our grandson, Eugene... or would you prefer that we start calling you William now?"

"My hopes are, Father, now that I know my birth name, is to have my legal name changed once more, to William Winston Collins, as long as that would not cause any grief to you or Mother."

"You are our son, Eugene... I mean, William. We love you the same, regardless of whatever name you choose to go by. And we are proud that you have included the Winston family name in your title. Now, tell us about your wife and our grandson, please!"

"As far as my wife is concerned, she is about three years older than I. She had a daughter when she was but fourteen years old, another daughter the following year, and then a boy. He was killed at Manassas when he was only fifteen. She has a younger sister who lives with us as well. Her husband was killed at Bull Run. She's a steadfast Christian woman, of remarkably strong character, and I love her more than life itself. She and her daughters nursed me back to health when I was wounded. My wounds were extremely serious, and I would have surely perished had it not been for their Christian kindness. As I healed, we fell in love and married fourteen months after I was brought there as a wounded soldier."

"And our grandson? Tell us about him!"

"His name is Christopher. He's four months old now, bearing a very strong Winston family resemblance, I might add, and he is the joy that defines the happiness in our marriage."

"And your wife's name..."

"Her name is Abigail Margaret, but I always call her, Abby. I could never adequately describe what she and little Christopher mean to me."

"And you say that you live down in Blanchard at present?"

"Yes, Father. Abby and I have a tobacco farm there. We raise a number of other crops there as well, but tobacco is our mainstay. Our farm covers twelve hundred and fifty acres, and we are southwest of Lynchburg. There is an additional eight hundred acres to our south which we hope to purchase in June. Blanchard is only a short half-hour ride from our farm."

"Do you think that you and Abby could possibly provide accommodations for two grandparents to come and see their grandson in the spring?"

"Ha! You will be received as royalty, and Abby will be absolutely delighted when I tell her that you're coming! We have three spare bedchambers upstairs, and one of them will be reserved especially for your visit!"

"Are you hungry, Eugene... uhhh, William?"

"I am starving, Mother!"

"Well then, let us step into the kitchen and see what we can do about that!"

On the morning of the following day, Will mounted his horse and proceeded to follow his father's directions to the farmhouse of Patricia Anne and her husband. It was a short journey of only ten minutes or less, and as he arrived at the farm of her residence, he took immediate notice that the man of the farm was at work at the barn, and appeared to be mending the metal spokes of a rake. Not wanting to meet with Patricia Anne without first obtaining her husband's permission, Will rode to the barn first and spoke directly to the man.

"Excuse me Sir, but are you Mister Robert Abington?"

"Yes Sir, I am indeed. What can I do for you?"

"May I dismount and speak to you for a moment?"

"Please do."

Shaking the man's hand, Will said, "Good morning, Sir. My name is Eugene Winston."

"Holy Jesus! We thought you were dead! Why are you here? What is it that you want here?"

"I'm not here to cause you or your wife any unnecessary anguish, Sir, I can assure you of that."

"Then answer me! What is your purpose in being here?"

"With your permission, and your attendance, I would like to request your approval for me to speak with your wife briefly. I swear to you that my motives are honorable. I only wish to pay my respects, and offer a Christian explanation for my disappearance six years ago, and then be on my way. I swear to you."

"As I said, Patricia and I thought that you were dead. We have children together... her and I... a boy and a girl."

"I know, Sir, my father and mother told me as much, and I'm extremely happy for you and your wife. I have a child of my own as well. All that I'm asking is that you give me an opportunity to explain my disappearance six years ago to you and your wife. I shall cause neither of you any distress, and we can all put the matter behind us and go on with our lives, and I shall never darken your doorstep again."

"Very well, Mr. Winston, your intentions do in fact seem honorable to me. Allow me to go inside and prepare my wife for what I am sure will come as a great shock to her."

"I understand completely. Take as long as you please. May I draw water for my horse while you are inside?"

"Certainly, you may help yourself."

As Will waited impatiently outside, Robert Abington went inside. From within the home, Will heard a loud scream, and then, silence. More than a half hour later, Abington summoned Will to the door and they stepped into the parlor where Patricia Anne was seated at a table, frightened out of her wits, and weeping.

"Patricia... Patricia... please don't cry. I've come here only to put you mind at rest. I swear it."

"You've been injured..."

"It's nothing, I can assure you."

Over a cup of coffee, Will explained to the nervous couple the events that had occurred which had caused him to disappear for six years. When the couple came to recognize that Will's surprise appearance was purely out of a concern to inform them of the truth, their meeting was quite cordial. Will told them everything about his injury in battle, his recovery while under the care of the Montgomery Family, and about his falling in love and marrying Abigail. William felt tremendous relief in seeing Patricia Anne again. He had seen with his own eyes that there was indeed the glow of love that existed in their marriage there, and it warmed his heart.

"I truly regret the grief that must have accompanied my absence. Had I not been injured and lost my memory, I would never have put either of you through such discomfort. I sincerely apologize."

"Robert and I understand now, Eugene, and we are grateful to you for coming here. The question of your disappearance has long been an agony to me, and I thank you for relieving me of that burden."

"Your children are truly beautiful, and I sense that you are both very happy in your marriage, and I cannot begin to tell you how comforting it is for me to know that."

Their meeting lasted for more than two hours, and ended on the best of terms. His parting words were given in the deepest sincerity. "It's oft been said that God works in mysterious ways, and He does, indeed. I sincerely apologize to both of you for any stress caused by my disappearance, and for any stress caused by my sudden reappearance. From the bottom of my heart, I will pray that God grants you long and happy lives together with your children."

Will shook Robert's hand, received a warm hug from Patricia Anne, and rode away with a sense of contentment in knowing that his visit had been both meaningful and comforting—to everyone concerned.

Will had accomplished much during his brief visit to Charlottesville, and had even visited with two old friends while he was there. Even in the merriment of renewing old friendships, Will was anxious to return to Montgomery Farm, where everyone called him, Will. He was uncomfortable with the name of *Eugene*, despite the fact that it had been the only name that he had known for the first twenty-five years of his life. With his old acquaintances having been reaffirmed, and explanations of his mysterious disappearance delivered to his loved ones, his Masonic Brothers, and his friends, Will was quite eager to return to Montgomery Farm and resume his life as William Winston Collins. On the twenty-eighth day of October he bid a warm farewell to his mother and father and left Charlottesville to go home.

In the duration of his two-day journey back to Montgomery Farm, Will had ample time to consider his current circumstances in life. His visit to Charlottesville had left him with the gratification that he had provided his friends and loved ones there with the earliest possible explanation for his mysterious prolonged absence. For that, his mind was at rest. But his visit to Charlottesville had also reaffirmed his love for his family at Montgomery Farm. He rode along the road from Charlottesville to Lynchburg with the sublime satisfaction of knowing that there was no one on earth that he would rather be than William Collins. He was beside himself with the magnificent anticipation of seeing his beloved family again, of holding little Christopher, and receiving the joyous affections of Abby and the ladies. He had been gone from Montgomery Farm for eight days, and cared never to leave again for such an extended absence.

For The Betterment Of The Family

"But if any provide not for his own, and specially for those of his own house, he hath denied the faith, and is worse than an infidel." 1 Timothy 5:8

Abby and Agatha had busied themselves with the task of bathing Christopher in a tub of warm water in the kitchen near the stove while Sarah and Elizabeth were in the orchard picking apples. In the midst of this busy day, Ezra knocked excitedly at the door. When Abby opened the door, Ezra cried out, "Mister Will is coming, Miss Abigail! He's crossing the creek right now and headed this'a way!"

"Oh! Thank God he's home! Finish for me, will you please, Agatha? I must run to greet him!"

"My Lord, Abigail, I wish to greet him as badly as you do!"

"Land sakes alive, Agatha, he's *my* husband!"

"I carried Christopher in my womb for nine months for you and Will, Abigail... how could I possibly keep from going to him? He's your husband, I know, but I can't help but love him, too. Please let me go to greet him, Abigail... please!"

"I understand, Agatha, I really do, and I always want you to be honest with me. Let us dry Christopher and wrap him in a blanket. We'll both go to him, dear. Knowing Will as I do, I fully expect he has enough kisses for all of us!"

Abby and Agatha quickly donned their coats, wrapped

Christopher in a warm blanket, and ran with Ezra to greet Will at the barn. Abby had never doubted that Will would return to her. Her anxiety had risen entirely from the uncertainty of what had awaited Will in Charlottesville. She knew nothing of Patricia Anne, nor the persuasive powers that she might have possessed. Her imagination had introduced a speck of doubt into her heart, and now her excitement over Will's return had eliminated all doubt, and she knew that Will's eyes would tell her everything else that she needed to know. She ran with Christopher to greet him, and once again look into the eyes that she had missed so greatly during the last eight days. The moment that she came close to him, she took the opportunity to study the way that Will was looking at her, and when she did, she knew that he was home to stay, and life would once again return to the normal, unfaltering happiness that the family had grown so accustomed to there at Montgomery Farm. Abby and Agatha smothered Will with kisses, and with Christopher in his arms, they walked to the house together, Abby holding onto Will's free arm and Agatha walking by his side.

"Where are Elizabeth and Sarah?"

"They are picking apples and pears in the orchard. They should be home any moment. Are you hungry, Will?"

"You bet I am!"

Sarah and Elizabeth soon returned and rallied with the others to greet Will. The family gathered with eagerness in the parlor that afternoon to listen to every detail of Will's visit to Charlottesville. While holding Christopher in his arms and giving him an occasional kiss on the forehead, Will satisfied their every question, and included a lengthy dissertation of everything that had transpired when he had gone to visit Patricia Anne Abington. After all, it was the details of his meeting with Patricia Anne that everyone wanted so desperately to hear. Everything else was but a secondary concern.

Agatha, Sarah, and Elizabeth gave Abigail a rest from her kitchen duties that afternoon so that she could spend more time alone with Will. Abigail and Will sat by the fire in the parlor, playing with Christopher, and the accommodating ladies in the kitchen soon had a hearty meal on the table. After offering the blessing for the food, Will couldn't resist the temptation to lend a little lightheartedness to the occasion by saying, "As I look around the table this evening, I can't help but wonder why God chose to place so many beautiful ladies right here in Montgomery House, and so very, very few in Charlottesville... but then, I would never question His judgment, instead, I'll just sit here and bask in the glory of it."

Abigail blushed slightly and added, "I shan't begin to tell you how much we missed you and your *William Collins* compliments."

"Which one of you lovely ladies made the bread?" He knew full well that Agatha had made the bread, but played dumb about it. Agatha answered him quickly.

"I did, Will. Why?"

"It tastes delicious, Agatha. You and Abby certainly have a way of making the best bread and biscuits in the county!"

Beaming with the immediate pride that Will had paid her a compliment, Agatha said, "Thank you, Will."

Agatha's lips began to quiver, almost as if she was about to burst into tears. Will realized that he had probably been errant in paying her the compliments that she had deserved, even though he had always been full of compliments for Abigail and her daughters. He quietly resolved himself to be more understanding of Agatha's tender feelings in the future, and less reluctant to pay her compliments. Will sensed that everyone at the table was aware of Agatha's momentary rush of emotion, and he quickly livened things up by introducing some lighthearted recollections of his trip to Charlottesville. It was a wonderfully cheery meal, and everyone seethed with the satisfaction of being together again.

Will's occasional humor was always a most glorious addition to the family meals. The ability to laugh together is an essential ingredient in the happiness and closeness of families, and laughter and merriment were the characteristics which best defined the sentiments during mealtime at Montgomery Farm. In their bedchamber that night, Will and Abby cuddled together in the luxury of their bed, enjoying their usual quiet conversation under the soft glow of a single lamp. Abby nestled closely to Will, kissed him on the cheek, and asked, "Tell me, Will, does Patricia Anne still have three breasts, darling?"

Spontaneously, and without any forethought at all, Will teasingly answered by saying, "Yes, Abby, bless her heart. However, her breasts are causing her and her husband a great deal of distress in their lives nowadays, and it just breaks my heart every time I think about it."

"Distress? Why is that, pray tell?"

"Well, Abby, you see, during the last six years, since I saw her last, her breasts have now grown to such an enormous size as to be very cumbersome for her. The one on her forehead now droops down to cover her eyes, and the poor thing is constantly walking into walls and other things. Her husband has to stand beside her at the supper table and raise it up so that she can feed herself... lest she would starve to death."

"Mercy, Will! What an irreverent imagination you have, William Collins! I can't even begin to tell you how good it is to have you home with us again, Will."

"It feels good for me to be home among the people I love, Abby, and I love you even more than life itself."

"I wonder sometimes if you have any idea of how boring and uninteresting our lives were here at Montgomery Farm before you came to us? As I think back, I can remember nothing but strife and anguish before you came to me."

"I thought we agreed not to dwell in the past. I'm here, and we're all happy now... that's all that really matters."

O   O   O

Although progressively fewer in numbers, suitors continued to occasionally call upon Sarah, Elizabeth, and Agatha. It seemed to be an ongoing nuisance that Will despised. Throughout the spring and into the summer, there was scarcely a Saturday to pass in which at least one or two gentleman visitors did not call upon one or the other of the ladies. To Will, the presence of suitors was disruptive to their accustomed privacy. William would make an effort to appear passive during these courtship visitations so as not to offend the ladies or their suitors, yet his distinct recollections of what had happened to Sarah at the hands of Timothy O'Donnell commanded that he remain quietly vigilant and observant. Will and Abby began to recognize that Elizabeth and Sarah, and even Agatha, seemed to display less enthusiasm during the times they were entertaining suitors. An extraordinary situation had evolved within the walls of Montgomery House. Unbeknownst to the ladies residing there, the presence of William Collins in the house and the resulting closeness that had developed between them, had unknowingly provided each of the ladies with a clearer understanding of the qualities each of them would require in their visiting suitors. In their minds, William Collins was on a pedestal which stood head and shoulders above all other men. Abby clearly recognized what was happening there and William had sensed the same thing, but for months, they kept their observations to themselves.

Will could not help but envision the visiting suitors as potential harbingers of unhappiness within his family. He loved his family deeply, and his detestation of visiting suitors was rooted in his overly zealous inclination to be the protector of the family which he loved so dearly. In truth, Will was unaware of the extent of his disdain for the aspiring suitors, or the effects that his overprotectiveness was having on Elizabeth and Sarah. He only knew that he loved his family dearly, and wanted what he thought was best for them. As far as Agatha was concerned, she relished in William's overprotectiveness, choosing to interpret it as an ongoing indication of his adoration for her.

The men who called upon Agatha seemed almost humorous to William. To him, the callers were all transparent fakes, hell-bent on obtaining a share of Agatha's wealth. Unbeknownst to William, Agatha was quite capable of looking out for herself, and had no difficulty in seeing the same untrustworthy qualities in those callers that William saw. Agatha had been badly abused as a child, and such abuse had weakened her mind in some respects, but she was nevertheless a very intelligent woman, capable of seeing through the lies and deceptions of greedy men. A genuine change had swept over Agatha in regards to the way that she perceived and regarded men outside of the family. During the times when she would sit on the porch with a suitor at night, she conducted herself as the perfect lady, no longer willing to allow men to have their way with her. If a man made such an audacious attempt, she would bid him '*good evening*,' ask him to leave, and quickly go inside, before the suitor even had an opportunity to apologize for his indiscretion. Her newly acquired attribute of '*celibacy*' provided Agatha with a confidence that grew even stronger each time she would reject the advances of an '*over-amorous*' suitor. Abby and William were unaware of the fact that Agatha had gained a new confidence in herself when it came to assessing the qualities of men. It became a game with her to toy with the visiting scavengers who sought to delve into her purse of wealth. She would lead them on, digesting their cunning and deceptive words, tantalizing them with sweet words of her own which were really '*bait*,' and when she felt as though her deceivers had reached a plateau of confidence in their attempts to deceive her, she would cleverly spring the trap by announcing that she was aware of their plot, and send them on their way with their tail tucked between their legs. For those few who wished to linger, and argue that their intentions were honorable, Agatha would simply pull a derringer from her purse, and her deceivers would abruptly '*high-tail it*' and leave Montgomery Farm much faster than they had arrived. The derringer was not loaded, but the fiends that went running had no way of knowing that. From the kitchen window one evening, Will had overheard one such conversation. He never mentioned what he had overheard to anyone, even Abby, but he went upstairs that evening with a new sense of respect for Agatha, and her constitution.

As far as Elizabeth and Sarah were concerned, William saw them as being much more vulnerable than Agatha. Will took his role as Elizabeth and Sarah's stepfather very seriously, and was equally as serious where Agatha was concerned. Many of the suitors had been frightened away by Will's ominous and piercing stares during their brief courtships, or his firm voice when he would step onto the back porch and announce, "It's nine o'clock, Sir, and time for your departure." With few exceptions, he saw the evil face of Timothy O'Donnell almost every time he looked upon the face of a gentleman caller. After an evening of courtship, he would often ask the ladies at breakfast the following morning what they had thought about the gentleman who had called upon them the previous evening. Elizabeth had paid one of the highest of compliments to one of her callers when she had answered Will's query by saying, *"He was alright, I suppose."* Other responses included, *"...he was a blabbermouth, ...he couldn't keep his hands to himself, ...he was quite boring, ...he was an idiot, ...his breath was nauseating,* or, *...he couldn't even carry on a decent conversation."* Such unenthusiastic responses came as a delight to Will's ears, reaffirming his confidence that the ladies were being particular when choosing the friendship of a male, and unwilling to compromise in their expectations. William was happy at Montgomery Farm, and he knew that he would inevitably worry about his stepdaughters when the day would finally come that they would marry and leave the protectiveness of his guardianship. He felt that any suitor who was willing to run the gauntlet of his guardianship and measure up to the grand expectations of his stepdaughters, most surely deserved a closer look, and he and the ladies were merely *'tossing the weeds out of the garden,'* so to speak.

As they had promised, Will's mother and father came to Montgomery Farm for a visit in the spring. It was a festive occasion in which everyone had the joy and privilege of getting to know one another. Their visit was intended to have lasted for two weeks, yet three weeks had passed before anyone realized it. Time has a way of passing much too quickly during visits such as that, and on the day of their departure, everyone was reluctant to say goodbye. It was a tearful event, and vows to have many more such future visits were exchanged between them as Will and his family watched their buggy disappear to the northeast. On the evening of the day Will's mother and father had left to return to Charlottesville, Will and Abby exchanged quiet conversation in their bedchamber.

"Your mother and father are the most delightful people I have ever met, Will. It's easy for me to see where you inherited your sweetness. And your father looks so young and handsome... just like his son."

"Father is handsome, I agree, but I don't think I take after him very much."

"I'm sorry to tell you, but you are woefully mistaken, Mr. Collins. You and your father could almost pass as brothers. Do you think it would be possible for us to visit them in Charlottesville someday?"

"Of course we can. We can hitch up the carriage and carry the whole family, just like we were going to church. We could spend the night in Lynchburg, on the James River. We'll see what kind of prices the remaining tobacco fetches at market, and if the weather permits, maybe we could ride up there in early autumn if you like."

"Tell me, Will, what has brought such a delightful smile to your face just now?"

"Oh, it's just because of the comment you made about my father and I looking like we were brothers, instead of father and son."

"What about it?"

"It just got me to thinking, Abby. You know, you were so young when Sarah and Elizabeth were born, that I swear sometimes when the three of you are together with Agatha, all four of you look like young sisters."

"Oh, Will!"

"It's true! You, Agatha, Elizabeth, and Sarah... you all look like young sisters to me."

"It's funny that you would say that. Sometimes I feel like Elizabeth and Sarah are my sisters. I was so young when they were born, that I feel like I have grown up with them. It's not easy for a young mother to raise two daughters without a man in the house—or I should say, without a man who could be trusted."

"You've certainly had no difficulty asserting your authority whenever the need occurred, although I'm seeing a lot less of your dominating over them, and more of a comradeship developing between all four of you."

"That's because of your presence here, Will. You're the head of this household now. You've relieved me of the need to assert my authority. Before you came to us, I simply did what I had to do in order to hold the family together... I swear, Will, I just..."

"Abby! You're weeping, darling, why?"

"I'm just going through a moment of female sentimental attachment, I suppose."

"What do you mean by that, Abby?"

"I'm happier here today than I have ever been in my life. I wish that things could remain the same forever. Just the thought of Elizabeth and Sarah marrying someday and leaving Montgomery Farm seems so dreadful to me. I want them to live full and happy lives, and I want them to experience the joys of motherhood someday... I just... I just don't want them to marry and move somewhere far away from us. The four months that Sarah was married and living in Baltimore were the most painful four months of my life. To have her *and* Elizabeth both leave us, well, when that day comes, I'll need to lean on you for support, Will."

"When that day comes, and sooner or later it will, I'll be here for you, Abby, I swear I will, but don't forget, you also have Agatha to lean on."

"I know, but Agatha will marry again someday, of that I'm almost certain. She's changed a lot in the last five or six months... I think she has become a much stronger woman."

O   O   O

Christopher had now celebrated his first birthday, the crops had all been planted for the season, and the family was comfortably awaiting the time of year when their labors would consume most of the daylight hours. They were enjoying a time of year when all of the chores were usually completed early in the day, affording the family time to engage in activities such as picnics, parlor games, and relaxing family conversation. Oft times, Will would read aloud to the family from the works of Shakespeare, Burns, or the family Bible. It was a time of year in which there was normally very little stress of any kind within the family, and it was a time of year which often found all four of the ladies quietly knitting as Will recited many marvelous passages of literature, or played the piano for an hour or two.

Without Will's knowledge, Abigail had been discussing a potential revelation of sorts with her sister and her daughters. She had every intention of proposing this startling revelation to William, but had not done so as yet. She wanted to have time to consider the impact that such a thing would have on the family before discussing it with William. More than forty days after the concept had come into her mind, and she had first discussed the idea with the other ladies, she felt as though the time had arrived in which she should bring her loving husband into her confidence. She was apprehensive as to how William would accept such a proposal, and even feared that such a thing might be insulting to him, or adverse to his Christian beliefs.

One rainy evening in April, Will and Abby had taken Christopher up to their bedchamber to retire early for the night and spend some quiet time together. Once Christopher had finished nursing and was sleeping soundly, Abby and Will snuggled him closely between them, admiring his beautiful sleeping face, and Abby quietly asked, "Would you tell me again how much you love Christopher and me, Will?"

"I love you and Christopher more than anything on this earth, but I surely think you must already know that, Abby."

"I do, Will, but I never tire of hearing you say it."

"And I shall never tire of saying it. I love you, Abby."

"Do you love me enough to give me a very special gift, Will, one that would mean everything in the world to me?"

"If it's within my power, I would gladly give you anything that your heart desires, Abby, you know that. Kiss me again, and tell me more about this very special gift that you want."

"More than anything else in the world, Will, I would like for you to give me another child. My prayers would be answered if Christopher could have at least one sibling to grow up with."

"My Lord, Abby. I've been trying as hard as I can to give you another child. I'm doing my part, or at least I think that I am. The rest is up to you, darling."

"I know it is, Will... I'm just afraid that I no longer have the ability to conceive, and it breaks my heart. I think that I have reached an age in my life that if I was going to conceive again, I would surely have done so months ago. Christopher needs a brother or a sister near his own age, and there's nothing that I can do about providing one for him. I wanted to give you a dozen children, Will, but it seems that I can't even give you one."

"This is not the end of the world, Abby, I suppose we'll just have to raise Christopher without a sibling... but that's not to say that I'm ready to stop trying to give him a brother or sister. We never know for sure what tomorrow might bring, and if it's all the same to you, I'd like to keep trying to provide a sibling for Christopher until the day I die. I refuse to believe that thirty-four years of age is too old for a woman to conceive. For goodness sakes, Abby, you're in your prime of your life."

"Perhaps so, but my failure to conceive thus far speaks for itself, doesn't it?"

"Don't be so willing to give up hope so soon, Abby, it's only been a few months... We'll keep trying and keep praying, alright?"

"Alright, dear, but..."

"But what, Abby?"

"Well... even though I'm a failure at conceivement, there's yet another alternative for us to have another child, Will..."

"Oh? What kind of alternative, pray tell?"

"Agatha and I have been talking a lot these last few weeks..."

"What's Agatha got to do with any of this, Abby?"

"Agatha has got a lot to do with this, Will... she has given us one child already, bless her heart..."

"And?"

"She could give us another."

"My Lord, is Agatha pregnant again, Abby?"

"No, of course she's not... not yet, anyway..."

"What, then? I don't understand."

"Think about it, Will. My wonderful sister, Agatha is willing and able to give us another child if we want one. We've talked about it for weeks and weeks now... more than a month."

"Oh my goodness... I can feel the blood starting to drain from my veins! And just to clarify what I think I'm hearing, Abby, what man would you propose to be the benefactor of such a conception, pray tell?"

"If any man other than you was the benefactor, it wouldn't be our baby, Will."

"Mercy sakes alive... I knew it! I should have guessed that you had something earthshattering to talk to me about when I saw that sneaky look on your face! Are you honestly and truly suggesting that I approach Agatha and ask her to bear another child for us... that I seduce her?"

"No! As I said, Agatha and I have already discussed the issue, and she has already told me that she is willing. I'm only asking that you consider..."

"And you would approve of me doing such a thing, Abby?"

"You're opposed to the idea, aren't you?"

"I'm stunned that you would suggest such a thing out of the clear blue like this... that's all! I never expected anything like this when I said that I would gladly give you anything you asked for..."

"She's my only sister, by blood, and I love her. You're my husband, by marriage, and I love you... and I desperately want a sibling for Christopher. Would it be asking too much for you to contribute to such an undertaking, Will, for the sake of our having another child? Don't you want us to have another child as much as I do?"

"Of course I do! I love children, Abby, and I love Christopher. I wouldn't mind us having ten or twelve children here in our home... even more... it's just that... you're suggesting that Agatha and I commit adultery together!"

"It is **not** the same thing as adultery!"

"Oh? Having intimacy outside of marriage is adultery, pure and simple!"

"Commissioning a surrogate mother to bear a child is an acceptable practice that goes all the way back to the Old Testament, Will, when Abraham and Sarah beseeched their servant, Hagar, to bear them a child."

"Yes, I know, but Sarah and Hagar soon came to hate each other afterwards. Have you considered that?"

"Agatha is not a servant, she's my sister, and we love each other. Sarah and Hagar never loved each other! They became jealous of one another, and such a thing as jealousy would never happen between Agatha and I. We love each other too much to let jealousy turn us against one another!"

"I've just... never given any thought to my doing anything like that with Agatha, of my own free will and accord. You're the one that I'm attracted to romantically, Abby... you're the one that I love with all my heart and soul, and you're the one who I married for life, not Agatha!"

"You told me that your previous union with her had been a pleasant experience. Can you not find it in your heart to repeat the pleasantry, for the sake of our having another child?"

"That's not fair, Abby! I was unaware that it was her in my bed that morning. I thought it was you! You know that, and it's very unfair for you to wave my own words in my face like that!"

"I am very sorry that I said that, Will, please forgive me. This would mean so much to me and our family. Agatha is willing to do this for us, Will. Won't you please consider it? I don't need an answer tonight. I can wait as long as it takes for you to feel comfortable with the idea. Just think it over in your mind and in your heart."

"How long have you and Agatha been discussing this between yourselves, Abby?"

"For more than a month, perhaps six weeks."

"You and Agatha have had six weeks to think about this, and so far I've had about six minutes."

"I know, Will, and I shan't rush you to a decision."

"What in the world would Sarah and Elizabeth say if they knew we were talking about the possibility of me voluntarily doing something like that with Agatha, Abby?"

"I keep no secrets from my family anymore, Will. My daughters are adults now. They were both present when Agatha and I first discussed the idea and they've been present during most of the discussions since. The only reason I did not ask for you to be there was because I knew that you would be too embarrassed to talk openly about such a thing in front of Agatha and my daughters."

"You were right, I'm even embarrassed to talk about such a thing in front of you. Tell me, Abby, what did Sarah and Elizabeth think about your scheme?"

"Please don't call it a scheme, Will. It's a proposal, suggested for the betterment of our family, and nothing else."

"Well then, what did Sarah and Elizabeth think about your *proposal*?"

"They understand how important it is to our family, Will. There's too much love between us for them not to understand. They know that you and I have been trying our best to conceive, albeit without success. If I am barren, and Agatha is not, I fail to see such a union as being a sinful or malevolent thing."

"I was unaware that you have such frank conversations with Sarah and Elizabeth. I suppose that I know now what you all must talk about whenever I'm not here."

"They're not children anymore, Will. I can talk to them nowadays about such things without being embarrassed. If you will remember, they were both there with me and Vivian to watch the birth of Christopher. They know where babies come from, and they are well aware of the part the father plays in contributing to the conception. Sarah has been married before."

"I'm well aware of the fact that they're not children, Abby."

"If I had the ability to conceive it would be different. I would never suggest for you to do such a thing if I could conceive. Please just consider this, Will. That's all that I ask."

"And how would such a proposed union between me and Agatha take place, Abby? Would you go downstairs one morning to prepare breakfast early again, so that she could sneak into my bed once more and pretend to be you?"

"That's not what I would prefer, Will, unless it was the only way that you would agree to comply."

"How then? Exactly what would you prefer? Would Agatha and I be required to copulate on the parlor table while the rest of the family looks on and cheers?"

"Please don't turn this into some sort of sinful joke, Will, it's not a joking matter and it's not sinful."

"Well, answer my question, Abby, where and how would this proposed exchange take place?"

"I would prefer for it to take place in the sanctity of our bedchamber, and I would hope that you would allow me to be present at the time of conception. With my approval, and my attendance, it would not be an act of adultery or betrayal... it would be an act of love, in its purist form, for the betterment of our family."

"I'm... not sure of how I feel about all of this, Abby."

"All that I ask, is that you give the matter its due consideration, Will. Think of Christopher. If you love me, and you want another child as much as I do, please consider this."

"I do love you, and I do want another child. I need to go downstairs for a while, Abby."

"Why?"

"I need to go out on the porch and get some fresh air, and I need some time to think this over for a while. I couldn't fall asleep right now if my life depended on it. I'll be back up a little later."

"I hope you know in your heart that I love you, Will."

"I know you do, Abby, I've never doubted that for a moment, and I love you, too... nothing could ever change that... and believe it or not, I also love Agatha, yet in a far different manner than I love you. I love Agatha because she is your sister, and because she is a beloved member of our family."

"And how about the fact that she has given us one child already, do you not love her for that reason as well, Will?"

"Of course I do, Abby. I realize that bearing a child is a difficult and painful thing. Not a day goes by that I don't thank God for what she did for us, and I no longer bear her any resentment for sneaking into my bed that morning. If she hadn't come into my bed and tricked me, we wouldn't have Christopher today, and I thank God every moment I'm alive for Christopher."

"So do I, Will. And now we have been presented with the glorious opportunity to have yet another child... a sibling for Christopher. Think of this as an honorable contribution to the future happiness of our family, Will, and not as some sort of sinful and disgraceful act of lust or betrayal, please."

"I'll think it over. That's all that I can promise you right now, Abby. Tell me something, is Agatha aware that you were going to present this amazing *proposal* to me tonight?"

"Yes, Will, Sarah and Elizabeth are aware as well."

"Lord have mercy, Abby! This puts me in a very awkward position among the family. I wish you had talked with me before talking with everyone else."

"I'm sorry. It was never my intention to do anything behind your back, I only wanted to be sure that such a thing would not be perceived as being sinful in the eyes of our family before approaching you."

"I understand, and I appreciate your motives, Abby. I suppose it's all up to me now, isn't it?"

"Make your decision with your heart, Will. Either way, I'll accept and respect your decision, and either way, I'll continue to love you with all my heart until the day I die."

"Tell me something truthfully, Abby... if I should decide that I do not want to do this, would you be terribly disappointed in me—never mind, you don't have to answer that, your answer is already written in your eyes."

O   O   O

As Will had promised Abby, he did a lot of thinking that night and the next morning. In fact, he thought of little else, and got very little sleep. After tending to the chickens and feeding the horses, he put some hay out for the cows and walked up to the house for his morning meal and coffee with the apprehension of knowing that he was about to face the family. Pausing briefly at the back door, he took a deep breath, and asked, *"Lord, help me..."* and went inside. The faces and the eyes around the breakfast table that morning were all focused inquisitively upon Will, as if they were trying very hard to read the expression on his face, and thereby determine his position in the matter. Without uttering a word, by their demeanors and their inquiring eyes, they were all telling him that Agatha's surrogate proposition was on everyone's mind, and by the looks of the family, it was thought to be a reasonable request, for the betterment of the family. It seemed as though everyone was having difficulty in understanding why Will would even hesitate to say *'yes'* to the glorious opportunity that Agatha was so unselfishly offering to the family. Will had never felt this uncomfortable in the presence of the ladies before, but then he had never been requested to do such an unconventional thing as this before. Abby had told him that every family member was aware of the request, a fact that was validated by the pleading expressions on everyone's face. Will tried to defuse the tense climate momentarily with an attempt to have casual conversation.

"I swear, Abby, your biscuits just keep getting better and better all the time."

"Thank you, Will, I'm glad you like them so much."

Will's attempt to generate conversation around the table seemed to fall on deaf ears, as the irritating quietness continued. He tried again, saying, "These preserves are really good, too. Who made them?"

Sarah spoke rather briefly to answer Will's query. "Lizzy and I made them last week, Will. We're glad that you like them."

In his peripheral vision, Will noticed that Abigail and Agatha were holding hands beneath the table, and neither of them were eating very much at all, they were merely picking at their food with disinterest. The climate at the breakfast table was uncomfortably tense, and Will's attempt to incite the family into casual conversation was an embarrassing failure. There was but one thing on everyone's mind, and Will knew exactly what it was. He knew that the issue would have to be addressed before any reasonable conversation or merriment returned to the table. He gave the matter further thought as he sat there eating the last of his eggs and biscuits. Abby was right when she had said that Christopher needed at least one sibling in his young life. The birth of Christopher had brought immense joy to the family, and another child or two would only bring the family more joy. Will looked around the table again at the pleading faces that looked back at him, and in a moment of self-denial and determination, Will made his decision. After breakfast, Abby walked out to the back porch to empty a pan of wash water. Will quickly drank the remaining coffee in his cup and arose to follow her outside, where he spoke briefly with her. The members of the family remained inside, fully aware of what Abby and Will would be discussing, and compliantly gave them the privacy on the porch that they needed. Straining their ears in an effort to hear a word or two of what was being said outside proved futile, so they sat there quietly. Out on the porch, Will wasted little time getting right to the point.

"I suppose that the reason everyone inside looks so gloomy this morning is either because someone very close to them has just died a horrible death, or because they are awaiting my decision. Which one is it, Abby?"

"We are *all* awaiting your decision, Will, every one of us. But I love you far too much to rush you into anything that you may be opposed to. If you wish to talk with Pastor Stephens first, you have my blessing. Take your time, and make your decision with your heart, Will. As I told you last night, I'll stand behind any decision you make."

"Please sit here beside me on the porch swing, Abby."

"Alright, darling..."

"Lord have mercy, Abby... Tell me, if I willfully do this with Agatha, in the aftermath of our intimacy, how would such a relationship here in Montgomery House define us as a family, in the coming weeks, months, and years?"

"If we all truly love one another, could we not be defined as a family that is so much in love that we defy definition? Does our family have to be precisely like every other family in the world? To me, our family is already unique unto itself."

"Our family is my very life's blood, Abby, and you are at the very pinnacle of my love, and always will be... You're my wife."

"I love you beyond explanation, Will. You are my husband, and in consideration of my failure to conceive, you are the only one capable of providing us with another child. I can't do it, or I would have before now. God has graciously provided Agatha to help us bring the promise of another child to life."

"You once told me that your first husband was an insatiable philanderer, and a man of devilish morals, lustful and deceitful.

If I willfully do this with Agatha, how could I possibly consider myself to be any different than him?"

"Don't you dare to even begin comparing yourself with Thomas Montgomery! It angers me to think that you would do such a thing! Thomas Montgomery had no soul, and he had no heart or conscience, Will! His pleasures were derived by his betrayals, and his lust for always taking what he wanted, despite the effect it had on his victims! He detested being around children unless he had the opportunity to molest them! If you only knew how much it hurts me to hear you compare yourself to him..."

"I'm sorry, Abby, I swear that I'll never do that again."

"I never intended to burden you with a lot of undue pressure, Will. I honestly thought that you would be elated when you learned what Agatha is willing to do for us."

"I am elated at the possibility of having another child, Abby. I'm just very nervous and unsure of myself, that's all... I suppose more than anything, that I'm afraid, Abby..."

"Afraid of what, Will? What is it that you fear?"

"That's just it, Abby... I don't know why I'm afraid, I just am..."

"I'll say this once more, Will, make your decision with your heart, and I'll stand behind whatever decision you make... of that, you have my solemn promise."

"I've already made my decision, Abby."

"You have?"

"Yes. I want another child as much as you do, and I'll do this for you, Abby."

"I would much rather that you did it for *us*, Will, and the future happiness of our family."

"Very well then, that's the reason I'll do it. I've told you before, I'll do anything it takes to bring happiness into our lives. And as I said, I want another child as much as you do, Abby, and you've helped me to see this as the opportunity it really is."

"Thank you, Will! And God bless you!"

"Wait a minute, Abby! Calm down! Before you get up and run inside to announce the glorious news to everyone, I will require certain stipulations and assurances before giving my final consent to doing something like this."

"Such as?"

"First and foremost, I want you to swear an oath to me by all that's Holy that my willful participation in this endeavor will in no way cause you to love me less. I couldn't bear the thought of such a thing, Abby. I'd rather for my life to end right here and now than to have you love me less."

"I swear that as a consequence, I will only love you more, if that's possible. You have my solemn oath to that effect."

"Secondly, I would require that Agatha swear an oath to us that she will abstain from any contact with other men. No suitors or other visitors, and no moonlight walks or even sitting on the porch swing at night with a caller. If she conceives, I would at least want the assurance that I was the sole benefactor of the child, and no one else."

"Agatha has been intimate with no one but you since James Brighton died last year. We both knew that you would require such assurance, and she has already given me her oath. This is one of the many subjects we discussed in depth. She has no desire to give birth to anyone's child but ours."

"You said that you wanted to be there with Agatha and I when this union is performed. Well, I've thought about it long and hard, and I just cannot do something like this in your presence."

"I understand, Will."

"And I would prefer that this union take place in her bedchamber—not ours."

"It will be as you say, I promise."

"Well then, if we're all in agreement, You can tell Agatha that I will come to her bedchamber tonight, if she wishes, and if it is what you both want."

"Tonight is not a good time for this, Will."

"Really? Last night and this morning you seemed so anxious to get this done, why in the world is tonight not a good night?"

"In three days, Agatha will cycle into a time in which she is much more likely to conceive. The time will be right then. I'm sorry, but that's the way it is."

"Mercy... That means I have three more days to think about this."

"Oh, Will, please don't change your mind during the next three days, I beg of you!"

"I'm not going to change my mind, Abby, I give you my word. I only hope that I can continue to maintain my sanity for three more days."

"I'm sorry, Will, but it's really best that we wait."

"You and Agatha would know more about those types of things than I do, Abby. I'll trust in you and Agatha to determine when the time is right. In the meantime, I'll try to busy myself with my work, and try to think about this as little as possible."

"I understand, Will."

"I know how much this means to both of us, I really do. Last night I told you that I wouldn't mind having a dozen children, and I was perfectly serious. I'm going to try and clear my head long enough to go down to the barn and help Ezra."

"I love you with all my heart and soul, Will Collins."

"I love you, too, Abby. And as I told you last night and this morning, I've also come to love Agatha, more deeply than I would have ever expected."

"Have you ever told her so, Will?"

"No, of course I haven't! I would never say such a thing to her or any other woman behind your back! That in itself would be a betrayal!"

"Then why don't you tell her now, Will? It would mean the world to her. She's right here in the kitchen."

"I could never bring myself to say anything like that to her in front of Elizabeth and Sarah, especially with them all knowing what our plans are now. I wouldn't be comfortable saying that at all."

"If I bring Agatha out here to the porch, would you feel comfortable in telling her then?"

"Yes, Abby... yes I would... as long as you would come back outside with her. I would insist that you be present when I tell her. As I said before, I want nothing said or done between me and Agatha without your knowledge and concurrence."

Abby went inside and quietly whispered, "Will has agreed to comply," and almost immediately Will could hear the hushed sounds of joy and cheerfulness emitting from within. With Abby's whispered words, everyone's spirits had been raised. Shortly, a very nervous Agatha walked out on the porch accompanied by Abby, where Will received her with a warm embrace. The warm embrace soon resulted in an equally warm yet somewhat brief kiss on the cheek. Will looked deeply into her eyes, cautious not to put too much passion is his voice in the presence of Abby, and said, "Abby told me last night what you're willing to do for us, Agatha, and I just want to tell you beforehand that this means the world to me and Abby. Someday it will mean the world to little Christopher as well. Please don't be offended by me asking you this, Agatha, but there is a question at the forefront of my mind. It's eating away at me, and I would be most appreciative if you would answer it for me."

"If I can, I will be happy to."

"Agatha, we've never discussed the issue of your wealth, preferring not to invade your privacy, but we know that you are a very wealthy woman."

"Yes, Will, I suppose I am..."

"With all your wealth, you could go anywhere in the world, live in the lap of luxury, and be waited on by servants for the rest of your life."

"I suppose so..."

"Instead, you choose to stay here, sewing, working in a hot kitchen, churning butter, putting up preserves, and washing laundry. And even with all that, you are now willing to suffer the pains of childbirth again? It would mean a lot to me if you would please tell me why you are so willing to make such a sacrifice as this, Agatha."

"All the money in the world could never purchase the happiness that I've found here with my family. I want to give birth again. I want to do it because of the love that I have for you and my sister, and the rest of the family. Christopher should have a sibling to grow up with. I don't see this as a sacrifice, Will, I see it as an opportunity to express my love to the family, by doing something worthwhile and contributing to our future happiness. During the months that I carried Christopher, I felt as though my life was meaningful. I want to feel that way again. I love you, and I love Abigail, and I love children. My family here means everything in the world to me, and whether you believe me or not, Will, I will consider it an honor to bring another child into the family."

Hearing such words from Agatha, Will was momentarily held speechless. Abby bowed her head and softly wept as Will put forth his greatest effort to contain his tears, and said, "I am ashamed of myself for asking the question, Agatha... I should have known without asking. You've touched me very deeply. Abby and I love you, Agatha, and when you and Abby say the time is right, you and I will endeavor to bring another child into the family, if you are willing to do so."

○   ○   ○

Will was now fully committed to the endeavor. And with the issue of his agreement having been settled, all of the tension and apprehension that had been at the forefront of everyone's thoughts were alleviated, although Will remained quite apprehensive regarding the part that he would play. Nevertheless, he made an effort to place the issue at the back of his mind, and spent the next several days earnestly attending to his farm labors.

○   ○   ○

Near the midnight hour, on the twelfth day of June, Abby kissed Will, took him by the hand, and walked with him down the hallway to Agatha's bedchamber. At Agatha's door, Abby kissed Will once more and returned to her bedchamber. Will stood there for a moment, then softly knocked and entered the room. Forty minutes later, Will emerged, and silently walked back to join Abby in their bedchamber. In the darkness, Abby embraced Will and asked, "Has it been done?"

"Yes, Abby, it's been done."

"I love you, Will."

"And I love you too, Abby."

"May I ask you a question, Will?"

"As long as it doesn't have anything to do with what just occurred down the hallway, you may ask me anything in the world."

"I understand... goodnight, darling."

"Goodnight, Abby."

○   ○   ○

To Will and Abby's consternation, Agatha did not conceive, and it became necessary for Will to make four additional '*midnight walks down the hallway*' on random dates during the following six weeks before Agatha confided in Abby, and told her that she had, in fact, conceived.

Setting all of the minor peripheral concerns aside, their ultimate mission had been successfully accomplished. Agatha was once again pregnant with Will's child, and the family was soon living their lives with very limited exposure to the world outside of Montgomery Farm. Will had also successfully managed to overcome most of the embarrassment he experienced when he was in the presence of Sarah and Elizabeth at mealtime. The daughters were obviously sympathetic to the reasons and the goals of such liaisons and therefore remained silent, never discussing the subject again, even between themselves. The entire family was also quite excited over the prospects of having another child in their future, and the circumstances by which the successful pregnancy had been achieved was deemed inconsequential and insignificant in the eyes of the family. Elizabeth and Sarah loved children as much as the rest of the family, and little Christopher was the undisputed center of attention whenever he was in the room. From time to time, Elizabeth and Sarah even had minor quarrels over the right to hold him, but it was all in fun. The family seemed to be in perfect harmony again at Montgomery Farm, and everything was going precisely as they had planned... that is, until the morning of July sixteenth.

July had brought about the time of year when the demand to do all of the many jobs that were involved in farming was at its peak. The annual harvesting of tobacco leaves had just begun. In addition, the year's supply of potatoes and corn needed to be harvested and properly stored away for the winter. The days were long and hot, and the menfolk worked from before daylight, until it became too dark to see outside. To make matters worse, tobacco worms had invaded the croplands of Montgomery Farm, rendering nearly twenty percent of their annual tobacco crop unfit to harvest. Every day for three weeks, seemed to find the family picking tobacco worms from their plants in an effort to save their crop. All seemed to be in a temporary state of chaos there on the farm. Even with the tender and compassionate heart that she had, Abby was unwittingly about to present an additional dilemma to Will and the family. She approached Will at the side porch as he was bringing in an armload of kindling for the kitchen stove. Will was perfectly familiar with Abby's facial expressions and demeanor when she had something on her mind, and from the look of things, he could clearly see that once again, something was bothering her.

"What's the matter, Abby?"

"I need for you to come to the well with me, Will. We need to talk about something important for a moment or two before we go back inside."

At the well, Abby took Will by the hand and had just started to talk to him when Sarah came out to draw a bucket of water. Then, Ezra arrived from the barn stating that he needed Will's help in repairing one of the wheels on the tobacco wagon. Abby recognized that the demands of the day had already precluded their having any privacy at all, so she kissed Will on the cheek and whispered, "Come to the house early for your noon meal, and we'll talk then."

Owing to the routine confusion of the morning, Will and Abby did not have a chance to talk to each other until everyone else was seated at the kitchen table for their noon hour meal. They went to the side porch, where Abby once again took Will by the hand, looked deeply into his eyes, and softly said, "I'm pregnant with child, Will."

"What!? You? You're with child? Lord have mercy, Abby, are you quite certain!?"

"Please keep your voice down, Will. I haven't told anyone but you that I'm pregnant yet."

"Praise God, Abby! Oh, my! This is wonderful news!"

"Are you disappointed in me, Will... that I did not conceive months ago, before we found it necessary for you and Agatha to produce a child together?"

"Disappointed? Ha! I would have to be a pretty sorry excuse of a man to ever be disappointed in someone as wonderful as you, Abby Collins! Besides, I've told you before, I wouldn't mind having ten, or even twelve children, and I meant every word of it!"

"I'm so embarrassed that I told you I was barren... I didn't know, Will, I swear I didn't!"

"My Lord, this is wonderful!"

"Does it cause you concern that Agatha and I are both with child now, at the same time, and only a month apart?"

"I am elated, Abby! This is what we've prayed for, isn't it? This is exactly what we've been asking God for! Let's go in and tell everyone!"

"**No**, Will! Please say nothing about this until I have had an opportunity to talk to Agatha in private."

"Why, Abby? What reason do we possibly have to be ashamed of this? My Lord..."

"I'm not ashamed in the least, Will. I'm so proud of myself that I can hardly stand it! It's just that she's my sister, and I love her dearly, and I do not want her to feel that my pregnancy is in any way, more important than hers. In my heart, I know that Agatha loves our family as much as I do, if that could be possible. We both carry a child for you, Will, and in the eyes of God, neither of us are more precious or important than the other. I want to tell her the news in a way that won't make her feel inferior to me. She's a precious person, and I want to make sure that she feels that way. And I want an opportunity to speak with Sarah and Elizabeth before I tell Agatha, so they will not show any partiality toward me, and risk hurting Agatha's feelings."

"I've never known anyone more thoughtful or kind than you are, Abby. Your presence in my life makes me beam with pride. I'm so happy that I can hardly contain myself!"

"You know how you greet me so lovingly each morning when you first come into the kitchen for your morning coffee?"

"Yes... what about it?"

"Would I be asking too much of you, if I asked you to try showing Agatha some additional attention, you know, like a compliment once in a while on how she's dressed, or a compliment on something that she's prepared for our family meals? I think it would help her to feel like she's a more important part of our family, and that she's loved. She's terribly insecure in life, and has always had a low opinion of herself. She's got no one to love her but us, Will, and it would comfort me greatly if I knew that my sister was happy here with us. If we provided her with a little extra attention from time to time, I think it would mean so much to her."

"Starting this evening, I'll try to remind myself to be a little generous with my compliments. In fact, I'll give all the ladies of my family more of the compliments that they deserve... Sarah and Elizabeth as well. Alright?"

"God has bestowed me with the kindest husband in the world. I've never been this happy in my life, and it's all because of you, Will."

Through Abby's marvelous ability to handle situations such as this with diplomacy and kindness, complete harmony continued to reign in the family. She met with Agatha that very afternoon, after talking with Sarah and Elizabeth, to tell her that she was with child, and the resulting conversation brought the two sisters closer together than they had ever been before. They both carried a child for the family, a circumstance which they both treasured equally. After they had finished their discussion, they brought Sarah and Elizabeth into the room, and the four of them celebrated together with much warmth and affection, and Will's generous bestowment of compliments became a regular attraction that bound them all even closer together as a family.

Elizabeth and Sarah's apparent disinterest in their suitors was an item of mild concern that Will and Abby had seldom discussed at length between themselves until a very warm and humid night in August. The heat had caused them to leave their upstairs bedchamber and sit on the back porch for an hour or two until the night air cooled the high temperature a bit. Abby initiated conversation on the subject, asking Will in a matter-of-factly manner, "Have you continued to take notice of how Elizabeth and Sarah seem to be rejecting so many of their suitors here lately?"

"How could I not take notice, Abby? They have even been rude and crass with some of their callers, in my opinion. Sometimes they even treat their suitors even worse than you used to treat me when I was first brought here, if such a thing seems possible."

"Please, Will, don't ever remind me of how poorly I treated you then... that's something that I'm trying very hard to forget, and my heart still bears the terrible scars of that shame to this day."

"Forgive me. I shall never mention the subject again, Abby."

"At their very best, Elizabeth and Sarah are very poor and somber conversationalists when they are entertaining suitors. I wonder sometimes if they even realize just how disagreeable they can be."

"I've noticed the same thing, Abby. Yet when their callers leave, Elizabeth and Sarah seem to immediately become their cheerful selves again. It's almost as if they are going out of their way to be discourteous to their callers. I don't understand it."

"I think that I understand it, Will... I just don't know what to do about it, or if I should even try to do anything about it."

"If you understand what's going on, how about explaining it to me, Abby?"

"I'm not sure of how you would react. Perhaps I should talk to Elizabeth and Sarah before you and I discuss it any further."

"Abby, please tell me what's going on. They're my stepdaughters, and a very important part of my life, and I don't need to tell you how much I love them."

"I know my daughters better than anyone, Will."

"I'm sure that's true, Abby. And I love them too much not to care what's going on. Please confide in me."

"Elizabeth and Sarah both still worship the ground that you walk on, Will. And please don't try to tell me that you are unaware of the fact. I'm sure that their love for you is not romantic in nature, like it once was. If anything, I think they are just unwitting victims of their own childish fascination with you. My Lord, it's written all over their faces. Every morning when you kiss them good morning, they practically melt with delight."

"Is it wrong for me to kiss my own stepdaughters, Abby? If it is, then I'll stop immediately."

"Of course it's not wrong! That's not the point that I'm trying to make here, Will. It's just that every suitor that comes here to call on them has his qualities measured against yours, and every single one of the young men are falling miserably short of Elizabeth and Sarah's grand expectations."

"Lord, have mercy... You mean that I'm the cause of their discontentment?"

"There is no discontentment, and I can assure you that you have only been a source of happiness for all of us here at Montgomery House, Will... all of us!"

"I deeply love everyone here, Abby, and I only want what's best for everyone. If I thought for one moment that my being here would interfere in any way with Elizabeth and Sarah's future happiness, I would..."

"William Collins, don't you dare suggest the possibility of leaving us! I would tie you to a tree with your own tongue if you ever mention such a horrible thing again!"

"Mercy! I surely wouldn't want you to tie me to a tree with my own tongue, Abby... it sort of gives me the shivers just to think about it! My Lord!"

"You can relax, dear, it was purely a figure of speech. My grandmother used that expression when she became angry with my grandfather. Your absence from Montgomery House would destroy four lives, not to mention little Christopher or the babies that Agatha and I now carry."

"I'm not going anywhere, Abby, I can promise you that."

"If Elizabeth and Sarah find such contentment in being here with us, why can't we just accept that? Not all women find their happiness by leaving home and getting married at such a young age. Some women simply do not aspire to that sort of thing."

"Sarah and Elizabeth are much too beautiful and full of life to stay here at Montgomery Farm and become spinsters for the rest of their lives. They deserve better lives than that, Abby."

"As selfish as it may sound though, I would not object if they each chose to live the rest of their lives right here with us at Montgomery House, and that goes for Agatha as well."

"That would give me great satisfaction as well, Abby, but I know in my heart that such a future would not be in their best interest. Somewhere in their future there is a couple of wholesome, handsome young Christian men waiting to be discovered by them, and somewhere in our future we will have a horde of grandchildren to look forward to, I know we will."

"Perhaps we could take the approach of encouraging them to take more of an interest in some of these young men who come here to call on them? Perhaps we could even tell them how much we approve of some of their callers."

"No! Absolutely not! I'll not hear of it! I did that once with O'Donnell, remember? I'll never do that again! I think we should do no more than encourage them to accept the visitation of suitors, and let them continue to make their own choices of who they like and who they don't like, just like they're doing now. That first time you and I talked honestly with each other in the barn that morning, we talked about facing life's little difficulties together. Since then, you and I have faced and conquered a number of difficulties together. I am proud that your daughters are so demanding in their expectations of a suitor, and very flattered that they would think so highly of me. I have every confidence that nature will soon seek its course, and they will each discover the man of their dreams."

"I think so, too, Will."

"What do you suggest, then, Abby?"

"I suggest that we continue to live our lives in the supreme happiness of which we have become accustomed, Will, and just take one day at a time. We'll pray about it, and accept whatever outcome pleases God. I believe you're right, as long as we are patient, the right young man will come along for each of them someday. Are you in agreement, Mr. Collins?"

"I could never bring myself to disagree with anyone as beautiful and wonderful as you are, Mrs. Collins."

Only A Minor Quarrel

"Let us therefore follow after the things which make
for peace, and things wherewith one may edify another."
Romans 14:19

By the last of September, the hard, demanding labors of farm work had slowly tapered off to a point that the family was once again afforded the opportunity to enjoy leisurely activities together, such as parlor games and picnics. The wives of both Josh and George had borne them children over the course of spring and summer, and aside from a short infestation of the coughing sickness, everyone at Montgomery Farm was in good health. Ezra had been the only exception, when he had been bedridden for nearly three weeks after being bitten on his groin by a tick. It seemed incomprehensible, that a man of Ezra's enormous stature could be sickened and brought to his knees by the single bite of a small insect. Will had immediately summoned Dr. Michaels to attend him, and even after receiving treatment, Ezra was slow to regain his strength and stamina. A month passed before he was fully recovered and back to the pursuits of his normal farm labors. Abby and Agatha were both progressing well with their pregnancies, and each morning would commence with Will's circuit of '*good morning*' compliments. The ladies of Montgomery Farm were so pleasantly contented in their everyday lives that no one would have anticipated the minor disturbance that was about to occur.

It was on the twenty-eighth day of September that Sheriff Homer Bellisle paid a visit to Montgomery Farm for the purpose of soliciting Will's assistance. A man in Boone's Hollow had been accused of robbing an elderly couple in their home, just outside of Boone's Hollow and beating the elderly couple within an inch of their life. The elderly couple reported the theft and assault to the sheriff in Boone's Hollow, and when the sheriff had gone to the alleged thief's home to arrest him, the man shot and killed the sheriff and hastily fled the area. He was thought to have taken up residency with his father and mother in the mountains, eighteen miles northwest of Blanchard. Sheriff Homer Bellisle had come to Montgomery Farm in order to solicit Will's assistance in bringing the man to face justice in a court in Lynchburg. There would always be enough work to keep Will occupied right there at Montgomery Farm, but with the harvest needs having tapered off somewhat, Will considered Bellisle's request. After all, they had become the best of friends, and friendships carried certain obligations with them. Families also came with obligations, and Will had a difficult decision to make. He knew that Abby would be opposed to his assisting Bellisle. Will wasn't comfortable with the prospects, and asked, "What about your deputy? Why can't he go along with you this time, Homer?"

"He could, I suppose, but someone needs to stay and watch over Blanchard. Besides, I'd rather have you with me. My deputy, Leroy, is a good-hearted soul, bless his heart, but he's dumber than a rock. This man's name is Orson Ashworth. He's killed one sheriff already, and I ain't hankerin' to be his second. I trust you, Will, and I know that together, we can bring this man to justice."

"I would suppose that the man knows full well that if he's brought in he'll most likely hang for killing the sheriff."

"Yes, with all the witnesses that saw him do it, I'm sure he knows that. But I still have to do my job, Will."

"Knowing that he'll probably hang if he's brought in isn't

going to make him very easy to handle, Homer. Desperate men are capable of doing very desperate things."

"I spect' I know that as much as anybody, that's why I'd like to have you along with me this time. I could go by myself, Will, but the truth of the matter is... two heads are better than one."

"When do you plan to leave?"

"There ain't no real hurry, Will. I know where he is probably holding up, and he ain't very likely to go nowhere. He most likely thinks no one will come looking for him up in the hills. He probably thinks that now that he's killed the sheriff, no one else will be foolish enough to come after him now."

"Well, if he thinks no one is foolish enough to come after him, he doesn't know *you* very well, does he?"

"What do you mean by that, Will?"

"I meant it as a joke, Homer, that's all. Don't get your feelings hurt."

"Well, how about it, Will? Can you come along and help me out?"

"Very well. Let me talk it over with my family tonight, and I'll meet you at your office first thing in the morning."

Leaving two pregnant women, two stepdaughters, and his baby behind and going in pursuit of a dangerous murderer was not a proposition that Will was taking lightly or looking forward to. However, Bellisle had always been there when Will had needed him, and Will was of the conviction that he could not turn a blind eye to the sheriff's request for help just because there was some danger involved. Bellisle had even volunteered to go all the way to Baltimore with Will when he had gone there to bring Sarah home. How could Will turn him down now? Will knew that Abby would frown on the prospects of him going off in pursuit of a criminal, but he had no idea just how angry Abby would become over the matter. He was about to find out.

At the dinner table that evening, Will announced that he would be leaving on a one, or possibly two day, expedition to assist the sheriff in bringing a fugitive to justice. This announcement instilled an immediate look of alarm on everyone's face. Will was able to pacify their concerns by placating them with exaggerated descriptions of how safe and simple the task would be. Everyone but Abby was mildly relieved, although they remained somewhat apprehensive. On the other hand, William could clearly see that Abigail was furious over the idea, even though she offered no opposing comments in front of the family at the dinner table. Having never seen such an angry expression on Abby's face before, Will knew full well that she would vent her anger in the privacy of their bedchamber later that evening, and Abby did exactly as Will had anticipated. Displaying a fiery temper and a raised voice that Will was taken aback by, she lashed out at him at soon as the bedchamber door was closed behind them.

"I'm terribly disappointed in your decision to go wandering about the countryside with Sheriff Bellisle, in pursuit of dangerous criminals! That's his job, Will, not yours, and I'm surprised that you would agree to do such a thing without first discussing it with me! Husbands and wives are supposed to discuss important issues like that before making a commitment!"

"It's like I told you downstairs, Abby, the man we're going to arrest is not really a dangerous criminal, and I should be back home in two days... maybe less."

"You've never lied to me before William, don't start now!"

"Why do you think I'm lying?"

"It's written all over your face! The man you're going after is a very dangerous man, isn't he? Tell me the truth!"

"Well... I don't know for sure, Abby... maybe, and maybe not. I've never met the man before. Why should I assume that he's dangerous?"

"What crime did the man commit?"

"Crime?"

"You heard me! What crime did the man commit?"

"Uhhh... he killed a sheriff up at Boone's Hollow... that's all."

"**He's a murderer**! And you claim not to know that he's a dangerous man? **How could you do this to your family**?"

"Abby, please don't raise your voice at me like that. I wish to have private conversation with you. I don't want everyone in the entire house to hear what we're saying."

"I'm sorry I raised my voice, William, but you must understand how I feel about this!"

Will glowered at Abby's petulant behavior, and sternly said, "I can understand you equally as well if we both talk in a normal tone of voice."

"Then perhaps you can tell me, in a normal tone of voice, how you can do such a thing with a clear conscience, William. If you should go off and get yourself killed, how would our family survive? If Agatha and I are both blessed to give healthy births in March, you would be abandoning two widows and three orphans! Not to mention, two stepdaughters who love you dearly. Elizabeth and Sarah worship the ground you walk on! Have you considered that, William?"

"Two widows? Agatha is not my wife, Abby, you are!"

"We both carry your child!"

"Why must you be so pugnacious all of a sudden, Abby?"

"**Why**?! I've already told you why I am so opposed to you going off with Bellisle! And I'm not being pugnacious!"

"Abby, there are times in a man's life when he has to do things that he doesn't necessarily want to do, but must. A man has to do what he thinks is right, Abby."

"Oh really? And leaving us behind while you go frolicking with the sheriff, searching for dangerous outlaws, is that the right thing to do, William? You almost died in battle when you were first brought here. You could have easily died when Herbert Meyers shot you. All this, and yet now you want to ride off and tempt fate yet another time! Such a thing is reckless behavior for a man who has the responsibility of being the head of a household, to say the least!"

"Be reasonable, Abby. I've never seen you act like this before."

"I've never felt this abandoned before! Agatha and I are pregnant with your babies and you want to run off with the sheriff and risk your life! Wouldn't we be in a fine state here at Montgomery Farm if something happened to you?!"

"I'm not going to argue with you about it... I love you too much to do that. Think about it tonight, Abby. Pray about it. Tomorrow morning, if you're still so opposed to my going, I'll ride into Blanchard and tell Bellisle to find someone else to go with him."

"I shan't feel any different tomorrow morning than I feel right now, William!"

"William? So my name is not Will anymore, it's William? Why not address me as Mr. Collins, Abby? That way your words could be twice as painful to me. Whether or not you feel differently tomorrow, I certainly hope that you'll behave differently tomorrow! I feel like I don't even know you when you're like this, Abby!"

"I can't help the way I feel!"

"You're treating me just like you did when I first met you, Abby, and it's breaking my heart."

The following morning Will awoke earlier than he normally would have. In the darkness, he reached over to find that Abby was not in the bed with him. This surprised him somewhat because he had never heard or felt Abby when she had left the bed. Given her harsh disposition of the night before, he assumed that she had left the bed sometime during the night. He lay there for a moment or two longer before he dressed himself and went downstairs to check on Abby. Abby was in the kitchen, preparing biscuits by lamp light, and she appeared to be an entirely different person than she had been the night before. In stark contrast to her demeanor the night before, when she saw him approaching, she brought forth a wide congenial smile, and cheerfully said, "Good morning, darling. I don't know why it is, but it seems like every time I have my hands in dough like this, my nose itches. Will you scratch my nose for me please, dear?"

"Sure. How's that?"

"That's wonderful, thank you. You're up awfully early this morning, Will."

"I know. I would have been downstairs an hour ago, but each time I attempted to get out of the bed, Agatha would pull me back into it."

"Agatha? Did she come into our bed this morning, Will, really?"

"No, darling, I was only joking with you."

"You devil! I love you, William Collins! I've never known anyone like you! You have the unique ability to anger me into laughter sometimes with your joking, and I love you for it."

"You weren't doing much laughing last night, Abby. All I saw was the anger in you, and plenty of it."

"I know, and I'm very sorry for the way I acted last night."

"Have you thought any more about what we were arguing about last night, Abby?"

"It wasn't an argument Will, it was supposed to be a discussion."

"If that was a discussion, I'd hate to be around to witness the hellfire in your eyes when you were in the mood to do some serious arguing."

"I'm so sorry, Will."

"Well, have you thought any more about our little *discussion* of last night?"

"I'm making two extra batches of biscuits, so that you and Homer can carry some along with you this morning."

"Does that mean...?"

"It means that I am begging you to forgive me for the way that I talked to you last night, Will. I think that my pregnancy is causing me to be very ill-tempered at times, and I hope you will forgive my behavior of last night. It's so selfish of me to treat you as if you were property, as if I owned you."

"Oh, but you do own me, Abby, I swear you do, lock, stock, and barrel. You own every ounce of my heart and soul."

"The fact that you always want to do what you think is right, is one of the many reasons that I love you as deeply as I do. I love you just the way you are, and last night I tried to change who you are to suit my own selfish wishes. Please find it in your heart to forgive me."

"I do forgive you, Abby. Let's just forget it ever happened, alright?"

"Alright."

"How long before breakfast is ready, Abby?"

"The coffee is just starting to boil, breakfast will be ready in about twenty-five or thirty minutes."

"Do I have time to run upstairs and finish what Agatha and I were getting ready to do?"

"You may crawl up there if you wish."

"Why on earth would I need to crawl up there, Abby?"

"Because you're about to have both of your legs broken, Mr. Collins! And maybe your neck, too!"

"Mercy! I suppose I'd better just sit down at the table and wait for my breakfast then."

"Ha! That's a very wise decision on your part, Mr. Collins."

As Abby worked to prepare breakfast, she bore an expression on her face which signified that she was deep in thought. After a moment or two of pondering, she walked over to Will, kissed him on the cheek, and quietly asked, "Please be honest with me about something, will you?"

"Of course I will, what is it?"

"Do you really have a desire to visit Agatha this morning? If you do, I want you to tell me the truth. I was joking with you when I said that I would break your legs. I hope you know that."

"I know that, Abby, and I love it when you joke with me like that."

"Be honest with me, Will, do you have a desire to go upstairs to Agatha?"

"I will not lie to you, Abby. No, I have no desire to go to Agatha this morning. I would never deceive or betray you, Abby."

"I know you wouldn't, Will."

"Given the surrogate nature of my past relationships with her, and the fact that she carries another baby for the family, and with our living in such proximity to one another, I have come to love Agatha in a way that far exceeds anything I would have ever expected, but you are my wife—the woman I love above all others. Surprisingly, my heart has no difficulty recognizing that my relationships with Agatha were committed for the betterment of our family. I bear no guilt for what we did, and not an ounce of lusting after her has entered my body or soul. I love Agatha for who she is and what she is doing for us, but my love for you surpasses any description known to mankind. Has my honesty clarified things in your mind, Abby?"

"Your honesty has given me comfort, as it always does, and I know that your words come from your heart. Agatha has given us so much, that I would have been disappointed if you hadn't found a place for her in your heart."

"I love you, Abby."

"I love you too, darling. Mercy, Will!"

"What's the matter, Abby?"

"My nose itches again."

Will stood and scratched Abby's nose again. They shared a long, sincere kiss, and afterwards, Abby looked deeply into his eyes and said, "I shall never be as overbearing as I was last night, but I beg of you to please be careful while you are away. Think about your family before allowing your bravery to do something that would destroy you. We all love you, Will, and we all depend on you more than you may ever know. We will pray for your safety until you return to us."

Shortly after sunrise, Will rode into Blanchard and met Sheriff Bellisle at his office. Bellisle was already prepared to depart when Will got there, so the two of them bid farewell to Bellisle's deputy, Leroy, and were soon on their way out of town. The weather was fairly cool for the twenty-ninth day of September, but the coolness made for a very pleasant ride. The sycamore trees were beginning to turn their early autumn shade of bright yellow, and if it had not been for the unpleasant nature of their travel, it would have been an otherwise beautiful day for riding. At mid-morning, Will reached into a sack that he carried in his saddlebags and handed the sheriff a biscuit to eat. Bellisle smiled from ear to ear when he saw the biscuits.

"I remember Abigail's biscuits after the funeral, when Mr. Montgomery died a couple of years ago, Will. I think she makes the best biscuits in the county."

"Thanks Homer, I think so as well."

"My wife's biscuits taste like sawdust, and sometimes they're hard as a rock. I've been living with her cooking for twenty years now, and I suppose if her cooking was gonna kill me, I'd of been dead years ago."

"What can you tell me about this man we're going after, Homer... this Orson Ashworth fellow?"

"He's a nasty kind of feller, Will. Before the war, he raped and killed a little negro girl up above Lynchburg. The judge ordered him to pay her master two hundred dollars, and that was it. He turned him loose."

"He killed a young girl, and got away with it?"

"The judge said that it was just a nigger slave. He said that it wasn't as if he had killed a white woman."

"That's disgusting! And the jury believed him?"

"There wasn't no jury. And if there had been, they'd a done the same thing, Will. It's just the way things are."

"And how about you, Homer? How do you think Ashworth should have been dealt with?"

"My way of thinking has changed a lot from what I used to think was right and wrong, thank God. I think the negro girl was a human being, with a heart and soul just like any white woman, and Ashworth should have been hung for what he done. Of course, I also happen to believe that the judge should have been hung right alongside him. We're all equal in God's eyes, Will, and the murder of that little colored girl shouldn't have gone unpunished."

"I'm glad to hear you say that. I agree with you."

"My way of thinking has changed about a lot of things since that night two years ago, Will."

"What night are you talking about, Homer?"

"You know damned good and well what night I'm talking about, Will... that night Herbert Myers and a bunch of hooded scoundrels showed up at your doorstep."

"Oh... That night is in the past now, its history now, Homer, and best forgotten."

"Still, I never said thank you for the words you spoke that night. They helped bring me to my senses, and helped me figure out what was right and what was wrong, and I'm beholding to you. I always will be."

"Forget about it, Homer, and tell me more about this fellow, Ashworth."

"Sorry, Will, but I'll never forget about it. Incidentally, that reminds me, the watch that belonged to Robert Marshall when he was killed is still in my desk drawer back at the office. It is indeed a valuable watch, and you need to take it home with you when we ride back through Blanchard. I don't like having something that valuable in my drawer."

"It doesn't belong to me, Homer."

"Marshall has no next-of-kin. He was working for you when he got killed. You paid for his burial. Nobody else has claim to the watch, just you. The watch is yours."

"Then perhaps you can assist me in finding a worthy disabled veteran there in Blanchard, and give the watch to him. Would you do that for me, Homer?"

"Oscar McDaniel lost both of his legs in the war. He has a wife and two children. Right now, he's depending on his neighbors and the church to help him and his wife along. If you wish, I would be proud to tell him that you want him to have the watch, Will."

"I would like that very much, only I would prefer that you tell him that the watch is from the people of Blanchard, in recognition of the contribution he made during the war. Now, tell me more about this Ashworth fellow, Homer."

"Well, it's like I told you yesterday, he shot the sheriff up in Boone's Hollow dead last week. He knows that if we take him alive, he's gonna hang, so he ain't likely to be too cooperative. He has a new Henry rifle and some kind of pistol, a Colt Army pistol, I think. He's a big man, more than six feet tall, and he's living with his mother and father, about six miles further up this here road. He deserted the Confederate Army in Georgia, and he's been living up here with his ever since. He's a hunter, and he knows danged well how to shoot."

"How old is he?"

"Thirty, maybe thirty-five, I don't know for sure. We ought to be where we can see the farmhouse in another hour or so... maybe less."

"Is there any way we can cut through the woods and come in from behind the house, Homer?"

"When we get to the creek up here, we can cut through the woods and follow the creek. That'll take us behind the house maybe a hundred yards or so, I think. It's been more than four years since I've been up this way, but I remember where the house is, and we can come in from the back alright."

"That's perfect."

"If you got some kind of plan worked up in your mind, Will, tell me what yer thinking."

"I think we should sneak around back and watch the house for a couple of hours... and see what's going on there. He most likely knows that someone will be coming for him sooner or later, so he's apt to have his attention on the road in front of the house. I think it would be stupid to try to come at him from the road, especially with him having a Henry rifle and knowing how to use it. You're the sheriff, and I'll do whatever you say, but I think we should watch the house for a while before we rush in there and put ourselves at risk."

"That sounds like a good idea to me, Will."

By three o'clock in the afternoon, Will and the sheriff had situated themselves in a thicket of persimmon and plum trees a hundred yards from the house, where they had a clear field of vision to the farmhouse. After almost an hour, the lone figure of a man emerged from the house and drew a bucket of water from the well, then went back inside. Will asked the sheriff, "Was that Ashworth?"

"I'm not sure, he was too far away to tell for sure, but it looked like him. The man was big enough to be Ashworth."

"If he knows that someone will be coming after him, why is he staying here like this? Why isn't he riding off to another state? Why doesn't he hide somewhere in the Blue Ridge mountains west of here?"

"I don't know, Will. It doesn't make any sense."

"Neither does killing a sheriff."

"Ashworth has always thought that he was above the law, especially after he got away with killing that girl. Maybe he thinks we're too scared to come after him, or maybe he figures he can make it to the woods and escape if anyone comes for him. I just don't know."

"How do you want to deal with this, Homer?"

"You got any ideas, Will?"

"Maybe. How about if we were to position ourselves closer to the well? He didn't appear to have a gun with him when he went for water just now. If we were closer to the well, we could shoot him in the leg before he gets a chance to run back to the house and get a gun. We could put the shackles on him while he was down, patch his leg, and haul his ornery ass back to Blanchard."

"I've got a wife and children, Will, and so do you. I don't want neither of us to take any chances with this critter."

"What are you suggesting, Homer."

"If it was anybody else we was trying to arrest, I'd say your plan sounded awful good. Ashworth has already killed two people, and it wouldn't make no never mind to him if he killed me and you, too."

"So, what do you suggest?"

"I say we do what you said, and shoot him next time he comes out for water, but I think we should be safe about it, and go ahead and shoot him dead."

"Are you positive that he's the one who shot the sheriff, and are you sure he's the one who killed that negro girl?"

"There ain't a doubt in my mind, Will... not one. He admitted to killing the colored girl when he was in court, and two people saw him kill the sheriff. No, there ain't no doubt in my mind."

"Then, whatever you say, Homer. Let's crawl on over to those trees yonder, and we can hide behind that pile of fence posts. We'll only be twenty or twenty-five yards from the well there. We can't miss from that distance. When he comes to the well, shout at him to put his hands in the air. If he takes off running toward the house, we'll kill him then. I just don't like the idea of shooting him dead without at least giving him a chance to surrender. Even a lowlife like Ashworth deserves an opportunity to surrender."

"Always the gentleman, huh, Will?"

"I'm not much of a gentleman, Homer, but I do have a conscience that I have to live with."

"Alright, Will, that's what we'll do then."

In order to remain unseen from the house, it took Will and the sheriff almost an hour to circle around through the woods and eventually station themselves behind a large stack of fence posts between the barn and the house. Much of the way, they had to crawl on their hands and knees. When they were finally situated in a strategic location, they resumed their vigil. An elderly woman came out of the house and emptied a pan of water, looked around for a moment, and then went back into the house.

"Was that Ashworth's mother?"

"I suppose so, Will, I don't know for sure."

A large black and brown dog came out of the woods near the barn and started sniffing around. Will and the sheriff were unaware of the dog's presence until the dog walked up to the sheriff and smelled of his boots and pant leg. It frightened the sheriff half out of his wits, and it was a good thing the sheriff didn't have his finger on the trigger of his rifle at the time. The sheriff leaned over and whispered to Will, "That damned dog just scared the hell out of me!"

"Me too, Homer. Quiet, I think somebody just opened the door."

A man befitting of Ashworth's description walked out of the house, went twenty or thirty yards, and proceeded to relieve himself, facing the southeast. His head moved from side to side as he scanned across the field toward the road.

"Is that Ashworth?

"You're damned right it is! I'd recognize that ugly face anywhere!"

"He doesn't have a gun with him, Homer. Go ahead and holler at him while he's pissing, and see if he'll surrender without making a fuss."

"This is the sheriff, put your hands up!"

Ashworth turned and immediately started running back toward the house, but Bellisle fired his rifle one time, and the lifeless body of Orson Ashworth fell to the ground. It had not been necessary for Will to shoot—the sheriff's bullet had done all that needed to be done, and Ashworth's life was ended in the same violent manner in which he had ended the life of the Boone's Hollow sheriff and the young negro girl. Will and the sheriff remained poised behind the pile of fence posts with their rifles trained on Ashworth's motionless body. There was no sign of even a twitch of movement coming from the corpse, so the sheriff rose to his feet and started to walk toward Ashworth's body.

"**Wait!**" Will cried out, but it was too late. A shot rang out from the doorway of the house and Homer Bellisle fell to the ground. Instinctively, Will fired a shot at the dark silhouette of the man who stood in the doorway, and the man suddenly disappeared back into the house. Will fired two more shots into the doorway and quickly dashed from behind the fence posts, grabbed the sheriff by his boots, and pulled him to safety back behind the pile of fence posts.

"Dammit, Homer! What have you gone and done to yourself!?"

"Well, for one thing, I just got myself shot up pretty good."

"Let me look at it!"

"I don't think it's all that bad, Will, I'm hit in my side here, and I think it just busted a couple of ribs or something. It hurts pretty bad, though."

"Dammit, Homer! That may be the stupidest thing I ever saw a grown man do! What in the hell were you thinking?"

"I don't know, I suppose that I wasn't thinking at all."

"This is the last time I'm going to do anything like this, Homer! You need to start paying attention to what you're doing. You could have got us both killed!"

"We're supposed to be friends, Will, don't kick me when I'm down like this. Wait till I'm back on my feet, will ya?"

"I swear, Homer, you beat anything I've ever seen!"

Will cut the sleeve off of his shirt, rolled it into a small bundle, and placed it over the wound in the sheriff's side.

"Hold this right here, Homer, I've got to keep my eyes on the house. The man who shot you is still in there, and it'll be dark in another hour. Keep your head down!"

The sheriff's condition was not life-threatening yet, but he would soon need the attention of a physician. Large splinters of rib bone could be seen in the gaping wound, but the bullet had passed through, tearing out a two inch gash of flesh and bone as it went. The crude compress that Will had placed on the wound had proved effective, and stopped the flow of blood temporarily. Eventually, the sun faded into the west, and about eight o'clock, a lamp was lighted from within the house. Will crept to a window and carefully looked inside to see an elderly woman sitting in a chair. At her feet, was the motionless body of a man about her own age. One of Will's bullets, though fired randomly at the doorway, had evidently found its mark.

Will knocked on the window and yelled, "Ma'am, come out of the house! Right now!"

The woman turned, looked toward the window, and shouted back at Will defiantly, "Go straight ta' hell! You've killed my husband and my son... you may as well come inside and kill me!"

Reluctantly, Will cautiously crept into the house to find that there was no one there, save for the elderly woman and her dead husband. Will left the man's body where it lay, and gathered up two rifles and two pistols. He retrieved a horse from the stable, and with great difficulty, he finally managed to load Orson Ashworth's heavy body onto the horse's back and secure it in place. Once he had tied the body in place, he went to the woods and brought up his and the sheriff's horses. When Will had assisted the sheriff into his saddle and they were ready to depart, Will went back inside the house, and spoke briefly with the old woman.

"Ma'am, the sheriff and I are leaving with your son's body. If you want, I can come back tomorrow and help you bury your husband."

"I have relatives that will help me bury my husband. And as for you, I hope your ugly ass burns in hell! Now git!"

Will climbed on his horse, turned to Bellisle, and said, "What a sweet old lady she is."

"Yeah, sort of helps a feller understand why her son turned out so rotten."

"Are you doing alright, Homer?"

"I'm doing fair, I suppose. Looks like I'll get to wake up Doc Michaels when we get back to Blanchard."

"With a half-moon like we have, we should be able to get you back there by one or two o'clock in the morning. Is the flow of blood still stopped?"

"Yeah, I'm doing fine in that respect. My pride is hurting me more than anything else right now."

"If you plan to keep doing stupid things like that, Homer, you need to give some consideration to retiring."

"I'll make a deal with you, Will."

"What kind of deal?"

"If you'll stop calling me stupid, I won't take my gun out and shoot you right between the eyes."

"That sounds like a reasonable deal to me... I accept!"

"I kinda thought you would."

The sheriff and Will arrived at the doorstep of Dr. Michaels' home about three o'clock in the morning. While Bellisle went inside to be treated, Will delivered the body of Orson Ashworth to the mortician. Documents attesting to the identity of the corpse would have to be prepared and witnessed the next morning, after which, the sheriff would have his deputy, Leroy deliver Ashworth's body back to his elderly mother for burial. Will then rode back to Dr. Michaels' house and waited for the doctor to finish his attendance of Homer. When the cleaning and bandaging of Homer's wound was completed, Will rode to Homer's home with him, and assisted him inside. Once he had Homer in his bed, and in the attendance of Mrs. Bellisle, he went outside and unsaddled Homer's horse, and enthusiastically rode off toward Montgomery Farm, and the family he loved so dearly.

Beware Of The Spirits That Dwell In A Bottle

"Woe unto them that rise up early in the morning, that they may follow strong drink; that continue until night, till wine inflame them!" Isaiah 5:11

I t was ten-thirty in the morning when William unsaddled his tired horse at the barn and walked wearily up to the house. He was soon in Abby's arms again, exchanging greetings with the others in his family. Abby and Will shared one delightful embrace after another, until Will sheepishly asked, "Is there any chance of a hungry man getting a late breakfast here at Montgomery House?"

Abby quickly answered, "Yes dear, you bet there is, we'll have something prepared for you in just a moment. Did you and Homer catch the criminal that you went after?"

"Yes, we did, Abby."

"That's good... And it would appear that everything went without any sort of serious incident, is that so?"

"Well... not really, Abby, it developed into much more of a serious incident than Homer and I would have preferred. We were forced to kill a couple of men, and Homer was wounded in the process."

"Oh my God! Was he wounded seriously, Will?"

"He'll be up and around in a couple of weeks... he was very fortunate, it could have been a lot worse."

"Will you tell us everything that happened?"

"After dinner tonight I will be glad to tell you everything about it. But right now, I'd like to eat something, and then I need to lie down for an hour or two. I haven't had any sleep for two days. I'm just happy to be home with my beautiful family this morning."

"I could never explain how much I worry when you're gone away like that, Will."

"I can imagine how much you worry, Abby, and I told Homer that I shan't be going off with him on any other escapades to capture criminals. You were right when you said that such a thing is too risky, and I'll never put my family through that kind of unnecessary torment again, I promise."

Will was elated to be at home among his loved ones again. Once he had eaten his breakfast, he bathed in a tub of warm water on the back porch, and after attending to a few other chores, he managed to sleep for an hour or two before he was awakened for dinner. As he ate his dinner that evening, his family could see the unusual and uncharacteristic weariness in his eyes. They were reluctant to purge him for conversation that evening, but because they were so anxious to hear the details of his and Sheriff Bellisle's confrontation with the Ashworth family they waited impatiently to hear the entire account. Will did not wish to share the gruesome particulars of his brief absence with his loved ones at mealtime.

After dinner that evening, Will did in fact, pour himself a larger than normal glass of bourbon, which was the first in a series of judgment errors that he made that evening. He told his adoring family exactly what had transpired while he was gone. The fact that Will had returned to them unscathed, and uninjured was a blessing that was foremost in everyone's mind that evening. Adding to their comfort was the fact that Will had vowed never to go on such a dangerous expedition again. With a warm fire in the parlor fireplace, and an even warmer fire aglow in William's belly and heart, the bourbon had a delightful effect on his physical and mental countenance... at least at first. Without paying due attention to what he was doing, Will had inadvertently drank three glasses of bourbon before he had realized the effect the strong spirits were having on him. His mind was focused on the vivid account he was giving the family of his and Homer's expedition to bring the fugitive to justice.

Will looked around him at his loving family who had gathered around the parlor table before him, and he marveled at the delighted faces that were so lovingly looking back at him. The wonderment of being in the presence of his loved ones induced him to throw caution to the wind, and partake of his bourbon without giving conscious thought to how much he was drinking. Without exercising prudence or caution, Will poured himself yet another large glass of bourbon and sat down beside Abby on the settee. Unwittingly, he had overindulged considerably in the amount of bourbon that he had consumed. Simply put, he had consumed entirely too much, too fast. Will had never been one who was prone to drinking in excess, and he had never experienced the mellowing and intoxicating effect of alcohol spirits on an intolerant and very weary body before. The journey with Homer Bellisle had taken a toll on the general constitution of Will's weary body, and the trip had nearly exhausted him. That, combined with the alcohol, had placed him in a state of intoxication never before witnessed by his adoring family, and never before experienced by Will. His jolly giddiness and occasional stammering of words was more of a pleasant amusement to his family than anything else... at least at first it was. No one could have foreseen that, before it was over, the night was going to evolve into one that everyone would remember for the rest of their life... although Will would most likely try his best to forget it. With an overly generous portion of spirits residing under his belt, Will addressed his dutiful wife, "Abby, my dear, I am very happy to be back home, and I feel unusually lifted up in spirit this evening for some reason."

Abigail had paid attention to the large portion of bourbon

that Will had drank, and simply replied, "I'm quite positive that you do feel... *lifted up*, dear."

"May I have your permission to address my wonderful family this evening? I have something very special that I would like to share with the people that I love most in this world."

"You're the head of our household, Will, you certainly don't need my permission to speak in your own house. Nevertheless, you do indeed have it. I'm sure that we would all like very much to hear what you have to say this evening, darling."

Perhaps the bourbon had plunged William Collins into the deceivingly sentimental disposition of allowing his innermost thoughts to flow that night, or perhaps he was truly moved by the overwhelming love that he had for his family. On this particular night, it was probably the larger than normal portion of bourbon that was responsible for loosening his lips, and permitting them to voice the feelings he had hidden away in the utmost depths of his heart. Regardless of the true cause of his honest candor, Will looked deeply and sincerely into the eyes of each of his family members, and addressed them individually, as they listened with pride and adoration, each of them attending to their knitting as they sat there waiting to hear what Will had to say.

Beginning with Sarah, and in the presence and full view of his surprised family, he took her by the hand as she curiously sat her knitting aside and stood up, seemingly uncertain as to why Will wanted her to stand. Once she was standing, he gently put his arms around her, held her firmly, and imparted upon her cheek a short but very sincere kiss. It was the first time that Will had kissed Sarah while having his arms around her, and even though it was a very brief kiss, it left Sarah momentarily mesmerized, and with her mother looking on, she was unsure of exactly how she should respond. Afterwards, Will said,

"Sarah, my sweet stepdaughter, Sarah, my Lord, but how you brighten up our days and our lives here at Montgomery House. I love your mischievous curiosity... You keep us all on our toes, Sarah, because we never know what you're going to come up with next... a characteristic that's only overshadowed by the purity and compassion in your lovely heart. I love your jolliness, and the way you smile that special smile of yours. You and Elizabeth are more like daughters to me than stepdaughters, and I wanted to make you aware of just how much your mother and I truly appreciate you."

In a state of entranced wonderment brought on by Will's simple kiss and his heart-warming words, Sarah was almost breathless, and nearly faint with emotion. She simply answered, "And I appreciate you and Mother too, Will... as we all do..."

Abby was as surprised as anyone by Will's sudden need to express himself so lovingly to the family, but knew by now that the bourbon was probably taking a toll on his ability to control his words and his actions. However, she did not voice any disapproval of Will's expression of sentiments, because she saw nothing in his behavior but Will's overwhelming love, and nothing that he had said thus far had offended her, it had only served to delight her. She saw the immediate satisfaction that Will's eloquent words had brought to Sarah, and it had warmed her heart. However, Will was starting to slur his words, and suspicions around the room that Will was becoming more than just a little tipsy began to rise, and were confirmed, as Will continued to throw censorship and caution to the wind, and went around the table to Agatha next. He pulled her up from her chair, wrapped his arms around her, and kissed her gently, yet fervently on the cheek. Agatha had dropped her knitting to the floor, and she had become weakened and limp by the time that Will pulled his arms from around her and said....

"Oh, Aggy, my sweet, sweet Aggy, there's not another like you in this world, my sweet. I appreciate the way you've always been there for Abby and me, and the rest of the family as well. That you are the mother of our child, makes me love you even that much more. That you carry yet another child for our family... well, Abby and I just love you, Aggy... and we want you to know that."

Dumbfounded, and even mildly aroused by Will's kiss, Agatha softly uttered, "And I love you and Abigail too, Will." She dropped back into her chair almost as a limp object when Will released her hands and walked away.

The fact that Will had called Agatha, 'Aggy,' had raised every eyebrow in the room, even Agatha's, and was perhaps the first genuine confirmation that Will's bourbon was now dictating his words as much, if not more so, than his lips. The bourbon had undoubtedly opened a doorway to his heart, and allowed his innermost sentiments to freely escape the confinement of his evaporated self-control. Will took another drink, and went to Elizabeth next. With the glorious anticipation of what words Will might render on her behalf, she quickly sat her knitting aside and enthusiastically rose to her feet to receive him. She had keenly watched as Will had kissed Sarah, and expected nothing less than the same for herself, and she could hardly wait for Will to put his lips to her cheek. While the others looked on with cheerful expectancy to hear Will's words, he imparted a kiss to her cheek and she turned her head slightly to look him in the eyes. The kiss, as simple as it was, had elevated Elizabeth into an immediate state of wonderment. Will looked deeply into her stunned, dilated eyes and said, "Lizzy, my dear, you are the essence of faithfulness, purity, and love. As I told Sarah, no father on earth has ever loved his daughters more than I love you and Sarah. Your eyes sparkle in such a manner as to give us all hope, and I love you for the hope that you have brought into my own life. Your mother and I love you deeply because of your gentle nature, your caring heart, and I love you simply because you're my wonderful stepdaughter, Lizzy. It shames me that I have been neglect in telling you this before now. Please forgive me."

The family remained quite stunned, yet tolerant of Will's adoring words and heartfelt kisses, because despite his being intoxicated, his words were warming the tender emotions of every heart in the parlor. There was not a dry eye in the family. By this time, Abby was anxiously awaiting her turn to be the recipient of Will's comments and kisses. In anticipation, Abby rose to her feet and eagerly received him. Will held Abby close to him, kissed her in a manner which far surpassed the emotional equivalence of any of his previous kisses, and said, "Abby, what could I ever say about the depth of love that I have for you that I haven't already said to you a thousand or more times, my dear? I could never find the words. You carry for us the promise of another child, even at great risk to your own life. You do so because of your faith in God, and your love for me and our family. I treasure your love, and I treasure each and every moment that we're together. I love you, Abby, and I shall love you until the day that I die!"

"And I truly love you, Will. I shall always love you."

Abby sat back down when Will released her. Having smelled the disgusting bittersweet stench of bourbon on his breath, and even tasted it in his kiss, Abby gently suggested, "It's getting late, Will, and I think perhaps you shouldn't have any more bourbon tonight, darling."

"Nonsense, Abby! I'm doing just fine. Please allow me to finish what I want to say, Abby, please? I've only just begun! I've never felt this sentimental before, and I feel as though there are things that I need to say to the people I love the most in this world... things that are long overdue for me to say. It feels so wonderful for me to stand here before you and be truthful to my family."

"Alright, dear," Abby said, as she embarrassingly rolled her eyes and looked at Agatha and her daughters while smiling and shaking her head. Will drank another large portion of bourbon and poured the last from the bottle into his glass. When he sat his glass down and turned his head to look at Sarah, Abby reached over and took his glass, and quickly hid it on the floor near her feet. Then Agatha reached down with her foot and slid the glass across the floor and under a parlor chest, completely out of Will's sight. In Abby and Agatha's opinion, Will had already had far too much to drink, and reluctantly, Abby was just about ready to put an end to his eloquent words and his blubbering recitals for the night. His drunkenness was becoming an embarrassment to her. She hesitated only because his words had touched everyone's heart in the parlor. As endearing as his words and kisses had been, Abby felt as though he may had already lost the ability to sensor his expressions, and she was somewhat leery of what his next words might be.

Will's eyes sparkled in the parlor lamplight from the infusion of bourbon as he went on with his alcohol-induced oration. His antics were still somewhat of a fascinating amusement to the ladies, but their amusement was about to transform into shocked disbelief of what they were about to hear.

"Anyhow, I know I'm a little dizzy from the bourbon, and I'm having a little trouble with my words, and for that, I truly pogolisize... I mean... apologize. But just let me say that when I was first brought here, I was nearly dead, I mean ta' tell ya' I was almost a goner. I was completely unconscious for a number of days, as you all well know. However, there was a number of days—I know not how many, that I was well aware of what was going on around me, even though I could not open my eyes, nor could I speak to anyone to say thank you. I could not even move my arms or my legs, but I heard you as you mended my injuries, as you gave me water, and as you provided care for me. I heard you as you softly prayed for me, and talked to me. I shall be eternally grateful for the loving care that you so unselfishly provided to me. You saved my life, and once my life was restored, each of you have given me a reason for living, and you are the only reason I have for living today."

"You need say no more, Will. We love you, darling. Why don't you consider retiring for the night, and I'll help you up the stairs, your legs seem to be rather unsteady."

"Oh, but that's where you're wrong, Abby my dear. I must say more, Abby—I'll burst if I don't, I swear I will!"

"Alright, dear. But please finish quickly so we can go to our bed. Your legs really do appear wobbly, and we wouldn't want you to fall and hurt yourself, now would we?"

"I will finish quickly, Abby, but my legs are as steady as a rock. Yes Sir... steady as a dadburn rock, I tell ya. Like I was saying before Abby interrupted me, I heard you as you mended my injuries, as you gave me water, and as you provided care for me, and believe it or not, I was even aware of all those times my wonderful nurses raised my bedsheet to look at my thingy."

Every face in the room immediately became wide-eyed and open-mouthed! With her daughters taking in every word, Abby was horrified by what she had just heard, and screamed, **"WHAT**?!"

"...that's perfectly alright, Abby. Don't be upset about it, I became very accustomed to it after a while, and it sort of gives me a warm feeling of pride deep inside, knowing my wonderful ladies here had such a great interest in me... that they would want to look under my bedsheet so often. I'll never tell a living soul, I promise, alright?"

"Will Collins?!"

Slurring his words terribly, Will quickly went on to add, "It was actually quite humorous as I look back on it now, and I treasured all the attention that my family was giving me..."

"William, come along with me! I'll help you up to your bed, dear. It's way past time for us to go upstairs."

"Wait a minute, Abby, I cannot allow myself to go to bed until my wonderful family answers one question for me first. It's something that I've wondered about for over two years, now. May I please have your permission to ask my one little bitty question?"

"Very well. As long as it's nothing vulgar or sinful, one question only, Will, and then it's off to bed for you and I. Guard your words and go ahead and ask your question, dear, and get it over with."

"Thank you, Abby. You are so sweet and understanding and thoughtful... and you really are beautiful, too! My question to my wonderful family is simply this; why did my poor thingy need to be examined so many times, when the injuries were on my head and my leg?"

"That's it! Come along, William!"

"But Abby, I'm just getting started. I haven't even mentioned that time that you locked the door and held that little bitty jar so lovingly while I..."

"NOW! Say no more, and I mean it!"

"Or those wonderful, wonderful times that Aggy came in the room at night and first taught me how to pee in a jar... That was soooo... nice of you, Aggy."

"I SAID NOW!"

"If it hadn't been for you and Aggy, I may have never learned how to pee again... Hey Abby, remember the night the jar was too small, and you almost twisted my poor thingy off?"

"WILLIAM COLLINS! Agatha, please help me get William upstairs to our bedchamber."

"Gladly!"

"Oh hell! I'm in very serious trouble now, I think—Abby is calling me *William Collins* again. That always means that I'm in trouble when she calls me that!"

"Come along with us, dear! I've got this arm, Agatha, you hold the other arm."

"Well... Goodnight, my sweet Ladies. I love you! As you can see, Abby wants me to go upstairs with her now. Oh, goody... Aggy's coming with us! The more the merrier, I always say! Lizzy, you and Sarah can come along too, and maybe I can show everybody how I can pee in a jar..."

"That's quite enough, William! Come along, dear!"

"I'm coming, Abby, my sweet, I'm coming... Give me a little kiss, Aggy, alright? Come on up Sarah and Lizzy, and I'll pull my pants down and show everybody my injuries. Ha! Ha! Ha!"

"If you don't be quiet and come along with us, William Collins, I'll see to it that you have an abundance of injuries to show everyone! And you won't have to pull your pants down to do it!"

"Mercy! I suppose I better hush my mouth... It sounds like Abby really means business this time. I'm coming, Abby... I'm coming. You're not going to tie me to a tree with my own tongue are you?"

"At this moment, I'm giving it serious consideration! Watch your step, William."

"Abby, please don't tie me to a tree with my own tongue... please?"

"Stop it!"

"Hey, can we play that game tonight where I put my mouth between your breasts and blow real hard? I love that game..."

"Stop it, I said!"

As Agatha and Abby helped William stumble upstairs to his bedchamber, Sarah and Elizabeth sat alone at the parlor table with their mouths agape, eyes the size of goose eggs, completely dumbfound over the bizarre revelations of the evening. A more shocking and candid display of intoxication had never been witnessed before at Montgomery House. When their mother and Agatha were far enough away so as not to hear them, Elizabeth looked at Sarah, held her hand excitedly, and asked, "Mercy sakes alive! What do you think about all that has happened here tonight, Sarah?"

"I haven't the faintest clue what to think, Lizzy! I'm almost speechless! Before tonight, I've never imagined Will to be one who was predisposed to overindulge in spirits!"

"Do you think Mother is angry with us... I mean because we cooperated so willing with Will's drunken orations?"

"I hope not. We'll talk to her about it at breakfast in the morning, but she didn't seem to be angry at us. She seemed to be enjoying everything about tonight until Will got so drunk that he started talking naughty like he did. I've never seen Mother so embarrassed."

"Do you think she is angry with us now, knowing that we peeked under his bedsheet that night?"

"No. That was more than two years ago, and from the way Will was talking, it sounds like Mother must have done a fair amount of peeking herself, and it sounded like she may have even done some touching, too. Lord only knows what Agatha must have done when she was alone with him. Mother stopped Will from talking before he revealed very much at all. We're all only human, Lizzy, and Mother is no exception."

"I wonder what Will was saying about peeing in a Jar?"

"It's hard to say. Did you see how Mother and Aunt Agatha were both blushing as they led Will up the stairs?"

"Yes, but you and I were blushing just as much as they were. I looked over at you once, and your face was as red as an apple. I knew that we should never have peeked under his bedsheet. I told you as much that night. I knew that it would come back to haunt us someday and it has."

"If I live to be a hundred years old, I'll never forget what has happened here tonight, Lizzy."

"Nor shall I. I shan't be able to sleep tonight. This has been the most interesting and peculiarly entertaining night of my life, Sarah. I feel a tremendous urge to talk about everything that has happened here tonight."

"Would you like to sleep in my room with me tonight, Lizzy? We can talk as much as you like."

"Yes. I would like that very much. Listen, Sarah—I can hear Will laughing up in his bedchamber. I wonder what's so funny?"

"Listen closely, Lizzy, Mother and Aunt Agatha are laughing as well, and it sounds like Will is singing or something. I swear it sounds like he's singing *The Blue Tail Fly*."

"I wonder what Will's doing to make them laugh so loud, Sarah?"

"In his present state, I can only imagine, Lizzy, I can only imagine..."

"Mercy! I've never heard Agatha and Mother laugh that loud before! It sounds like they are hysterical! And it sounds like someone is stomping on the floor as well!"

"I would give anything to be a fly on the wall in their room and see what's so funny."

"Me too, Sarah. Do you think Mother will tell us in the morning what was so funny?"

"We can ask her, but I doubt it. Whatever is going on in there, Will is probably doing something naughty, and I don't think that Mother would want us to know."

"I swear... I just don't know what to think about all of this..."

"Neither do I, Lizzy."

As one might have anticipated, all of the faces around the breakfast table the next morning still remained embarrassingly reddened... from the shocking mortification of Will's astonishing exposés of the night before. Any and all secrets lingering within the household had been irreverently brought to the light of day and revealed before a shocked audience. Will's repeated apologies for his outlandish behavior soon managed to displace the humiliated grimaces on everyone's face somewhat, and with his marvelous ability to make amends, their scowls were soon replaced with slightly embarrassed, yet mostly adoring and sympathetic smiles. All was well again at Montgomery House, and perhaps even better than it had ever been before. Will summed up his remorseful sentiments best at the breakfast assembly of his loved ones, when they all held hands for the morning blessing of their food.

"Before I ask God to bless the food, I would just like to say that I have always detested the behavior of a slovenly drunkard, and last night I allowed myself to become that which I detest. I am sorely ashamed of myself. I truly apologize for my ill-mannered behavior last evening, and I especially regret my crude language and the disrespectful things that I said. I remember only small portions of what I said last night, but what I do remember brings me the deepest of regrets. I truly love each of you with all my heart and soul, and I always will. Like I said, I'm regretful for the way I behaved, and I can feel God's disfavor bearing down on me this morning. You have my solemn promise that I shall never overindulge in spirits again."

In the adoring presence of his family, all heads were bowed as Will offered the blessing of the food. "Father, we stand here before you this morning, not as individuals, but as a family...

unified by the grace that you have granted us and by the love that we have for each other. We ask that you bless each of us, Father, and we ask that you bless the lives that Abby and Agatha now carry in their wombs. We are thankful for the food we are about to eat, and most thankful for our loved ones who have prepared it. Forgive us of our trespasses, and keep us safe. And, I ask particular forgiveness for my shameful trespasses of last evening, Father. Amen."

Initially, few words were spoken as they sat to eat. Halfway through breakfast, Abby broke the silence that loomed over the family table.

"How do you feel this morning, Will?"

"To tell you the truth, Abby, I feel as though someone has tied me to a tree with my own tongue and taken a hammer to my head."

"Will?"

"Yes, Abby?"

"While we are in the presence of the family this morning, I would like to apologize for raising my voice at you last night, dear."

"Unless my memory serves me wrong, I deserved a lot worse than just a raised voice, Abby, and I would prefer that we never discuss last night again. Can we change the subject, please?"

"Not until I finish with what I want to say, Will. In your absence this morning, we had a family conference before you came downstairs, and…"

"My Lord, Abby, I haven't been vanquished by the family to live the rest of my life in exile at the barn, have I?"

"Just let me finish, Will. As I said, we've all talked between ourselves this morning before you came downstairs, and I would like to say a couple of things to clear the air between us… if you will give me your permission to do so."

"Please do… I've got it coming to me, I'm sure."

"First, we have come to recognize that your body has an intolerance for excessive alcohol spirits… wouldn't you agree?"

"Yes, Abby, I agree wholeheartedly, and I have already given you my solemn promise not to do anything like that again."

"Secondly, because of this intolerance, and because we are adverse to ever having a repeated performance of your antics of last eve, we recommend careful monitoring of all of your future alcohol consumption. Wouldn't you agree?"

"I most assuredly do, Abby."

"Thirdly, and I fully expect you to listen carefully to this one, as it is the most important one of the three."

"Go ahead, Abby. I fully deserve anything that you're about to say to me, I'm sure, so why don't you go ahead and get it over with?"

"Our consensus is that you do in fact deserve what I am about to say, indeed."

"Please go ahead and say it, Abby, and get it over with..."

"Alright, dear. Will Collins, you are undoubtedly the most wonderful thing that has ever happened to us here at Montgomery Farm."

"What?! Did I hear you correctly?"

"From all of us, we sincerely mean that. And just because you became a little loose with your words last night, is not sufficient cause for us to bear any long term ill feelings. We know that you said nothing cruel or spiteful, you only spoke the truth. And we know that your words of love came directly from your heart. We also feel certain that we will never see a repeated performance of last night's transgressions, and with that in mind, we've agreed to forgive and forget... everything but your wonderful words of love and your sweet kisses, we shall never forget them."

"I don't quite know what to say..."

"We love you, Will, each and every one of us."

"Thank you... all of you. I love you as well."

"And to show our appreciation, we are going to prepare a special meal for you tonight, dear."

"Mercy! For me? Really?"

"We'll have chicken and dumplings, biscuits and gravy,

black-eyed peas, and corn, and Sarah and Elizabeth are even going to bake a cake—all as a special treat to show you how much you are appreciated here. And as a special treat for the women in our family, there will be no bourbon served to the men tonight. Are you in agreement with that, darling?"

"Yes, Ma'am, I'm in complete agreement."

"Would you mind playing the piano for a few minutes after breakfast before you go to the fields?"

"Under normal circumstances I would be most happy to, Abby, but I swear, my head is hurting so badly that I would prefer not playing until this evening, if that would be alright."

"We understand, and we will look forward to this evening."

"Oh my! Please excuse me, I think I'm about to be sick..."

With that, William dashed out the back door. The ladies could hear the distant sounds of his miserable gagging and stomach distress. As the ladies continued with their breakfast, Abby simply said, "Poor Will... he brought all this on himself, bless his heart."

O   O   O

Later that morning, Will left to go to work in the fields as the ladies washed the breakfast dishes and gathered the day's laundry together. They talked giddily between themselves, and Will remained their primary topic of conversation. As she sorted the dirty laundry, Sarah commented, "When I get married, I pray that I will be able to find a man just like Will."

Abby looked at Sarah and retorted, "I don't think there is another man quite like him, but I'm sure that you and Elizabeth will both find someone whom you will love just as much as I love Will."

Agatha added, "Have you ever stopped to consider just how miserable our existence was here at Montgomery Farm before Will came along?"

Elizabeth responded, "Yes! The transformation has

been remarkably amazing!" Then she faced her mother and asked a question that she and Sarah had spent half the night contemplating.

"Mother, if Sarah and I asked you and Aunt Agatha an important question, would you promise that you will give us an honest answer?"

"Well of course we will. We have no secrets between us here at Montgomery House, and I have never lied to you. What is this important question, pray tell?"

"It's just this, Mother; last night, after you and Aunt Agatha took Will to your room, Sarah and I have never heard so much laughter in our lives. Why were you both laughing so hysterically?"

"Oh my, Elizabeth! Please, darling, I prefer not to answer that! Ask me anything in the world but that, please!"

"Mother! You promised that you would answer our question truthfully!"

"Only because you tricked me into making that promise!"

"Nevertheless, you did make a promise! Sarah and I will die of curiosity if you don't keep your promise and tell us what happened! Please, Mother!"

"Should I tell them, Agatha?"

"If you do, I'm afraid that I will start laughing again."

"Mother please! Tell us! Sarah and I are adults now, deserving of your confidence!"

"Very well. But you must swear an oath that you will never repeat what I am about to tell you! Will was terribly intoxicated at the time, and he doesn't even remember anything that happened up in our bedchamber. I would never want him to know what he did up there, so you must swear an oath to keep it a secret."

"We swear! Now please tell us before we burst!"

"Well... It happened like this... Agatha helped me take Will upstairs into the bedchamber to tuck him into bed as you know..."

At this point in her explanation, Agatha broke into irrepressible laughter, which caused Abby to start laughing as well. Sarah and Elizabeth were becoming highly frustrated because Abby was laughing so hard that she could not finish her explanation. Finally, after wiping tears of laughter from her eyes, at Sarah and Elizabeth's persistent pleadings, Abby continued with her account of Will's outrageous behavior of the night before.

"We managed to help Will sit down on the bed. Agatha pulled his boots off while I unbuttoned his shirt and together, we both helped him undress down to his undergarment. We turned our backs to him long enough to fold his shirt and trousers, and lay them across a chair, and to our complete astonishment, before we could get him into the bed and under the covers, he dashed off his undergarment and began dancing perfectly naked around the bedchamber and singing before our flabbergasted eyes!"

"Oh no! Mercy!"

"It seems that your stepfather is a very talented and extremely agile dancer, which has been a fact unknown to me, but his nakedness while dancing so splendidly dexterous, incited Agatha and I into such an immediate fit of laughter that we lacked the power to subdue ourselves." Abigail and Agatha burst into uncontainable laughter again, leaving Sarah and Elizabeth desperate to hear more.

"Please stop laughing and finish telling us what happened, Mother!"

"I can't control myself... Agatha, would you please tell them the rest?"

"I'll try... Well, as Abigail just said, the sight of a naked man dancing and singing was absolutely more than we could bear. We tried desperately to contain ourselves, but it was simply impossible... you see, when a naked man dances... Ha! Ha! Ha!"

"Aunt Agatha, please finish!"

"Well... uhhh... let me see, how can I best explain this without embarrassing everyone or using vulgar words? Uhhh... when a naked man dances... certain unmentionable things sort of bounce and swing around, and when bearing witness to such a ghastly entertaining event, it's utterly impossible to keep oneself from laughing, especially when the man is singing *The Blue tail Fly*! I fear that I shall never again be able to hear that song without recalling images of Will and bursting into laughter!"

"Abby composed herself long enough to add, "It was several minutes before Will finally tired of his drunken folly and collapsed onto the bed, but it took much longer than that for Agatha and I to recover from our laughter. We laughed until we feared for the health of the babies we carry. If I live to be a hundred years old, I shall never forget the sight of him dancing naked in our bedchamber while singing *The Blue tail Fly*!"

Having finished sharing their accounts, at that point all four ladies lapsed into a rather disorderly fit of laughter. They laughed so hard that Abby had to leave the room, and Agatha held her sides and fell onto the settee. Abby and Agatha were both in the final months of their pregnancies, and it was incumbent upon them not to cause undue stress to the babies they each bore by laughing so hard.

By the twilight of evening, Will's headache had vanished, and he serenaded his family with his marvelous piano music as the ladies sat around the piano quietly attending to their knitting and sewing. It was a pleasant and marvelously sedate evening, that is, until Agatha decided that it was time to liven things up with a little laughter. In a mood to be mischievously naughty, Agatha impishly asked Will if he would play *The Blue tail Fly*. Not remembering his drunken bedchamber antics from the night before, Will cheerfully and naively complied. But shortly into the song, the ladies broke into hysterical laughter, and laughed so enthusiastically that they were forced to stop singing. Perplexed, Will ceased playing momentarily and asked, "What in the world has come over everyone? Why is everyone laughing all of a sudden? Would one of you please stop laughing long enough to tell me what's so funny?"

Abigail gathered her composure briefly and replied, "It's nothing, darling. Please forgive us..."

For months afterward, if any of the ladies desired to liven things up among the other ladies, all they had to do was clear their throat and sing, *"Oh... Jimmy crack corn and I don't care... Jimmy crack corn and I don't care... Jimmy crack corn and I don't care... My Master's gone away..."*

Agatha was correct when she said that life at Montgomery Farm truly had changed from the threatening, misery-ridden, and dreary days before William Collins had arrived.

Epilogue

"But he answered and said, It is written, Man shall not live by bread alone, but by every word that proceedeth out of the mouth of God." Matthew 4:4

After the stunning night of Will's alcohol-induced escapade, Abby jokingly supervised the portions of bourbon that he was permitted to consume, and Will was entirely in concurrence with her half-hearted mandate. Will had never been intoxicated before in his life, and as Abby would so delicately characterize his state of inebriated behavior; *"Once was quite enough to last an entire lifetime."* The women of the family rapidly recovered from their shock and embarrassment over Will's admissions, and the family soon returned to living their normal, harmonious daily lives together... albeit with a much better understanding of each other. From that point on, there truly were no secrets residing within the Montgomery-Collins family. Will's bestowment of his traditional morning and evening pleasantries continued to be an element of binding contentment for the family, only now they were distributed with much more caution, self-assurance, and prudence than the unruly night of Will's intoxication. Instead, they were performed with more pomp and circumstance than before. It brought added warmth into Abby's heart each time she looked around the family's meal table and saw the glow of happiness in the eyes of her family. Disturbing recollections of the war and all of the tragedies that were once vivid daily nightmares there at Montgomery Farm had faded into the oblique corridors of the family's past, and the residents there had been emancipated to live their lives free of the encumbering burdens of their dreary heritage.

○   ○   ○

To the supreme joy and happiness of the family, Abby and Agatha were both blessed to give birth to healthy children that spring. As unconventional as it would have seemed to the prying eyes of the outside world, Sarah and Elizabeth were once again in attendance to assist Vivian as the infants were brought forth. Birthing was traditionally an event that was never attended by women who had not previously given birth themselves, yet Abby wanted her daughters to be well trained and familiar with all phases of the procedure, in preparation for their roles as future mothers. Agatha was the first to give birth, bringing forth a beautiful baby girl, and was followed within a week by Abby, who presented Will with his second handsome son. For the first time in her life, Agatha was liberated to experience the joy and freedom of being able to raise her own daughter, legally named, Vera Collins, as her very own child, and she rejoiced in such freedom and love. The entire family bustled with excitement over their newborn children, and the house seemed to take on a more joyful personality with the introduction and arrival of each new life. When Will's mother and father received news of the births, Abby discretely told them in her letter the true circumstances involved in the double births and the generous surrogate role that Agatha had performed for the family. Abby thought it best that as Will's parents, the family should be honest and truthful with them. Will's mother and father wrote back that they were quite sympathetic and understanding, and nonetheless elated over the births, regardless of the circumstances by which the children had been conceived. They visited Montgomery Farm again that year to bask in the glory and pride of having three grandchildren, in fact, they visited twice more that year, and their visits were always welcomed with the grandest of celebration.

○ ○ ○

Owing to the fact that the family was abiding in the grandest state of supreme happiness right there on Montgomery Farm, William Collins was never inspired to establish a law practice, regardless of the fact that his education had endowed him with both the credentials and the wisdom to be a fine attorney-at-law. William had found such happiness on Montgomery Farm that any vocation aside from raising his crops and attending to the needs of his wonderful family could have only provided him with disappointing changes in the way of life to which he had become so fond. William had grown to have little tolerance for conflicts, and after all, conflicts were a part of the daily life of an attorney. It's not surprising that Will wanted nothing to do with it.

○ ○ ○

Days and months have a way of passing much too quickly in our lives, and most especially in the lives of people who are living in the splendor of happiness. Such was the case in the lives of the people residing at Montgomery Farm. Elizabeth had become betrothed during the following three months, but aborted her betrothal for reasons known only to herself and the residents of Montgomery House. And as odd as it may have seemed to onlookers, young, vivacious Sarah had also rejected a marriage proposal. The sisters remained steadfast in their convictions to remain highly discriminating when considering the qualities of men, and Elizabeth and Sarah eventually rejected all but a select few suitors who came to call upon them. Even Agatha, by choice, had rejected all suitors that came to call upon her, preferring to raise her daughter without the distraction of superfluous male interests outside of the family. After rejecting two marriage proposals over the span of the next seven months, the suitors finally seemed to get the message, and eventually stopped calling on her altogether. It was as though she had found some new kind of peace in her life, right there at Montgomery Farm, and chose not to leave.

When a new schoolhouse was erected just two miles from Montgomery Farm, Elizabeth became the first teacher there. Given her love for children, she was perfectly fit for the job, and greatly endeared by both her students and their parents as well. On many days, Sarah went to school with her, and even substituted for her sister on many occasions. The sisters had always been close to each other, and each new year found them drawn even closer.

Sheriff Homer Bellisle, after being wounded again by a Mississippi migrant farmer, retired from his sheriff's position, and took a job as a furniture builder and salesman there in Blanchard. At least once a month he would ride to Montgomery Farm, where he would visit with his best friend, William Collins. He always enjoyed sharing the company of Will, and he never turned down one or two of Abigail's hot biscuits when he came to visit. It was more than just a coincidence that his visits always seemed to occur in the mornings, at a time when Abigail's fresh biscuits were coming out of the oven.

Ezra and Vivian continued to live happy and fruitful lives there on Montgomery Farm with their children and grandchildren. They remained endeared to the Collins and Montgomery family, and their family was always an important part of the regular Sabbath picnics there as well.

O O O

An extraordinary turning point in the lives of all who resided there at Montgomery House occurred during the year following Abby and Agatha's delivery of babies. Christopher now had two adorable siblings, and happiness reigned supreme in everyone's heart there at Montgomery Farm. To everyone's utter surprise, that February, Sarah announced her betrothal to Robert Brumfield, the handsome young son of the family's attorney, Lawrence Brumfield. Sarah had finally found a man whom she loved and adored, and whose quality of character she truly respected. Equally astounding, and almost as a miracle, Elizabeth soon followed, when she and Michael Stephens announced their betrothal in March of that same year. Michael Stephens was the son of Rev. Mitchell Stephens, and the perfect husband for Elizabeth. Both sisters married in May, and both sisters took residency on nearby farms with their new husbands within two miles of Montgomery Farm. Abby, Agatha, and Will missed the presence of Sarah and Elizabeth there in the house, but with everyone living so close together, seldom did a week go by in which there wasn't a visit or two. And with three young children, there never seemed to be a dull moment there at Montgomery House for Abigail, Agatha, and Will.

To the great satisfaction and joy of William and Abigail Collins, Elizabeth and Sarah were blessed to have husbands who absolutely doted upon them, and the coming years soon found them providing grandchildren for Abby and Will. Holidays were made all the more merry at Montgomery Farm as the family grew. Mere words could never express the delight that had overtaken Will and Abby's hearts when they first looked upon Sarah and Elizabeth holding their newborn children. Only a grandparent would ever understand such joy. William never saw himself as a stepfather to Sarah and Elizabeth. Nay, in the deepest corners of his heart, he loved them as only a true father could love his daughters.

No one ever questioned Agatha as to the amount of her wealth, but it seemed as though she was always there to render assistance to any family member in need. Her joy in life was in giving, and she never flaunted her wealth or spent her money on items of opulence.

As for the Collins and Montgomery family, with two attractive young women such as Abigail and Agatha, and one handsome young man such as William Collins living under the same roof, it was unavoidable that at least a few surreptitious rumors would circulate through the local population from time to time. But the family was so beloved by the community that the rumors were never spiteful or vicious in nature. Will's family was known to be God-fearing and righteous, and generous to a fault. They had donated most all of the money for the construction of the new schoolhouse, and were among the most prominent supporters of the Blanchard Benevolence Fund, a fund used to provide financial relief for distressed widows and orphans. As Agatha began taking Vera to church with her and sitting with the family, the community could have speculated viciously on the possible relationship between the occupants of Montgomery House, but they did not.

General suspicions notwithstanding, perhaps that's a circumstance that is best left uncertain in the eyes of the hypocritical world. God knows the truth, and God quite obviously extended many blessings to the family. That's all that really matters.

In 1871, Abby and Will further delighted the community of Blanchard when they adopted two orphaned children, aged six and seven, and brought them into the love of their family. Then again in 1872, they adopted two orphaned twin daughters, five years of age. Abby and Agatha reveled in the delight of raising their children. Will had once told Abby that he loved children, and wouldn't have minded having a dozen of them. With seven children abiding in the household now, there was never an idle moment there at Montgomery House, and there was seldom a moment in which a smile did not adorn the faces of everyone there.

Sadly, in 1875, William's father passed away in Charlottesville with pneumonia after a short illness. Will's mother, Edna, moved to Montgomery House in the spring of 1876, where she provided invaluable assistance to Abigail and Agatha in the raising of all the children. An addition was added to the house in order to accommodate the four adults and seven children now residing there, and the addition was complete with two lavatories. Two buggies were needed each Sabbath in order to provide transportation to and from their church. Abigail and Agatha became as daughters to Will's mother, and visitors to Montgomery House had little problem in noting that love was the dominating theme there.

Perhaps an even better understanding of the love that prevailed within the Montgomery-Collins family could have been obtained by paying a visit to Montgomery Farm in the early evening hours during a specific spring day in the year of 1921. Two elderly women sat there in their rocking chairs on the front porch of Montgomery House that evening, amusing themselves with quiet conversation. There were no children running about the household or the grounds... by all evidence, the children had likely grown to adulthood years earlier. It would be evident to an observant visitor that most all of the residents of Montgomery House had vanished and gone to live their lives elsewhere, save for these two frail women who seemed to be there alone. The barn was in near ruin, the chicken house had long since rotted away, and there was a floorboard or two missing from the front porch. The crop fields were overgrown from years of idleness and the house was now in an ill state of repair, but these two women occupants appeared to be living contentedly there, and seemed immensely satisfied with their current stations in life, even when considering their aged circumstances. They were in the waning years of their life. The spark of youthfulness had long since disappeared from their bodies, and their hair, gathered in simple buns at the back of their heads, was as white as a freshly fallen snow. Their wrinkled and crooked hands were involved with their sewing, as long as the sunlight would permit. But the daylight was declining, and it would soon be too dark for their poor eyes to see well enough to sew, and their sewing would have to be taken inside. They talked quietly between themselves as they sat there, reminiscing of earlier days—days in which time had not yet taken its cruel toll on their earthly bodies. If a visitor were to draw near enough, they could hear the elderly ladies as they spoke to one another...

"Tell me something, do you remember the night that he got so drunk that we had to help him up the stairs to his room...?"

"Mercy sakes alive, how could I ever forget that night? That was the one and only night he ever got drunk, but he was fit to be tied that night! If you will recall, that was the night that he danced for us... remember? My Lord, what a sight that was! I've never seen the like!"

"Oh my goodness! I can see him dancing around the room now! My goodness, but he could dance!"

"One of the things that I remember most about him was the look of joy on his face when he would read the Bible to the children in the evenings, and the way they always seemed to gather around him so closely when he read. My Lord, but those children loved him, didn't they?"

"I'm afraid that we all loved him."

"You know, it always amazed me that he had the strength and courage to stand up against all of those hooded hoodlums that night and spit right in their eye, yet he wept the morning that Christopher was Baptized. He had a heart of pure gold, didn't he?"

"Yes he did. I can sometimes still hear him singing *The Blue-tailed Fly* when I close my eyes at night, and it always seems to bring a smile to my face."

"I think about him every time I walk by the old piano."

"My Lord, he could really make that old piano talk, couldn't he?"

"And who among us could ever forget his wonderful antics at Christmas time, when he would go up in the attic and dress himself in that colorful green costume, then come downstairs and bestow all the children with gifts?"

"Who indeed? I'll certainly never forget!"

"The good Lord only made one man like him, that's for sure."

"Hardly a moment of the day passes by without me thinking about him."

"I miss him terribly sometimes… No, I suppose I miss him most all of the time really. Especially in the evenings like this when it's quiet, I can almost hear that soft voice of his sometimes…"

"I know, dear… I know… I miss him too… it's hard to believe he's really gone, isn't it? Sometimes I expect to see him walk out the door at any moment with a cup of coffee in one hand and a biscuit in the other and just sit down to talk to us."

"We've been very blessed. God allowed us to have him here with us for sixty-seven years!"

"Sixty-seven wonderful years!"

"Lord have mercy, that man really was something very special, wasn't he?"

"That he was indeed, dear… that he was…"

"Oh……. *Jimmy crack corn and I don't care…*"

"Stop it, Agatha!"

CPSIA information can be obtained at www.ICGtesting.com
Printed in the USA
LVOW08s1018090115

422047LV00002B/17/P

9 781489 703439